Salvaged Soul

The Ignited Series
Book Three

Desni Dantone

LAINED
PUBLISHING

Salvaged Soul

This is a work of fiction. Names, characters, and incidents are either the product of the author's imagination or are used fictitiously. Any resemblance to actual persons, living or dead, or events is entirely coincidental.

Cover design by Najla Qambar
Edited by Jennifer Leisenheimer

Published 2015 by Laine D. Publishing

ISBN 13: 978-0-9895090-5-3

The Ignited Series:

Ignited

Sacrificed

Salvaged Soul

Avenging Heart (Coming Soon)

Chapter 1

{Nathan}

Some conversations were easily forgotten. Some were never forgotten. And then there were some that you would give anything to forget. Take, for instance, the conversation I just had with Gran. Nothing short of a lobotomy could have made me forget that conversation, no matter how badly I wanted to.

There were some things no grandson should *ever* be forced to talk to his grandmother about. Sex was one of those topics. I knew this because I just suffered through it for ten horrifying minutes. There was only one person I could think of to blame for the uncomfortable subject matter forced on me that morning, and I was on my way to find her right now.

I knew exactly where Kris would be. Her schedule was as regimented as an army recruit's. The Kala had ensured that, to know exactly where she was and who she was with at all times. Now, she would be eating breakfast with Micah in the mess hall.

The Kala's orders for her to be accompanied by either Micah or her appointed bodyguard, Kim, everywhere she went was something I had been forced to accept. Fortunately, I was good friends with one of the supervisors, so I had also worked it out that she could be with me without Micah or Kim tagging along. And *that* was something I'd had the luxury of watching Micah bitterly accept.

It was the one time I had used my connection to Jared for personal reasons. Since we had first met over a decade ago, when we were both young hybrids going through the early stages of development together, we had formed a friendship that had survived even after I left, and he ascended to a leadership position on the island. He had no problem granting me access to Kris. Of course, since he knew me so well, it hadn't taken him long to figure out why I had requested it.

It was Jared who suggested I keep my relationship with Kris on the down low. Because she was destined to become the world's most powerful Skotadi, the Kala feared her. It was in her best interest to maintain a low profile. To be seen in a relationship with a Kala—especially a well-known one like myself—would put an even brighter spotlight on her than there already was.

At least none of them knew she was also a demigod of Incantation, and capable of yielding magic like her goddess mother, Hecate. Well. . . she couldn't yield anything yet, but she had been practicing it in secret while under the protection of the Kala here on the island. Since Incantators were feared even more than the Skotadi, her identity as one was something else we were forced to keep hidden.

We hoped her future as an Incantator would free her from her ties to the Skotadi. All she had to do was figure out how to do it. And I had no doubt that she would find a way.

She *had* to find a way.

Because there was no way in hell I was going to lose her now. Not after coming as far as we had. Not after realizing just how much she meant to me. Not when we had a lifetime yet to spend together. Knowing what we had to look forward to made pretending I wasn't absolutely crazy about her more tolerable. However, my strength wavered a little every time I saw her.

I didn't spot Kris in the mess hall when I entered. I glanced at my watch. 9:07—only seven minutes late. For a girl, that was pretty much considered on time.

The dining area was packed with Kala of all ages and stages, though the leaders dined in a roped off area separated from the rest of us. This morning, the three head leaders sat at their round table, sipping their coffees and eating their pastries as they likely discussed the most recent Kala-Skotadi war developments with the mid-level supervisors.

Each mid-level headed up their own department, based on one of the twelve specialties we were gifted in. All matters and decisions pertaining to those specialties went through them. Jared was a low-level supervisor in the leadership department, and was one of many put in charge of organizing and executing missions. There were often multiple missions going on at one time, so Jared was a busy guy.

So far, since returning to the island, I had not been called up for a mission, but I knew it was only a matter of time. Since I had left the island seven years ago, and had avoided following the rules of the Kala, they labeled me a troublemaker. Not that I cared, but I figured I was due to be taught a lesson in Kala etiquette soon.

Avoiding the supervisors, I moved through the food line, grabbing an assortment of bagels and pastries. By the time I turned with a full tray, Kris was setting her bag down on a table in the dining area. Micah and Kim were both at her side.

I bit my tongue on the not so nice words that instantly came to mind, and limited myself to a hard glare directed at the center of Micah's forehead.

"If looks could kill."

I turned to the familiar voice beside me. Finding a grinning Alec staring at me, at one time, would have brought about an intense need to punch something. Not so much anymore. If anything, the guy had become an ally of mine. Only because he hated Micah, too. More than he hated me.

And I wasn't so sure he hated me anymore.

And I wasn't so sure I hated him anymore.

Well, not as much.

Like Kris, Alec was destined to become a Skotadi against his will. And also like Kris, he was under constant supervision. His bodyguard was a beast of a man that not even I would mess with. Bruce towered over me by six inches. And he was big. Really big. Apparently, he had been the top-ranked fighter in his class. He had been serving as a Kala soldier for about ten years now, making him a little younger than me.

Despite being a lot bigger than me, he seemed to admire me a little. Maintaining his position behind Alec, Bruce gave me a stoic nod, which I returned before shifting my attention back to Micah.

"I can't believe I'm going to say this," Alec continued, turning to follow my gaze, "but I think you might actually despise him more than I do. And that's a lot."

"I'm sure you're a close second," I returned.

He took a moment to ponder that, then shook his head. "No. I think she might have both of us beat."

If the look of absolute boredom on Kris's face wasn't enough, the way she moved away from Micah when he leaned close to whisper something to her, and the ensuing roll of her eyes in response to whatever he said, suggested plenty.

I knew I had nothing to worry about—as long as Kris's destiny didn't eventually force her into Micah's arms. As far as who she *wanted*, I knew that was me.

I offered Alec a grin before leaving him and Bruce to navigate the food line as I worked my way over to Kris's table. She had just started to stand when she saw me. Her eyes lowered to the assortment of sweet deliciousness on my tray, and she smiled.

Familiarizing myself with her likes and dislikes hadn't been hard considering I had kept a watchful eye on her for fourteen years. Some things, like the type of donuts she favored, had been instilled in me without even realizing it, which was why it didn't come as a surprise when she plucked the chocolate donut with sprinkles from my tray the second I set it down.

"Saving me a trip?" she asked as she claimed the pint of chocolate milk I had also gotten for her.

"I thought you might want a break from your entourage for a few minutes." I may have been speaking to Kris, but my gaze leveled on Micah.

He and Kim had to get their food yet. I knew that. From the smirk on his face, he knew that I knew that. I looked away from him as I took a seat beside Kris, leaving Micah with no choice but to walk away in defeat.

Other than my knee grazing hers, we didn't touch. At times, like now, maintaining an acceptable distance between us bordered on painful. Surely anyone watching us closely enough would see through our charade, but most had no idea what was really going on between us, or what our stolen glances and subtle touches really meant. I had to remind myself that it was better that way. At least for now.

So, as much as it pained me to hold my hand back from brushing that unruly strand of hair that kept falling in her eyes, I did. I refrained from touching her. Until later.

Speaking of which . . .

"So . . ." I mumbled around a mouthful of donut. "I had an interesting talk with Gran this morning."

Out of the corner of my eye, I noted the hesitation of her hand before it moved to tuck that chunk of hair behind her ear. Her method of stalling.

Which meant she knew exactly what talk I'd had with Gran earlier. Which meant she had to have been behind it somehow. Which meant . . .

Oh, shit.

Anyone within a five foot radius had to have heard me gulp as I turned my head to look directly at her. Her head shifted fractionally, but not enough to permit eye contact. Her tongue flicked across her lips quickly, the tell-tale sign that she was nervous.

"Kris?"

"Hmm?"

"Is there—" I stopped, suddenly unsure how to proceed. Apparently there was much we needed to talk about if she was approaching Gran about sex, but I had no idea where to begin. I wasn't exactly sure what she had said to Gran to prompt Gran to give me *The Talk*. I wasn't sure where Kris's head was. Until now, I honestly hadn't suspected that she had given it any thought.

I stared at her without saying anything for so long that she eventually turned her head far enough to lift her eyes to mine. She waited, and still I said nothing.

I was saved by Alec as he plopped into a chair across from us. *Really? What happened to me, that I am actually glad to see Alec?*

"You'd think they would have better variety," he muttered as he poked at his food with a frown. "We eat the same crap every day."

"Limited resources," I quipped. "You know, being on an island and all."

Granted, the Kala traded with the citizens on the mainland and had more than enough finances to import a better variety of food. They chose to fund better weapons instead. There had been an ongoing complaint over the subject for years. Not once had it been given consideration by the supervisors.

"I happen to like eating donuts every morning," Kris said.

Alec and I both stared at her as she shoved the last bite of a donut into her mouth.

My girl, ever the lady.

She had the right idea though. Spying Micah over Alec's shoulder as he approached the table, I decided that a speedy breakfast would be wise. I finished off a sausage, egg, and cheese croissant in three bites, and stood with my Styrofoam cup of coffee as Micah was pulling a chair out.

Kris looked up at me, her brown eyes wide and questioning.

I shrugged. "Gotta run. Jared wanted me to swing by the Command Center before class."

"Again?"

Since I had arrived back on the island, Jared asked for me to come by often, usually to discuss the investigation of potential spies on the island. One of the first things I had done upon arriving was to inform him of the spy that had set Kris and me up for the Skotadi back in Kentucky. Travis had been surprised to see me, but not as surprised as he was when security apprehended him. He hadn't ratted anyone else out yet, but Jared was convinced there were more like him. He had made it his mission to find out who they were, and why they were working for the Skotadi.

"I guess he missed me while I was gone," I joked.

"I'll see you later then?" Kris flashed me a smile—sweet with a dash of sexy—that made me want to forget all about hiding our relationship.

It took a tremendous effort on my part to not cave. Only my eyes, which were fixed on her, hinted at the torture I suffered. "Yeah. I'll see you later."

Alec gagged, causing me to break my gaze from Kris. "No

one, least of all me, wants to see the two of you making googly eyes at each other," he whined.

I shook my head at him, and left.

The Command Center wasn't far from the mess hall. Conveniently, most of the main buildings bordered the village center, a large horseshoe-shaped clearing with far too many benches and palm trees that opened to the beach on one side. Though easy to get to, gaining access to the Command Center proved more difficult.

Security stood at every entrance. The building had always been guarded, but it was my understanding that security had been increased recently. I wondered how much that had to do with the potential spies on the island, and how much that had to do with the three Skotadi now living here.

In addition to Kris and Alec, Lillian had also been brought back. While Kris and Alec weren't full-blown Skotadi yet and were permitted some freedoms, Lillian was not. As the Skotadi put in charge of tracking down Kris and ensuring Micah's demise, she was considered extremely dangerous, and thus heavily guarded. Apparently, they were treating her conversion to a Skotadi as an illness, and she was being held in the Infirmary which was in the same building as the Command Center.

The guard at the main entrance took down my information before letting me through. Another two guards stood outside the door that led to the Infirmary wing, but I passed by without slowing. I knew more guards waited inside the Infirmary, and that their presence increased the closer I got to Lillian's room.

I knew because I had visited her a few times. Not necessarily *her,* because in her evil state of mine, she hated me and wouldn't have wanted to see me. Mostly, I conferred with the medical staff and inquired about her progress. There hadn't been any good news yet.

The Kala had no idea how the Skotadi had turned her, and no idea how to convert her back. Even after we had supplied them with the information we had acquired in West Virginia—that Incantation had been used somehow—they didn't know what to do.

Probably because any Incantator that could help wouldn't dare step forward to do so. Incantators were often persecuted because of fear of their power. That was why we had decided to keep Kris's identity as an Incantator a secret, and why she worked on her skills in secret with Micah, away from the eyes of Kala leadership.

Only Jared knew. But I knew he could be trusted with that information. He was just as eager as I was for her to reach her potential. Especially if it could save herself, Alec, and Lillian all from living the rest of their lives as Skotadi.

The guard stationed outside of Jared's office knew me by name, apparently. "Morning, Nathan." He opened the door for me, but I hesitated to look at him before entering. He must have guessed what I wanted to ask because he supplied, "It's Rodney."

I nodded. "Thanks, Rodney."

As he shut the door behind me, I smirked at my old friend. "It doesn't look natural. You sitting behind a desk."

Though his head remained tipped down as he studied a stack of papers on the top of his oversized mahogany desk, I glimpsed the curve of a smile on Jared's face. "A lot has changed in the seven years you've been gone, buddy." Finally, he looked up and flashed me an over-the-top grin that showed off his perfect teeth.

According to most of the girls on the island, Jared was— what did they say?—dreamy. I didn't get the 'Tom Cruise from *Top Gun*' label he had acquired amongst the female Kala. But then, I had once navigated the Mohave Desert with him for five days without a shower or a shave, and forever had the 'Tom Hanks from *Cast Away*' image of him burned into my memory.

"So I've noticed," I muttered as I sat in a plush leather chair opposite him. I leaned forward, resting my elbows on my knees. "What do you need me for this time?"

"I wanted you to hear it from me first," Jared started, taking on that authoritative tone which sounded odd coming from the guy I'd once witnessed skinny dip off the pier for ten bucks. "We flushed out another mole. He's not talking any more than Travis had. Not yet anyway."

"Where was he stationed?"

"In Geography. He worked directly under Travis, so we're going through that entire division. There have to be more hiding there."

Geography was a part of the 'prophecy specialty' division given the task of tracking Skotadi movements around the world. If there were spies in there, they could easily hide the locations of the Skotadi's strongholds, and *that* would be a very bad thing for the Kala.

"You've got to get them out of there, Jared."

"No shit." He laughed humorlessly. "We're working on it. I

could really use an extra set of eyes that I can trust."

I groaned. "I'll keep my eyes open, but I'm not going to take on any kind of official role. You've got me busy enough with that damn class anyway."

"We'll get rid of the class," Jared offered quickly. Too quickly, like he'd been giving this some thought.

While it would be nice to not have to instruct the two combat classes I had been given upon moving back to the island, I knew that if I gave them up I would have no excuse not to become more involved with the Kala system.

"No," I responded firmly.

Jared sighed in defeat. "Fine. Stay a measly instructor."

"I didn't even want to be that."

"Well, you have to do something while you're here. It was either that or a custodial job."

"I guess you expect me to thank you?"

He grinned at me, and for the first time since I had walked into his office he wasn't Jared the supervisor, but Jared, my friend. "You and I both know words like that don't come out of your mouth easily."

"You're absolutely right," I agreed with a chuckle. I stood to let myself out. "I've got to get to class. I'll let you know if I see or hear anything."

"Nathan! One more thing," Jared called. "You asked about Callie last time?"

I stopped with my hand on the door handle, and turned to face Jared. "Any change?"

He shook his head. "Only getting worse."

I nodded glumly and let myself out.

Only getting worse. . .

Though I had yet to tell her, Kris's best friend was in trouble. Big trouble. Callie was sick in a way that could only be caused by Incantation, and there was nothing anyone could do as her life slowly slipped away. There were two people who could potentially help her. One was Kris—an Incantator in training who struggled with the basics. The other was being held a mere fifty yards away and, in her current state, laughed demonically when asked what she had done to Callie.

Lillian. The girl I used to love, the reason I had left this island seven years ago, and the one who had brought me back to it now. The one central to everything. The one who needed to be saved . . . before everything was lost.

And we had no idea how to do it.

Chapter 2

{Kris}

"You're not focused enough!"

The sound of Micah's voice had a way of doing the opposite of what he coached. He said focus; I wavered. Well, in actuality, my focus simply shifted. Instead of trying to move the rock with my mind, as he wanted me to do, I imagined what it would be like to make his head explode. That was when it happened.

The rock exploded.

"Holy shit!" Alec laughed hard. So hard he doubled over, clutching his stomach, and looked close to falling over and rolling in the sand.

My lips twitched from watching him, but my anger held the smile back. I picked the tiny pieces of rock shrapnel out of my hair and tossed them to the ground. "I'm done for the day."

"You still have ten minutes before you need to leave for class. We need to keep working," Micah argued. "You made something happen. You can't stop now."

I spun on him quickly, forcing myself to bite back the

truth—that the rock had nearly been his stubborn head. "We worked all morning, and we've been working nonstop since lunch. I need a break."

"Micah, why don't we call it quits a little early today?" Gran placed a gentle arm around my shoulders. She often came to my aid when Micah pushed me too hard, and I welcomed her comfort.

Alec often did as well, though usually with threats against Micah's life. That was, of course, when he wasn't the one dying from an unstoppable fit of laughter.

"Fine," Micah relented. "We'll try again tomorrow."

I gave Micah a look to portray just how *not* excited I was about that. For now, I was just eager to get away from him. As far as he would allow me anyway. As my appointed guard while we practiced, I couldn't really go far without him now.

We had decided to keep Kim out of the loop as far as what we did on the beach every day. Since we were practicing my Incantation skills, along with strengthening my specialties, it was best not to involve anyone that we didn't need to involve. Alec's guard, Bruce, kept a good distance, usually hanging out on the pier while we practiced, and though he knew some weird stuff was going on, he didn't know the half of it.

I picked up the spell books I carried with me and dusted the sand off of them before slipping them into my backpack. Coming up alongside Alec, who had finally managed to pull himself together, I whispered, "That rock? It was nearly Micah's head."

He snorted. "I figured as much from the look on your face." He cast a glance over his shoulder at Micah as we walked away.

Lowering his voice for my ears only, he asked, "How's that stone working out for you?"

My hands instinctively reached for the charm that hung around my neck. Gran had given one to both Alec and me last week. She had enchanted it to weaken the wicked impulses we both tended to have from time to time as a side effect of our souls gradually spiraling down the drain of evil.

Gran wasn't a natural Incantator, but she had always had a special interest in it, and had taught herself a few spells that really anyone could do—just not as well as a true Incantator could. She wasn't great, but she was better than I was right now.

Her charm actually seemed to work. Most days.

"It might have been the only reason it *wasn't* his head that exploded," I admitted with a grin. I glanced over my shoulder. Micah remained a few feet behind Alec and me, visibly moping as he trudged after us. His always present protector, Richie, followed closely behind.

Alec pulled his charm out from under his shirt and kissed it gingerly. "I think mine has saved me a few times, too. Otherwise, he might be fish food by now."

We both chuckled. Alec and I often bonded over our mutual dislike of Micah. Since Alec had recently admitted to being in love with me, but still chose to let me go, and even approved of my blossoming relationship with Nathan, moments with Alec were at times strained. When we ganged up on Micah, things flowed easily between us as they always had before the big L-word came between us.

It wasn't that a part of me didn't love Alec in return. I did. In fact, a big part of me would always have loving feelings for him after what we had shared. Those feelings just weren't nearly as strong for him as they were for Nathan.

I glanced at my watch excitedly. Ten minutes until class started.

The Kala leaders had insisted that I take a combat class to hone my skills while I stayed on the island. Little did they know I had a hidden romance with the instructor they put in charge of that class. It filled me with a sense of naughty goodness every time I thought about it. Luckily, I fought the other students during drills and not Nathan, otherwise our cover would have been blown by now. As Callie had once said, anyone who watched us fight would know that there was something going on between us.

Not that I cared. I didn't want to keep our relationship a secret. But Nathan insisted that it was in my best interest, and so I dealt with it.

Grudgingly at times. Especially times like now.

As we moved through the village center, we ran into a large cluster of Kala, many of whom I recognized from the combat class. A few stopped to let Alec and I pass. Others skirted around a tree to avoid crossing our path. Their actions didn't bother me anymore. I had grown used to their skittishness around us in the few weeks we had been here. No. That didn't bother me.

The two girls giggling in front of us bothered me. Every day, and I meant *every* day, I stood behind them in class and listened to them swoon over Nathan. I couldn't help but suspect that the excitement on their faces now had something to do with the fact that they would be getting a glimpse of him soon.

I said goodbye to Alec before following the annoying gigglers into the Education Building. I didn't look back, didn't acknowledge them, but I knew Micah and Richie followed me. They had to, until I got to class, and Nathan took over.

Except Nathan wasn't there yet.

Regardless, I turned to Micah in the doorway, and said, "You're dismissed."

Micah glanced into the classroom behind me. "Where's Nathan?"

"I'm a few minutes early. He'll be here. Just go. It's fine. You know I won't go all *Carrie* and kill everybody in the two minutes before he gets here."

Micah made a face. He didn't like discussing what I was, and he definitely didn't like me making jokes about it. "Yeah, okay. I'll see you later then."

"Yep," I said with far more gusto than I felt. I hated that I had to have a babysitter everywhere I went. I especially hated that Micah was often that babysitter.

Fortunately, I got to stare at a sexy, sweaty Nathan for the next hour and a half. Along with the rest of the class. At least they were all in the dark, blind to our stolen glances and the festering heat between us. But then, that meant I was forced to bite my tongue instead of confronting those who found it necessary to drool over him like a bunch of hormone-crazed groupies.

I took my usual spot in the back and dropped my backpack to the floor with a thud. The two girls in front of me turned to look over their shoulders—briefly halting their Nathan worshipping—and I returned their stares with perfect indifference. They regarded me warily before tipping their heads together to continue, now in whispers.

I sure wasn't making many friends among the Kala.

Not that I cared. These Kala girls were a unique breed. Very much like the typical teenage girls I had experienced in high school, only worse. In fact, pretty much all the students on the island were spoiled brats. They were like the popular kids on crack, and with a much bigger god-complex. Probably because they were actually part gods.

They all acted the part perfectly.

"Kira said she saw him in the Infirmary the other day." My ears perked up as the brunette's voice drifted back to me.

The other girl, the blonde, was quick to wave it off. Quicker than I was. "Yeah, but probably only because he feels like he should. Sure they have history, but it's been a long time."

"Well, Kira doesn't think they'll ever figure out how to change her back. Even if they do, it's not going to stop Kira from making a move now that he's back."

They were definitely talking about Lillian. And Nathan visiting Lillian. And some girl named Kira making a move on Nathan.

I had the sudden urge to hit something. Or someone. Specifically, the girls in front of me. And this Kira, whoever she was.

I instinctively reached under my shirt, withdrew the charm from around my neck, and twirled it between my fingers.

Technically, I couldn't feel it working, but at times like this, I knew it had to be doing something.

Something kept me from banging their heads together like a couple of cymbals.

Nathan's timing couldn't have been better. He walked in with his usual oversized duffel bag slung over his shoulder. Dressed in black mesh shorts that dropped to his knees and a black sleeveless shirt that hugged his upper body in all the right places, he looked every bit the part-god that he was. As all female eyes in the room followed him, it was obvious that I wasn't the only one who thought so. Even the boys surveyed him with respectful admiration.

He dropped the bag and turned forward. His eyes darted to mine quickly before skimming over the rest of the class.

I knew it immediately. Something was off. Something was wrong.

"Group drills," he declared, effectively silencing the chatter in the room. "Count off by fours."

I smiled to myself. This was his "lazy lesson." It was the one he did when he had something on his mind and didn't want to bother teaching something new or difficult. With group drills he could hang back and watch the class spar, only offering assistance when it was necessary, thus freeing himself to mull over whatever he had on his mind.

And he thought he knew *me* so well.

I ended up calling the number three, and ventured across the room to where the rest of the threes had assembled. One of the boys grumbled under his breath while two of the girls exchanged catty glances when I joined the group.

"Yeah, yeah . . ." I muttered as I dropped my bag to the floor with a thud. "You all hate me. Nothing new to me, and I really don't care. Can we get started now?" One at a time, I met their eyes with a hard stare. "Who's going first?"

The group stepped back as the two other girls took positions. While they sparred, I pretended to watch and critique. In reality, my gaze remained fixed to the front of the room, on Nathan.

Though I knew something was bothering him, I hadn't mastered the ability to tell what exactly that was yet. One thing I had learned about Nathan was that if he didn't want me to know what was troubling him, he wouldn't make it easy for me to figure out. While things between us were far from where they had started, some things had never changed.

* * * * *

The only thing worse than unintentionally blowing up a rock two days in a row was getting hit in the face by the shrapnel produced by one of those rocks. It hurt. A lot. At least I was capable of healing abnormally fast, and stopped bleeding after a few minutes. By the end of the day, not even a scar would remain.

As I stormed off the beach, leaving everyone behind me, I realized that my anger was fueled more by the frustration I felt with my difficult-to-control specialties than it was by any concern I had about my face. Only one thing—or person—could make my barely contained rage worse.

Micah.

"Hey, wait up," he called from behind me.

I didn't slow. If anything, I sped up. "Just once, it would be nice of you to forget your babysitting duties," I tossed over my shoulder, and glimpsed Richie as he scrambled to catch up to us.

"Never." He chuckled as he took a few quick steps to come up beside me. "It could be worse . . ."

"I doubt that."

"You could be stuck with Kim."

I scoffed. Though Kim was a tough and very intimidating Kala, she wasn't nearly as annoying as Micah. And she at least gave me some space. Micah, on the other hand, knew no boundaries. Apparently, since he thought we were soul mates, he thought he was entitled to get within my comfort zone, despite me repeatedly telling him he was not welcome.

"Where are you going?" Micah asked.

"To the gym."

I didn't need to elaborate. Micah knew why I was going to the gym, and who would be there this time of the day. Nathan always worked out during the hour he had free between the end of his morning combat class and when he met us for lunch.

Micah's steps faltered briefly, but he quickly caught up. Despite his silence, I sensed the agitation rolling off of him in waves. I waited for one of his snarky remarks that I had grown accustomed to hearing, and good at ignoring, but he said nothing. As the gym came into view, Micah's steps slowed to a sulky crawl.

He knew as well as I did that if Nathan was there—and he would be—then Micah would promptly be dismissed. The one thing Micah hated more than anything was relinquishing any sort of control to Nathan, especially when it had anything to do with me.

His behavior annoyed me, and frequently pissed me off to the point that I was grateful for the charm around my neck. But never had I been more grateful for that charm than now, and for once, it had nothing to do with Micah.

Stepping through the front door of the gym, my eyes immediately found Nathan amongst all the sweaty, hard-bodied Kala. In my opinion, his was by far the finest. Apparently, I wasn't the only one who thought so.

In the weeks that I had been on the island so far, I had tried to not let the constant attention Nathan received bother me. Some of the guys regarded him as an idol, since he had helped train many of them in their younger years. That was okay, but the girls with their doe-eyes that followed him everywhere he went and their unsubtle attempts at flirting got on my nerves.

Then there were girls like the one I saw now. The type who thought the way to get a guy to notice her was to expose as much skin as possible and to practically throw herself at him.

Either Nathan had grown accustomed to thwarting off girls like her over the years, or he was clueless. The only thing that kept me from going Skotadi-crazy on the girl was his blatant disinterest in her as she pretended to spot him at the bench press. The charm around my neck probably helped, too. That was until he finished his set, sat up, and his eyes shifted to the door. The resulting smile on his face when he saw me could quiet even the feistiest of demons.

He said something to the girl before making his way over to where Micah, Richie, and I stood by the door. Once he was within earshot, I let a brief pang of jealousy take control of my mouth.

"Kira?" I asked him.

"What?"

I thrust my chin forward, eyeing the girl where she still stood by the bench press, watching.

Nathan followed my gaze, then glanced back at me peculiarly. "Veronica, one of the other instructors."

"Of course there's more than one of them," I muttered under my breath. From the look on Nathan's face as he glanced at Micah and Richie in confusion, I realized that I had said it loud enough for him to hear.

Micah threw his hands up defensively. "Not my problem you have your girlfriend on your old playground," he said to Nathan. Turning to me, he said, "I guess you're with him now, so I suppose I'll see you later?"

"Yeah, sure," I said with a wave of my hand. When and where I saw Micah again was the least of my concerns.

Nathan watched as the door closed behind Richie, then he turned to me. "Do I even want to know what that was all about?"

"Probably not," I said quickly. "Are you still working out?"

"I'm done. Let me grab my stuff."

He trotted back to the bench, said something to Vivian, or Venice, or whatever her name was, and slung his bag over his shoulder. I kept my mouth shut because, surrounded by Kala who didn't exactly trust me, I had to, but my eyes, when they briefly met hers, clearly portrayed the *'mine'* I desperately wanted to scream to the entire island.

Chapter 3

{Nathan}

As the door shut behind us, my thoughts were on what Micah had been talking about. *Girlfriend . . . playground.* I didn't get it. I was curious about this Kira, and even more curious as to why Kris looked like she had bit into a lemon when she said her name.

Before I could ask, Kris grabbed my hand and steered me around the side of the building, where we were hidden amongst a cluster of palm trees and white sand dunes. She stepped close to me, and I held my hands up as if to ward her off.

"I'm sweaty and gross," I warned.

"I happen to like you like that."

She gripped the front of my shirt and pulled me in, raising up onto her tiptoes to meet me. Though something felt off, two seconds into the kiss I remembered that I was a guy . . . and I didn't really care. And I concluded that I would make every attempt to be sweaty and gross in her presence from this moment on.

Not even the voices from a group of Kala walking out of the

gym behind me could halt the rapidly growing heat brewing between us. I only vaguely registered that they were too close for comfort. Without breaking contact, I pulled Kris behind a high sand dune. There, I turned to put my back against a broad palm tree, and in one swift motion, pulled Kris into my lap as I slid to the ground.

Perfect. We were more hidden, and my hands were free to slip under the hem of her shirt without worry. My fingers skimmed her smooth skin, eliciting a trail of goosebumps in their wake. Feeling her body come to life beneath my hands ignited something inside of me, something I had grown accustomed to holding back with her in the past. But not right now.

I was so absorbed in her, in her mouth, in her body against mine, that I didn't hear the approaching voices until they were practically on top of us. I recovered my hands and smoothed her shirt back into place, but it was too late. Whoever it was had busted us.

"Oh, yeah," a young Kala boy called, "way to go man."

Kris immediately pressed her face into my neck to hide.

"Hey, that's our combat instructor," the boy whispered loudly to another boy trailing behind him.

Kris groaned and buried her face deeper. She realized that there was a fifty-fifty chance that the boys were in the same class as she was. I wasn't about to tell her that I recognized them, and that they were in her class.

"Stay hidden," I whispered to her. "They don't know it's you."

I watched them closely as they walked away, high-fiving each other for some weird reason. They weren't the ones making out with a girl.

Once they were out of sight, I said, "They're gone."

Kris tilted her head to look up at me, though she still remained partially hidden in my neck. "That was embarrassing."

"They didn't see you."

"Yeah, but now the whole island is going to hear about you making out with girls behind the gym, and other girls are going to think they have a shot—"

"Whoa, wait a minute," I interrupted her before she took a hard turn into Crazyville. "Where is this coming from?"

Even as I asked, I feared I already knew the answer. And if so, her comments from earlier suddenly made sense. I still wanted to hear it from her though. I pushed a curtain of hair out of the way, revealing her face and rosy cheeks. "Kris? What's going on?"

She shrugged. "I've overheard girls talking about you, about how hot you are, what they would like to do to you . . ." She made a gagging motion, then continued quickly, "I'm just sick of hearing it every day."

I grimaced. "And one of these girls was named Kira, I assume?"

"No, I overheard her sister talking. I don't know who Kira is."

"That makes two of us," I said, making a poor attempt at a joke.

Kris didn't laugh. "She knows who you are. You must have left quite an impression on her."

I noted the sarcasm and chose to ignore it, because she had a point. There were lots of girls I didn't remember. *What does that say about me?* Nothing good, I knew, but I was different now. I had changed.

"I'm sorry you have to hear that stuff."

"It's not your fault," she muttered as she got to her feet.

I didn't have the nerve to tell her that it might actually be my fault, not yet, and took her extended hand as I rose to a stand beside her.

"Sometimes . . ." she continued softly, "I wish I could tell them the truth, even if just to make them shut up. It's hard to pretend we're something that we're not."

I nodded but said nothing. *What could I say?*

I knew it sucked for me—to not hold her hand in public, to not steal kisses whenever the mood struck, to not be seen together often enough to cause suspicion—and I knew it was worse for her, considering she was ostracized by the majority of the island. I was one of the few she had in her corner, and for her safety, I had to maintain an appropriate distance.

In public anyway.

I shot her a grin. "Come on. Let's head back to the dorms. I need to shower, and we could *not pretend* for a while, and grab a late lunch."

It sounded like an amazing idea to me, and from the shy grin that emerged on Kris's face when she realized what I was suggesting, I knew that she agreed.

Ten minutes later, back in my room, I turned to her with a teasing smile. "Do you mind if I take a shower now, or would you rather I stay all gross and sweaty?"

She shoved me in the general direction of the bathroom with a smile. "Go."

I waved a hand around the room. "Make yourself comfortable."

The fact that I was able to leave the room, with Kris sitting on the edge of my bed, was a miracle. The fact that I managed to get through a shower amazed me. But nothing was more impressive than the idea that came to me in the middle of that shower. I was so impressed with myself that I sped through the rest of it in record time.

After my inadvertent screw ups earlier, this would definitely get me back in her good graces, and I was going to win brownie points as world's best boyfriend. For one with limitations anyway.

She was sitting cross-legged on the bed, my trainer's manual on her lap, when I emerged from the bathroom. She lifted her head and that stubborn strand of hair fell forward, partially covering her right eye. Usually, I would have been struck by the urge to put it in its rightful place, but this time my footsteps faltered at the sight of her.

She has no idea how beautiful she is.

"Checking your manual to see what torture you have planned for us next," she said as she tossed the book on the nightstand, completely unaware of what she had done to me.

I turned and pretended to examine the scruff on my chin in the mirror while I regained my composure. "You already know most of it," I tossed over my shoulder. "You're the best one in the class."

"That's not saying much," she snorted.

I turned around, but decided it was best, for now, to prop myself up against the dresser, on the other side of the room from her. At least until I told her about my brilliant idea.

"Hey, um . . ." I started, suddenly unsure. Suddenly nervous. *Why do I have to turn into a bumbling idiot around her all the time?* "I thought of something while I was in the shower."

Her eyebrows raised. "That sounds interesting."

She made it really hard to keep my distance. I looked at the floor to keep from looking at her, because looking at her made it too difficult to maintain the five feet between us. And being too close to her meant I wouldn't be able to explain my idea.

Two minutes. I could wait two minutes . . .

"I was thinking about earlier," I finally managed, "about what you said about us not getting to be ourselves, and thought maybe it would be a good idea for us to get off the island for a little bit."

"You think they'll let me off the island?" She sounded skeptical.

Honestly, so was I, but I had friends in high places. Friends who could get things done. Well, one friend really.

"I think I can make it happen," I said.

"And do what?"

I lifted a shoulder. "Anything. I don't know . . ." Only now did I realize that I probably should have planned this out a little better. Precious brownie points would be lost for poor presentation. "We can go somewhere, do something stupid . . ."

"Stupid? Oh, well, that sounds tempting."

"I don't mean stupid. I mean . . . simple. We've never done simple."

"I think we're way beyond simple."

"Yeah, but wouldn't it be nice to not have to pretend? Just for a few hours? It would be nice to get a chance to be us, without having to worry about someone seeing us."

Kris's face scrunched up, and eventually broke into a smile. "Are you asking me out on a date right now? Because if you are, you're seriously bad at it."

"Give me a break. I haven't done this in a long time."

I finally pushed away from the dresser. As I angled closer to Kris, her teeth caught her bottom lip. It was a nervous habit, but *oh, my God.* Something in me came unhinged at the sight, and I had to remind myself to behave. But then her tongue flicked across her lips—a move so quick I wouldn't have noticed if I weren't staring at them—and I knew there wasn't a chance in hell I would be able to keep my hands off of her now.

"I may be bad at the asking part," I said, lifting my gaze from her mouth to her eyes. "But what I'm good at more than makes up for it."

I reveled in the fact that sometimes I managed to make *her* nervous. Her eyes were everywhere but on my face by the time I reached her. Bending down until my nose nearly touched hers, I placed my hands on either side of her legs, essentially trapping her. Her eyes widened when she finally met my gaze, then just as quickly as the nervousness appeared, it was replaced by the bravado she always managed to muster up.

That was one of the many things I loved about her.

"Oh? And what exactly are you good at?" she breathed.

"This." I yanked her legs out from under her, forcing her to fall back on the bed with a squeal. I followed and hovered over her long enough to register the gleam of excitement in her eyes before taking her mouth with mine.

I kissed her deep and slow and controlled. My plan had been for hot but brief, for the simple reason that I couldn't handle kisses this incredible for too long before I started wanting more. The moment her fingers dug into my shoulders, pulling me in, I knew my plan was shot to hell and I was in trouble.

My hands were still on her hips, where I had grabbed her earlier. Now, my grip tightened to pull her against me as I shimmied farther up the mattress until no part of either of us touched the floor. My mouth slid from hers, only for an instant, but long enough for a tiny whimper to pass her lips. That sound shattered what little self-control I had left. I reclaimed her mouth with a wild and desperate need. In that moment, I knew I had never wanted anything more than I wanted her.

And that was exactly why I had to do what I had to do. Cringing against the physical pain it caused, I pulled away. Not far. Just far enough to not kiss her again.

Her eyes, when they flew open, were full of questions. And then understanding, because this wasn't the first time I'd had to pull the brakes. She didn't say anything, but that might have been because she was struggling to catch her breath.

It even took me a moment to catch mine. And then she bit that damn lip of hers again, and I had to close my eyes to keep myself from losing it.

Breathe in . . . breathe out.

"Nathan?"

I grinned and opened one eye, thinking that was safer than two. It wasn't. "Just give me a minute?"

I felt her shift beneath me as she settled into the pillow and made herself comfortable. Risking a peek, I observed the cutest expression of patient boredom on her face as she stared at the ceiling. When her eyes shifted and she saw me watching her, she smiled.

That was bad because it made me look at her lips again. But I had regained my composure enough to control myself. Instead of kissing her again, as that smile demanded, I asked, "Will you go out with me?"

Her smile widened. "That was much better."

"Is that a yes?"

She nodded. "Definitely a yes."

*　　*　　*　　*　　*

Having friends in high places had its perks. That didn't mean Jared would necessarily agree to my idea. It just meant that he might actually hear me out before shutting me down. And so far, from the skeptical curve of his eyebrows, I saw this whole conversation ending with a big fat N-O.

Time to pull out the big guns.

"We've known each other a long time, man," I said. "You know I can handle this."

He leaned forward to place his elbows on the desk, and

cupped his chin in his hands. The sharply curved eyebrows softened . . . just a little.

Knowing he was close to caving, I added, "I need this. *Kris* needs this."

The look he gave me let me know how big of a pain in the ass he considered me, then with a loud sigh, he opened the top drawer of the desk and withdrew a stack of papers. He flipped through them, scanning over a few. At last, he said, "Tonight. O'Brien's on the dock. He can get you the boat, and he won't ask questions."

I grinned. "O'Brien? The little shit I beat the snot out of before I left?" That had been, what, nearly seven years ago? But, oh, I remembered him. And I knew he wouldn't ask any questions.

Jared nodded once. "That would be the one."

I couldn't help but chuckle. Jared looked up with a stern expression, but I saw the hint of a smile hiding under his mask. "Don't push it," he warned.

I threw my hands up in surrender, and promised, "I'll be good." Not like I cared anymore about whatever girl we had been fighting over then. As long as he kept his eyes off of Kris tonight, his nose would remain unbroken.

"You know Skotadi are in the area," Jared warned. "They're always snooping around the mainland, trying to figure out where we're hiding . . ."

"I know, I know. Don't let them track me back to the island. Don't get killed. I know the rules."

Jared made a noise that fell somewhere between a snort and

laugh. "Doesn't mean you know how to follow them."

I smiled as I backed out the door. "Stranger things have happened," I said, and then I got the hell out of there before he changed his mind.

I had a grin ready for every guard I passed on my way out of the building. Once outside, I headed toward the beach. My usual hour at the gym was shot by now anyway, and I was too excited to wait until lunch to give Kris the good news. I kicked off my sandals before stepping onto the sand, and made my way toward the cluster of bodies on the far end of the beach.

Considering they were experimenting with Incantation, they kept out of sight as much as possible. Very few Kala ventured that far down the beach, and those that did usually did so in the evening, and for privacy of an entirely different type.

As I neared, I was able to make out the individual faces. Kris, of course, was the center of attention, and appeared to have Gran and Micah both instructing her in some sort of exercise. Alec had taken up a position a few yards away, and appeared to be working on something of his own. Regardless, he maintained a watchful eye on Kris.

I didn't mind that so much anymore. Now, I considered it a good thing that he cared about her as much as he did, and looked out for her in my absence. Despite the stormy start to our relationship, I was glad that Alec was such a big part of Kris's life, simply because it was important to her. Because she insisted on maintaining a friendship with him, I chose to overlook the few lingering glances he shot her, only because they were becoming less frequent and slightly less pathetic.

The bodyguards were present as well. Richie, serving as Micah's protection, kept his eyes fixed on Kris as she and Micah worked together. Though he appeared relaxed where he sat in the sand, I noted the rigidness of his shoulders, and knew he was prepared to spring at the first sign of aggression toward Micah. Bruce, on the other hand, wasn't even near them, choosing instead to whale watch—or whatever he was doing— from the pier.

Richie was the first to spot me, and quickly scampered to his feet in a defensive posture before he realized it was only me. His abrupt reaction caused the others to take notice of me. Kris immediately dropped what she was doing. Literally. A wall of sand, suspended midair by nothing but her mind, fell to the ground as she spun around to meet me.

"That's—umph." I swayed slightly as the weight of her—as insignificant as it was—crashed into me.

"Awesome?"

I nodded. "New trick?"

She beamed. "I'm having a good day. Haven't blown anything up yet. What are you doing here?"

I glanced around at the others, most of whom had continued about their own business and weren't paying any attention to us. The exception was, not surprisingly, Micah. He had been on the other side of the sand wall, working directly with Kris, and was now left with nothing else better to do than stare at us.

The seconds ticked by as I glared at him, until he finally shifted his gaze and, at least, pretended to look preoccupied. Though I knew his ears would be staining to pick up everything exchanged between us, and his mind would attempt to pluck anything he missed out of Kris's head, I finally explained to Kris my reason for tracking her down.

Her reaction wasn't what I expected.

"Tonight?" she squeaked.

I tried not to let her lack of excitement deflate my swollen ego . . . too much. "I thought you wanted to get off the island, go do something *stupid*." I tried to lighten her suddenly sullen mood by making fun of myself. It didn't work. She nibbled on her lip like she was starving, and it was a chocolate donut. "Kris? What's wrong? You don't want to go?"

"No, I do!" she responded quickly, as if realizing for the first time her lack of excitement. "I definitely do. I just thought it would be a few days from now, and I would have more time to prepare."

"You don't have to prepare anything. I'm taking care of it."

Though she nodded, and offered me a small smile, uncertainty still lined her eyes. After a moment, she mumbled, "I have no idea what I'm going to wear."

Sometimes I didn't understand girls. "It doesn't matter what you're wearing. You'll look great in anything," I said diplomatically. At least I had been around them enough to know the right things to say in most situations.

Not that it mattered in this case. Kris was in her own little world, silently suffering her odd case of anxiety about tonight, and dwelling on her wardrobe shortcomings.

"Kris?" I stooped slightly to force her into making eye contact with me. "You okay? You still want to do this? Because you don't really seem so sure anymore."

Finally, I got a full smile—a real smile. "Trust me. I do. I'm just surprised it's tonight, that's all."

"Okay." I wasn't convinced, but didn't want to push it. "Meet you at your room at five?"

She nodded, already distracted by her thoughts again. I hesitated, debating briefly whether or not I should push her into telling me what was really bothering her, but ultimately decided to let it go for now. I nodded to Richie as I passed, maintaining a calm exterior despite the churning in my stomach.

It was only the short notice, and apparent lack of girl-approved attire, that had her acting strange. Nothing else. Nothing was wrong. Nothing of real importance anyway.

"Nathan!"

I stopped and looked over my shoulder as Gran trotted after me. I wiped the shit-eating grin from my face before she saw it. Really, all things considered, she moved well for her age.

"You'll remember what we talked about?" she asked me.

I hesitated. Surely her mind wouldn't be the first to go. "Talked about what, Gran?"

She gave me that look—the look that made my inner child cower and scamper off to his room for time out. "You know damn well what I'm talking about. The other morning—"

I groaned when it finally clicked. *That* talk. How could I have forgotten? "Seriously, Gran? That conversation will stick with me until the day I die. And not because I enjoyed it that much."

"Well, it doesn't need to stick with you for long," she returned. "Just long enough—"

"For what, Gran? Long enough for what?"

"For you to be smart about . . ." She trailed off, for once looking as comfortable as she should have been considering the subject. "*Certain things.*"

I sighed. "It's just a date, Gran. We can go on a date."

"Yes, but . . ."

"But what?" I paused, and glanced over her shoulder at Kris. She had turned away from us, and faced Micah in some sort of challenge of the minds or something. "What's bringing this on, Gran? What did she say to you?"

Gran shook her head softly, and I knew I wouldn't get a straight answer. Cryptic, coded messages were Gran's thing. "She's thinking. But I question if it's because she's really ready for a physical relationship, or if she feels like she should be ready. Remember, you're older than her, more experienced than her. . ."

"I know, Gran. I know."

"I just fear that's pushing her before she's ready," Gran concluded.

"I'm not . . ." I stopped. I haven't been pushing for anything. Have I?

"I'm not saying you are," Gran corrected quickly. "I think she's pushing herself . . . for you."

Huh. I had not expected that.

Gran smiled as she patted me on the back. "Just do what's right for her. You always have. Don't let that change now just because things have changed between the two of you."

"That will never change."

That was a vow I meant full-heartedly. No matter the

40

context, there was nothing I wouldn't do for that girl, and nothing I would ever do to hurt her. No matter how embarrassing it may have been for the words to come from Gran of all people, they stuck with me. As I walked away, I couldn't help but wonder if she was on to something I had been blind to.

What if a wardrobe crisis wasn't the only cause of Kris's anxiety about tonight?

Chapter 4

{Kris}

Nathan had been right. We needed some time off the island to be ourselves.

He had planned an exceptional evening. From the moment Kim handed me over to him at the door, to the moment our feet hit the sand on the mainland, everything had gone off without a hitch. Even the Kala stationed at the boat dock had practically rolled out the red carpet for us.

And it was still going well.

Better, even, because we were now alone, and enjoying our first taste of real—not prepackaged and mass produced, cafeteria-style—food in weeks. Sitting at a secluded, candlelit table mere feet from the ocean's gently crashing waves, with soft music playing in the background, and the best-looking, most attentive date ever across from me was the highlight of all of my eighteen years. I couldn't have wiped the smile from my face if I had wanted to.

"How much time do we have left before the boat comes back for us?" I asked as I scooped the remainder of my dessert—something that resembled a chocolate cake, but named something I couldn't pronounce—onto my fork.

He checked his watch. "About an hour and a half."

"So what's next?" I asked as I tossed my napkin onto my empty plate.

"Whatever you want," he returned casually as he removed several bills from his wallet and placed them on the table. "Across the street is a dance club, where I will go if you insist, and behind me is one of the world's most beautiful black sand beaches waiting to be explored."

His tone and hopeful expression made it clear which option he preferred. I nibbled my lip as I considered the beach over Nathan's shoulder.

"But it's dark," I said timidly. "We won't be able to see much."

He smiled at me in that way he did when I said or did something that wasn't exactly bright, but he resigned to love me regardless. He propped his elbows on the table and stared at me in silence for a moment before it dawned on me—he hadn't actually meant for us to *explore* the beach. More like explore each other . . .

"Beach," I answered quickly. "Definitely, beach."

Fifteen minutes later, I concluded that nothing could beat a romantic, leisurely stroll to wrap up the perfect evening. Aside from a few small sand creatures, we were alone. We walked hand in hand until the restaurant's lights were nothing but a faint glow behind us. The half-moon overhead gave us just enough light to see each other. Conversation flowed easily, and for once didn't center on all the danger and drama that filled our lives.

"This is probably the warmest water you will ever swim in." Nathan drew to a slow stop, and pulled me after him as he angled closer to the waterline.

"Haven't swam in it yet," I said.

"What? Micah won't let you take swim breaks?"

I gave him a hard look. "No talking about that stuff, remember?"

He pressed his lips together and lifted a hand in surrender.

Smiling, I kicked off my sandals to let the water lap over my feet. He was right. It was warm. Especially for the ocean. "I always liked to bury my toes," I mused as I dug them in the sand, and then watched as the next wave washed it away.

A distracted grunt came from behind me, and I turned to see what Nathan was doing. I watched, first in confusion then in awe, as he unbuttoned and shrugged out of his shirt. I eyed the magnificence of a bare-chested Nathan with silent interest, but when his hands moved to the waistband of his pants, I couldn't keep quiet any longer.

"What are you doing?" I asked. My voice sounded sturdier than I felt. My legs, on the other hand, shook like I straddled a fault line.

His carefree shrug didn't do much to placate me, considering he now stood before me in nothing but a pair of boxer shorts. And while that was awesome in its own way, I was too confused—and if I wanted to be completely honest with myself, a little nervous—to thoroughly enjoy it. The last time I had seen this much of Nathan, he had been near death, and it had been out of necessity to save his life. Now? Now, he had willingly stripped for a completely different reason.

"I'm taking you for your first swim." Advancing a few steps toward me, he added, "It's just like wearing swim trunks."

"What about me?" I gestured to the capris and halter top it had taken me all afternoon to decide on wearing. I wasn't about to get in the ocean wearing them, and the thought of stripping down to my underwear in front of him scared the daylights out of me.

Of course, I had done it with Alec once before. Hell, I had stripped *naked* in front of him. Though I had been in Skotadi mode when it happened, and wasn't exactly fond of the fuzzy memory, he found ways to remind me of it frequently. Regardless, if I could play a game of basketball in my underwear with Alec, I should be able to swim in my underwear with Nathan.

Except . . . this situation scared me more. With Alec, I had felt confident that nothing would happen between us because I hadn't wanted anything to happen. With Nathan . . .

Well, I wanted something to happen. Very much so. It was only a matter of when.

He stopped beside me, took one of my hands in his. "It's just like wearing a bikini," he insisted, completely unaware of the thoughts behind my delay.

I wasn't so much worried about the underwear versus bikini debate as I was nervous about what would happen when I got into that water with him.

I watched as he waded in. Once he was in up to his knees, he turned. "You coming?"

He was tempting . . . very tempting. I knew I would get in, eventually, but I needed another minute. I folded my arms over my chest. "What if I'm wearing ugly granny panties?"

He grinned. "You're not."

"How do you know?"

His head tilted and he gave a lazy shrug. "Lucky guess."

He was right of course. But I wasn't about to tell him that I had dressed in my nicest matching pair of undergarments just in case a moment like this arose—though I had anticipated something that involved a little less salt water. And not this much skin exposure.

No, it's okay. I can do this.

Before I changed my mind, I lifted the halter over my head like my stomach wasn't about to jump up my throat. Whether Nathan watched me or not, I would never know because I refused to look at him the entire time I undressed. I didn't risk a glance at him until after I was safely submerged in the water . . .

And immediately wondered what I had been so nervous about.

He had waded out far—farther than I could touch, actually—and only his head and shoulders bobbed above the surface. The moonlight bouncing off the gently breaking surf reflected in his eyes and caused the tiny silver specks to shimmer brightly. Accentuated by his reassuring smile, his eyes reminded me of the guardian angel I had once thought him to be. I knew I would be safe with him. No matter the circumstance.

His hand found mine under the water. "Come here."

"I can't touch the bottom." Though I could tread water, I would hardly consider myself a decent swimmer. The thought of my feet not touching something solid rattled me. Not to mention, only six months had passed since I had nearly drowned in the car accident.

From the look on his face, I knew that Nathan understood the reason for my water anxiety. If anyone understood my fear, it was him. "I can touch," he soothed. "It's okay, I've got you . . ."

With a gentle tug, he pulled me toward him. Propelled by momentum and water current, my body collided with his, and our legs entangled as I kicked like a panicked bug stuck on its back. Nathan swayed slightly, but righted us quickly and easily.

"Stop squirming," he murmured into my ear as he pulled me against him.

"I'm not a good swimmer." While true, I wasn't about to admit that I was more squirmy than usual because of the bundle of nerves in my stomach—and it wasn't all because of the water.

"Here . . ." His hands found and gripped my flailing legs, and positioned them securely around his waist.

Physically, on the outside, I felt instantly grounded and safe. Inside, the bundle of nerves multiplied and forced a shaky breath to pass my lips.

"You're nervous." Nathan's eyes were on me, observant.

My gaze met his briefly, before quickly skirting away. "Large bodies of water scare me," I answered as I scanned the dark horizon over his shoulder.

"It's not that," he said. "It's me. You're nervous being with *me* right now."

Damn him and his unnatural ability to read me like a book. I didn't respond. I didn't need to. We both knew he was right.

"Why?" he pressed.

There was no point in trying to blow it off as nothing. He always knew when I tried to do that. Absolute honesty remained my only option. All I had to do was determine what exactly I was so nervous about.

"Well, for starters, we're half naked in the ocean," I answered. Just saying the words out loud sent a wave of heat up my neck and into my cheeks.

Nathan nodded, a playful grin curving his lips. "And I'm seconds away from kissing you . . ."

I tried to swallow to wet my throat—though it sounded more like a gulp to my ears—and still I only managed a weak whisper. "Then there's that."

His grin widened, bringing out his dimples. "Nothing is going to happen, Kris. That's not what this is, okay?"

My eyes flicked to his, but this time I locked in on the irresistible blend of silvery-blue that gazed back at me. Once locked, I found it impossible to look away. I stared in awe. Because, once again, he knew. Like he always did. While I'd had a difficult time pinpointing the exact reason behind my anxiety, *he knew.*

"You're not ready," he continued, then added with a short laugh, "I know that now."

My jaw dropped as I pushed back to see his face more

clearly. With his arms wrapped tightly around me, I couldn't move far. "Was this some sort of experiment?"

"No. That wasn't my intention," he said quickly. "But the last two minutes have answered the question I've been wondering ever since I had that talk with Gran."

Crap. I thought I had dodged that. I silently thanked God that it was dark enough to hide the redness I felt deepening on my cheeks. Then I pulled together the necessary bravado to get through this conversation, and maintain my cool. Well, as cool as I could manage under the circumstances. "Oh? What question was that?"

"If you've been thinking about taking the next step in our relationship."

"Hmmm." I surveyed him like a lawyer cross-examining a witness. "So, because I'm jumpy right now, you believe that I have *not* been thinking about it? Correct?"

He narrowed his eyes, seemingly unsure how to take the sudden shift in my confidence level. His shoulders shrugged with uncertainty.

Finally! Finally Nathan was wrong about something!

I smiled knowingly. "Well, actually . . ." My smile grew as his face fell and his eyes widened slightly. He was five seconds from reaching his 'deer in headlights' face, and I reveled in knowing *that* about *him*. "Just because I'm nervous doesn't mean I haven't been thinking about it."

"Oh." And there it was—the boyish, jittery side of Nathan I enjoyed seeing every now and again. I especially liked that I seemed to be the only one capable of bringing out that side of him.

"In fact . . ." With a sudden burst of confidence, I nuzzled closer, wrapping my arms tighter around his neck so that not even the water could slip between us. "I had hoped for at least a heavy make out session tonight, which is why you were right earlier. I'm not wearing granny panties."

His breath caught, and he muttered something under his breath that I didn't quite catch. I wasn't sure which one of us moved first, or maybe we both moved at the same time, but, in the next instant, our mouths crashed together like it was our last minute together on earth. Hands gripped and pulled, and held everywhere and everything at once. Breathing dropped far down on my list of priorities, as everything about Nathan consumed me.

Nothing mattered more than the feel of him beneath my exploring hands, his hands tightening around my waist, and his lips moving fiercely over mine. Even when a swell of water washed over us, causing our lips to part momentarily, we didn't stop. If anything, that brief separation made us both more desperate, more frantic, in our need for each other.

The fact that we were entangled as we were with very little clothing between us no longer filled me with anxiety, but with a yearning for more. I didn't know what came next, but the way he brought my body to life with his mouth and his hands made me want to find out.

Suddenly, Nathan pulled away, though from the sound of the noise coming from the back of his throat, it wasn't something he wanted to do. "Maybe this wasn't such a good idea," he grunted. His eyes squeezed shut and his forehead rested against mine, like breaking that kiss had taken everything out of him.

I knew he had stopped for my benefit, because he didn't want to push me too far too fast. He had been doing that for weeks, every time things started to get a little . . . too hot between us. And though this was definitely the hottest it had ever gotten, I wasn't scared. Not at all.

"I told you I wanted to make out tonight," I said lightly, hoping to persuade him to continue.

He groaned. "I'm thinking about a hell of a lot more than that right now." With his eyes closed, he missed the look on my face, but my silence must have clued him in to my shock. His eyes squeezed tighter, and he shook his head like he couldn't believe what he had admitted to. "What am I saying?" He finally looked at me, his eyes wide. "That's not me. That's my twenty-two-year-old body talking."

"I happen to like your twenty-two-year-old body," I returned with a playful smile. I had to smile to cover the renewed anxiety his admission induced.

Granted, I had been thinking about more than just making out too, but hearing him admit that his thoughts were going there kind of brought back the uncertainty I had felt before. But he would never know it.

Because despite being nervous, I knew that Nathan was *the one*. And when the moment came, I would gladly and willingly take the next step with him. I figured it was only natural to be nervous when considering something so momentous. Being nervous wasn't going to stop me. Not when I knew that I wanted to be with Nathan.

Eventually. Because even though I knew what I wanted, I wasn't so sure that *now* was the ideal time. It took him saying what he said for me to realize it, but I knew now that he had been right about one thing earlier—I wasn't ready. Not yet. But close to it.

Nathan stared at me for a few long, heavy seconds, as if debating his next move. Or considering my ability to handle his next move. Though I felt a small pang of disappointment, a bigger part of me was relieved when he finally looked away. His deep breath signaled that the decision he had made hadn't been an easy one. As his chest heaved against mine, his grip on me loosened, though only fractionally since he still had to hold me up in the water.

Though a palpable uncertainty still lingered, one thing was certain. Our swim was over. With the aid of the surf, Nathan moved us closer to the shore. He let me go once I could touch the sandy bottom, but his arms remained around my waist, and he dropped his head to give me an insanely slow, sweet kiss. A kiss that signaled an end to not only the swim, but also to whatever might have happened in the water had we stayed there.

As we redressed and prepared to return to the dock, and the island, I held on to the sweetness of that last kiss. Because it was the type of kiss that reminded me of how lucky I was to have the love of someone like Nathan, and I knew that when the time was right for us to take the next step in our relationship, I would be the luckiest girl in the world to get to experience it with him.

*   *   *   *   *

We were met by a dark and quiet island, the path from the dock to the dorms empty, aside from us. We were out much later than I had thought we would be, and I worried that Nathan would get in trouble for having me off the island as long as he had. Of course, he reassured me that he would be fine.

"I hope so," I sighed as we stopped outside the door to the girls' dorm.

He turned to face me. "It doesn't matter. Tonight was worth anything Jared could throw at me," he said, and when I started to fuss, he quickly added, "but that's not going to happen, because Jared won't care."

As Nathan kissed me goodnight, I forgot all about the potential consequences of our late night. And I realized that I didn't want our evening to come to an end.

He regarded me warily as my eyes lit with a brilliant idea. "It's already so late," I said, "why don't you just spend the rest of the night with me?"

His eyebrows hooked with bewilderment in a way that almost made me laugh.

"Before coming here," I continued, "we were together all the time. We've shared a bed more times than I can count. I miss it, and even if it's just for one night, I want to do it again."

By the time I finished building my case, his grin had morphed into a frown. "I know, Kris. I miss that too."

"So . . . what do you say?"

He eyed the building, then shook his head. "There's one big

problem." He nodded his head toward the entrance, and I followed his gaze to the glass doors. "Kim."

Ah, yes, my formidable body guard, who I could now see sitting on a chair just inside, reading a magazine—obviously waiting for me. She wouldn't expect Nathan to come along, and I doubted she would let him in my room at this hour.

I reluctantly accepted that extending our date wasn't going to happen.

"Yeah, okay," I sulked, then cheered when I remembered that morning was only a few hours away. "Breakfast tomorrow?"

"Absolutely."

Nathan kissed me goodnight one more time before he ushered me into the building. Despite the disappointment that I would be going up to my room alone, I bounced as if walking on clouds. The date had been wonderful, Nathan had been wonderful, the swim . . .

Oh, God, the swim. I would *never* forget that.

Kim stood as I approached. Without so much as a *'how was it?'*, she escorted me to my room. I wished I could talk to her. If anything, to have someone to talk to about the things that I couldn't talk to Alec or Nathan about. There was Gran, of course, but the last time I asked her something she lectured Nathan about sex.

Times like now, I missed Callie the most. I wished that I could pick up a phone and call her. We would undoubtedly be up half the night talking about my evening with Nathan. Callie would dissect it moment by moment, and give me tips for our next date. Because that was what Callie did.

But she wasn't here.

That left Kim. And I just wasn't sure about her yet. So far, my weak attempts at getting to know her had failed. Actually, I gave up trying about a week into our arrangement. Maybe I should try again, now that she has had time to see that I wasn't all that bad.

By the time we reached my room, I decided to give Kim another shot. But not tonight. I was in too good of a mood to risk another failure.

I gave her a friendly smile as I shut the door behind me, leaving her at her post in the hallway. She didn't smile back. But she didn't scowl either. Her scowls had diminished. That had to be a good sign, right?

I quickly gathered up a pair of dry undies and a t-shirt, and went to the bathroom to dress for bed. I brushed my teeth at lightning speed and removed the makeup from my face. Finally in more comfortable, and dry, clothes, I was ready to crash for the night.

If only Nathan were here . . .

I had never been one to believe in the power of wishes, which was weird because I was supposed to be capable of yielding magic, and possibly capable of making a few wishes come true. The truth was—I wasn't good at it. And, well, I had never actually seen a wish come true.

Not until I walked out of the bathroom . . . and Nathan appeared in my room like magic.

Technically, I had nothing to do with it. Technically, I caught him as he stepped through the open balcony door. He had come from outside, though I had no idea how that was possible unless he had scaled the side of the building like Spiderman.

Either way, he was here in my room, looking all kinds of fine.

And once again I was in my underwear.

His eyes lifted to the ceiling with a slight shake of his head. "This was a bad idea," he muttered.

I glanced down to take inventory. At least I had picked boy shorts, and not something skimpy. And I had on a shirt. "This is more than I had on earlier."

"It was dark earlier."

Keeping my eyes fixed on him, I walked backwards a few steps and flicked the switch to the overhead light. We were left with the soft glow from the bedside lamp. "Better?"

"Not really." He was at least looking at me now, but the rigidness of his posture and his hands fisted at his sides hinted at his internal struggle.

I figured a change in subject might settle him down. "How did you get in here anyway?"

"Climbed from balcony to balcony," he answered. My mouth dropped open, and he added, "I used to do it all the time when I was living here before. Actually, we all did it. I'm sure everyone still does. It's about the only way to get around the dorm rules."

"Oh, well, good to know there are ways around them." For future use, I thought, but didn't say it out loud. He looked ready to flee any second, and I didn't want to scare him off. "So now that you're here, I assume that you're staying?"

Please, please, please . . .

His eyes lowered, and I felt the heat of his gaze as it washed over me. His throat jumped. "I don't know," he hedged, then glanced down at himself. "My clothes are wet. . ."

I held up a finger to silence him, and moved to my closet. I withdrew a pair of mesh shorts from the top shelf, and tossed them across the room to him.

He looked at them peculiarly. "Are these mine?"

"Yeah," I admitted. "They got mixed in with my stuff."

He had no more excuses for not staying now. Other than not wanting to, and we both knew that he wanted to.

He nodded, almost as if surrendering. Or telling himself he could do this. He pointed a finger in the direction of the bathroom. "I'll be right back."

I let the breath I had been holding out the moment the door shut behind him.

He's here. He's staying.

I almost couldn't believe it. I nearly pinched myself to make sure I wasn't already asleep and dreaming. Then the door opened—damn, that was fast—and he stood in front of me. I nearly stopped breathing entirely.

Holy six pack. No, wait. That stomach flirted with eight pack territory. Oh, what have I gotten myself into?

"Second thoughts?"

The sound of Nathan's voice pulled my eyes up . . . up over insanely hard pecs . . . to his eyes. "Not at all."

"Good. Because I'm definitely not leaving now." He took a step closer to me, a grin tipping the corners of his mouth up.

"And I'm definitely not tired."

I stepped into him, placing my hands on his ribcage. They were just as hard as they looked. "If we're not going to sleep, whatever will we do?"

He answered me with a kiss.

Chapter 5

{Nathan}

I woke to an empty bed. I stared at the ceiling, listening to the shower running in the bathroom for several moments before I registered the sound of a knock at the door. Micah's muffled voice coming from the other side shattered the hope I had for a great day and killed my happy buzz.

Spurred by the sudden burst of rage his presence induced, I jumped out of bed and swung the door open with authority, like I had every right to be there.

Micah's mouth dropped, and he took in my attire—or lack thereof—with visible distaste. I crossed my arms, barely stifling a smile at his discomfort.

"What do you want, Micah?" I growled. A quick glance over his shoulder confirmed my suspicion that this was part of the morning routine. Kim had already left, leaving Kris to Micah's and Richie's supervision. I should have expected their presence this morning, but I forgot. I also didn't care.

"Kris and I are supposed to go to breakfast together now,"

he said, adopting his usual air of cockiness.

"Well, she's going to breakfast with me this morning." I attempted to shut the door in his face. He threw an arm out to stop me. We stared at each other, neither saying anything for several seconds.

Finally, barely loud enough for me to hear him, Micah muttered, "I can't wait for you to screw this up."

I laughed. Once, and not because I found his statement funny. "Not going to screw it up." Again, I tried to shut the door. And again, he stopped me. Little did he realize the injury to his arm he risked in doing so. Next time, I wouldn't hesitate to slam it shut on his forearm. Broken bones and blood didn't faze me, and I wasn't scared of Richie.

Micah smirked, like he knew something I didn't.

I popped my jaw to keep from popping his. "I'm not going to screw anything up. Not with her," I insisted.

His smirk morphed into a taunting grin, and I suspected he wanted for me to think he knew something. But he didn't. He couldn't. I hadn't done anything.

"Being a prophet sure has its perks sometimes," he mulled.

My heart clenched slightly, but I maintained a blank expression. "You want me to think you had a vision of something?"

"Oh, I know I did."

Fortunately, I had mastered the ability to portray confidence even when it wavered. Like now. I refused to let this son of a bitch know the impact his words had on me.

He's a prophet. He saw me screw up with Kris, enough to put that shit-

eating grin on his face.

Nope. Not going to happen. I knew that. Even Micah knew that. He wanted to get under my skin. Nothing more. "And what is it that you *think* you saw, Micah?"

He looked down the hallway like he had somewhere better to be. "Maybe a smoking hot Brazilian," he said casually. Then he turned and looked me squarely in the eyes. "You know anyone who matches that description?"

I laughed, for real this time. Because his suggestion that Lillian would ever come between Kris and me was that funny. And I suspected now that he was making it all up. Lillian getting in the way was an easy assumption for him to make. Almost too easy. He was bluffing. And I had almost been worried. If only for a second.

Micah chuckled humorlessly in return. "We'll see who's laughing when you break her heart, and I'm there to pick up the pieces."

Before I could reply, the bathroom door opened behind me. Because I was glaring at Micah, I saw the way his eyes shifted downward in a way that they shouldn't. A quick glance over my shoulder confirmed that Micah was getting a nice view of a scantily clad Kris. She squealed at the sight of him in the doorway, and I shifted to block his gaze as she scurried to grab something a little more concealing.

Micah shot a murderous look in my direction, before looking back at Kris. "Are you having sex with him?" he demanded, thrusting a thumb in my direction.

Kris, now dressed in the baggy pair of sweats that had taken up residence in the corner of her room—probably for weeks—stepped up beside me. "First of all, that's none of your damn business," she said. "Second of all, what are you doing here?"

Micah turned all sorts of shades of red and purple as he stared at Kris, and I knew that he was desperately trying to read her mind, to search for the answer to the only question he cared about at the moment. I grinned when I realized that he had hit a wall Kris had thrown up.

Apparently, her training had paid off.

Kris crossed her arms, looking pleased with herself, and repeated, "Micah, what are you doing here?"

His head shook slightly, and he seemed to give up on picking her brain. For now. "Uh, breakfast," he muttered miserably.

"As you've probably already been told, I'm going with Nathan this morning," she said. "I'll see you later."

With that, she pushed the door shut. I didn't know if he was in shock, or if he respected Kris's wishes more than mine, but he stepped back, letting the door close.

With him finally out of sight, I retreated to the bed and plopped down onto my back with a sigh. Though I didn't necessarily believe him, his words had stuck with me, and I knew that they were going to eat away at me.

. . . when you break her heart . . .

Never. I could never break her heart. I would rather die than do such a thing.

. . . and I'm there to pick up the pieces . . .

Ugh. I had done what I'd sworn to never do. I let Micah get to me.

The bed shifted as Kris sat beside me. "What's wrong?" she asked.

I folded my arms behind my head so that I could look at her instead of the ceiling. "Nothing. Micah just gets under my skin."

She didn't buy it. "What did he say to you?" she pressed.

Kris shifted so that she leaned over me, with one of her arms bridged across my middle. Her eyes leveled on mine in a silent plea for the truth.

I took a deep breath. I didn't want to tell her what he said, but when she looked at me like that, I caved. "Micah said he can't wait for me to screw this up, and that when I do he'll be there to pick up the pieces."

I left out the part about his claim that it was a vision, and Lillian's involvement. Kris was already uneasy enough about her being on the island. No need to make that worse. Especially when I knew that he was full of shit.

She wrinkled her nose at the mention of Micah waiting in the wings for her. But that wasn't the part I wanted her to concentrate on. I needed her to understand.

I took her chin in my hand, and held her gaze with unwavering earnestness to emphasize what I needed her to know. "I'm not going to screw this up," I vowed. "I would never do anything to hurt you."

"I know."

She said it with such certainty that I had to kiss her. I pulled her to me, and I sealed my promise to her the best way I knew how. And there we stayed, breakfast forgotten, for the rest of the morning.

*   *   *   *   *

I had just enough time to grab a bagel and a coffee, and made it halfway to my morning class when I got word that it had been cancelled. Apparently, I was the last to know.

"Jared wants to see you," the wannabe-supervisor runt told me before he ran off to his next task.

I suppressed a groan as I turned for the Command Center. I couldn't have cared less about the class, but I dreaded finding out what Jared needed to talk to me about if it warranted cancelling it. Perhaps another spy got busted? Or Callie . . .

God, I hoped this had nothing to do with Callie.

Security gave me no trouble as I made my way through the building. A guard, whom I had never seen before, stiffened as I rounded the corner leading to Jared's office. His gun raised fractionally before recognition registered in his eyes. He lowered his weapon with a nod as I passed.

This had nothing to do with Callie, I determined. I had a nagging suspicion that something had happened—or was about to happen. Jared's usual personal guard, Rodney, stood outside Jared's office, his eyes wide as he scanned the hallway.

"They're in Meeting Room One. Down the hall," he told me.

I slowed as I contemplated asking him what was going on, but instead I veered off in the direction he indicated, growing more confused with each step.

They?

Surely this had nothing to do with Kris. It was just a

coincidence something was going down the day after I snuck her off the island and slept in her room, and the same morning I had a standoff with the Kala's golden boy.

Micah. That little shit. What had he done now?

When I pushed the doors open to the meeting room, and saw the collection of Kala already waiting in the room, I knew it had nothing to do with Micah. Or Kris.

The Skotadi were up to something. Lucky me to have been selected as a member of the team about to be sent out to intercept them. I had been in on a few of these meetings before. I knew what they looked like. Though I had never seen any of the head Kala leaders participate in a meeting before, let alone all three of them.

They sat at the front of the room, heads tipped together as they scanned the soldiers that had already arrived. Supervisor Jeffries, the hot shot mid-level in charge of the leadership department, sat next to them. Younger than them by at least a hundred years, he looked to be in his forties with grey tinted hair that matched his grey eyes. He carried a flair of self-righteousness, common among the up-and-coming supervisors, and squared his shoulders when he met my gaze.

Ignoring him, I took a seat next to a veteran Kala I recognized from my previous years on the island. As I looked around at the others, I noticed that they were all experienced older Kala. No newbies. No training. All business. Which meant whatever this was, it was big.

Two more entered after me. Jared and a brunette girl I might have recognized, but when her name didn't immediately come to mind, I looked away, not wanting to stare. She took the last seat, next to me, as Jared moved to the front of the room.

"This looks like everybody," he said to the leaders. To the rest of us, he said, "As you all have probably guessed, the eleven of you have been called up for a mission. I'll be the mission leader. Before you leave, you will be given a packet which will contain your temporary IDs, passports, and profiles. We will be traveling in pairs or small groups so as not to alert the Skotadi, and we will be meeting at a predetermined rendezvous point. This is a top secret mission. You will not be told of the specifics until we meet at the next location . . ."

A wave of audible grumbles swept through the room. No one liked going into a mission not knowing what they were heading into. Myself included.

"We'll be leaving the dock in three hours," Jared continued, unfazed.

A thick manila envelope with my name scribbled across the top was tossed onto the table in front of me. I stared at it numbly while everyone else ripped into their own envelopes.

"A recommended packing list is in your packets. Take the next few hours to pack, say your goodbyes, and learn your new identities. Know them well before we hit the mainland. We'll be splitting up there immediately," Jared concluded.

He glanced at the Kala leaders, and Supervisor Jeffries stood to address us. "As you all know, every mission we handle is important in the war we are fighting against the forces of evil. Though you do not know the specifics yet, I want you all to know that this mission is of the utmost importance. I expect you all to give us your best."

I snorted quietly. As if we had any other options.

Jared beamed me with a look as he cleared his throat. "See you all at the docks at noon."

Chairs scraped across the floor in an ear-splitting chorus, accentuated by the grumble of voices around me. No one openly complained. Every person in this room was a seasoned Kala warrior. We knew better than to openly question orders, especially in front of our superiors.

I hesitated in my seat, staring at the envelope in my hands, reluctant to open it. My concern wasn't over the mission itself, but over leaving the island. Worse than being separated from Kris was the deeply rooted fear I had of being in a position that rendered me helpless in the event that she needed me. Though she wouldn't be left completely alone, I didn't feel comfortable leaving her. Especially now.

"What a load of shit, huh?"

My head swiveled toward the quiet voice beside me. I was met by smiling green eyes that looked at me like they knew me. I squinted, trying to place the brunette. I knew her. From somewhere.

Her hand thrust out in front of me. "Kira Johns, class seven-oh-three."

Kira? Her name sounded familiar. *Recent* familiar, like it hadn't been years since I last heard it. No . . . wait. Kira was the name of the girl Kris had been in a tizzy about the other day.

I took her hand to shake it and opened my mouth to introduce myself though, apparently, an introduction wasn't necessary.

"Nathan Young," she said for me. "Top five in our class, and if I remember correctly, I believe even *the* top fighter."

Despite not being able to place her, she obviously knew me well. I shook her hand and withdrew quickly before the situation crept any further into awkward territory.

"That's me," I said diplomatically as I stood, the words *'walk, don't run'* repeating in my head.

She laughed, a flirty, seductive laugh that kicked my defenses into high alert. A few years ago, I would have happily flirted back to see where it would go. Things were different now. I disliked shallow girls, hated when they played games, and had one hell of a good girl unknowingly encouraging me to be a good boy. Especially after the conversation I'd had with Micah that morning . . . hell, yeah, my defenses shot up.

She was saying something, but I was too busy plotting my escape to catch on right away.

". . . this time we're going to be spending together, it could be just like before . . ."

I stared at her dumbly. "What?"

She winked, pulling out all the stops. "I'm really looking forward to this mission, honey."

Honey? Who in the hell was this girl? Either I'd lost my touch, or I had missed some important part of this conversation. I shook my head. "Seriously, what?"

She lifted the envelope in her hand, with her name across the front. "The mission? Our identities?" She must have realized from my blank stare that I had yet to look at my identity. She looked all too pleased to clue me in, however. "You and me? We're newlyweds," she said. With a flirty bump into my side, she passed by me. "Looking forward to the honeymoon."

At that, she finally left, sashaying away in that way girls did when they wanted you to check out their ass. I took pride of the fact that I didn't look.

Chapter 6

{Kris}

He was dead. *Dead.*

The boat was set to leave in two hours. I knew because I'd heard everyone—*everyone*— talking about it. The whole island knew who was going on this mission, and were getting in their final moments before the time came to say goodbye.

Tears, well wishes, and hugs surrounded me.

Yet Nathan was a no-show. Since the moment I first heard the news, and heard his name dropped, I turned this island upside down looking for him. Now I sat, defeated, on a bench between the village center and the beach. Kim hovered just behind me and, though she remained silent, I felt her presence.

I lifted my chin out of my hands when I saw Alec approach from the direction of the mess hall. He shook his head solemnly and I lowered my head again. A moment later, I felt the bench shift slightly as he took a seat beside me.

"We've looked everywhere, Kris," Alec said.

"I know," I mumbled.

"He's probably looking for you while you're looking for him."

"That's why I've decided to stay here. He has to come by here at some point." Worse-case scenario was a public, hasty goodbye when he passed by on his way to the dock.

My shoulders slumped under the weight of Alec's heavy arm, but I didn't care. He was there, and the weight of his arm comforted me in a way mere words couldn't. I instinctively leaned into him, pressing my side against his.

There was nothing romantic about it. Not anymore. I knew that. Even Alec knew that.

For the longest time I hadn't been sure if it were possible for me and Alec to be *just friends,* but as time went by, I had felt the shift in our relationship. It was more than just the fact that we were both born Skotadi, and going through a slow, agonizing change neither of us wanted. Though that connected us to each other in a way others could never understand, it was only a small piece of the very complex puzzle that connected us.

And I was always grateful to have him by my side.

Suddenly, his arm lifted. "Man, are you in trouble," I heard him say, and I lifted my head to look for the target of his comment.

Nathan's arms spread to his sides in exasperation as he approached. His gaze shifted from Alec to me, and he mouthed the word, *sorry.*

I jumped to my feet. "Where have you been?" The words came out a little squeakier than I intended, and I inwardly cringed at my weakness.

"Fighting with Jared," he returned as he came to a stop in front of me. His arms started to reach out for me, but he caught himself, and held them back. He looked pained, tormented—the same as I probably looked.

"I still have to pack yet," Nathan continued. Glancing over my shoulder at Kim, he added, "Maybe you could come with me while I do that?"

"I'll be back here in two hours," Kim said to me as her answer.

Two hours. Then Nathan would have to board the boat to the mainland. Until then, he was mine. We kept up with the charade for public appearances until we reached his room. The moment he shut the door behind us, I found myself enveloped in his arms.

"I'm so sorry," he murmured into my hair. "As soon as I got out of the meeting, I tracked Jared down, tried to persuade him to get me out of it. I just . . . I don't want to leave you."

"Couldn't persuade him?"

"No." He pushed me back so that he could see my face. "He always said he trusted me more than anyone else. Apparently, he needs me on this one."

"So . . . you're still leaving."

He nodded solemnly, and I suspected that he worried more about leaving me behind than he worried about the mission. Whatever it was.

"Where are you going? What is the mission?"

"I don't know. It's top secret. They won't tell us until we meet at our rendezvous location."

I scoffed. "What's the point of that?"

"To ensure that no lovesick sap tells his girlfriend everything before he leaves." He looked at me pointedly before releasing me and turning to his closet.

I watched as he tossed an assortment of clothes on the bed. As he dashed into the bathroom to grab the necessary toiletries, I picked up a shirt and started to fold it for him. If anything, to keep my mind off of the obvious.

They didn't even know what they were going to be doing? Top secret? To me, that meant dangerous . . . life-threatening dangerous. My worst nightmare was unfolding right in front of me, and I was powerless to stop it.

It took me a moment to notice Nathan crouched in front of me, holding the shirt I had intended to fold. His eyes were lined with worry. For me. Always for me.

"Kris? Are you okay?"

I snapped out of my daze, and shook my head in a moment of absolute honesty.

He cupped my face in his hands, forcing my eyes to meet his as he offered me a reassuring smile. "Everything is going to be alright. I'll be back before you know it."

I huffed. "I'd rather you not leave in the first place. Why did they have to pick you?"

He shrugged. "Everybody who is going has a lot of experience. I'm one of the most experienced guys that they have."

Nathan stood, rolled the shirt up hastily and tossed it into the large duffel bag laid open on the bed. Apparently, he didn't concern himself with wrinkles. The rest of his clothes quickly followed until the bag was stuffed and zipped shut.

He looked at me triumphantly. Packing had taken all of five minutes. Only Nathan could pull that off, and still look incredible in whatever he took with him. Wrinkles and all.

"Now it's you and me time," he said.

The moment I had been waiting for. No sooner than I stood with a smile on my face, a knock at the door wiped it off.

Now what?

Nathan hesitated as if debating whether or not to answer it. Ultimately, he decided to risk it. I heard his heavy sigh when he saw the wide-eyed errand boy standing in the hallway.

"What does he want now?" Nathan demanded harshly.

"Jared wants to see you in his office."

"Again?"

The boy shrugged, glancing at me. For help? Perhaps for me to remind Nathan of the golden rule to not shoot the messenger? He wouldn't get any help from me. He was lucky I hadn't already tackled him to the floor.

"He wanted to make sure I enforced you to come." The kid visibly gulped, and I knew he was wondering how in the hell he would manage to force Nathan to do anything.

I started to feel a little bad for him.

"Fine," Nathan gritted out, waving a hand at the boy as if to dismiss him. "I'll be there in a minute."

The boy scampered away, and Nathan shut the door. He turned to me, a silent apology written all over his face.

I forced a small smile. "Go get it over with."

Nathan nodded solemnly as he closed the distance between us. He took my face in his hands, stilling me for a quick kiss. "I won't let this take long," he promised. "Meet me at the rocks in thirty minutes?"

I put on the bravest face I could muster. That would leave us with a little less than an hour. Not nearly enough time as far as I was concerned but, at this point, I would take what I could get.

Fear that it might be the last little bit we ever got gnawed at my gut.

*   *   *   *   *

One good thing came from separating from Nathan for a few minutes. Back in my room with nothing else to do, I enchanted a stone with a protection spell that I found in the big spell book. It was nothing more than a cheap souvenir shop stone set in a golden chain necklace, but that didn't matter. It would hold a spell.

I just hoped it worked. Though my abilities were getting better—some days anyway—my spell casting was inconsistent. It seemed to depend on my mood, the weather, who I was with . . . a lot of variables. The only thing I knew for sure was that confidence was necessary for success. I put more focus and confidence into this protection spell than anything I had done up until that point.

More than anything, I *needed* this spell to work.

It took about fifteen minutes. Once finished, I slipped it into my jeans' pocket and headed for the rocks.

That was what Nathan called his special spot and, according to him, it was his. He claimed to be the only person who visited the place. I couldn't understand why. It was a beautiful and tranquil spot hidden away from the drama that infested the rest of the island.

Then again, I doubted anyone else knew it existed. As I climbed over the large boulders and ducked under low hanging tree limbs, following what I hoped was the right trail, I couldn't help but wonder how he had found it. I sure wouldn't have ventured down this path unless I knew that it would lead me to something worth my efforts. But I didn't specialize in nature either. Not like Nathan.

When I jumped down from the last large boulder onto solid ground again, I saw my destination up ahead. Massive rocks, five and six times my height, grouped together in a large mound that resembled something like a large bowl. A crack, barely wide enough to permit Nathan to squeeze through, served as an entrance to the cavern created by the rocks. Inside was a deep pool of clear water fed by the small creek that snaked through the island. A narrow band of light filtered down from above, through a five foot gap in the rock roof. It served as the only source of light in the otherwise dark space.

I kicked off my sandals, and sat at the edge of the pool with my feet in the water to wait for Nathan.

Such a nice spot. Such tranquility despite the turmoil raging in side of me. Such a nice place to spend final moments with someone you loved.

He better hurry.

*   *   *   *   *

{Nathan}

I cast Rodney a look he wouldn't challenge before bursting through the door to Jared's office. Jared sat at his desk, looking at a stack of papers, and didn't bother to look up when I entered.

"Nathan . . ." His lips curled into a sly smile. "Won't you come in?"

"Cut the crap, Jared. I just saw you. What do you want now? And make it fast."

"Got somewhere to be?" He finally looked up.

"As a matter of fact, I do."

His smile grew as he set the papers down. "Wonder where that is . . ."

"Doesn't take a genius to figure it out," I returned. "Now what do you want?"

He gestured toward the chair in front of his desk. "Have a seat."

"I'm not staying long enough to sit down. What do you want?" I repeated impatiently.

Since Jared and I went way back, he had come to expect attitude from me when warranted. Otherwise, I would have found myself in a heap of trouble for talking to a supervisor the way I talked to him now. He more than likely knew he was being a douche for dragging me in here now of all times, so he let it slide.

"I couldn't ask you earlier because we weren't alone," he started. "How was last night?"

I hooked an eyebrow. "Really? You brought me back in here to talk about my date?"

"I don't care about your date," he corrected hastily. "Everything else. It went well?"

I stared. "What exactly are you asking, Jared?"

He sighed as he leaned forward in his chair. "There have been reports of increased Skotadi on the mainland," he admitted. My eyebrows shot up, forcing him to add, "Don't repeat that to anyone."

It was common knowledge that small groups of Skotadi often searched the mainland for signs of the Kala. They knew we were in the area, but didn't know our exact location. An increase in their numbers may indicate that they were getting closer, and was something the Kala would need to watch carefully.

"How many?"

He shrugged. "Not sure exactly. But we do know a large number arrived last night. If I had known, I would have never let you leave the island. You and Kris got lucky."

No kidding. I blew out a puff of air, having realized the bullet we had barely dodged. "I didn't see anything out of the ordinary," I told Jared, "but then again, I wasn't looking."

Jared nodded, satisfied with my answer. His demeanor still seemed off. "They don't seem to know where the island is at least."

"That you know of. They're not increasing their numbers for

nothing." The severity of the situation hit me, and I leveled my gaze on my friend. "You can't send eleven of our best soldiers on a mission *now*, when there are Skotadi sniffing around nearby. We should stay here, and you know it."

What if they figured out where the island was while we were gone? What if they decided to attack? At least Jared looked as conflicted as I felt about it.

"This mission is coming from the top," he said in defense. "They're requesting the best, we have to give them the best."

"The top? Who?" Jared shifted uncomfortably, so I pressed harder. "What is this mission? Where exactly are we going, Jared?"

He hesitated as if debating what, and how much, to tell me. Finally, he decided to be truthful. "Mount Olympus," he said. "The gods themselves have asked for our assistance. Do you want to be the one to tell them no?"

*   *   *   *   *

Shit.

Shit, shit, shit.

Shit.

I was due to meet Kris . . . now. But I had one more previously unplanned, but now necessary, stop to make.

Bruce and I exchanged cordial nods as I rapped on Alec's door.

"Well, well, well," he drew as the door opened. "Coming to say goodbye to me before you leave? I'm honored, really, but I don't care about you *that* much. Could've saved yourself the trouble."

"Funny," I muttered as Alec stepped back, inviting me in with a wave of his hand. I made sure to shut the door behind me. What I had to say to Alec was for his ears only. "We need to talk."

Reacting to the severity of my tone, Alec's trademark grin dropped and I got a glimpse of his rarely seen serious side. He took a seat on the edge of the computer desk, facing me with his arms crossed. His eyes were alert and ready, his unspoken question visible.

"This mission is worse than I thought," I started, causing Alec's eyebrows to raise in curiosity.

I was well aware of the enormity of what we were about to do. No Kala hybrid had ever been to Mount Olympus. As far as I knew, no modern day Kala had ever met one of the demigods that lived there, let alone a god. Certainly, neither had ever asked for the Kala's help before. Whatever had prompted them to do so must be huge—something they feared enough to not deal with it themselves.

Which meant we were about to go into something that could likely get each and every one of us killed. Because that was the only reason I could think of that the demigods wouldn't have taken care of it themselves—fear of their own demise. Sure, the gods were immortal, but the demigods were not. And we, a small group of Kala, were expendable in their eyes.

"We're going to Mount Olympus," I told Alec.

My statement was met by silence as Alec absorbed the

gravity of it. He opened his mouth a few times as if to say something, but the words never formed. Finally, he shook his head as if he thought he hadn't heard me right. "Mount Olympus?"

I nodded.

"As in *the* Mount Olympus?"

"The one and only."

"As in the home of the gods?"

"Yes," I snapped.

He cleared his throat and stood to pace the room. "I'm not a Kala so I don't know for sure, but my guess is that this is a first?"

"For us to be asked to go there? Yes, it's a first."

"For them to ask for your help?"

"That's a first, too."

"Well that can't be good," he concluded.

"That's why I'm here." Finally, now that his shock had worn off, we could get down to business so I could get back to Kris.

Kris. No way could she know about this. Not until I was gone.

"Whatever we're going there for must be something huge."

"Obviously," Alec muttered. He hadn't stopped pacing the room and my eyes followed him as I continued.

"There's a possibility that it may be related to what's going on with Kris, and with you . . ."

Alec pointed a finger at me like I had just connected the dots to a thought he had been struggling to connect.

No one had suggested that Kris or Alec had anything to do with the mission; I had reached that assumption on my own. The demigods had to be getting nervous about the impending maturity of two Skotadi powerful enough to challenge them. I wondered, too, if they had discovered that Kris was also a demigod, and therefore even stronger than initially thought. Regardless, this sudden trip to Mount Olympus had me anxious for her.

"I'm going to find out as much as I can." I hesitated to take a deep breath. I was a Kala soldier. I had been prepared my entire life to sacrifice for the Kala if necessary. But the words had never been this hard to admit before.

"You need to know that there's a chance none of us will be coming back," I finally said. "*I* might not come back."

Alec stopped pacing and faced me. He was sullen. Surprisingly so.

"Kris can't know about this," I continued.

Alec huffed. "No shit."

"If I find anything out, I'll get in touch with *you*, and . . ." This next part was the hardest, but also the most important, part of my reason for visiting Alec. "If anything happens to me . . ."

I didn't finish the thought, but I didn't need to. Alec knew what I wanted to say. "You don't even have to ask," he said with surprising sincerity.

"Keep Micah . . ."

"Goes without saying," he said with a grin. "He won't get within a foot of her if I can help it."

A look passed between us then, and I knew that coming here had been the right thing to do. Alec was the right one to go to. Alec, in my absence, was the only other person I entrusted with

Kris's wellbeing, because if anyone could love her as much as I did, it was him. If anyone could continue this quest to save her, it was him.

"There's one more thing," I said, and Alec shot me a look as if to ask, *what now?* "Jared said that there are a number of Skotadi converging on the mainland. No one knows what they are doing yet, but if anything happens while I'm gone, make sure you keep her away from them."

"You know I will," Alec vowed.

I nodded, and started for the door, having done what I came here to do. As much as I hated the thought of anyone else making a lifetime of memories with her, I was relieved to know that she wouldn't be completely alone.

"Hey . . ." Alec stopped me at the door. "As much as it pains me to say this to you of all people, be careful over there."

Despite our rocky start, something transpired between Alec and me in that moment. We were no longer enemies, no longer rivals. I had long stopped despising him, but now? Now, I considered Alec a friend.

Chapter 7

{Kris}

Our time at the rocks ended much too soon, and before either of us wanted. We walked hand in hand, both of us wanting to remain connected as long as possible. Once the heart of the island, and pretty much every Kala living on it, came into view, Nathan dropped my hand.

Twelve Kala were leaving on the mission. From the size of the crowd gathered on the beach near the dock, it looked like everyone on the island knew at least one person leaving.

Kim waited for us on the bench closest to the beach, along with Gran. Surprisingly, Alec, Micah, Richie, and Bruce were also there.

Alec's presence I welcomed, and would most certainly seek the moment the boat left with Nathan on it—the moment I would need his friendship the most. Micah's presence, however, I could have done without.

The look I shot him portrayed my annoyance with him. He shrugged his shoulders like he couldn't help himself. He probably thought he couldn't. He probably thought it was his duty as my soul mate to be there for me when the man I really loved left. I would have to set him straight later.

"Nathan . . ." Gran rose from her seat with a forced smile on her face. "I know I don't need to tell you to be careful, but because you're my grandson, I'm going to do it anyway. *Be careful.*"

She pulled him in for a hug. He had to bend down for her to plant a grandmotherly kiss on his cheek, and stayed there long enough to quietly murmur something to her.

As Nathan exchanged handshakes and goodbyes with the others, I glanced around the beach. Those who were leaving were easy to spot. They were all surrounded by friends and family, and were the ones hugging everyone. Like Nathan, each one was poised and ready for whatever awaited them, while the rest of us struggled to hold back our emotions. I wondered if it was always like this when a team left on a mission, or if everyone shared my fears about this mission.

A group close to us seemed even more upset than the others. Nearly all of them were girls, and most of them were crying. I spotted the two girls I stood behind in my combat class in the group. The brunette girl was clinging to another brunette with a similar body type, and the same green eyes.

Her sister perhaps?

As if she heard my thoughts, the older girl glanced at me briefly before her gaze drifted behind me. I didn't have to guess what, or rather who, had caught her eye.

"*Shit.*"

This came from behind me. I tossed Nathan a curious look over my shoulder. His eyes, when they lowered to mine, were wide with near-panic. "I'm going to go ahead and apologize now for what is about to happen," he muttered.

Before I could ask what he meant by that, her voice stopped me. Confident and sultry, it was practically a purr. And it was targeted at Nathan. My eyes hardened as her manicured fingers ran up his bicep, and she stepped between us as if I didn't exist. Only a warning head shake from Nathan kept me from punching her in the throat.

"Kira," he addressed her stiffly while shrugging away from her touch. His eyes darted to mine at the moment it hit me.

Kira? That was the name of the brunette girl's sister alright—the name of the girl that apparently had a plan to get her claws hooked in Nathan. Thank God for the charm around my neck. That, and that alone, prevented me from jumping on her back and having a good, old-fashioned girl fight in the sand.

She shifted and turned enough to register me standing there. She flashed me a fake smile while speaking to Nathan. "Bring your little sister to the base?" I knew from her tone and the curtained iciness in her eyes that she knew damn well I wasn't his sister. But then, I doubted she really knew who I was . . . and she was curious.

Nathan opened his mouth to answer, but I would never know what he intended to say, because I interrupted him with a response of my own. "I'm Kris," I said. "I'm not his sister, but you might have heard of me. I'm the resident Skotadi on the base. Nice to meet you."

Her face fell. She looked to Nathan, to me, then back to Nathan. "Are you kidding me?"

Nathan shifted uncomfortably and raised his hand to the back of his neck. His guarded smile and silence served as his answer.

"Were you the one who brought her here?" she asked, her voice approaching shrill territory. How she wasn't already aware of that fact eluded me, but clearly she had no idea Nathan was the one responsible for bringing the dreaded Skotadi to the island. Until now.

He nodded and she scrutinized me. I stared back for several seconds before I lifted an eyebrow, silently daring her to say something to give me an excuse to really let her know what I thought of her. Unfortunately, she didn't take the bait.

She shifted and turned back to Nathan as if the last thirty seconds hadn't happened. Flipping her hair over her shoulder, she leaned in close to him, and dropped her voice. "Finish your goodbyes and I'll see you on the boat . . . *hubby*." She said the last word with a seductive wink before slinking away. I recognized the swivel in her hips as the *check out my ass as I walk away* walk.

Nathan watched her walk away, but his eyes at least seemed to be boring into the back of her head, not her ass, and I was pretty sure he only did so to avoid looking at me. He should know by now that he wasn't getting off the hook that easily.

"Hubby?" I repeated Kira's last word to him.

Nathan's gaze lifted to the sky as if pleading for divine assistance before reluctantly settling on my waiting eyes. He opened his mouth, and closed it again without saying anything.

"That's her," I said, jabbing an accusatory finger in her general direction. "That's the girl I told you about."

"I know."

My eyes popped. "You said you didn't—"

"I didn't remember her until I ran into her at the mission meeting," he explained quickly.

"And she's going on the mission too?"

He nodded.

"What was with the *hubby* thing?"

Nathan sucked in a deep breath. From the way he gnawed on his bottom lip, I knew the truth wasn't something I would want to hear, nor something he wanted to tell me. I crossed my arms, lifted an eyebrow, and waited. I avoided the snickers coming from behind me. I would deal with Alec, and his apparent amusement with my standoff with Nathan, later.

"It's, uh . . ." Nathan started. He stopped to clear his throat before continuing, "It's our cover."

What the hell was that supposed to mean? "Your cover?"

"We're all splitting up, taking on temporary identities to avoid detection by the Skotadi, and regrouping at a rendezvous point later," he explained and I nodded along, waiting for the point where the hubby explanation would come in. He paused, then said it in a rush, "Kira and I are supposed to be newlyweds on our honeymoon. That's our cover."

"Oh, man. Where's a camera when you need one?"

This time I shot Alec a glare over my shoulder.

"Sorry." He threw his hands up, as if he could ever pass for innocent. "I just love watching you two fight."

"We're not fighting," I hissed at Alec before turning my attention back to Nathan. I had lied to Alec. We were *so* fighting. "Were you ever going to tell me?"

Nathan shrugged and looked at me like a five-year-old trying to bargain his way out of time out. "I didn't want to worry you for no reason."

"No reason?"

Playing house with another girl, let alone an attractive one who obviously had her sights set firmly and determinedly on him, was hardly something he should expect me to brush off as *'nothing.'* This was the guy who seemed to know me better than I knew myself. He had to know that *I* thought there was reason to worry about this situation.

Nathan grabbed my elbow and steered me away from the watchful eyes of our entourage. There, he dropped his voice for my ears only. "You have to trust me," he pleaded.

I did. Or so I had thought. Shooting a look in Kira's direction, I muttered, "It's her I don't trust."

"But if you trust me, that shouldn't matter, right?"

I shrugged lamely.

"Because it doesn't matter what Kira says, or does," he continued. "It doesn't matter if she thinks she's in any position to try something. It won't ever work. You know that, right?"

I stared at him wordlessly.

"Okay, Kris?"

My gaze swung to Kira, and I burned a hole into the back of her head as she laughed at something one of the girls in her group said. Not surprisingly, her friend looked back at us. More specifically, at Nathan. Bitch.

"*Kris.*" He growled, and shifted to block my view of Kira completely. "You know that, right?"

I reluctantly looked up at him. "Yeah, okay." I still wasn't happy about it, and my tone let him know that. But I did trust him. He had never given me a reason not to trust him.

"I really want to kiss you right now," he said with a small smile.

"That's pretty random." I couldn't keep from smiling in return—not when he flashed those dimples at me.

"Not really. It's called making up after a fight."

"Then it's really too bad that you can't do anything about that."

My words lifted with a challenge, and for a moment I thought Nathan would cave. His eyes clouded, and I thought he might kiss me right there, in front of everyone. So close. But Nathan had always been good at self-control. This time was no different.

He glanced over his shoulder at the dock, where those selected for the mission were gathering to get onto the boat. Time had run out.

"I have to go," he murmured.

Not wanting to hear the emotion I knew I would hear in my voice, I simply nodded. Even that felt numb. Like it wasn't my head that nodded, but someone else's.

Some other girl was saying goodbye to the love of her life.

Some other girl was hoping it wasn't for the last time.

His hand grazed my cheek in a subtle display of affection. It lingered there as his eyes swept over my face as if trying to memorize what I looked like—as if, he too, thought it might be for the last time.

"Love you," he whispered.

I tried to return the same words, but had to settle for mouthing them. If I tried to vocalize them, my voice would crack, and the tears would come. And they wouldn't stop.

He abruptly turned, like he knew that if he didn't do it now, he would never do it. Watching him walk away, without running after him, was agonizing.

He will be okay. He will come back . . .

"Nathan, wait!"

He stopped and turned as I hurried after him.

"Here." I reached into my pocket and withdrew the necklace I had nearly forgotten to give him. "This is for you."

He held his hand out to take it. "Branding me before I leave?"

"It's enchanted." I pressed it into his palm and folded his fingers around it.

"Enchanted?"

"With a protection spell. I'm not positive that I did it right, and don't know how well it will work but . . ." I looked up at him with a sheepish shrug. "I want you to have something."

He opened his hand to study the necklace. "Should I wear it?"

I nodded, suddenly feeling foolish. "It doesn't mean you should try to be a hero or anything. It might not work."

He cupped my face in his hands, and the necklace dangled in

the air between us. "Thank you. I won't take it off." He sealed that promise by pressing a hasty kiss to my forehead. Then he turned and walked away. Again.

And it was just as hard watching him go the second time around.

I glanced away just long enough to be sure that no one had seen the brief kiss. Though innocent enough, it surprised me that he had done it at all. Everyone seemed to be absorbed in their own grief, watching those that they loved step onto the boat.

All but one.

My eyes swept over her at first. Belatedly, I realized that she was looking directly at me, and I returned my gaze to meet hers. Kira already stood on the boat. Far away, but not so far as to miss the smile on her face.

It wasn't friendly.

It was a challenge.

Chapter 8

{Nathan}

Either Kira took acting classes as a child, or she enjoyed her role as the blushing bride a little too much. To anyone watching us, I undoubtedly looked like a big asshole, but no way was I about to take our cover as newlyweds to the level of embarrassing displays of PDA. Fortunately, we never encountered any Skotadi on our way to the airport, so I wasn't forced to up the act.

By the time we were securely in the air, leaving Costa Rica, she had relented a little. Probably only because I had requested a set of headphones before take-off, and pretended to be sleeping to the sounds of eighties hits by the time we hit cruising altitude. I had a hell of a time biting my tongue on the lyrics to the Aerosmith in my ear, but Kira knowing I was awake and free to talk to her was much worse.

The previous late night with Kris eventually caught up to me, and I fell asleep sometime after we crossed the Gulf of Mexico into the United States. After a few hours of sleep, an elbow to the ribs served as an effective alarm clock. My eyes snapped open and Kira smiled at me, but it wasn't a happy smile. I didn't need to know *her*—I only needed to know girls in general—to pick up on her aggravation. She said something, and even though I couldn't hear her with the headphones on, I could read her lips.

We were descending.

I sat up straight in my seat and fastened my seatbelt, but the headphones stayed on. I had every intention of holding onto those for as long as possible. Unfortunately, it didn't stop Kira from lifting them from my ear every now and again to suggest some place for us to visit . . . or catch dinner . . . or see a play.

With a groan load enough to catch the attention of the older woman across the aisle from us, I whipped the headphones off and turned to glare at Kira. Because I had drawn a small audience, I lowered my voice. "You do know we're not actually on our honeymoon, right?"

Daggers shot from her eyes before she put on her fake, happily married face. "Our connecting flight isn't until tomorrow morning. What do you expect us to do for the next few hours? We at least have to eat something."

I had planned on greasy take-out and a cheap pay-per-view movie. But being in the hotel room longer than absolutely necessary, alone with Kira, probably wasn't a good idea. Not with the way she took this whole honeymoon thing so seriously.

"We'll see," I grumbled, and turned to watch out my window as the ground drew closer. On the outside, I appeared simply interested in the landing. Internally, my thoughts were in overdrive.

Kira was taking this way too seriously. I knew it was more than just obeying orders and personating a role. She was playing a game. She was playing to win, and I was the prize.

Surely she would let up once we met back up with the others, but for now? I feared a long night ahead.

* * * * *

We ended up eating at a bar and grill that had a large screen television on every wall. It was a compromise. Better than the greasy fast food I'd had my heart set on, but far from the romantic fine dining she had suggested. And this way, I could watch the baseball game on the screen over her head while pretending to be halfway listening to her.

After dinner, I adamantly refused to take a stroll through downtown like she wanted, but upon returning to the hotel, I wondered if that hadn't been the smarter, safer choice. It was just the two of us now, alone in the suite. One king bed. Great.

I set my bag down on the sofa in the sitting area adjacent to the bedroom. Kira narrowed her eyes, but said nothing as she rummaged through her own bag.

"I'm going to take a shower," she announced.

I glanced up from the television with a nod before I resumed flipping through the channels. I kept a wary eye on her, and didn't relax until the bathroom door shut behind her, and I was finally alone.

I considered leaving before she got out of the shower, and walking around until I was certain she had fallen asleep. But with the jet lag and lack of sleep the night before, I opted to make that plan B. I could find a movie and pretend to be so into it that I couldn't be bothered with distraction. That sounded plausible, but I worried that she might want to watch it with me, and try to get cozy on the couch. The baseball game from the bar was over, so that was out.

I spied the phone on the table next to the bed. It would have been nice to call Kris, to hear her voice, to reassure her. Because no matter how bad this was, I suspected her imagination had something far worse conjured up.

Then again, maybe not.

The bathroom door swung open, and Kira emerged. Kira and little else.

I was reminded of a scene from a movie I had seen a long time ago, where some girl approached a guy wearing a whipped cream bikini. Kira wasn't actually wearing whipped cream, but from the way she pranced into the room in a tight, short and . . . *oh, my God* . . . totally see-thru night gown, she might as well have been donned in whipped cream. Like the girl in the movie, Kira knew exactly what she was doing.

I couldn't remember what the guy in the movie had done. And I really wanted to remember so that I could follow his lead, because my thought processes were a little slow on the uptake right now.

On second thought, the guy probably did what every other warm-blooded male on the planet would do in that situation, and that wasn't something I wanted to copy.

My eyes dropped to the television. "What are you doing?"

I glanced up as Kira shot me a look of surprised innocence. "I'm getting ready for bed, silly."

She wasn't fooling anyone. Least of all me. I waved a finger at her . . . *outfit?* . . . before focusing on the television again. I had no idea what was on the screen, but it was safer than looking at Kira. "You can't possibly sleep in that."

"Actually, I prefer to sleep without any clothes on."

When I glanced up again, the look of innocence on her face had morphed into something else entirely. I swallowed the lump that had formed in my throat, and pulled at the collar of my shirt. Either my throat had swollen shut from the steak fajitas I had for dinner, or my shirt had shrunk. And the room was hot. Way too hot. And small. Like the walls were closing in on me. On us. I was trapped in a room with a half-naked girl—one who wasn't my girlfriend. This was bad, so very bad.

I wondered if I was in the middle of one of Kris's nightmares. For some reason, that thought grounded me, pulled my head out of the clouds of panic, and brought a faint smile to my lips. I wiped it clear before Kira thought I was smiling for another reason.

"You have a habit of dressing like that in front of guys you barely know?" I asked without giving her the satisfaction of looking at her. I had every intention of making it known that what was on the television was more interesting to me than her. Whatever it might have been. Because I honestly didn't know.

I heard a scoff, but didn't look up. "Barely know?" Her voice dripped of venom, and I knew the girl-claws were seconds from coming out. "You know it's not like you haven't already seen more of me."

I knew it. I knew there had to have been some history between us for her to come on this strong. I hated that I didn't remember what she remembered. I hated that I had been one of those guys. My mood sobered, but my voice stayed firm. "That was a long time ago, Kira. Things are different now."

Another scoff. "Why? Because your dear Lillian is alive after all?"

"This has nothing to do with Lillian."

"Who then?" Kira laughed, but it lacked humor. The claws were definitely out now, and she spat her next words. "That little Skotadi girl?"

My gaze slid wordlessly to hers. I wondered how she knew. Then again, I always suspected that anyone watching Kris and me closely enough would see through our charade. Apparently Kira had, though I wasn't about to let her know that she was right.

If anyone on that island could make life more difficult for Kris, Kira could.

"No, Kira," I said calmly. "I'm just not interested in anything more than completing this mission right now."

"What happened to you?" she sneered. "After Lillian disappeared, you were a party animal, and *this* . . ." She pointed to herself, drawing my attention again to the scant clothing, and the body it barely covered. "This was how we had fun."

No. The truth is that I had been so immersed in grief that I did anything I could to numb the pain.

I stood and tossed the remote in Kira's general direction. It bounced on the bed beside her. "The room is all yours," I said as

I started for the door.

"Where are you going?"

I stopped with my hand on the knob, but didn't turn around. "Anywhere but here."

Kira didn't stop me as I walked out.

I found myself grateful that our overnight stay was in New York, and I had places to go and things to do late into the night when most towns would shut down. A bar kept me entertained for a few hours, though I only allowed myself two beers the entire time. The bartender kept eyeing me up like I was a closet alcoholic trying, and failing, to maintain his sobriety. I didn't return to the room until nearly two in the morning. As I had hoped, Kira was asleep. But in avoiding her, I spent another night getting very little sleep. With an early morning flight, my alarm was set to go off only two hours after I finally laid down on the couch.

Not good considering we were due to arrive in Greece tomorrow, and would be in the shadow of Mount Olympus in less than two days.

*   *   *   *   *

If Kira thought I had been grouchy the day before, she quickly learned how much worse it could have been. Two nights with five total hours of sleep had turned me into a cranky grizzly with a thorn in his ass. And Kira was the thorn.

I spent the entire nine-hour flight either asleep, or pretending to be asleep with the earphones on. Kira barely looked at me.

We landed in Athens without incident. With the time difference, it was late evening when we arrived. Once again, we had reservations set up for us to stay the night. But unlike the previous evening, Kira showered and went to bed with barely a glance in my direction. I slept on the couch's pull-out bed.

The following morning, we boarded a train, and arrived at the small village of Litochoro shortly after lunch. The village was nestled between two gently rolling hills at the base of Mount Olympus, and was our final stop.

Litochoro was a low-key tourist hub for anyone wishing to climb the mountain. On any given day, hundreds, if not thousands, of tourists flocked to the village to explore the mountain or the nearby beaches. As I had learned by reading the information packet the Kala leaders had supplied each member of the team with, most of the locals were aware of the truth behind the mountain. They knew the gods and demigods existed, and resided there.

They also knew about us, and though no Kala had ever visited Mount Olympus before, they were all very excited for us to be there. They made sure to keep that excitement toned down in front of the tourists, though the girl that checked Kira and I in to our room at the Gods and Goddess Inn was a little intense.

Despite that, she was helpful, and explained that half of our team had already arrived, as she'd had the privilege of checking them all in. She had heard that the other half was due to arrive on the next two trains, and that in addition to the twelve members of our team, there were members of the European and Australian

Kala colonies arriving as well.

At that, Kira and I shared a look, and my stomach dropped a little.

Three teams?

That was bad. That was very, very bad.

Alone in our room, I engaged the deadbolt and secured the chain lock while watching through the peephole to ensure that the check-in girl was in fact leaving. Once she disappeared out of sight, I spun around.

Kira stood in the middle of the room, one hand covering her mouth. "How bad is it?"

I shook my head. "I think we'll be fine. She left. There are plenty of other Kala here for her to obsess over."

"No, not her." Kira's hand dropped and struck her thigh with a *thwunk*. "The mission. How bad is it if they called in three teams?"

I shrugged in an attempt to downplay the fact that I had the same worry she had. "I'm sure it's nothing we can't handle."

Kira nodded, but it wasn't convincing, and I saw the worry on her face as she turned. She didn't believe me any more than I believed myself.

*　　*　　*　　*　　*

Jared knocked on the door around dinnertime, and suggested that we powwow mission details over some authentic Greek food. Just me and him, which was nice because, for one, it got me away from Kira for a couple of hours, and secondly, I hadn't had a good gyro in years. Most importantly, Jared informed me that the two of us were a part of the six-man group chosen to ascend the mountain tomorrow morning to meet with the gods. Apparently, only a small group was needed to discuss the mission specifics with the gods, and to relay the information to the rest of the team members.

Once again, sleep eluded me as I tossed and turned most of the night. Come morning, I didn't care how much—or how little—rest I had gotten the night before. Pure adrenaline had me pumped and raring to go with the sunrise.

In addition to Jared and me, the small team climbing the mountain included the other two leaders and their two top soldiers. The two European guys spoke with thick French accents that made it difficult to understand them, but I understood enough to determine that their names were Pierre and Louis. They appeared bored with the feat before us, though looking at the mountain from the edge of the village, I imagined we were in for something far from boring.

The Australian guys, named Callum and Seb, were much more excited. Perhaps a little too excited, and maybe even a little oblivious to the magnitude of what awaited us. Still, they were much more fun to hang out with than the French guys.

We signed up for a self-guided tour so that we didn't have to explain anything to an unsuspecting tour guide. They couldn't help us anyway. Though every one of them had been all over that mountain, looking for the entrance to the home of the gods, none of them actually knew where it was.

No one did. Not even the team leaders were told exactly

where to find it. We were walking blind. Our only instruction had been to climb to the base of Mytika's Summit. That was it. Where we went from there was anyone's guess.

It took us a few hours of fast-paced steady hiking to get there. It was obvious from where we stood, with the summit still a several-hour climb above us, that we weren't going any farther without some serious climbing gear . . . or godly intervention.

Jared dropped his backpack to the ground with a sigh, and moved to stand under the shade of a small tree. The trees had dwindled in number and in size during the climb, to the point that now the amount of rock greatly outnumbered the amount of foliage. Right now, that lone tree off the side of the trail was our only sanctuary, and the rest of us followed Jared there, seeking refuge from the unforgiving sun.

I withdrew a bottle of water from the backpack I had purchased that morning just for the hike, and downed half of it in one gulp. Then I dumped a little on my head, but it did little to cool me down.

"Now what?" Seb grumbled.

Jared stepped out from under the tree and walked around in a wide circle. He appeared to inspect the rock walls that surrounded us, though it was anyone's guess as to what he was looking for.

"The entrance to the *Hall of the Gods* is at the base of Mytika's Summit," he mused quietly as he ran a hand over the gray stone. "There has to be something around here . . ."

"We split apart?" Pierre stammered in broken English. "That what Americans speak it?"

I squinted at him as I tried to determine what he was gibbering about.

Jared apparently had no trouble interpreting him, and nodded. "Yeah. We'll split up, cover more ground. Nathan, you're with me."

The look I shot Jared let him know just how I felt about walking around, looking for something none of us would know on sight. But, I supposed Frenchie was right—splitting up and searching for *something* was about our only option.

As I fell into step beside Jared, he said, "This is all you, man. I might be a natural leader, but you're the nature freak." He waved his arms out in front of him, as if shoo-ing me away. "Go. Track the gods down."

I shot him a look that said, *'you're an idiot'*. "Yeah, because I'm sure the gods would leave obvious footprints in the dirt for me to track."

Jared shrugged when he realized I had a point. "Well, then look for signs of a hidden door or something. I don't know. You have a better idea?"

"You think the gods aren't already aware that we're here?" They were probably all sitting around, watching the cameras in their high-tech security room and laughing at us.

"Another good point," Jared mumbled as he fell behind me.

The trail narrowed as we rounded a large rock formation, permitting only one person through at a time. Since I was in the lead, I was the first to see her.

Perched on a boulder, head cocked to the side in amusement, was a sight that could only be described with the word, *apparition*. She was real, I was sure of that, but her form looked . . . fuzzy and incomplete, like she was a hologram produced by a defective laser.

Or a goddess in-between realms?

I recognized her immediately, and my jaw dropped in awe. After all, she was the source of the very tracking expertise we were discussing.

Artemis.

Though I expected nothing less of a goddess, her natural beauty, combined with the charisma that radiated from her, was an overwhelming combination. Enough to stop my feet beneath me so suddenly that Jared plowed into my back with an *'oomph.'*

She slid off the boulder with a small smile, and a gracefulness that would put a dancer to shame. "You are the two I am looking for," she said. Even her voice sounded like softly strung harp strings to my ears.

I stood, transfixed. As Jared came to a stand beside me, I saw that he too was in awe. I didn't doubt that we looked like a couple of pimple-ridden prepubescent boys watching their first peepshow.

Our reactions didn't faze Artemis. With a wave of her hand, she said, "Come with me."

I started forward as Jared said, "There are four others with us."

Artemis glanced over her shoulder, but didn't stop. Her long tan robes nearly covered her sandal-clad feet. Though they moved beneath her, she appeared to float along the trail. "The two of you will suffice."

We followed closely behind her as we navigated the steep terrain. I cast Jared a concerned look when I saw what lay in front of us. Sure, a vertical rock wall might not have been a problem for an *immortal* goddess, but there was no way Jared and I could climb it. Not without some climbing gear.

"Stay close to me," Artemis instructed.

I didn't know what she was talking about because I assumed we would be stopping. There wasn't anywhere left to go but up, and that wasn't happening unless we grew wings. But then she walked into the rock wall. . .

And then the wall wasn't really there anymore. It was, sort of, but in a blurry kind of way. Sort of like Artemis had appeared at first. Now, she was solid, standing on the other side of the blurry wall of stone. She turned to wait for Jared and me. Right up until the moment I passed through the wall unscathed, I expected to make hard and painful contact with rock.

Artemis smiled at the amazement on our faces, and kept walking. We were on a trail in this realm too, but it was covered in a thick fog that enveloped us. I could only see a few feet in front of me—just enough to keep an eye on Artemis. I felt Jared at my back, staying close, as we followed her.

Seconds turned to minutes, and the fog thickened until I couldn't see my own feet, but I dared not slow down for fear of losing track of Artemis. My foot hit something hard and unforgiving, forcing me to lurch forward. Throwing my hands out in front of me, I connected with more stone.

"Step up . . ."

Though I could no longer see her, I could hear her. In front of me. And a little higher . . .

I lifted my foot, finding the first step, then another, and climbed through the fog until she came into view again—six inches from my face. Jared's hands were all over my back like a blind lab rat trying to find the cheese at the end of a long tunnel. At this point, I didn't care how stupid we looked, and I reached behind me to grab a hold of his shirt as I ascended the stairs after Artemis.

Though I had no way of knowing just how high we were, I knew we were high. The air felt thin, I had poor balance, and I just *knew*. And still we kept climbing.

I imagined that we were ascending to the top of Mytika's Summit . . . from inside the mountain? It was a difficult concept for me to grasp, and I assumed there would be a few more things in the coming minutes that I would have a hard time believing.

"Close your eyes now."

I did as Artemis instructed. That didn't stop me from wincing from the sudden burst of bright light that assaulted my eyes through my eyelids. A hand came down on my shoulder, stopping me from taking another step.

"Take your time, and open your eyes when you're ready."

"I think I'm blind," Jared muttered from beside me.

I used my hands to shield the light as I slowly—very, very slowly—opened my eyes. Even then, I looked down at my feet until my eyes adjusted.

Finally, I looked up, and took in a sight that belonged in a high-budget fantasy movie. Not real life. Even seeing it with my own eyes, I couldn't believe something this spectacular could exist in the world without being computer generated.

We stood on a balcony at the top . . . of the inside of the mountain. Its rocky peak towered fifty yards above us, but that was nothing. No, the truly phenomenal sight lay beneath us.

An entire community had been chiseled out of the odd cone-shaped structure created of stone. An elaborate network of stairs connected the balcony on which we stood to the bottom. Along the way, large golden doors that stood three or four stories high opened into the side of the mountain, and I could only imagine where they led. At the very bottom lay an enormous garden, with a thin but tall waterfall pouring out of the side of the mountain into a central pool of the clearest water I had ever seen.

Though they resembled ants from our height, dozens of individuals mingled amongst the lush and colorful garden. Others passed to and fro through the many, many doors.

Gods. All of them. I had always wondered how they lived on Mount Olympus. It had never made sense to me until now. Because now I knew they didn't actually live on the mountain. They lived *inside* it.

And I was there. I was standing inside the *Hall of the Gods*.

Chapter 9

{Kris}

Days were now labeled in terms of how long Nathan had been gone. Today wasn't Thursday. It was day number three. Three whole days since he left. I had once heard that time numbed the pain of separation, but I disagreed. Each day without him was worse than the previous, and he was all I thought about.

I wondered where he was. I wondered what time it was there. I wondered if he had started the mission yet. I wondered if he had completed it. I wondered if Kira had tried to make her move yet. When my mind wandered to thoughts of her, my inner Skotadi fought a little harder to come out and play.

My training hadn't been going so well the past few days. I knew why. Everyone knew why. My head wasn't in it because my heart was gone, and I didn't know when it would come back.

Top secret mission. How long could it take? A week?

"I was talking to Gran the other day about your specialties." Alec sat across from me at our usual table in the mess hall, with Kim and Bruce between us. We had been talking about the progress we both had made so far, but somewhere between fire yielding and charming, my mind started to wander.

"Uh-huh." *Two weeks tops. Definitely couldn't be more than two weeks.*

"And we both think that maybe some of the things you're trying to do aren't working because . . ."

How am I going to make it two weeks? What if it ends up being longer?

"So I was thinking about giving up girls, and maybe try the gay thing for a little while . . ."

What if it's a month or more? What if . . .

"There are some hot gay guys out there. Some even as hot as me . . ."

What if it's forever? What if the last time I saw Nathan is really the last time?

"Actually, I did try it once. I was drunk, and one thing led to another . . ."

What?

"What?"

"Ah," Alec said over the cup of coffee lifted to his mouth. Though I couldn't see his lips, the twinkle in his eyes suggested that they were slanted in an Alec-style grin. "So coming out of the closet is what it takes for you to pay attention to me?"

Bruce snorted into his cup, spilling a little bit of coffee. Kim remained silent, though I detected the tease of a smile on her face. I stared at her a few seconds longer than what was socially acceptable, and when her gaze drifted to mine, the smile was gone, replaced by a wary frown. Not that it mattered now, because I knew I hadn't imagined that smile.

Kim had actually smiled.

And Alec was still waiting for me to acknowledge him.

I shook off the moment of astonishment, and offered Alec a smile as an apology. "I'm just really distracted right now."

"That's actually the point I'm trying to make." Alec leaned forward, resting his elbows on the table. "You're not focusing enough."

I groaned. "You know who you sound like?"

Alec pointed a finger at me. "Don't you dare compare me to him."

I shrugged. "It's not my fault you said the same thing he says . . . *all the time.*"

"Whatever." Alec waved his hand dismissively, letting the Micah insult bounce off of him surprisingly well. He must have been wearing his charm. "You need to stop worrying about Nathan. He's a big boy. He can handle himself. You need to start worrying about yourself. Time is running out, Kris."

I sat up a little straighter in my chair. "I know it is."

"Then put your game face on."

It was a warning—a stern one—that I already knew I needed to heed. It wasn't just my future in jeopardy. Alec's was too, and he was counting on me. *Everyone* was counting on me because *everything* was at stake. It was so much bigger than simply what would become of Alec and me, and much more important than my relationship with Nathan.

Besides, all the worry I did over Nathan would be in vain if he returned from the mission to find that I had become the monster we were trying to keep me from becoming. So, yeah, I knew I needed to focus on me first.

I squared my shoulders, lifting my head high. "I got it, Alec."

His head tilted with a broad smile. "There's your game face. Good. Now I can eat." He stabbed the mountain of scrambled eggs on his plate with a fork, but stopped just before shoveling them into his mouth. "You do know I'm not gay, right? I was just messing with you earlier."

I smiled into my cup of orange juice. "You said you were drunk. Who am I to judge you?"

"No, seriously . . ." The scrambled eggs were dropped, completely forgotten. He jabbed a thumb into his chest. "Right here? Straight as they come. Got it?"

"Sure," I said, but my tone suggested uncertainty.

I glanced at Bruce, and saw the faint smile on his face. At least he recognized a joke when he heard one.

Alec leaned forward with his hands on the table, his eyes wide as they darted between the three of us. I suspected that he was about two seconds from jumping up and proving his sexuality with the next girl that walked by. Or Kim. I decided I had better stop teasing him before he got into trouble for offending some Kala princess, or had his jaw broken by Kim.

"Alec . . ." A slow smile spread across my face. "I'm joking. I know you're not gay." If anyone knew just how non-gay Alec was, it would be me.

"That's not funny." He finally took a bite of his eggs.

"It was kind of funny," Bruce muttered quietly.

Alec grunted something unintelligible, and dove into his

breakfast with renewed urgency. Apparently, now that his sexual preferences had been confirmed, he realized just how hungry he was. He had nearly cleared his plate before he looked up again with a groan.

"Incoming," he said in warning. "Looks like you're about to get branded, Kris."

Before I could ask what he was talking about, Micah plopped into the seat beside me. With a bracelet in his hand. I had to admit it was gorgeous, with a dozen or so tiny, sparkly gems strung together on a silver chain. As spectacular as it was, it didn't look like something that had come out of a *Tiffany's* magazine.

"What's this?" I asked him.

"Something you need to wear."

He grabbed my hand, but I pulled it out of his grasp before he could slip the bracelet on. "Why?"

He dropped the bracelet to his lap with a sigh, and his eyes lifted to mine. The sadness in them caused my heart to stutter a beat before falling into its natural rhythm again.

That protective instinct—the need to shelter Micah from any kind of pain, both physically and emotionally—came from somewhere deep inside of me. Somewhere very, *very* deep, and it clashed with the other half of me that yearned to rip his head off. It was as if I were riding on a very unsteady seesaw that bounced back and forth randomly and forcefully. The daily battle did a hell of a job messing with my head. Because even if I didn't particularly like Micah, I didn't really hate him either. Not like the Skotadi in me did.

But I also didn't really care for him. Not like my mother's

bloodline had programmed me to do. However, that love-crossed version of me seemed to be in control of the seesaw this morning.

"I've been doing some researching," Micah explained, and I tried to ignore the injured-pride tone to his voice. It did weird things to my heart—without my approval. "I've been staying up late for weeks now, trying to find a way to help you, and I think I found a way. A lot of spells require the use of certain stones or gems, right?"

"Yeah, I know. I have a few in my room." My favorite was the black tourmaline crystal placed under my pillow that kept Micah from invading my dreams. "We've had a hard time finding the rest."

"I found them." He lifted the bracelet. "I went through the books and found every single one that you might need and had the Earth Department supervisor order them."

I gingerly took the bracelet from him, and marveled at the raw beauty of the gems as I rolled them between my fingers.

"I thought maybe if you wore this all the time, you could draw from their energy," Micah continued. "And when you need them, when you do a spell, they will already be with you."

My eyes remained fixed on the gems as if they held me in a trance. Who knew what strength I might gain from having these on me when I attempted spells?

"Thank you," I whispered, finally meeting Micah's eyes.

I chose to overlook the gleam of admiration I saw in them, and fastened the chain around my wrist. It didn't necessarily make me feel any different, any better, but just knowing the possibilities gave me a renewed sense of empowerment.

Having the bracelet, and all the gems that I needed to reach my potential in my possession, gave me the confidence I had been lacking all this time. I had the feeling that this was exactly what I needed to get over the hump that had stalled me.

It would all be thanks to Micah. I couldn't believe he had gone to all this trouble for me.

No. I actually could believe it. That was one thing I could always count on Micah for. He would stop at nothing to help me, and he had proven that once again today.

I felt a little bad now about how I had been treating him. It wasn't his fault we were destined to be soul mates, and it wasn't fair to take it out on him. True, he was okay with letting it happen—perhaps a little too okay with it. But I supposed I went a little too far in letting him know how unhappy I was about having my fate determined for me.

I made a conscious decision to be nicer to Micah. Starting now.

When I looked up and caught Alec's gaze, he hooked a dark eyebrow in curiosity. I couldn't imagine what his reaction would be when I told him about my change of heart regarding Micah.

*   *   *   *   *

My new and improved opinion of Micah lasted about twenty minutes.

The downward spiral started when he suggested we try something different with our practice that morning. Because I was eager to see how well the gems around my wrist would work, I was game for anything. Even going somewhere alone with Micah—well, with Richie tagging along of course. Kim took a break, while Alec went down to the beach with Gran and Bruce. That left the three of us to enter the Infirmary that morning.

This wasn't my first trip to the Infirmary. Shortly after arriving, the island doctor had checked me out. I had no idea what he had been looking for, but he had apparently decided that I was worthy enough to live on the island while they helped me find a cure for my evil. As if it were a medical condition.

But today, Micah had something entirely different in store for me.

Security regarded Micah as if he were some Kala prince, and wrinkled their noses at me like I was something that they would throw in the dumpster. But since I was with him, the guards held the doors open until I had passed through, rather than shutting them in my face.

Security also seemed to know exactly where Micah was going, and it finally occurred to me what he planned for me to do.

Healing diamond injury.

I came to a halt as the last door opened in front of us, and I caught a glimpse of the Skotadi in the room—on the other side of a glass wall.

"I'm not sure I'm ready for this, Micah."

"There's only one way to find out," he returned. "You have to learn some time."

"I will. I'm just . . . not sure I want to do it now. I don't know what to do."

"I told you what to do. I explained what compounds are used, and exactly how to use them." He pulled the vial he always carried with him out from under his shirt, and lifted the chain over his head. Holding it out to me, he added, "You have everything you need right here."

I didn't take the vial from him. If anything, I recoiled from it.

I didn't want to do this for two reasons. One, we hadn't reviewed how to perform the ritual enough for me to feel comfortable doing it on my own yet. And two, I didn't exactly agree with the method in which he practiced the skill.

A quick glance at the Skotadi behind the glass confirmed my suspicions. While all Skotadi looked like death, this one in particular looked like he had been dead, buried, and dragged through the pits of hell no less than a dozen times. I didn't doubt that he had been Micah's practice dummy for some time. My opinion of the Skotadi was as low as anyone else's, but that didn't mean I thought it was okay for the Kala to kidnap them for the purpose of practicing diamond injury healing.

I had experienced diamond injury. I knew how badly it hurt. Skotadi or not, I wouldn't wish that experience on anyone. Unless, of course, they tried to kill me or someone I loved. Then it was injure to kill. Not injure to practice healing.

"Micah, no. I'm not comfortable with this."

He regarded me with a hint of compassion, and for a moment I thought he would respect my wishes and call off this exercise. Then his eyes flicked to the see-through glass wall behind me, and he said, "You have about thirty seconds to get comfortable with it."

"What?" I turned to see what he saw.

Three Kala guards had entered the small room with the Skotadi. One of them carried a knife. From the shine radiating off of it, I recognized it as a diamond coated weapon.

"Stop them," I said to Micah.

He looked at me, but said nothing.

Behind me, I heard a shout as two of the Kala engaged the Skotadi, and I turned to watch the scuffle on the other side of the glass. Considering how weak and sickly he appeared, the Skotadi didn't stand a chance. The Kala easily maneuvered him into an exposed position—one that made it easy for the third Kala to use the knife.

"They're going to do an easy one, Kris," Micah said to me quickly, as if that made it all okay. "It's going to be a shallow scrape, it's going to be placed far from his heart so that you will have plenty of time to heal him."

I scoffed, refusing to look at Micah. The Kala with the knife did just what Micah said he would do—he cut the Skotadi on the wrist in a move so quick I nearly missed it. The horrendous howl that erupted from the Skotadi indicated that the knife had found its mark.

As the Kala retreated from the room, I spun to Micah. "Do something!"

He held the vial, dangling from its chain, out to me again. "This is all you."

Something inside of me snapped. Something deep, deep

inside of me wanted to destroy the self-righteous brat in front of me with nothing more than my bare hands. But that same small part of me longed to turn and help my suffering kindred just feet away. Whatever admiration I, as his star-crossed soul mate, had for Micah was drowned out by the absolute disgust emitting from my Skotadi half. She was winning the battle for my body at this moment, and I hated him even more for giving her that power.

I glared at Micah, and snatched the vial out of his hand. "I hate you," I seethed.

Micah's eyes widened as he looked at me, but I didn't have time to concern myself with what he saw. My Skotadi was pissed, but as much as she wanted to extinguish Micah's life, she wanted to save that Skotadi more.

The Kala guards moved aside, allowing me to enter the room. I kept my head down as I passed, to hide my eyes from them. Though surging wasn't a phenomenon I could necessarily feel, I had come to realize that the angrier I was, the more my eyes surged with the evil residing inside of me.

The injured Skotadi in the room snarled when I first entered, then regarded me with curiosity when I looked up and our eyes met. He saw them. And he didn't know what to think.

He howled again, gripping his injured arm in agony, and seemed to forget about me. The pain dropped him to his knees, and I followed, stooping in front of him as I twisted the cap off of the vial. I dumped the mixture of compounds—certain healing stones that had been ground into a bluish black sand-like powder—into my hand.

"I'm going to heal you," I told the Skotadi.

"Not my first . . ." he ground out. If anything, he seemed angrier by that admission.

Of course. My suspicions had been right. They had done this to him before, and Micah had healed him. Likely many, *many* times before.

Now it was up to me to heal him, and I didn't know if I could do it.

I tossed one last hard glare at the glass. Though I couldn't see through it, I knew Micah stood on the other side, watching. Then I took the Skotadi's injured arm and placed the palm of my hand, and the healing compounds, against the gash.

It was superficial, at least. But the beginnings of diamond poison had already begun to creep up his arm, evidenced by the black streaks marking his skin. The streaks disappeared beneath the sleeve of his shirt just above the elbow. Once the poison infiltrated the heart, healing would be impossible and it would be game over in a matter of minutes.

Concentrate.

I blocked out the Skotadi's wails, and put my focus into the meditation part of the healing. That much I remembered. But there were supposed to be words to recite . . .

"Micah, I don't remember the words!" I shouted.

There was a click over the intercom, and then his voice filled the room. "*Sanaret terram aerem.*"

As if I understood Greek.

Bastard.

I touched the charm around my neck for strength and reigned in my inner demon long enough to focus on the task at hand. Even if it was she who wanted to save this Skotadi, the other half of me—the Incantator demigod—was the one who had to do it.

I repeated the words, pronouncing them to the best of my ability. At the same time, I pushed out my energy—also to the best of my ability, because that was a weakness that I had been working on—and attempted to envelop the negative energy in the Skotadi. Being the first time I was attempting to heal diamond injury, I had no idea what its energy felt like. All I had were Micah's instructions coming over the intercom, adding to what little I remembered from when he had first explained the process.

The hand I had placed over the Skotadi's wound warmed with energy. My grip strengthened, and I repeated the words again. And again, more forcefully and with more conviction each time. I put everything I had into pulling the poison out of the Skotadi, but he just wasn't responding.

His moans intensified until they drowned out Micah's voice.

"Micah! Help me!"

Though I struggled to hear him, I thought he said, *"Keep trying."*

I used my free hand to lift the sleeve of the Skotadi's shirt, and saw that the streaks had passed his shoulder and disappeared behind the shirt where it covered his chest. If the poison weren't already to his heart, it would be soon.

"He's going to die! I can't do this!"

Nothing but silence answered me.

I turned back to the Skotadi, lowered my head, and pushed

harder, murmuring the words quietly over and over until the Skotadi's cries quieted. His arm went slack in my hand, and I knew I had failed. I gently lowered his arm to the floor, then stood and backed away from the motionless body, unable to look at him directly.

The scraping of a foot on the floor behind me spun me around—with thoughts of vengeance on my mind.

Micah stood in the doorway. "You did it right."

"He's dead."

"You did all the steps right," he insisted with a shrug. "Maybe if you had started sooner . . ."

"Maybe if you hadn't put me in this position in the first place," I returned.

"You need to practice, Kris. Before I got good, plenty of Skotadi died in here."

"That's sick. *You're* sick."

"It's necessary. We're fighting a war. If more of us can learn to heal diamond injury, the Kala could finally win it."

I knew the reasoning for practicing this skill. I knew it made sense, but right now? After failing and holding myself partially responsible for this Skotadi's death, I wasn't in the mood to hear it. Not to mention, I was still struggling to hold my own alter ego back, and every word that came out of Micah's mouth only angered her more.

I needed to get away from him. I took several steps toward him, and the door, but stopped in front of him before exiting. I needed him to know one thing. "I will never forgive you for this."

"You will, Kris." He smiled at me confidently. "Besides, he's just a Skotadi."

I scoffed. "In case you didn't notice, I was almost Skotadi a few moments ago. Because of you, and what you did," I spat viciously. I grabbed Gran's charm around my neck again, and said, "You're lucky I was wearing this, because you nearly pushed me over the edge." I moved to go around him, to get away from him, before that still happened.

He grabbed my arm to stop me. "That would never happen, Kris."

My teeth were clenched, and I hissed between them. "It still might if you don't let go of me right now."

I yanked my arm free and stormed away. The guards at the door were smart enough to let me through.

And Micah was smart enough to maintain a safe distance as he followed me out of the room. He and Richie stayed behind me as I left the building, and sought the relative safety of my dorm room.

Kim was sitting in the hallway, and scampered to her feet as I approached. "Don't let him anywhere near me," I told her before slamming the door shut behind me.

Never before had I been happier to barricade myself inside the walls of my room. But I would do whatever it took to keep Micah out of my sight until I was confident enough that I wouldn't kill him the next time I saw him.

Chapter 10

{Nathan}

Artemis gave Jared and me a moment to take it all in before she led us to the heart of the gods' home. Fortunately, there was an easier way to get to the bottom of the mountain than taking the stairs.

Behind us towered a tall golden door. It opened to reveal a small room with buttons on the wall, similar to what would be found in any standard elevator. But we weren't in just any standard elevator that steadily lowered us with the aid of gears and cables. Artemis pushed a button, and the doors *immediately* opened to the grand garden. I stepped out on legs that wobbled as if I had just ridden the world's fastest rollercoaster. But then my eyes swept over the grand garden, and I forgot all about the elevator.

It was all so very . . . green. Trees and shrubs and other plants I had no name for, of all sizes and shapes, filled the massive space. Splashes of vivid colors, thanks to the thousands of flowers, broke up the green and lined the paths that snaked throughout the grounds. The only other break came from the large pool of water in the center.

Gods were everywhere. On benches under trees, lounging on the rocks surrounding the pool, walking the paths. They all regarded Jared and me with the same look of recognition, like they had been expecting us.

Artemis led us past the pool before taking a turn down another path. This one ended at another large golden door. It glided open without a sound as we approached.

"Wow," Jared breathed. "This place keeps getting more and more awesome."

"This way." Artemis stopped under the golden arch and, with a wave of her hand, ushered us through with a smile.

I didn't know what to expect, and if I were being completely honest with myself, I had a small pang of uncertainty as we crossed the threshold. Jared and I emerged into the center of a round stadium-like room. I spun around, only to realize that the door we had stepped through wasn't there anymore. Elevated above us were large seats chiseled out of the stone. Twelve seats exactly.

"The seats of the twelve Olympians," Jared muttered.

"I think so," I agreed.

Artemis was one of the twelve Olympians. But, like the door, she too had disappeared.

"Where d—" I started to ask Jared, but a loud, booming voice cut me off.

It came from above and behind us, and we both turned to find the source. Standing before one of the seats, his hands on the railing as he leaned over to get a better view of us, was Zeus. I nearly stumbled backward from the shock, but the surprises didn't stop there. Another god walked out of the stone wall behind him as if it were an open door. Then a third appeared to his right in the same manner.

Poseidon and Hera.

It was like meeting the President, the Queen, and the Pope at one time.

I stared at Zeus because, well, he was Zeus. But it was his wife, Hera, who addressed us.

"We understand you are the two that we need to speak to," she said softly.

Why Jared and I were so important, I didn't understand. Unless this did have something to do with Kris, and they somehow knew we were linked to her.

Who was I kidding? They were gods. Of course, they knew exactly who we were.

"So, tell us . . ." Zeus boomed. "What is the status of the thirteenth demigod, born of Hecate?"

My pulse jumped, because, dammit, this *was* about Kris. I wondered what they meant by 'status.' They didn't know? Before I had a chance to ask for clarification, Jared posed a question.

"What exactly do you want to know about her?" he asked.

"Are her loyalties to the blood of her mother, or to that of her many fathers?" Zeus rephrased.

I hadn't been aware that she had a choice, but the fact that Zeus had asked filled me with some hope. But then, I didn't know how to answer the question without throwing Kris under the bus.

Fortunately, Jared was good at the diplomatic stuff. "She intends to be loyal to her mother," he answered, "however, the blood of her fathers makes it difficult at times."

"Is there a way to help her overcome her evil bloodlines?" I asked.

Zeus and Poseidon shared a quick look, but I didn't miss it. Whatever their thoughts were, they didn't share. But Hera did.

She cast them both an amused glance before turning to Jared and me with a smile. "They don't actually know the answer to that. We haven't experienced another like her. She's the first to have such a strong mixture of both good and evil."

"But Hecate is under Hades' control . . ." Poseidon started before trailing off under Zeus's heavy gaze.

His words had my thoughts spinning. There was still much I was unsure of, but there was one thing which had me hopeful. The fact that Hecate's blood ran through Kris's veins meant that she might have a chance of avoiding a future as a Skotadi. But why would Poseidon be worried about Hecate being under the control of Hades? What impact did that have on Kris?

The hard look on Zeus's face kept me from asking.

"She has not reached maturity yet?" The tone Zeus used was sure and certain, like he was stating a fact, not posing a question.

I didn't know which answer would be in Kris's best interest, but I knew lying to the gods to protect her wouldn't go over well. "No, she hasn't," I admitted reluctantly.

I held my breath as they conferred, and tried to interpret if her not having reached maturity yet was a good thing, or a bad thing, as far as they were concerned. I glanced at Jared once to gauge his understanding of the situation. His head shook once, and I knew he was just as confused as I was.

I picked up a few words, mostly from Poseidon, who seemed the most temperamental of the three.

"Long time . . ."

"Pesky demigods . . ."

"Done away with . . ."

"They are our children," Hera stated fiercely, squaring her shoulders to Poseidon.

"And they are rising against us!" Poseidon fired back.

The floor vibrated beneath my feet, and I glanced at Jared to see if he felt it, too. His mouth curved into a frown as he surveyed the walls surrounding us. I followed his gaze, and eyed a crack in the stone that hadn't been there a minute ago.

No way could he bring Mount Olympus down on us. Right?

I worried more about what had caused Poseidon's outburst. *The demigods were rising against the gods?* The demigods were obviously not on the gods' good side from the bits and pieces of conversation I picked up.

"With Hecate's daughter, we will have three," Hera said softly to Zeus.

"The other two are lost to Hades," Poseidon argued.

"Not if we get to them first."

From what I saw, Hera and Poseidon were on opposite sides of a disagreement, with Zeus stuck in the middle. I knew Kris was involved somehow, but wasn't exactly sure how, and I didn't know if I should be rooting for Hera or for Poseidon to win this argument.

Zeus regarded Jared and me with curiosity, and I figured he was close to making a decision. "How close is she to reaching maturity?"

Jared and I shared a glance, then he answered, "We have no way of knowing."

"There is no guarantee to which side she will fall," Poseidon said as if reminding Zeus of something they had discussed multiple times.

"She is Hecate's daughter," Hera chided.

"We know nothing of Hecate's condition. Not enough to rely—"

"Enough," Zeus interrupted Poseidon. "I've heard enough. We must act now. We cannot wait for the girl to mature. We will send the Kala to rescue our two captive demigods, as planned. *They* will get the job done."

"And the girl?" Poseidon growled.

"We will wait," Zeus ordered. "She could be very valuable to our cause."

From the smile on Hera's face when she turned back to Jared and me, I knew she had gotten her way. From the sounds of it, I gathered that was the best thing for Kris. Hera seemed to be sticking up for her, while Poseidon . . .

I wasn't exactly sure what he wanted, but I didn't think it was anything good for Kris.

And what about these other demigods?

Finally, Zeus turned to us with some answers. "Our children, the demigods born to many of us, have made the poor decision to rise against us, their gods."

"How do they plan to do that?" Jared asked.

"They have found a way to achieve immortality for themselves and their army," explained Zeus. "If they are permitted to go through with this plan, they will be indestructible."

The Skotadi. It had to be, but something was off. "Which demigods?" I asked, hoping my intuition was wrong.

"Six of them so far have turned against us," Zeus explained. "Only two of our children have remained loyal—Isatan and Permna."

"All six are from the side of . . . good?" That was the part I had a hard time grasping. That the so-called 'good' demigods were the ones who were contemplating overthrowing the gods.

"Yes," Poseidon gritted. "My son and his friends."

No wonder Poseidon was so bitter.

"And the four who have sided with Hades?" Jared questioned.

"We see no alliance between the two groups," Hera answered.

"*Yet*," Poseidon added bitterly.

As it stood now, six demigods were on the verge of acquiring immortality. If they were successful, I saw no reason that Hades' four demigods wouldn't want to follow.

"Isatan and Permna will need to destroy the others before they are able to go through with their plan," Zeus continued. "However, they are under siege, held captive by a group of Skotadi in a village near here. That is why we have requested your assistance. We need you to rescue them before they are destroyed, and our hope is lost."

"We believe Hades is sending a demigod to destroy them," Hera added. "You must rescue Isatan and Permna before he arrives. Until the daughter of Hecate has matured, these two demigods are our only chance to prevent the uprising."

I stifled a groan. As bad as I had expected this mission to be, it had ended up being much, *much* worse.

"How big of a Skotadi presence will we be up against?" Jared asked.

"We don't know."

I rubbed my eyes to thwart off the dull ache that had settled behind them. It didn't help.

"How have they managed to hold the demigods?" Jared asked, and I looked up.

Good question. They were *demigods*, blessed with supernatural powers and strength. How could a group of Skotadi have managed to hold them hostage?

"We believe they have access to a skilled Incantator, who has created a compound capable of weakening demigods," Hera answered.

So now we were dealing with an Incantator too? I didn't have a good feeling about this mission. At all. And I was especially concerned about their intentions for Kris.

"And what of Hecate's daughter?" I asked, though I feared the answer. "When she reaches maturity?"

Hera smiled, and I noticed that she seemed very fond of Kris, for not knowing her. "Being the daughter of Hecate, and having four other pure bloodlines, she will have a power that reaches far above the other demigods. That strength will be needed for this great feat."

Shit.

So they wanted Kris, once she reached her potential, to help them destroy the other demigods. Though they claimed she would have an advantage over them, it still made me nervous. Anything that risked Kris's safety made me nervous.

"What about the demigods who have sided with Hades?" Jared asked, thoughtfully. "If the six turned demigods are destroyed, won't the balance of good and evil shift?"

Zeus nodded. "Yes, and that is why the demigods must be destroyed systematically. When one of ours is destroyed, one of theirs must be also, until all are gone."

All are gone? I didn't like the sound of that. "Except for Isatan, Permna, and Hecate's daughter, right?"

Zeus glanced at Poseidon, before he answered, "Yes."

That hesitation was enough to convince me that the gods could not be trusted. Given the elevated power that she would possess, there was no way they would allow her to continue to exist. They would use her, then get rid of her.

And I wasn't going to let that happen.

I tuned out as Jared requested the specifics regarding the two demigods who were sequestered nearby. I would participate in their rescue, of course. I would complete this mission to the best of my ability, but already my thoughts were on how to get Kris out of the mess she unknowingly had been thrust into.

As always, she was my priority.

*   *   *   *   *

All thirty-six soldiers were assembled and debriefed within minutes of our return to Litochoro a few hours later. Arrangements were made for the entire team to head out on the very next train the following morning.

It was a two-hour train ride, followed by a two-hour drive through the most remote parts of Greece to get to the isolated village of Ichalia, where the demigods were held captive.

I spent a large portion of the train ride writing letters to Kris and Alec, detailing everything that had been discussed with the gods, and everything I had learned about Kris. At the train stop, I dropped the letters in the mail, confident that Kris would not only be taken care of if anything happened to me, but that she would know what the gods wanted of her.

A few of the Australian guys managed to persuade a local bus driver to drive us the two hours to Ichalia. According to the driver, no one had been to the village in months, and most stayed far away from it now. Though no one knew exactly what, they suspected something peculiar was going on there. Many blamed a curse for the disappearances of those who had gone there, and never returned.

It was a long drive on a narrow and ridiculously bumpy road. On more than one occasion, I thought the bus would get stuck between two rock walls. At one point, one of the French Kala was rocketed out of her seat and onto the dirty floor. Conversation was pointless.

I was seconds from insisting on walking the rest of the way when the bus ground to a noisy halt. I looked out the window, but only saw endless rows of wheat and the road as it snaked through the brown field. The road disappeared around a bend and into a patch of trees a few miles ahead.

I lifted my eyes as Jared walked down the aisle from the front of the bus. "This is as far as the driver goes," he announced. "We're walking from here. Everyone grab a bag."

By the time I disembarked the bus, someone had already removed all the equipment bags from the storage compartment and tossed them to the ground. I selected one and placed it over my shoulders. It didn't matter which bag I took. They all contained the same—various weapons and combat gear, a water canteen, three days' worth of food, and a change of clothes. The straps bit into my shoulder from the weight.

As the bus bounced away with a chorus of screeching metal and exhaust backfire, we began our trek. Since none of us knew exactly how much farther it was to the village, we kept off the road, and blended into the wheat fields on each side as we approached the bend in the road. We ducked into the trees and cut across at an angle until the road reappeared on the other side. There, nestled between the tree line and a steep mountain wall, lay the village of Ichalia.

I dropped my bag to the ground and rested against the broad trunk of a tree as the three leaders convened. A few of the others followed my lead, and found their own tree to rest against. Most, however, stood biting their nails or wringing their hands in anticipation.

I didn't see the point. The mission sucked. We all knew it. Some of us were going to die. There was no way around it. No point getting anxious about it. Anxiety dulled the reflexes, and I had a feeling I would be needing them pretty sharp.

I had just shut my eyelids to block out the fidgeting when Jared dropped to a knee beside me.

"We're going to send a scouting team," he said.

I looked at my friend with one eye open. Scouting missions were always done by the nature specialists. I suspected that Jared had volunteered me as one of the scouts.

"I volunteered you to lead it," he added.

Both eyes popped open. "You've got to stop volunteering me for shit."

Jared grinned. "Ah, come on. You live for recon jobs. Besides, you're the best scout we have."

"How do you know I'm the best scout?" I returned, and pointed to a French guy propped against the tree next to mine. "How do you know he's not the best?"

"Because I've met a lot of Kala," Jared said evenly. "I've done a lot of missions, and I've seen a lot of action. I know what most of these guys are capable of, I know what you are capable of, and I know you are the best scout here."

I dropped my argument, because he was probably right. I was a good scout. And if I were about to head into battle, I wanted to make sure the best Intel had been gathered ahead of time. The only way to ensure that was to do it myself.

*   *   *   *   *

Four of us sat atop a cliff overlooking the village below. Pierre and Callum, both of whom I had met the day before while climbing Mount Olympus, were sprawled out on their stomachs to my right, and a guy I had just met, named Jas, hunkered down behind us, taking notes of our observations.

So far we had counted fifty-plus Skotadi, confirmed that there was one road in and one road out of the village, and had sketched a rough map of the structures that made up the village. Ten large buildings were grouped in the center, with twenty-three small huts that littered the outskirts. We saw no villagers.

"Does anybody else find that odd?" Jas questioned in a thick Australian accent.

"They're in there somewhere," I said in return. "We'll need to take precautions when we go in to make sure no villagers are injured."

"I think the big . . ." Getting hung up on his words, Pierre pointed to what he was attempting to say.

"Building?" I smirked.

"Yes. I think they there."

I shook my head at his poor English, but he had made a good observation. I instructed Jas to make a note of the two biggest buildings in the center of the village. Both of them were good options for the location of the demigods, or villagers.

"What I want to know is . . ." Callum started, and pointed to something in the field outside the village. "What is that?"

I had been wondering the same thing, and had been contemplating what to do about the small rectangle shack in the middle of the field. It didn't fit. It didn't make sense to be there. "Go check it out," I said to Callum. "See if it's anything worthwhile."

Callum muttered something unintelligible before he slinked away.

Thirty minutes later, we had every detail of the village studied, noted, and were ready to leave. Problem was, Callum hadn't returned yet.

I had seen him enter the shack, but hadn't seen him since. From the small size of it, I didn't understand how it could take him so long to inspect it. I was about to organize a search and recovery party when he plopped down in the dirt beside me.

The odor that came with him nearly made me gag, and I scooted as far away from him as the tree behind me would allow. "What in the hell is that smell?"

"Sewer." His clothes were soaked and stained, and he smelled like he had taken a bath in it. He looked way too happy for someone who had fallen in by accident. But then, he had good reason to be happy. "The shack is an old sewage maintenance building," Callum explained. "The tunnels run under the village."

As Callum requested the notebook, and began drawing a map of the tunnels that ran under the village, I felt a glimmer of hope. Using the tunnels, getting into the village would be a piece of cake. While getting in wouldn't be a problem, getting out was what worried me.

Chapter 11

{Nathan}

If there was one thing the Kala were good at, it was waging war. Kala leaders had always ensured that we had the most sophisticated combat gear when battling the Skotadi. That was especially true for this mission. There were gadgets and weapons in my bag that I had never seen or used before . . . and I was a combat instructor.

My weapons of choice for tonight's mission were a standard assault rifle with diamond-coated bullets and a diamond-coated knife that fit into a strap on my bullet proof vest. As I glanced around at the others, identical to me in their all-black combat uniforms, night-vision goggles, heavy vests, and loaded down with enough ammo to take down the entire Skotadi fleet, I imagined that this was what the end of the world would look like.

I had a bad pseudo-psychic feeling that I couldn't shake. Not that we weren't prepared for this raid. We were very prepared, and we had a good group of soldiers to pull it off with, but that knowledge couldn't drive away the strange sense of doom I felt.

Once it set in, the best I could do was push through it.

We were split into six teams. I had been assigned as leader of one of the two offensive teams that would converge on the two large buildings in the center of the village. Under my command was the youngest American from the Costa Rican base, named Caleb, and three Australians: Jeremiah, Denis, and Pete. The five of us were to find and secure the two imprisoned demigods, while the defensive teams sought and eliminated Skotadi resistance. Thanks to the elaborate maps the recon team had crafted of both the village and the sewer tunnels, each team knew exactly where to go and what their objective was.

The raid had been planned out with the attention to detail I had come to expect of Kala missions. Lack of preparedness wasn't the cause of my bad feeling. Something else was . . . something out there in the darkness beyond the village. I couldn't see it, but I felt it.

The only thing that made me feel a little better about the unknown were the two Kala positioned a mile up the road that led to the village. Their job was to watch for any sign of Hades' demigods. I felt a little better at knowing we had a small cushion, a window of time to potentially escape their wrath if they showed up tonight.

We approached the sewage maintenance shack under the cover of darkness, and entered the tunnels two at a time. They were wide enough to allow two to walk shoulder to shoulder, but at the first split, the teams parted into two groups. I continued down a narrow tunnel with about twenty soldiers trudging along behind me. The water level rose the farther we traveled, until we were wading through knee-high filth. Each step tested the strength of my gag reflex. Somewhere behind me, I heard someone lose their Kala-issued prepackaged meal.

"Come in, Team Loser, come in." Jas's Australian drawl buzzed in my ear.

All six team leaders were equipped with a headphone communication set. Jas had been put in charge of the other offensive team, and was somewhere behind me.

With a grin, I pushed the button below my jaw. "You can't do any better than Team Loser?"

"Like Calvin is better."

"I didn't pick your name, remember?" The guys who came from Australia with Jas had already taken to calling him Calvin because, well, he looked like he could be a Calvin Klein model. He got a lot of shit from the guys because of his pretty boy looks.

"Exactly," he returned. "Lack of originality, mate."

"Hey, Dipshit, shut up!"

Jas ignored the voice of another team leader in our ears. "I just want to know what you're going to owe me when my team finds the demigods first."

"How about a muzzle?" A French accented voice suggested over a wave of static.

"I second that," I chuckled.

"I was thinking something more along the lines of money," Jas said. "Say . . . five hundred?"

I choked out a laugh. "Keep dreaming, Calvin."

I paused at an intersection, and glanced down at a copy of the map Callum had sketched before veering to the right. One defensive team behind me would follow. Jas's team and a second defensive team would go the left.

"Jas, make sure you go the right way at the intersection," I said.

"Right? I thought I was going left?"

"Left is the right way."

"You Americans make no sense," he grumbled. "I'm going left."

Other than the sloshing of our feet moving through the sludge, we entered the perimeter of the village in silence. Above us, moonlight filtered down through slits in the manholes, broken up by the occasional shadow cast by a building. I heard no voices from above, but that didn't mean the Skotadi weren't nearby.

"Five hundred might have been a little steep," Jas continued in a hushed voice. "How about two-fifty?"

I reached a ladder and glanced down at the map for confirmation. This was it—my team's point of entry. Using a series of hand signals, I instructed Jeremiah to climb the ladder and undo the screws securing the manhole.

"Respect," I spoke into my device quietly. "That's all you'll get from me."

Jeremiah signaled that his task was complete, and I motioned for him to climb down. One thing I insisted on, as a leader, was to be the first man to step foot onto enemy grounds. I would never ask one of my men to go first.

"I'll guess I'll take that bet," Jas sighed. "In addition to bragging rights, of course."

I climbed the ladder to the top.

The street above me was illuminated by an unusually bright light cast by the full moon. I preferred total darkness so we would have more of an advantage with our night vision goggles. With a bright moon, the Skotadi could see us just as easily as we could see them.

The unease in my gut twisted tighter.

The ladder vibrated as the rest of my team ascended beneath me, and I whispered into my radio, "Offensive team one, in position."

Seconds, and then minutes, ticked by as the other teams announced that they were in position. Only the pounding of my pulse in my ears filled the silence between. No matter how many missions I had partaken in over the years, and how different each of them were, the underlying current of fear never changed.

Men would die tonight, and not just the enemy. As always, there was a chance that I may not come out of this one alive. Despite that very real fear, my composure remained unshakable.

"May the best man win," I said quietly into my radio.

Jas didn't answer, but another voice I recognized did. With the words, "All teams, go," Jared ordered the start of the raid.

I pushed the manhole open, and climbed into a narrow alley wedged between two buildings—it should have been *the* two primary buildings, but I waited to consult my map. As the rest of my team climbed to the surface, I squatted low to the ground and provided cover with my gun pointed at the mouth of the alley. Once all four of my men were out, we moved into shadows cast by the building.

There, I gathered my bearings with the aid of the map. Our

target building was behind us; Jas's target was the one across from us. They would be entering it from one alley over, once they found a point of entry, which was something I had to do yet.

Using hand signals, I instructed my team to fall in, and led them toward the front of the building, where I hoped to find an entrance. Quickly moving shadows darted across the intersection, and I fingered the trigger of my gun before I recognized them as one of our defensive teams.

"Alley's clear," I spoke into my radio.

"Copy that," returned a voice I recognized—Jared. "Entrance of building one had two guards. It's all clear now."

"Copy." I picked up the pace as Jared's team moved out of sight.

At the intersection, I signaled for my team to stop, and glanced around the corner to the front of the building. Two small crimson spots stained the ground in front of the doorway ten yards away, but because we were all using diamond, there were no bodies left behind.

We entered the building, and my guys fanned out to secure the large entryway. It didn't take me long to realize what kind of building we were in. The faint smell of chalk and floor polish, and the echo-inducing openness, screamed schoolhouse.

Sounds of a small scuffle spun me around in time to see Caleb hovering over a Skotadi's body before it dissipated. He stepped back from the expanding puddle of blood left on the floor, and lifted a hand with the 'okay' signal.

I radioed Jas as we moved down the wide hallway. I noted the smugness in his voice as he informed me that the building they were sweeping through was a type of administrative building. Of course. The demigods would more likely be found there than in a school.

At this point, I didn't care who found the demigods. Getting everyone out alive was my priority.

Jared piped in to inform us that one defensive team had moved in on the administrative building to assist Jas's team, while Jared's defensive team was sweeping through the school, coming from the other side.

"You had better not shoot my ass when we meet," he added.

"Yes, sir," I returned.

I slowed outside the first closed door we came to, and instructed my team to take flanking positions. I palmed the knob, found it unlocked, and pushed the door open slowly. I moved out of the way as Jeremiah and Caleb entered the room together, guns readied, then followed quickly behind them.

The smell of rotting flesh hit me like a tangible wall of death, and I nearly doubled over and threw up on my shoes. Blinking away the involuntary wetness in my eyes, I took in the sight before us. Bodies—some bagged, most not—in varying stages of decay lay in heaps on the floor between desks, on top of desks and the counter that ran parallel to the large windows along one wall. Forty, maybe fifty, bodies of all sizes filled the room—men, women, and children.

Denis spun around to retch in the corner behind me as I stooped to take a closer look at the body closest to the door.

Jeremiah squatted beside me. "They're not hybrids," he observed in a hushed voice.

Villagers. All of them *human* villagers. There would be no recovery as part of this mission. The villagers were all dead, and I suspected that this was only one of many rooms stuffed with bodies we would find before the raid was over.

Jared's voice buzzed over the radio in my ear. "We've encountered human casualties."

"Same here," I returned. My voice sounded distant, faint, like it didn't belong to me. I gathered up a blood-stained white sheet, and draped it across the body at my feet before rising.

My team stood, facing me. Grown men—hardened, seasoned Kala soldiers—with tear-rimmed eyes, looked to me for direction as I fisted my hands to keep them from shaking. I craved a steadying breath to compose myself, but didn't dare. Not yet. Not in that room. Taking a deep breath of air polluted by death would send me running for a corner to throw up in.

I pushed past the guys, moving for the door. "Let's keep moving," I ordered in the best fake-composed voice I could muster. "There might be some still alive somewhere."

The fresh air in the hallway helped alleviate the souring in my stomach, but did nothing to erase the images burned into my memory. I doubted anything ever would, but I at least had regained enough control over my emotions to trudge forward.

The other team leaders barked in my ear, distracting me from what I had just seen.

A heavy Skotadi presence had been discovered on the other side of the village; Jas's team and their accompanying defensive assistance were moving through the administrative building, and suspected that they were closing in on the demigods based on the number of Skotadi they had encountered; Jared reported three rooms with bodies in addition to the one my team had found.

The strain in his voice hinted at his own struggle with the discovery. It seemed the school was being used as the village morgue, and we were the unlucky ones to discover it. At least we were spared from a heavy Skotadi presence in the school. I suspected my guys weren't at the top of their game after finding that room, so the less Skotadi resistance we encountered the better.

We cleared three more rooms. Each room we found empty pushed the visions that haunted me farther away, and helped to strengthen my confidence. Each step I took replaced my lingering sadness with anger and a need for vengeance. By the time we reached the end of the first hallway, I was back in warrior-mode and ready to make every one of the Skotadi pay for the devastation they had caused this village.

My team took flanking positions as we rounded the corner into another hallway—a short one with only two doors. The one closest to us was an extra tall set of double doors, and I suspected they led to a cafeteria or gymnasium.

As we entered, it became immediately obvious that it didn't matter what the large room was, because it could have been any room and the only thing that mattered was the bodies that filled it. Again, the stench of death hit me, though not as powerful as it had been in the smaller classroom.

Before us stretched row upon row of narrow cots, occupied by bodies.

There had to be hundreds of them...

"This one is still alive!"

I followed Caleb's voice, and stepped closer to the cot closest to the door, and noted the slight movement of the man's chest. Barely. I glanced around the expansive room filled with pale and wheezing villagers. Each raspy breath I heard sounded like someone's last. By some miracle, they all hung on to life.

"What do we do?" Denis asked.

I spoke into my radio, "Jared, we've got about two hundred survivors in the gymnasium."

"Skotadi?"

"None."

"On our way."

I moved down an aisle with cots lining both sides, hoping to find a villager coherent enough to speak. They all looked to be at about the same stage of illness—whatever illness it was that they shared. Looking at their reddened eyes, ragged breathing, and frail bodies, I was reminded of a movie I had seen where a whole town had been infected with hemorrhagic fever. Though these villagers weren't actually bleeding from their orifices, the redness in their eyes resembled blood.

Belatedly, the thought occurred to me that whatever had plagued the village could have been contagious. Then I remembered that we were dealing with Skotadi-caused devastation, not the work of nature, and I suspected that the people in the next town over might have been right about one thing. The village might have actually been cursed, and this might have been the work of a seasoned Incantator.

The question remained as to why. Why this village? Unless...

I remembered the kidnapping of humans I had witnessed in West Virginia. We had never really discovered what the Skotadi were doing with humans there, and I wondered if the people of that small town were now inflicted with the same illness—or curse? How many other small towns were there that the Kala were unaware of? And why weren't we aware?

We had a system, an entire department put in charge of tracking stuff like this . . .

Jared's voice in my ear put a stop to my running thoughts. He and his team were on the other side of the gymnasium's doors, and I instructed my guys to watch their trigger fingers as they entered.

Their reactions at the horrific sight matched my team's initial reaction. Once they composed themselves, they spread out to help my team assess the villagers.

Jared moved to my side. "What do you make of this?"

I shook my head without a word. Other than scattered and incomplete theories, I had nothing to offer.

A gurgling noise from the cot behind us spun Jared and me around instantaneously. The man that lay there had managed to lift one of his arms, and held it out to us as if pleading for help. I didn't hesitate to take his hand as we stepped closer.

His lips moved, but I heard nothing.

Jared fumbled under the cot and stood holding something that looked like an identification card. "Shit. He's only twenty-four years old."

Looking at the man's sunken eyes and wrinkly skin, I would have guessed at least sixty.

"Attis?" Jared addressed the man, and he managed a weak nod.

Again, his lips moved, but I couldn't make out what he said. I dropped my head to put an ear closer to his mouth, and I finally heard his whispers.

"Bewitched by the devil . . ."

I lifted my eyes to his, and asked, "A curse?"

His head shook fractionally. *"The children . . . seek the essence of their youth . . ."* I recalled the room filled with bodies. Though I hadn't wanted to look closely at the time, I had noticed that most of them were small. So the Skotadi had cursed the village, and were killing its inhabitants—starting with children—because they sought the essence of their youth?

I shifted to ask him if he knew who was behind it, but an onslaught of chatter in my ear stopped the question on my tongue.

"Demigods located . . ."

"Building cleared . . ."

"Moving out . . ."

"All defensive teams maintain a perimeter," Jared ordered over his radio. "Nobody move until the demigods are secured at the rendezvous point. Jas, haul ass."

"On it," Jas said.

I turned to Jared. "What do we do with the survivors?"

His brow furrowed, and his eyes were lined with guilt when they met mine. "I don't know what we can do."

"We can't just leave them here."

Jared's gaze swept the room. Finally, he muttered, "If we can eliminate all the Skotadi, secure the entire village . . ."

Then, and only then, could we risk moving the villagers. No way could we sneak two hundred villagers out while Skotadi prowled outside. Our 'stealth extraction' mission was about to become a 'locate and kill' mission. It guaranteed more casualties on our end. I didn't even know how many men we had already lost, and if we had the manpower to muster up a successful attack. And that was assuming Hades' demigods didn't show up, because it would take us at least a day to get all the survivors out.

Jared had a big decision to make, and he didn't take it lightly. When he made up his mind, he lifted a hand to his headset to make an order, but he never got to make it.

"Team three taking heavy fire! Requesting immediate assistance!"

Everyone in the gymnasium heard the plea, and we all moved for the doors as one. Ahead of me, Jared barked out orders for every team to converge on the residential huts on the east side of the village where team three had been assigned. Except for Jas—his orders remained to secure the demigods.

Stealth was no longer needed. Not with the battle cries coming from the far side of the village. The Skotadi knew we were here.

The slapping of our feet on the blacktop echoed off the buildings and through the otherwise quiet street, giving the impression that we numbered far more than a ten-man wave of reinforcements. Rounding the corner, and catching my first glimpse of the battle amongst the crowded huts, I knew ten extra guys weren't enough.

I spotted five Kala positioned behind the cover of a bullet-ridden vehicle, taking heavy fire from at least thirty Skotadi. Between the two groups, several bodies writhed in diamond poison-induced agony on the ground, but not enough to account for the amount of blood that had already been spilled.

"I want five guys flanking!" Jared shouted with a wave of his hand to the right.

I ducked behind a row of huts, running in the direction Jared had indicated. All four of my men followed, while Jared's team dug in and opened fire on the mass of Skotadi from the street. We emerged on the other side of the huts in an excellent flanking position. We spread out between two buildings, dropped low to the ground, and started firing.

Already, Jared's men had dwindled the number of Skotadi, and my men took down another six before they scampered behind cover from our position.

Through my headset, I heard Jared order another Kala team that had arrived to join and render aid to the trapped Kala team. With the cover fire supplied by the rest of us, they got in easily.

"A dozen Skotadi coming in from the west!"

I didn't recognize the voice, but it didn't matter. I scrambled to my knees and spun, gun raised, as a wave of Skotadi barreled down on my team. Though my men hadn't heard the warning I heard, they followed my lead. A collective burst of ammo from all of us took down the first line of Skotadi before the rest of them were on us. In the lead was a burly Skotadi with a shiny knife pointed at my chest.

He hit me hard, driving me to the ground on my back. The blade made contact with my vest, but didn't pierce my skin. I drove both of my feet into his midsection and flipped him over my head. He landed with a chorus of crunching gravel and curses before I rolled on him with my own knife.

With a swift stab to the heart, I ended him quickly, and spun to assist the rest of my team. Two of them were engaged with two Skotadi in a knife fight. Jeremiah stepped to my side and we assisted them in finishing off those last two Skotadi.

When it was over, there were four of us. Caleb was gone.

"His gun jammed!" Jeremiah's eyes darted to mine. "I saw it. Caleb's goddam gun jammed!"

He picked the gun off the ground and smashed it against the wall in a fit of rage. I put a hand on his shoulder, but before I could offer any words, an urgent voice interrupted me through the radio.

"All team leaders, two demigods incoming. Two miles out."

Jared followed with an immediate order. "All teams, pull out!"

I cursed as I scanned the battle scene. Their timing could not have been worse. We still had men cornered by Skotadi. Though the Skotadi presence surrounding them had been significantly reduced, it wasn't enough.

I turned to what remained of my team. "Hades' demigods are coming. You know the plan. Go, get out."

Four guys raced past us, hauling ass out of there. I recognized them as Jared's team. Not surprisingly, Jared wasn't with them.

I waved my hand after them, and said to my team, "Go with them. Get to the trees."

I didn't wait for any of them to respond, or watch to make sure they left. I spun and raced back to the main road, where my team had split from Jared's team.

As I approached, I spotted the barrel of a gun propped up on the hood of a parked vehicle as it fired round after round into the Skotadi. I slid behind the vehicle, coming up alongside Jared, and positioned my gun beside his. Only the slight curve of his lips hinted that he knew I was there.

From what I could see, only three Kala remained. A group of five Skotadi separated them from us. From their line of escape.

"Ooh," I sucked in between my teeth. Make that four Skotadi left. To Jared, I asked, "How much time do you think we have left?"

"From two miles out? Less than ten minutes."

I had been thinking closer to five minutes. Ten was better. Five to ten minutes to free the sequestered Kala and get the five of us out of this village before the hand of Hades dropped on us.

Keeping one finger on the trigger, I reached under my vest and grasped the stone Kris had enchanted with a protection spell. I hoped she had done it right, because I had a feeling we would need it to get out of there.

Chapter 12

{Kris}

I couldn't stand to be around Micah, and he knew it. I only tolerated his presence during practices on the beach, and even then I sought Gran's and Alec's assistance before his. Despite that, he remained my shadow, and I had to deal with it because the supervisors insisted that he assist me with my training.

They may have claimed it was because we were equals as far as strength, but I was increasingly convinced that was only an excuse for them to monitor my screw ups and tendencies for evil through the watchful eyes of Richie.

I was determined not to let Micah or Richie hamper my progress. Every day, I felt better and stronger. I still had a long way to go, of course, but I was more optimistic than I had been in a long time. The gems I carried around my wrist seemed to have helped. Though I hadn't admitted it to Micah, the smug smile on his face told me that he had noticed.

It didn't take long to learn that fighting and fire yielding were my strongest specialties. I could now conjure a fire almost effortlessly, and had learned to extinguish it without causing myself or others third degree burns.

Most of our efforts were spent on practicing Incantation. I ran through multiple spells a day—usually the same basic ones. I had yet to make myself invisible, but I managed to turn my hair fire red for about an hour this morning before it faded out, and I could now move bowling ball-sized rocks a few yards—without blowing them up—using nothing more than my mind and a few precisely chanted words.

The two specialties I had yet to make progress with were charming, and summoning the dead. While Alec said he hadn't figured out how to communicate with the dead yet, he had mastered the ability to charm people. Not surprisingly, that was his best specialty.

"You have to maintain eye contact," Alec explained to me. "Don't let them look away. If you do it right, if you hook them quickly enough, they won't be able to look away. When their eyes glaze over, you know you have them."

We sat side by side on the beach, facing the water, and I absentmindedly drew a heart in the sand between us with my finger. "Have you ever charmed me?"

Alec grinned. "Honey, I don't need to use my paranormal skills to charm any girl, including you. It's called charisma, and I have it."

I shook my head with a laugh. "I'll take that as a no . . ."

"It's actually easy once you get the hang of it," he said, pulling the conversation back to charming—of the supernatural sense. "Communicating with the dead, on the other hand, I have no idea. Nothing I've tried works."

"I tried it once," I admitted. "But I tried to reach Gran . . ." I glanced over my shoulder at my adoptive grandmother as she conversed with Micah. Obviously, it hadn't worked because she was still very much alive. "I'm afraid to try to communicate with my friends."

Though my eyes were on the crashing surf, I saw Alec's head swing toward me. "The girls that died in the car accident?"

I nodded my head.

"They were your friends. What are you afraid of?"

"I don't know . . ." Maybe that they blamed me somehow, or hated me for surviving when they hadn't? "I dream about them enough. I don't need to try to communicate with them when I'm awake."

"You dream about them?"

"At least once a week," I answered.

"You're doing it," Alec said excitedly. "That's a form of communication. Actually, I think it's the most common method of communicating with the dead."

"Really?"

"Yeah. I learned a thing or two in my brief Skotadi education. You're good at it without even trying. Now, all you need to work on is your *charming*." Alec glanced at his watch. "But first, you have to help me."

I spent the next ten minutes coaching Alec on fire yielding. By the time I left for combat class, he was producing decent flames with his hands. He needed help with aiming and extinguishing those flames, but that would have to wait for another day.

Kim met me by the bench between the beach and the village center, and trailed me as I hurried to class. Not that I was excited about class. Not anymore. But I sure as hell didn't want to get caught coming in late.

The instructor who had taken over the class in Nathan's absence was a tool. In a complete reversal of what I was used to with Nathan, this guy hated me—like went out of his way to have me 'accidentally' decapitated hated me.

Most of the students in the class were all too happy to volunteer to be the one to take the Skotadi-girl down. But I was usually paired with Tyson. He was the next Nathan. Only bigger. And meaner. And he hated me too.

I took my place in the back, behind the same two girls I had stood behind every day for weeks. As usual, they each shot me the occasional cautious glance, like they expected me to suddenly turn evil. I took the opportunity to catch and hold the brunette's gaze the second time she looked at me. I smiled in an attempt to hide my intentions. "Will you be my sparring partner today?"

Her head spun quickly toward the blonde, whose lips curled into a grimace. One of them muttered, "Ew" before the brunette turned back to me with wide eyes. "Um, no?"

As their heads tipped together to mask their whispers, I practically heard Alec's voice in my head, shouting, *"Don't ask. Demand it. Take charge."*

Instructor Kand walked in, putting an end to my weak attempt at charming. He promptly split the class into pairs— grouping me with Tyson once again.

Tyson glanced over at me with a wicked grin. I held his gaze as I crossed the room to him. When only a few feet separated us, I said, "You're going to take it easy on me today." I stared at him a few extra seconds, willing him to succumb, and waiting for his eyes to glaze over, but they never did.

He scoffed. "I don't think so."

Ninety minutes later, I left class with a new set of bruises and a slight limp. Kim followed as I went back to my dorm room to recuperate. She frowned at the sight of my swollen and bloodied lip, but said nothing. It wasn't like she could do anything about it.

I supposed there wasn't anything anyone could really do. Alec would likely kill Instructor Kand, and Micah . . .

While he was the best option for getting results, I decided I would rather suffer a little extra abuse than speak with him any more than absolutely necessary. Besides, the bruises would be gone in an hour or two. I healed that fast.

I stretched out on my bed, and closed my eyes to get a little rest before dinner.

When I awoke again, my feet were in the ocean. The moon shined high in the sky, and bright enough to illuminate the pier to my left. I backpedaled until my feet hit dry sand.

I wore the same clothes I had on earlier, and saw no trace of my shoes. I had no recollection of what I was doing on the beach, or how I had gotten there. Goosebumps prickled my arms from the cooler night air, and I rubbed my arms to chase them away.

I wanted to turn away from the water, to return to the

warmth and comfort of my room, but I couldn't. My feet were frozen beneath me, as if stuck in quicksand. I looked down, and wiggled my toes. They worked fine, but the connection between my brain and legs wasn't functioning.

I looked out over the water. Gentle waves rolled toward me, but I felt the pull of something bigger, something unseen, and I took reluctant steps forward until my feet met with water again. I stopped as a shadow moved into my periphery, between me and the pier, and I squinted to get a look at what had caused it.

"Alec?"

He blinked rapidly a few times before swinging his head toward me. "Kris? What are you doing here?"

"I have no idea," I answered.

Alec turned to stare at the ocean. "Do you feel that? It's like something is pulling me . . ." He jutted his chin forward. "Out there."

"I feel it too," I admitted. "What do you think it is?"

Alec was silent as he gazed out at the water, and eventually I turned to stare with him. The sensation of being pulled forward intensified, like liquid metal ran through my veins and the ocean was a large magnet. No . . . it wasn't the ocean. Something just out of sight, beyond the horizon, called to me—to us.

Perhaps as close as the nearby Costa Rican shore?

The sensation pulsed suddenly, causing a deep ache in my legs, and then disappeared completely. It wasn't until then that I realized how straight Alec and I stood, and we both sagged in relief at the same time.

He turned to me, his mouth dropped open, but he said

nothing. For a long time, we just looked at each other, caught in our own thoughts. After a minute, Alec dropped an arm over my shoulder and steered me away from the water.

Several more minutes passed in silence as we made our way to the trail that led us to the village center and the dorms, before Alec said, "Let's keep this between the two of us. At least until we figure out what just happened."

"Okay."

That was probably best. We were already the black sheep on the island. The others would only regard us with more caution if they knew we were being summoned to the ocean in the middle of the night by some unseen force. Speaking of . . .

"How did you get out of your room without Bruce seeing you?" And how did I get past Kim?

Alec shrugged. "I have no idea."

In order to keep them in the dark, we needed to get back into our rooms the way we had left. The only way I knew how to do that was to climb up the building using the balconies as Nathan had done. I had always wondered how hard it had been for him to do that.

As it turned out, it wasn't that hard.

*   *   *   *   *

Considering the peculiar walk on the beach the night before, my day started off uneventfully. Breakfast with the usual gang, Incantation practice on the beach during which I managed to change Alec's hair color to bright yellow for ten minutes, lunch, then another hour of specialty practice before combat class.

Class passed in the same manner as usual, but the moment it was over, my day changed drastically. I knew something was up when I saw both Micah and Alec, and Bruce and Richie, waiting for me outside the classroom.

I didn't have a chance to ask before Micah rushed to my side with an explanation. "Callie arrived about twenty minutes ago."

"Callie?" I pushed past him, eager to see my best friend. "Where is she?"

And what was she doing here? She was supposed to be back home with her family, and adhering to a sentence of lifelong grounding under the watchful eyes of her parents and two Kala guards entrusted with the job of protecting her from Skotadi.

Alec put a hand on my shoulder to stop me. "She's sick, Kris."

"What exactly do you mean by *sick*?" I looked back and forth between Alec and Micah, and didn't like what I saw in their eyes.

"Remember when Callie said Lillian put some sort of spell on her?" Micah started tentatively, and my stomach hollowed at the mention of it. I hadn't forgotten, but when nothing bad had happened afterward, I thought Lillian hadn't completed whatever it was she had been trying to do. "They think Incantation is behind Callie's sickness."

"And it was likely Lillian," Alec added.

As if I needed another reason to hate that woman. She had tortured me, almost killed Nathan . . . and now she had infected my best friend with some Incantation-induced illness?

I raced toward the exit. "I assume she's in the Infirmary?" I shot the question over my shoulder.

"Yes, but . . ."

I spun on Micah, gritting my teeth. "But what?"

"They might not let you in," he answered.

My laugh resembled a witches taunting cackle. "Oh, they'll let me in, because I'm with you. You've gotten your way with everything else. What's stopping you now?"

Micah's lips tightened as his eyes flashed with anger. Finally, he muttered, "Fine. Let's go."

As Micah led the way through security at the Infirmary, Alec filled me in. From what he had heard, the Kala guards assigned to protecting Callie noticed that she was showing signs of an illness shortly after she returned home. Her parents had taken her to numerous doctors, but no one had been able to help her. The guards started to suspect Incantation was behind it a few weeks ago, and started to make arrangements to bring her here with the hope that the Kala might know what to do. So far, everyone was baffled by what they had seen.

The moment I walked into her room, I understood why.

The girl I saw now was nothing but a ghost of my best friend, with ashen skin and sunken in, bloodshot eyes. The prominence of her elbow bones hinted at the thirty pounds she had lost. Despite that, her chapped lips curled into a small smile when she saw me.

"I'm guessing from the expression on your face I look as bad as I feel," she rasped.

I choked out a laugh as I swatted a tear away from my eye. Running my hands through her dry hair, I repeated a phrase she had said to me on more than one occasion. "You could use a few highlights."

Callie started to laugh, but covered her mouth when it resulted in a fit of coughing. When she recovered, her voice was hoarse, forcing her to whisper, "So I guess that bitch did something to me after all."

"Yeah." I glanced up at Alec, who stood across from me, on the other side of Callie's bed. "We're going to find out what she did, and we're going to fix it."

Alec nodded, and lifted an eyebrow as if to say, *'Ready when you are.'*

I took Callie's hand and squeezed it. "We're going to go get this mess figured out. Don't go anywhere until I get back."

Callie settled on a small smile as her response.

Alec and Micah filed out of the room behind me, and we were met by Bruce and Richie in the hallway. I ducked past them without a word, and started for the other side of the Infirmary.

"She's not going to tell us anything," Micah said as he hurried to my side.

"We can find ways to make her."

Micah scoffed. "How do you plan to do that?"

Honestly, I had no idea, but she had messed with my best friend and I was pissed. The swing in my stride portrayed a confidence I lacked internally, but no one would have known that from my poised and determined demeanor. Faking it made me feel better, and like I actually had a plan.

When we reached the first set of guards blocking the entrance to the wing where Lillian was kept, I turned to Micah.

"Get us in."

With a sigh, Micah approached the guards. Their frowns vanished as he explained our situation, and even went so far as to claim that the supervisors were aware of our intentions. They weren't, but I had yet to witness a guard on this island question Micah, and wasn't surprised when they stepped aside.

I heard them radio to the other guards, informing them that we were coming. No one got in our way until we reached the last door to her room. There, a stone-faced supervisor stood with his arms crossed over his chest.

"This area is restricted," he announced.

Micah stepped forward as our spokesman. "Are you aware of the human girl that was brought to the island about an hour ago?"

"Yes, I know, but that doesn't change the fact that no one is to come in contact with this Skotadi." His eyes leveled on Alec, and then me, with visible distaste.

"She's the one who cast the spell on my friend," I objected. "We need to find out what she did!"

Micah turned to look over his shoulder, fixing me with a hard look. Alec's hand came down on my shoulder as if to calm me down.

Fine. They wanted me to play nice? I could play nice.

"Alec?" I whispered. "Can you charm him?"

When he didn't respond, I glanced over my shoulder. His eyes were already leveled on the supervisor. "Just waiting for him to make eye contact."

"I understand you want to help, but you kids are going to

have to—"

Alec suddenly stepped past me, catching the supervisor's gaze as it swept over us. "You're going to let us see Lillian."

The supervisor's eyes glazed over, and I knew Alec had him. He blinked once slowly, shaking his head as if he knew something wasn't right.

"You're going to let us in the room to talk to Lillian," Alec repeated, slower.

Micah's mouth opened, but I shut him up with a sharp shake of my head. The last thing we needed was for this to fail, and Alec to get busted for attempting to charm a supervisor. And that was bound to happen if Micah opened his big mouth.

"Absolutely," the supervisor said. He resembled a well-groomed zombie as he opened the door to let us enter.

I didn't know what I expected to see, but the sight of Lillian pacing a room stripped of everything but a bed on the other side of a glass wall wasn't it. Another door still separated us from her, but that was all. No more guards or supervisors stood in our way.

Alec stayed in the hallway to instruct the supervisor to go for a long walk, and to forget our conversation, before coming up to stand beside me. "How do you want to do this?"

"You and I will go in," I said. "You can charm her if she doesn't talk. And Bruce?" I turned to look for him. "Can you come for protection, since she has a knack for hurting me?"

He nodded once in answer.

I looked to Alec for strength before I swung the door open to face my nemesis for the first time since I had put a bullet in her stomach. Granted, she had deserved it, and I would do it again in a heartbeat. Preferably, I would aim a little higher if given a second chance.

Lillian spun around at the sound of the door opening. I was convinced by now that the frown on her face was a permanent fixture, but when she saw me, her lips curved into a grin that could easily have won an award for 'world's most evil.'

I spoke first in an attempt to gain the upper hand. "Not expecting to see me?"

"I thought maybe it was that guy you're so in love with coming to annoy me again," she retorted. "What's his name?"

I ignored the choking sound coming from Alec beside me and the warmth that rose up my neck at her mention of Nathan coming to see her in here. I had never asked him why he found it necessary to do so, and didn't want my jealous streak to get in the way of what I had come here to do. Yet, somehow Lillian knew exactly how to rattle me.

"This has nothing to do with Nathan," I returned coolly. "This is about the spell you did on my friend."

"Oh . . ." Lillian laughed humorlessly. "The gullible human girl? I assume she has fallen ill?"

My eyes narrowed. "What did you do to her?"

Lillian shrugged lazily, and I knew she wouldn't talk . . . willingly.

My eyes met Alec's. With a nod, he stepped closer to Lillian, forcing her gaze to shift to him. "You're going to answer us," he said. "You're going to tell us exactly what you did to Callie, and how we can fix her."

Lillian glared at him for a few heavy seconds. I turned to

make sure Bruce was near, because I had no idea what Lillian might do. Her eyes didn't appear glazed over, but what did I know? I wasn't the charmer here. Alec was.

"Lillian?" Alec asked cautiously.

Her head tipped back with a sinister laugh. Drawing in a breath, she said, "You actually thought you could charm me? Have you forgotten how powerful an Incantator I am?"

I scoffed. "So powerful you can't even get yourself out of a locked room?"

Lillian's lips pressed together and her eyes hardened on me. "Your friend is going to die, and there isn't anything you can do to stop it. The plan has been set into motion. In time, you will all know the truth, but by then it will be too late."

"Too late for what?" Alec asked.

Her gaze flicked between Alec and me. "For everyone."

* * * * *

Sleep was a lost cause as Lillian's cryptic threat replayed over and over in my head. I stared at the ceiling for hours, considering every possible explanation for Callie's illness and Lillian's hidden agenda—whatever it was—and how the two could be related.

Before I could unravel Lillian's plans, I had to find a way to fix Callie. She was my priority. Around midnight, I gave up on sleep and opened one of the spell books I kept under my bed.

We knew Incantation had caused Callie's condition, so Incantation should undo it—if I could find the correct spell. Multiple pages in the book had already been dog-eared from my never-ending search for a spell to save Alec and me from our evil futures. I skipped over those pages, and focused on spells that healed the body rather than the soul.

Though the search would be an uphill battle, I would fight to the end. I wouldn't give up. Lillian may have been a powerful Incantator, but I was Hecate's daughter. If anyone could undo Lillian's spell, it would be me. Saving Callie fell on my shoulders, and I vowed to not let her down.

After two hours of searching, I found something promising. I checked the list of ingredients, and rummaged through the collection of stones stored under my bed. I had been collecting them for months, since I first started learning about this part of my life, and had acquired quite a variety. Micah, of course, had completed the collection with the bracelet. But this stone—the one I needed now—had been one of my first.

I had learned that it didn't have the healing properties I needed it for. But perhaps Callie could get some benefit from it?

I finally found the dark green malachite stone, and slipped it into my jeans' pocket.

Kim looked up as I opened the door to my room, blinking her eyes rapidly as if trying to wake herself up. Surely, she wasn't reduced to sleeping on the floor in the hallway outside my room? Kala leadership wasn't that heartless, were they?

It wasn't until then that I realized the thought had never occurred to me before. "When do you sleep?" I asked her.

She hesitated as if contemplating whether or not to answer me, then finally said, "During the day when you're on Micah's or Nathan's watch."

Which meant she didn't sleep much now, since Nathan was gone and I currently refused to be around Micah more than absolutely necessary. I nodded, and walked past her without a response because, really, Kim's sleep schedule wasn't important right now. Tomorrow, I would suck it up and let Micah hover over me so that Kim could have a break. For now, I had somewhere to go. I knew Kim would follow, and that was okay. I had nothing to hide.

The Infirmary was quiet at this time of night. There were fewer guards to contend with, and I navigated the halls without resistance. The young Kala that stood outside Callie's room nodded when he saw me, and I realized that I recognized him. Though I had only seen him briefly a few months ago, I remembered him. Jake something? He was one of the Kala who had been sent back to Boone to protect Callie.

"I have something that might help her," I said to him in explanation for my sudden late night visit.

"Go ahead," he said. "I'm not going to stop you."

"Thanks." I smiled as he opened the door to let me inside.

The room was dark, aside from a faint glow coming from the bathroom light. It was enough to illuminate Callie's sleeping form under the sheets . . . and someone else sprawled out beside her on the tiny bed. I walked half way across the room before I realized who it was.

Alec, his face peaceful in sleep, lay curled up on his side with Callie snuggled in his arms. My heart clenched at the sight of their conjoined hands on top of the rumpled sheet.

Careful not to disturb them, I slipped the small stone under

Callie's pillow and recited the words I had memorized. With one last look at the two of them, I crept out of the room, my heart fuller than it had been in a long time.

Chapter 13

{Nathan}

The first fireball made its appearance as the last Skotadi fell.

Lighting up the sky as it soared over our heads like a falling asteroid, the car-sized ball of fire was the first sign of the demigods' arrival, and that the son of Hephaestus—Derona—was one of them. As it crashed into the building behind us, triggering an immediate inferno, we ran.

Golf ball-sized chunks of brick and burning splinters of wood rained down on us, but didn't slow our retreat. If anything, my feet pounded the blacktop harder and faster at knowing that whoever had produced that fireball was coming up fast behind us—along with another demigod of equal strength in whatever skill he specialized in. I didn't plan on waiting around to find out who it was.

The five of us dodged the steady string of fire that rained down on the village as we ran. Our goal was the field that lay beyond the village, and ultimately the forest beyond that. I only slowed when the realization that the school—along with the surviving villagers—would, if they weren't already, be caught in the blaze. My feet inevitably kept moving because I knew there was nothing I could do to help them now.

We rounded the corner of one of the last buildings not already engulfed, and the tree line came into view. Two hundred yards away. Across an open field.

The shadows of several members of our team were visible just inside the line of trees. I wasn't sure what they were waiting for. It wasn't like they could provide cover for us as we sprinted across the open. Not against Derona.

We came to the edge of the village, and slowed only long enough to slide beneath the wooden fence that separated the village from the wheat fields. Fortunately, harvesting season was near, and the wheat was high.

High enough to somewhat conceal us as we ran like hell for the cover of the trees.

A flaming tractor crashed into the field fifty yards to our left, causing the guy beside me to spit out a string of French words. The sudden brightness forced me to lift the night vision goggles off my head before it blinded me.

"Split up!" Jared called.

Though I hated to split up, Jared had a good point. We could never fight back against the demigods—one hundred of us no better than the five of us. At least by splitting up, we would be less visible and harder to track through the field. If we were lucky, we would all reach the trees without being burnt alive.

But then, the tree line didn't exactly provide instantaneous protection either. By the time I reached it, the other Kala were long gone, and the first twenty yards of the forest was already burning.

And now I was alone.

The deafening sound of crashing trees and rapidly spreading flames drowned out any footsteps I might have otherwise heard. In my periphery, I saw a shadow, accented against the glowing orange backdrop, running parallel to me, but couldn't make out who it was. He wasn't stopping to look for the others, and neither was I.

Several moments of steady running put the blaze safely behind me, but I still didn't slow. Not yet. Not with Hades' demigods involved, and no way to know for sure if they were still in pursuit. Without the light from the fire, and with the moon blocked by the heavy tree canopy, the woods were dark. My goggles were long lost, and more than once, I got tripped up by fallen tree limbs or dips in the uneven ground.

The worst was the full-sized toppled over tree in my path that I didn't see until I slammed into it. My legs collided with the thick trunk at full speed, but my arms thrown out in front of me kept me from somersaulting over it. Forced to a stop for the first time since I started running, I allowed myself a glance over my shoulder.

The village fire was nothing but a distant glow. A path had been seared several hundred yards into the forest, but had fizzled out far behind me. The question was whether or not Derona had turned back, or was still following us—only now without lighting everything he came in contact with on fire.

My guess was on the latter.

I wasn't about to turn back and risk stumbling upon the demigods, but I had no idea where to find the rest of the team either. The last I had heard, the plan was to meet at the tree line, and that plan had been shot to hell with the appearance of the first fireball.

"Shit!" I slapped a hand down on the hard bark of the tree. *Now what?*

"Nathan?"

I took a step back from the fallen tree, wishing more than ever that I hadn't dropped my goggles so that I could see the source of the voice that had called my name. It was low to the ground, and I thought I recognized it.

"Kira?"

"Down here."

I turned in the direction of her voice. "Keep talking."

"I tripped on something . . ." I vaulted over the fallen tree, following the sound of her voice. "Twisted my ankle. I think it's broken."

My foot connected with something soft. I dropped to a knee, and Kira's soot covered face materialized out of the shadows in front of me. "Can you stand?" I asked her.

"I can try . . ."

I hooked my hands under her arms and helped her up. I kept my hands near and ready as she tested her ankle. She wobbled, and I shot them out to catch her before she fell.

Kira walking out of here on her own accord wasn't going to happen.

"Alright. Come on . . ." I slid one arm around her waist to

steady her as she draped an arm across my shoulders. We weren't going to make much progress, and there was a good chance that we would be overcome by the demigods if they were still following, but I couldn't leave Kira behind.

I wouldn't leave anyone behind.

"Do you know where everyone else is?" I asked her as we started moving.

"The French leader said he saw a clearing on a map on the other side of the forest," she explained. "They thought it might be about four miles. The plan was to meet there and regroup."

Four miles on the other side of the forest? For the nature-gifted Kala, finding it would be easy, and the others would tag along. Problem was, I hadn't seen the map, and didn't know which direction we needed to go to reach the clearing.

"Which way were they going?" I asked, hoping she had an idea. I could work with an idea.

"I heard . . . east. I think."

At least we were already heading east. That was promising.

We trudged along slowly, hampered by Kira's injury. From her reliance on me as a crutch, and her occasional cries of agony when she put too much weight on her ankle, I didn't doubt her claim that it was broken. Over an hour passed with me supporting the bulk of her weight. My arm was tingling by the time I saw the first signs of a sunrise on the horizon.

"Need a break?" I suggested.

Kira breathed a heavy sigh of relief. "Yes."

I eased her down onto the trunk of a fallen tree. The break wasn't so much of a break as it was an opportunity for me to search for signs of the rest of our team. Now that I had some light to assist me, I wanted to make sure we were moving in the right direction.

I saw no visible tracks from where I stood. I called to Kira, told her that I would be back in a few minutes, and expanded my search area. I moved farther east, and found my first footprint a few hundred yards from where I had left Kira. Twenty feet from that one, I found approximately a dozen more, all moving in the same direction. The tracks were a few hours old, but from the drag marks I saw, I suspected injuries had slowed the group's progress. Perhaps enough that Kira and I could catch up to them.

I hurried back to get Kira before we lost any more time. Through the gaps in the trees, I saw her sitting exactly where I had left her. As I closed the distance, I quickly realized something was wrong.

She stood, leaning heavily to the side of her good ankle, with her hand stretched out to something I couldn't see. I picked up the pace, putting a few more trees behind me, and saw what she saw. Only I saw it for what it really was.

"Kira, no!"

Her eyes shifted to mine, and I saw the glimmer of unshed tears in them. "It's my mother," she whispered. "Isn't she beautiful?"

Not from my angle. What Kira thought was her mother was something far more ominous. A nekro—a dark spirit of the underworld—and there was only one way that it could have been here.

The demigod of the dead, Hades' very own son, was near.

"It's not your mother, Kira." I took her outstretched hand and placed it around my neck. Ducking my head to avoid eye contact with the walking corpse, I quickly steered Kira around it.

The nekros created illusions to deceive their victims. That meant Kira truly believed she was leaving behind her dead mother, and fought me the first several steps. Until a second nekro appeared in front of us. And another. Each as ghastly as the first.

"Nathan? What's going on?"

I had never experienced a nekro in the real world, until now. They were rare because they could only be called up by Nakurlas, the demigod of death, and he stuck predominately to the confines of the underworld. I flashed back to my development years, and what I had learned about them.

"They're nekros," I answered, and Kira sucked in a sharp breath. "Don't look at them." Making eye contact gave them the opportunity to create an illusion of a lost loved one that was difficult to resist.

"He's near then . . ."

"Yeah. We have to move fast."

I had to give Kira some credit. She pushed hard and fast despite her broken ankle. But then having the demigod of death and his minions breathing down our necks was pretty good motivation.

For nearly an hour, we dodged the spirits of the dead that wandered the forest. They were sporadic, at least, and didn't slow our progress much. From the ease with which we evaded them, I suspected that Nakurlas was far behind us, didn't know our exact location, and was fishing. By ignoring the nekros, we were able to avoid detection.

An hour after we dodged the last nekro, I saw a splash of color through a break in the trees. A few more yards, and I saw movement.

Our team—or what remained of it—had reached the clearing, and were stopped. Half a dozen injured lay on the ground while the rest of the team administered aid with the help of the two rescued demigods.

Jared glanced up as Kira and I emerged from the trees. His sprint to close the distance between us was the second fastest I had ever seen him move. I greeted him with a grin before he wrapped both arms around me in a tight hug, far from the usual one-armed, tough guy back slaps I was used to. He squeezed tight once before grabbing Kira's shirt and pulling her into the hug with us.

"Oh, thank the gods you two made it," he murmured.

I eyed the remaining Kala in the clearing over Jared's shoulder. "How many did we lose?"

He released us and dropped his head. "Fourteen."

"How many from our base?" Kira asked.

"Counting the two of you now, there are seven of us left," Jared answered, then turned to Kira. "Go on over and get fixed up. We're going to have to move soon."

As Kira limped away, Jared said to me, "Permna is using her prophecy powers to watch the demigods' actions. They've returned to the village for now, but they will be coming after us with another Skotadi army. We have to keep moving. We won't be safe until we get to Mount Olympus."

"How are we going to get there?"

His answer was exactly what I suspected. "We're going to have to walk."

*   *   *   *   *

A two-hour train ride plus a two-hour bus ride equaled a hell of a long walk back to Mount Olympus. Fortunately, hybrids were blessed with extraordinary powers of healing, and the injured were at full health by the second day. Another day and a half of fast-paced hiking put us within sight of the mountain.

We were again greeted by Artemis at the base of Mytika's Summit. This time, she led the entire team inside the *Hall of the Gods*, along with Isatan and Permna. Isatan led us to a quiet corner in the garden near the waterfall to wait while he went with Artemis to find his father.

"How badly do you want to jump into that pool right now?" Jared asked as he walked up beside me.

"I'm surprised they haven't forced us into it." Sewer-stained combat clothes plus four days of hiking in eighty degree temperatures had left the entire team smelling . . . exactly as bad as it sounded.

Jared mulled silently a moment, then asked, "What do you think is going to happen now?"

I shook my head because that wasn't something I wanted to think about yet. The good news was that the gods had their two loyal demigods back. Together, they could strike back against the wayward demigods before their plan to achieve immortality was seen through. I hoped Kris could avoid involvement in it, but I wasn't optimistic. Not if she would grow to be as powerful as they expected.

I also had a bad feeling that this mission wasn't over yet . . . that the *real* mission was only getting started.

I glanced over my shoulder at the enormous golden door behind us, impatient for someone to come out and tell us something . . . *anything*. I didn't see either of the demigods, or Zeus, or anyone who had the answers I wanted. But someone else stood there.

A goddess, though I didn't know her name. She wasn't any of the twelve Olympians, and wasn't one who had passed on a specialty to the Kala. I had never seen her before, though she stared at me like she knew me. She pushed away from the wall, and walked toward me. As she approached, I realized her eyes weren't necessarily on me, but something on me.

Her hand reached out to grab the stone hanging from my neck. "This is the work of Hecate."

"Her daughter, actually," I returned.

"Yes." She smiled as she examined the stone. "I see it worked."

Puzzled, I looked down. The quarter-sized stone had a small chip taken out of it. I took the stone from her to look closer, and I realized what had caused it. The Skotadi's knife that had been intended for my heart. I knew it had pierced my vest . . .

I hadn't been stabbed because the blade had hit the stone.

I swallowed the lump in my throat, and managed a weak

smile. *Good job, Kris . . .*

"I'm Circe," the goddess said. "I'm glad to finally see the excellent work of my sister."

I dove into my memory banks, grasping for what knowledge I had of Circe. She was a lesser known goddess of magic, I knew that, second to Hecate, who was far superior in her abilities. She was supposedly Hecate's daughter, which made her . . .

I looked up to take in the goddess who was Kris's sister, but words were lost to me.

"You know my sister well?" Though it was a question, she spoke with such conviction, I suspected Circe already knew the answer.

"Yes."

She smiled again, and lifted her hand. It had been empty a moment ago, but now she held a small vial of fluid out to me. "I believe you may have some use for this potion."

I took it from her hesitantly. "What is it?" I asked.

"I made it myself using a potential spell," she answered proudly. "The soul of whoever drinks it will find their true potential, and will find security and protection from evil influence, after a three-day deep sleep."

I studied the fluid in my hands. "I don't know what that means."

Circe glanced around as if searching for eavesdropping ears. Jared stood the closest to us, but he had discreetly wandered away when she approached me. She stepped closer, and dropped her voice. "Theoretically, a soul darkened by evil, with the potential for good, may find its way to the light."

"Okay . . ." A few uses for something like this came to mind, and I wondered how exactly she intended for me to use it.

"One drop of this fluid will create another full vial," she said. "I suspect you will find your uses for it."

So I could use it on more than one . . .

My head snapped up with a question, but she was gone. As I spun around to look for her, Jared caught my eye, and he walked over.

"What was that all about?" he asked.

"Not exactly sure," I murmured. She hadn't stuck around long enough for me to ask my final, and most important, question.

Was this potion intended to sever Kris's connection to evil? Did Circe intend for it to bring out Kris's true potential—of goodness?

I thought, yes. That was her intent. She knew I could get the potion to Kris, so she had given it to me. As I wrapped my head around what had happened, and the possibilities of what the potion in my possession could do, the golden door swung open and Isatan approached us.

He nodded to Jared and me. "My father wishes to speak with you now."

I felt the eyes of the other Kala on us as we walked away with Isatan. He led us to a room—not the same one as before, with the twelve seats chiseled out of the stone, but another cold stone-walled room. Zeus, Hera, and Poseidon stood in the center, waiting for us.

Hera greeted us with a smile. "Thank you for rescuing

Permna and Isatan."

I stuffed my hands in my pockets with a nod as Jared said, "It was our honor. We lost many men, but I understand the cause will be worth their sacrifice."

"We will see to that," Zeus vowed. "The corrupted demigods will be tracked down and destroyed. The sacrifice of your men, and the loss of the innocent villagers of Ichalia, will not be in vain."

I assumed Isatan had filled them in on the villagers. I wondered what they knew of the situation. Was it a curse? Who had been behind it? And how was it related to the corrupted demigods' plans to achieve immortality?

"What has been determined of the villagers' situation?" I asked, fishing for information.

"Not much," Hera answered with a small smile.

Zeus shot her a scalding look, and I had a feeling he didn't like looking incompetent in front of measly hybrids. "We now know that a small group of Skotadi are working with the devious demigods, and they are using humans in their quest for immortality with the aid of a powerful Incantator."

"And Hades' demigods?" Jared probed.

Zeus and Poseidon shared a look, and Poseidon answered, "I always suspected they were involved."

I thought it was obvious—they were. Otherwise, why had they been summoned to the village by a group of Skotadi that was in cahoots with a group of demigods that was rising against the gods? I agreed with Poseidon—they were in on it too. Which meant there were now ten corrupted demigods to deal with . . .

against two.

"This curse," Hera said softly, "is more than just a curse. They seem to be draining the life forces of a large number of humans. If enough human life is sacrificed at once, and the correct magic is used to capture the essence of their souls, the demigods can use that power to gain their immortality."

Zeus murmured something to Hera that I couldn't hear, and she shook her head in return. It resembled something of a marital dispute, which was an odd sight to witness between two gods.

Finally, Hera turned to Jared and me with a tight smile, but she still spoke to Zeus. "Nothing will be hurt by them knowing the truth. Besides, they are friends of Hecate's daughter, and she will be our ally."

Poseidon made a noise that sounded suspiciously like a snort, and I decided that, when it came to Kris's safety, he couldn't be trusted. Hera was definitely on Kris's side, and Zeus seemed on the fence. I hoped that, when the time came, Hera would have the influence over Zeus she seemed to have today.

Zeus grumbled, then spoke to us. "We will be needing the girl's assistance as soon as she is able. With the level of Incantation being used in this curse, she may be the only demigod we have capable of stopping it. Hecate would be ideal, of course, but she cannot help as long as she is imprisoned by Hades, and Circe doesn't have the strength to do it."

Jared glanced at me before responding. "We will inform you upon her reaching maturity."

Zeus nodded. "Until then, I ask for your assistance in the pursuit of the corrupted demigods. I know your men are tired and injured, but if you could spare an army to assist our demigods, we would be grateful."

And that was the ball I had been waiting for to drop. Just as I had suspected . . . the mission had only begun.

Chapter 14

{Kris}

"What about this one?"

I flipped the massive book around and pointed to the spell half way down the page. *'Repairing a damaged vessel.'* It had taken me some time to get used to the language used in these ancient spell books, but I now knew that *'vessel'* meant body.

And Callie's body was definitely damaged. If only we knew exactly what Lillian had done to cause the damage, we could find a more specific spell. Right now, generic spells like this one were all we had to work with.

Micah read the specifics, like what materials were needed and how the spell was performed, and nodded his head. "Tag it. We can try it."

By *'we'*, he meant me. I would be the one to try it since I was the practicing Incantator of the group. Micah and Alec were there to help me find the right spell, and for moral support. Because I really needed it. Because I wasn't very good at this whole Incantation thing. Which really sucked, because now was when I needed to be good. I needed to be able to do what I was supposed to be able to do now more than ever.

Because I would never forgive myself if Callie died.

"That makes three," Alec announced.

I had learned the hard way that I couldn't attempt more than three complicated spells at a time, and even that was taxing. The first time I tried to do a bunch, I thought I was going to die. I ended up sleeping the rest of the day, and then needed a four-course meal when I woke up. Apparently, casting spells expended a lot of energy. The more involved the spell, the more it took out of me.

"I can swing by the lab to pick up the materials and meet you there," Micah volunteered.

"Yeah, okay." I looked at Alec. "You coming with me?"

"You bet." Alec gathered up the two spell books, and stood.

"I guess that means I'm going too," Kim said, her tone brusque and business-like as usual. She had hovered in the background the past few days while we searched for a way to help Callie, and though she hadn't said or offered much, I suspected that Kim had come to care about what happened to Callie. That was one thing about Kim I had been able to determine with confidence. She took her role as a Kala seriously—especially their credo to protect humans from the forces of evil.

"Let's go. That girl isn't going to get better with us hanging around here." Bruce opened the door and ushered us out ahead of him.

Once we reached the village center, Micah and Richie split

from the rest of us with a promise to meet up in the Infirmary in a few minutes. As I watched them walk away, I realized that even Richie had become a source of support. The extra spring to his step, and eagerness that I rarely saw from him, came purely out of concern for Callie. The guy might not like me because of who—and what—I was, but after all the time he had unwillingly spent around me, there seemed to have been a truce developed between us somewhere along the way. He still watched me cautiously around Micah, but I had also seen him let his guard down a few times. He never would have done that three months ago.

The rest of the island . . . well, they still treaded carefully around me.

Except for the moron who came out of nowhere, bumped into me, then spun around and slammed into Alec.

"Hey! What the hell is your problem?" Alec shoved the kid so hard his feet lifted off the ground, and I was convinced that the only reason he didn't land on his ass was because he was graced with the superhuman balance of a hybrid.

Bruce jumped to attention, though I wondered if he intended to protect the Kala, or defend Alec and me. But then, the kid didn't really stick around for the ass-kicking Alec appeared ready to dish out.

I doubted he realized who exactly he had plowed into. "Sorry," he muttered as he scampered off. Almost as if it were an afterthought, he glanced back to offer an explanation. "They're back."

My feet froze as I watched the boy dash away—in the

direction of the beach. *They're back.*

They? As in . . .

My feet started moving toward the beach. To the docks, along with what appeared to be the rest of the island, all of whom must have just gotten the same memo.

They were back.

Pushing through the horde that had assembled on the narrow trail leading to the dock, I spotted the boat. I caught glimpses of a few unfamiliar faces still on it, and spotted a few that had already disembarked, but I didn't see the face I longed to see.

"Excuse me," I said, pushing past two Kala who were talking and laughing like this was any other day. Obviously they weren't eagerly awaiting someone's return. Not like I was.

The crowd thinned once I reached the beach. Like the day the team left, clusters of Kala scattered all over, waiting for their loved ones. A few lucky ones were already entangled in an embrace. A few others hung their heads in tears. Most, like me, looked toward the boat with a hopeful expression.

I finally got a good look at the few who remained on the boat, and my stomach dropped.

Where is he?

I turned in a slow circle, taking in the scene around me. Only then did I realize that most of the waiting Kala were crying, or close to it, and only a small handful were rejoicing. From what I saw, I determined that only half of the team had returned. I scanned the horizon through blurry eyes, looking for a second boat.

There had to be a second boat because the alternative wasn't acceptable. Each second that ticked by made it more real. More painful.

Seeing no sign of another boat, I spun around to search the beach again.

Alec stood in front of me. "Kris . . ." His expression was grim, his voice soothing. He held a hand out to me, but I didn't take it. I wouldn't take it, because it was a gesture of pity, and if I took it then I would be admitting what I was too afraid to admit.

That Nathan wasn't on the beach. He wasn't on the island.

He hadn't come back.

"No." I shook my head and ran past Alec. The crowd on the trail had doubled from moments ago as more Kala hurried to the dock. I pushed against them, needing to get as far away from there as I could.

"Kris!"

I tuned Alec out, and kept pushing through the thick crowd. He called my name again, but I didn't stop, didn't turn. I hit a wall of Kala blocking my escape. Choking back the sob rising in my throat, I tried to go around them.

I couldn't cry yet. Because once I started, I wouldn't stop.

"Kris!" Fingers grazed my hand, and I snatched my arm back as if I had been jolted with electricity.

I didn't want to be touched. I didn't want sympathy. If Alec thought I needed a friend right now, he was wrong. I needed to put distance between me and that damn beach.

I started to elbow my way between two Kala girls, cutting off their excited chatter, when the hand found mine again. This time, it grabbed me firmly and pulled, spinning me around in the process. I had a few choice words ready for Alec, but they were forgotten the moment I saw blue.

The sob I had been holding back finally escaped as I threw myself into Nathan's arms. His strength enveloped me, and my feet lifted off the ground as he pulled me close. My face nuzzled the side of his neck—his rough and stubbly and perfect neck—as relief washed over me.

"I didn't see you," I mumbled. "I didn't. . .and I thought. . ."

Nathan's arm tightened around my waist. "It's alright," he crooned. His fingers combed through my hair in a soothing gesture. "I'm here. It's alright."

Nathan swayed slightly when a Kala bumped into us, reminding me that we weren't alone. My ears picked up a few hushed whispers, and I realized we were causing quite the scandalous scene. We were surrounded by an island of Kala who weren't supposed to know about us, but I didn't care. I had Nathan back, and I wasn't ready to let go of him yet.

"Kris?" Nathan leaned away, and I reluctantly vacated the sweet spot under his chin. But then I got to see his face, and that was pretty great, too. His lips were parted like he wanted to say something, but whatever thought he had drifted away the moment our eyes met.

His gaze dropped to my mouth, and his lips quickly followed. Right there, in the middle of the trail, surrounded by a crowd of stunned Kala, Nathan kissed me. An insanely soft and slow *I missed you so much and I want to remember what your lips feel like* kind of kiss—the kind of kiss so intimate that anyone watching had to look away to give it the privacy it deserved.

Though it would have been nice to imagine that Nathan and I were in our own little world with each other, I felt the penetrating stares of many Kala on the back of my head. That, and that alone, was probably the only reason Nathan cut the kiss short. He peeled away slowly, and I felt his sigh of agony against my lips just before he set my feet on the ground.

One arm remained firmly around me as his eyes scanned the crowd over my head. "Looks like the cat is out of the bag," he mumbled.

I met the curious eyes of a passing Kala girl with a challenging glare. "I don't care. I'll take whatever they dish out if it means you'll kiss me like that more often."

Nathan chuckled as his grip on me lessened. But only so he could slip his fingers between mine. His head tipped down so that we were nearly eye to eye. "Are you okay now?"

He was alive, so yeah. I nodded. "Where were you?"

His lips curled into a lopsided smile. "I was the first one off the boat. We must have passed each other in the crowd. I spotted you when you started running off."

I guessed that had been him calling my name then, not Alec. Speaking of . . .

I looked around, but only saw a bunch of Kala I didn't know casting me uneasy glances. "Did you see Alec? He was here a minute ago."

Nathan's chin jutted forward. "Yeah. They're back there, waiting at the top of the trail."

They? That likely included Micah. Ugh . . . wait . . .

Callie!

I gasped when I remembered where I had been going before hearing the team was back. "I have to go," I told Nathan.

"Oh. Okay." His brow furrowed. "What's going on?"

"They brought Callie to the island," I explained quickly. "She's sick. Really sick. They think Lillian put some spell on her, and . . . no one knows what's wrong or what to do, so we're trying a bunch of different spells to break the one Lillian did. We were on our way to the Infirmary when . . ." I gestured to Nathan. His return had temporarily put everything on hold. But now I had to get back to my best friend.

His grip on my hand tightened, and then he started moving, pushing his way through the crowd and pulling me after him. With him leading the way, Kala who would have otherwise laughed in my face moved to the side. A few raised their eyebrows at our conjoined hands, but no one spoke up.

We reached the others quickly, which wasn't surprising. Nathan cared a lot about Callie, and like the rest of us, I knew he would stop at nothing to help her.

"Welcome back," Alec greeted Nathan with a grin. Surprisingly, he looked and sounded genuine.

Micah, on the other hand, looked like he had swallowed a bug. He said nothing as we made our way through the village center to the Infirmary.

The guard opened the door ahead of our entrance, and nodded at Nathan as we passed. He was either greeted by name or acknowledged with a respectful head nod by every guard we encountered as we worked our way through the building.

"Does everyone on this island know you?" I whispered to him.

"Pretty much." Nathan pushed through a set of swinging doors and stopped. "Which way?"

"Down here." I led the way now, with Nathan's hand still entwined with mine and I had no intention of dropping it.

Jake stood outside Callie's door, and smiled as we approached. "Here to do a few more spells?"

"I'm going to try," I muttered as I passed by him.

I entered the room first, and was the first one to see the difference another day had made. I hadn't thought it possible for her to get worse, but she had. Her skin was even more pale, her eyes more bloodshot. Her breaths now came in shallow, rapid wheezes.

I immediately went to her side and smoothed a few stray hairs out of her face. Her thin lips curved and her eyes drifted over my shoulder. Only then did I realize that my hand was free, and Nathan wasn't beside me anymore.

"Well, look who finally showed up," Callie said, her voice barely a whisper.

I looked over my shoulder in time to catch the anguish etched on Nathan's face before he covered it with a smile. A fake smile, but a smile for Callie.

"Like I could stay away." He stepped forward, coming up beside me to take one of Callie's hands in his.

If it were possible, I fell even more in love with him.

"How did this start, Callie?" he asked gently.

She tried to laugh, but ended up coughing. By the time she

caught her breath, her voice was hoarse. "Everyone thought it was mono."

"You don't remember any more about what Lillian did, or what she said?"

She shook her head instead of speaking.

"We've tried a few spells already," I offered. "Nothing has worked yet."

"We have three more to do now," Micah spoke from the doorway, reminding me, as if I had forgotten.

I hadn't, of course. But I also wasn't all that optimistic that any of them would work. Maybe if the right spell were done by a capable Incantator. We were fishing in the dark, and I didn't know if I had the skill to pull something like this off.

Nathan shifted to look at me. I saw an unreadable emotion in his eyes, but one thing I knew for sure—he was thinking. The wheels were turning in his head, and I really hoped he came up with a good idea, better than what we had tried so far.

"Do what you came here to do," he told me. "I've got to go find Jared."

"Now? You can't stay while . . ." *While I try some spells that probably won't work anyway?*

"We learned something in Greece," he said quickly. "I can't be sure, but . . ." He looked down at Callie, who had decided that keeping her eyes open took too much effort.

He had been in Greece? While I was surprised to hear how far they had traveled for the mission, I wondered what he had learned there that caused him to look at Callie with that worrisome look in his eyes.

"You think it has something to do with what's happened to her?"

Nathan nodded wordlessly, his eyes never leaving Callie. "Maybe."

Chapter 15

{Nathan}

I took a chance and headed for Jared's office, assuming he had made it off the beach by now. Before we left Greece, he had promised to send the gods another team of fresh soldiers to assist in tracking down the demigods. He had a busy few days ahead of him, and I assumed he would get started with the planning right away. Besides, his office was close, just on the other side of the building from the Infirmary, so I wouldn't waste much time if he wasn't there.

No one was stationed outside his door, but it was unlocked, and I waltzed right in.

He glanced up with a wry smile on his face. "Miss me already?"

"They brought Callie in while we were gone."

Jared straightened. "Is it as bad as we were told?"

"It's bad." I paused to let that sink in. Jared, like all Kala, didn't like to see any human suffer at the hands of the Skotadi. "Jared, she looks like those villagers. Same pale skin, rapid

197

breathing, and imminent death. It's identical."

"I thought you said Lillian did something to Callie."

I nodded as I gathered my thoughts. This was the hard part for me to understand, let alone explain. "The gods said an Incantator was working with the demigods, and was the one behind the curse, and that a small group of Skotadi were helping them, right?" I paused, and waited for Jared to nod so that I knew he was following me.

"Yeah," Jared muttered. "That didn't make any sense to me. What would the Skotadi get out of helping them?"

"Nothing makes sense anymore!" I threw my hands up. "Why do we have Kala on the island working as spies for the Skotadi? Who's to say there isn't a small group of Kala out there working for them, too?"

"Okay . . . okay. Calm down."

I took a deep breath. "The point is, Jared," I said slowly. "Lillian was the one who did this to Callie. I think Lillian is the Incantator who has been working with the demigods on this immortality thing. There were others, I'm sure of now, back in West Virginia. The Skotadi there were kidnapping humans. We didn't know why at the time, but I would bet the same curse was placed on all of them too. Lillian was behind it. I know it."

"Even if you're right, we're not going to get anything out of her. Not with the way she is now."

I smiled and dug the vial I had been holding on to since we left Greece out of my pants' pocket. "And that's why we're going to give her this."

Jared frowned. "What is that?"

"Circe gave it to me. She said this . . ." I held the vial up between my thumb and index finger so that the light hit it. "This could bring Lillian back."

*   *   *   *   *

Our first stop was to the lab, where we grabbed two more small vials. Jared looked at me like I was crazy while I poured a small amount of the fluid into one of the empty containers. We glanced at each other, then bent down to watch magic in action.

And nothing happened.

I stood up straight. "I don't understand. She said just a drop of the stuff would make another vial."

I needed two more vials . . . for Kris and Alec. No way would I give it all to Lillian, and leave them with nothing.

"I told you that didn't make any sense." Jared picked up the near empty vial and tipped it so that the small amount of fluid slid from one side to the other. He tipped it back again, then swirled it around—not that there was much fluid to be swirled. He set it on the table and shot me a look that said, *now what?*

I replayed the conversation with Circe in my head. She hadn't said much, but she had said a drop would make more. So why hadn't it?

Maybe if I added another drop? Maybe it needed a little bit more.

"Ah, would you look at that?" Jared proclaimed. "It is working!"

I bent down to watch as the drop of fluid expanded until the bottom of the vial was covered. Then it moved up, slowly—so slowly it was impossible to visually see it rising. But over time, over the course of a few minutes, the single drop of fluid had multiplied until the container was full.

Just like Circe had said it would. I looked at Jared with a smug grin, and he gave a lazy shrug.

"Okay," he said, drawing the word out. "I'm impressed."

"And?"

"And?" He paused, and a slow reluctant smile tipped the corners of his mouth. "And . . . you were right. I was wrong. It doesn't happen often, so I'll let you bask in the glory . . . for now."

I looked away from him with a shake of my head, and placed a drop in the second empty vial. This time, Jared and I patiently waited as the process repeated. When it was over, we had three full vials of the magical fluid—potion?—or whatever it was. One each for Kris, Alec, and Lillian.

I decided that Lillian should be first to take it, for two reasons. One, I was convinced that we would need Lillian's help if Callie was to have any chance at recovery. And from the looks of Callie, we didn't have any time to waste. Two, I wasn't about to give Kris some mystery magical water until I knew it wouldn't cause anything bad to happen to her. I supposed the same went for Alec. Though my reasoning made me feel like an asshole, Lillian was the chosen guinea pig.

"If this actually works . . ." Jared led the way from the lab to the wing in the Infirmary where Lillian was kept. I could tell from how fast he was moving just how excited he was about the possibility.

"This could change everything," I finished for him.

We reached the heavily guarded area that had been sealed off from non-important Kala. Since I had been permitted through to check on Lillian's progress a few times, the guards were used to seeing me. Having Jared with me only sped the process up, and we were ushered through without a problem.

Getting Lillian to actually drink the stuff in the vial would be our biggest hurdle.

Jared left to find the island's doctor, leaving me alone in the small observatory room adjacent to Lillian's exam room. The wall separating the two rooms was made up of a large one-way mirror. Though she couldn't see or hear me, I could see and hear her clearly.

That was how it had been since the day we arrived on the island, aside from the few times I had attempted to talk to her. She didn't know how many times I had come to check on the progress the doctors were making. She wouldn't have cared anyway. Not in the state she was in now.

Those first few days, she had spent every minute trying to find a way out of that room. Free objects had to be removed to prevent her from hurting herself, or the medical staff when they entered to care for her. Aside from the bed, which had been bolted to the floor, she had nothing in the room with her.

She had long given up trying to escape. Now she spent her days pacing the room. Meals were delivered by guards, and I had heard that she had given up attacking them when they entered. The fire in her eyes had dimmed, but the evil residing underneath was still very visible.

To others it appeared that she had given up, but I suspected that she was merely biding her time. She was still very dangerous. Though hopefully not for much longer.

Jared returned with Dr. Ribbons, a tall and lanky weasel of a man. I wasn't sure why he had been appointed as the Kala's island doctor. I had always thought that doctors were supposed to have compassion and actually care about the people they were helping. From the few interactions I had with him, I determined that he didn't seem to care about anyone but himself. I didn't doubt that his eagerness to 'cure' Lillian was more about getting her out of his hair than helping her.

"You're sure that this is safe?" he asked Jared. "I don't want to get into any kind of trouble if anything happens to her."

Jared glanced at me, and I shrugged.

"This is coming from the gods," Jared answered. "It's safe, but if anything happens, I will take the fall for it. Not you."

"The problem will be giving it to her," I said. "If she knows what it is, she'll dump it."

Explaining to Lillian that we were trying to help her wouldn't do us any good. She didn't want help; evil Lillian wanted to be evil.

Dr. Ribbons glanced at his watch. "Dinner will be served in twenty minutes. We could slip it into her beverage."

My eyes met Jared's from across the room, and he nodded.

We stuck around long enough to make sure Lillian drank the potion. As I discussed the specifics with Dr. Ribbons—like the fact that Lillian would likely sleep for three days—one of the guards let out a shout of alarm.

Through the glass, I saw Lillian crumbled on the floor as two guards rushed into the room. Dr. Ribbons quickly followed.

Jared and I watched through the mirror as the doctor rolled Lillian over onto her back. He pulled a stethoscope from the pocket of his lab coat and placed it on Lillian's chest.

My heart sunk as Jared muttered, "Shit."

This can't be happening.

The thought crossed my mind that Circe deceived us—deceived me. I had no idea why she would do that. It didn't make sense. I was sure she had meant for me to give the potion to Kris. But it was my understanding that they wanted Kris—they *needed* Kris—to help them get rid of the corrupt demigods. It didn't make sense.

Thoughts of a conspiracy came to sudden halt when the doctor looked up, his eyes settling close to where Jared and I stood on the other side of the mirror, and shook his head. "She's just passed out."

"Damn," Jared chuckled. "That shit works fast."

"No kidding." She had literally just finished her meal, and drink, before standing up to return the tray to the shelf by the door. It had knocked her out in, maybe, two minutes. The guards lifted Lillian off the floor and put her in the bed, where she would stay for the next three days.

In three days, everything might change. I couldn't wait to tell Kris the great news. After making sure the doctor didn't need any more assistance, I left to go find her. Jared insisted on coming with me, to check on Callie. As we approached the room, I tried to prepare him for what he would see.

Much like mine had done earlier, his feet froze under him inside the door, and he stood gaping at the once very pretty girl withering away in her bed.

Callie looked the same. Her condition had not worsened in the last hour, but it hadn't improved either, which meant that the spells were not working despite Kris's best efforts.

Kris stood at the foot of the bed, and looked up as I approached. Her eyes were bloodshot and heavy, and she swayed unsteadily as she fought to keep them open.

"What the hell?" I barked, glancing over my shoulder to glare at the others in the room. "Is this what happens when she does spells?"

I steadied Kris with my arms, and bit back a grimace as Micah's voice floated toward me.

"Only the elaborate, difficult ones," he answered.

"And you guys just stand back and let this happen?" I shot back, beaming Alec with a hard glare.

I had asked him to look out for her while I was gone. And this? This was not what I would consider looking out for her best interest.

Alec's eyes lowered to the floor before he answered. "It's Callie. She wouldn't let us stop her because it's *Callie*."

"I can't help her," Kris murmured softly. She swayed, and likely would have crumbled to the floor if my arms hadn't tightened around her when they had.

"Not like this you can't." In one swift motion, I put an arm behind her knees and scooped her up. She was too exhausted to protest, and her head dropped against my shoulder as I hurried out of the room.

If I had anything to say about it, the only thing Kris would be doing for the remainder of the day was rest in her room. The guard at the main entrance saw us coming, and opened the door for me. I nodded my appreciation as I stepped outside, squinting against the sun.

As I turned for the girls' dormitory, I heard Micah coming up behind me.

"She wouldn't have it any other way," he said.

"I don't care, Micah. She needs rest right now."

"I know that," he insisted. "We all know that. She's the one who won't give up. It's her best friend."

I stopped and turned so suddenly he nearly ran into me. "There's another way. I think I found it. I'll know more in a few days."

"Callie might not have a few more days."

"She has to hold on, because this—" I nodded to Kris's limp body, "—isn't working, and she can't keep doing this to herself. I'll talk to you, and everyone else, about it later. Right now, I'm getting her to bed."

Any other time, I would have expected Micah to object or to make a snide comment. With Kris in her current condition, not even he could argue with me.

Chapter 16

{Kris}

I dreamt that Nathan was back, Callie was better, and the three of us were celebrating with cups of hot chocolate. We were in Boone, sitting with our feet dangling off the edge of the bridge over the river that had changed my life. Usually, dreams of that river were bad dreams, spurred by bad memories. This one wasn't so bad. Well, it started off okay anyway.

When Megan and Lauren rose out of the water, both encased in an angelic white glow, a familiar sense of harmony flowed through me. That peacefulness was something I had only recently started to feel when dreaming of them. The sight of my friends no longer frightened me. Now, they usually had reassuring messages and smiles for me, and that was always great.

But this time their focus seemed to be on Callie, and that worried me.

"Over here!" I wanted to shout to draw them away from her, but in this dream, my mouth didn't work.

Lauren floated in front of Callie, and Callie smiled as

Lauren's hand reached out to her. Callie didn't sense what I sensed. She was happy, and I was suddenly very scared.

"You can't take her!" My plea went unspoken, and unheard.

Lauren's hand brushed Callie's cheek, and I watched silently, powerless to stop whatever happened.

What was happening? Was this it? Was Callie being collected—to join my other friends, because she too, should have died that night? Was fate finally catching up to Callie?

"Not yet." Lauren's soft voice echoed through the valley.

It repeated louder in my head . . . and louder . . . and louder. And then I wasn't safe on the bridge anymore, but submerged under the water, looking up at a blinding light above. It grew brighter as I kicked for the surface, but I never broke through. A pressure settled in my chest as I realized that I was back in the familiar drowning dream.

I jolted awake, clutching my chest as I gasped for air. On a deeper level, I knew I was only suffering the remnants of a dream, but it took a few moments longer for my body to get the memo. Sweat beaded on my forehead, my breaths came in rapid, shallow bursts, and my pulse pounded like I had just run a marathon. The ceiling slowly came into focus above me, and I realized that it was early morning, and the sun had just started to rise.

It took me another moment to realize that I heard a voice calling my name. A face shifted into my line of sight, and I saw Nathan.

My breathing steadied, and I managed a smile. "What are you doing here?"

"I slept here." His brow creased as he studied me. "Are you okay? What just happened?"

"Bad dream," I answered lazily like it didn't matter. And it didn't, not now. But I could tell from the way his eyes remained fixed on mine in silent analysis that Nathan wasn't satisfied with that simple answer. For his benefit, I added, "It was the river."

He nodded once. "Same as usual?"

"Pretty much." Also, as usual, I didn't want to talk about it. That was something he had learned to accept—to not push me into dissecting my nightmares. When they were over, I wanted to forget about them. Not dwell on them.

Especially this morning. Finding Nathan hovering over me within seconds of waking was a good reason to forget the unpleasantness behind my awakening. I pushed through what little distress still lingered from the dream, and focused entirely on the here and now with Nathan. Because he was back, and I couldn't be happier about that.

I lifted a hand, and brushed my knuckles against the stubbly shadow on his jaw. "How long has it been since you shaved?"

"A few days." He leaned into my touch. "Does it bother you?"

His tone suggested that he knew it didn't, but I answered anyway. "Not at all." In fact, I thought it was sexy. Not a full beard. But a few missed shaves' worth of stubble? Hell, yeah I thought that was hot.

"You sure about that?"

The mischievous gleam in his eyes caused my pulse to jump. I didn't know what he was up to until his head lowered to mine. I prepared for a kiss—and expected it to be another wonderfully glorious moment. But no. I didn't get a kiss. Instead, I got roughed up by a stubbly chin against my cheek.

"Ah!" I screeched, and pressed my palms against his chest. My hands warmed from the sudden contact with hard, smooth skin. Of course, his chest was bare. And of course, I didn't manage to budge him at all.

And I wasn't so sure I really wanted to now. Not with pecs like that at my fingertips.

Nathan took advantage of my moment of weakness. Tossing the bed sheets to the side, he threw a leg over both of mine and rose above me, pinning me beneath him. At the same time, his mouth moved to my ear, his stubble mercilessly scraping against everything in its path.

"Say uncle?" His breath tickled the sensitive spot behind my ear, causing me to squirm in I'm-being-tickle-tortured agony.

"Never!" I pushed against him, harder this time, because I was really ticklish there—and the jerk knew it.

He grabbed my wrists and pinned them above my head. As if I ever stood a chance. He nuzzled my neck, continuing his stubble-faced assault as I twisted and squealed beneath him, completely at his mercy.

"Uncle! Uncle!"

I felt the vibration in his chest as he chuckled. "That's what I thought," he murmured dangerously close to my ear.

This time, his breath against my skin didn't tickle so much as it . . . felt good. Really good. So good a tiny, barely audible moan snuck past my parted lips. Nathan stilled, and the rush of his breath stirred the hair that had pooled on the pillow beneath me. He paused there, for only a moment, before his lips were on the move again, trailing a line of soft kisses along my jaw, coming closer. Closer. . .

His head lifted and his eyes pierced mine the moment before his mouth closed in on mine. It didn't take long to register the difference with this kiss. Whereas Nathan was usually the voice of reason and the advocate of holding back, this time he was neither. Not that I was complaining. My lips readily parted beneath his, allowing him deeper access.

Nathan released one of my wrists, and slipped his free hand between us. My t-shirt had ridden up some during our playful struggle, and when his hand grasped my hip, he was met with bare skin. From there, his touch moved up, seductively slow, until he met fabric. That didn't stop him. As his fingers pushed my shirt higher and grazed my ribcage, his lips broke away from mine to sear a trail across my jaw to my neck, allowing a moan to pass my lips.

Nathan stopped suddenly, his mouth pressed to the side of my neck, over my pounding pulse, and his hand froze with the tips of his fingers just under the lace of my bra.

"Kris?" His voice was rough. "I need you to tell me to stop."

"What if I don't want you to?" I whispered.

With a heavy breath, his head dropped to rest against my shoulder. He shook it once, and I wondered if it signaled defeat on his part. Had he reached a point that he would let this happen?

Every other time we started to get close, he pulled the brakes because he knew I wasn't ready yet. And, to an extent, he had always been right. If he said the same thing now, he would still be right. But I had come to the conclusion that this was something that I would never feel completely ready for. Because it was scary as hell thinking about having sex.

The seconds ticked by with Nathan suspended above me, frozen so still I might have suspected that he had fallen asleep if it weren't for his labored breathing. I knew what he was doing— gaining his composure so that he could think reasonably.

Sometimes I wished he would let his twenty-two-year-old body do his thinking for him—like every other guy did. Sometimes he was too damn considerate for his own good.

"You know," I murmured thoughtfully. I traced a finger over the hard bicep positioned next to my head as he held himself up. "One of these days, you're not going to be able to pull the breaks, and it's just going to happen . . ."

He shuddered, but I wasn't sure if it was from my touch or my words. "I'm having a difficult enough time right now." His indecision was audible in the gruffness of his voice. I waited another moment, and was about to make another suggestive comment, when his head lifted with a, "I'm good."

I didn't hide my disappointment. "Okay."

"I'm not going to let anything happen until I know it's what you want."

"How do you know that's not what I want *now*?"

His smile was tender. "Because I can hear it in your voice," he answered. "Just like I can see it in your eyes. And here?" He shifted his hand so that it was pressed against my heart, which was admittedly racing pretty damn fast. "I can feel that."

"What? I'm not allowed to be nervous?"

He delicately traced my cheek before wrapping a strand of my hair around his finger. "Nervous, yes. Uncertain, no. Not about this." His eyes shifted to mine, driving home the message.

I supposed I got it. Sex was a big deal. Maybe not to him so much—not anymore—but it was to me. He knew it was to me, and he was doing everything in his power to make sure that, when it finally happened, it would be the experience he thought I deserved.

Okay, so I probably had the best boyfriend in the world.

With a teasing smile, I said, "I hate you sometimes."

"Yeah? Well, I love you."

He kissed me again, and we tested his ability to keep his composure a little bit longer, before a growling stomach—we weren't even sure whose—reminded us that we needed to eat. By the time we grudgingly rolled out of bed, it was midmorning.

Nathan left for his room to shower and get ready while I did the same. Before he left, he made plans for us to meet in the mess hall in an hour. Sure, we needed to eat, but there was something he needed to tell me. And Alec. He told me that the two of them would meet me there.

I considered every possibility while I showered and fixed my hair, but by the time I left my room and started toward the mess hall with Kim, I hadn't come up with any explanation for the excited glint in his eyes.

I ran into Micah and Richie at the door. Apparently, Nathan had requested for their presence as well, which only added to the mystery.

What could he have to tell me, Alec, *and* Micah?

This time of day, the mess hall was mostly empty, and it only took a quick scan of the tables to see that we were the first to arrive. I picked through what was left at the pastry bar, and ended up with a wrinkled chocolate donut hard enough to use as a weapon if necessary.

As I returned to the dining area, Nathan, Alec, and Bruce arrived. Nathan smiled, while Bruce outright laughed at something Alec said. The sight caused my feet to stop working in the middle of the large room.

What had happened to them? Not that I wasn't happy that Nathan and Alec were no longer plotting each other's demise, but it was . . . well, it was weird to see them cordial with each other.

No, cordial wasn't even the word. They were actually *friendly*.

By the time I shook off the surprise and started moving again, Nathan was watching me peculiarly. I gave him a reassuring smile as I slid up beside him.

"You alright?" he murmured. His eyes leveled on mine with an intensity that slammed me with a movie-reel flood of images from that morning.

I couldn't help smiling like a giddy moron at the memory. "Perfectly fine."

"Good." He planted a kiss to the side of my head, before pulling out a chair for me to sit in. He took the seat next to me as the others settled in around us.

"Alright, Natey-boy," Alec said. "You've got us all here. What's the big news?"

"You never got a letter from me, did you?" he asked Alec, surprising everybody with the randomness of the question, but none more so than Alec.

"You wrote me a letter?" Alec repeated, a teasing grin forming on his lips. Then recognition flashed in his eyes, and he told Nathan, "No, I never got it."

What in the hell was going on? Nathan writing Alec letters? Alec looking at Nathan like they shared a secret that no one else was in on? I felt like I was living out an episode of The Twilight Zone.

Nathan leaned back in his chair with a shrug. "It's coming from the middle of nowhere in Greece, so it'll probably take a while."

The serious look on Alec's face disappeared, and he now stared at Nathan with a grin. "Care to save me from all this nervous anticipation, and tell me what it was about?"

Nathan held up a finger. "Waiting on one more person."

Before anyone could ask who, the double doors at the entrance banged open. Every head at the table whipped in the direction of the noise as Jared entered.

"Sorry I'm late," he said, though his tone suggested he could have cared less. He shot Nathan a look that I couldn't interpret as he took a seat next to Alec.

"*Now* we're all here," Nathan chided.

Jared took a drink from the Styrofoam cup he had brought with him, and eyeballed Nathan over the lid. But the visible curve of his lips behind the cup made him appear anything but menacing.

"You all know that Jared and I were on a mission together," Nathan started, drawing everyone's attention. "What most of you don't know is where we went."

There was a stretch of expectant silence. Though I knew they had been in Greece, I didn't know why, and I was just as curious as everyone else to hear.

It was Jared who spoke up, and we all turned to him. "We went to Mount Olympus."

Bruce's jaw dropped at the same time my own went slack. Micah had been picking his nails like he had no interest in being a part of this meeting, but dropped his arm to the table with a *thwunk*. Someone gasped, and while I never would have guessed it if not for the look on her face, I suspected it had come from Kim.

"You saw the gods?" Micah asked hesitantly.

"Yes, and they had a specific mission for us," Nathan answered.

Everyone listened with enraptured silence as Nathan spun a wild and dangerous tale of betrayal, uprisings, curses, and immortality. When he finished, no one moved for several long seconds.

It was Micah who finally broke the silence. "Why would the Skotadi be helping the demigods? That doesn't make any sense."

"We're still looking into it," Jared responded brusquely.

"That's not the important part right now anyway," Nathan said, drawing everyone's attention back to him. Micah scoffed like he couldn't disagree more, but Nathan continued unfazed. "All of that was just background information to get to the reason we're here."

My teeth came down on my lip, trapping the air in my lungs. If demigods cursing humans to achieve immortality so that they could start an uprising against the gods wasn't the *Big News*, I was afraid to hear what else Nathan had to tell us.

"One of the goddesses gave me something while we were there—a potion of sorts. She said that whoever drank it . . . the true potential of their soul . . . would be secured and protected." He said that last part with a shrug, like he didn't really know how to word it.

Looking to Nathan, Jared said, "It can basically protect a soul from evil." Nathan nodded, and Jared added, "Or it can save a soul that has already been possessed by evil."

"Return a soul to its true potential," Nathan clarified. "That's what Circe said."

Jared grinned. "Basically, it's chicken soup for the soul."

As the two of them had been fumbling over their explanation of this potion, the rest of us had been swiveling our heads back and forth between them. Now, everyone sat still, staring silently at the table, as the gravity of what they said sunk in.

"Circe?" Micah questioned. "You got this potion from Circe?"

Nathan nodded. "That's right."

"You do know who she is, right?" Micah continued.

I didn't, but then I didn't know who half of the gods were. Every day I was reminded of just how little I had retained from my junior high Greek Mythology class. It was either that or the version taught in schools was bogus.

"Hecate's daughter," Nathan answered Micah between clenched teeth.

My head whipped around. "Daughter?" As in . . . my sister?

Nathan peeled his gaze away from Micah, and his eyes softened when they lowered to mine. "According to most legends, Hecate had a daughter with her lover, Asclepius, before Hades imprisoned her. Because she was born to two gods, Circe is a goddess. She has the powers of both of her parents—the power to yield magic from Hecate, and the ability to heal from Asclepius."

Powers of magic and healing? If anyone could produce a potion that could do what they were claiming this potion could do, it was probably her. Right?

But, oh my God . . . I had a half-sister?

"Other legends have pinned her as a sorceress," Micah countered. "Of *black* magic."

Oh. I didn't know much about magic yet, but one thing I had learned was that black magic was bad.

"You met her," Alec said to Nathan. "Can she be trusted?"

Nathan glanced at Jared before answering Alec. "I think so."

Micah chuckled humorlessly. "My guess is that you want Kris to take this potion to save her soul, right?"

Nobody said anything for a long time as Nathan and Micah exchanged glares.

"We are hoping that this is the solution we've been looking for," Jared eventually said.

I looked from Nathan to Jared, and found him looking

directly at me.

They thought this potion could be the thing to save me from the life of evil I was meant to have? It sounded promising, if what this goddess told them was, in fact, true. But something held me back from getting too excited. What exactly that was, I couldn't put a finger on just yet.

"We gave it to Lillian yesterday," Nathan blurted suddenly, interrupting my train of thought. He shifted to face me directly. "If it works, if it can bring her back . . ."

Then there would be no reason not to believe Circe's potion was legit, and he would want me to take it. There was no mistaking the sound of hope in his voice—hope that he had finally found a way to save me. But . . .

I finally pinpointed the problem I had with this idea.

"You said this potion will secure a person's soul to its true potential?" I chose my words carefully, and only when I had finished my question did I look up to meet Nathan's waiting eyes. He nodded slowly, and I glanced across the table at Alec. "But we were *meant* for evil. That's the whole reason we were created. To be evil. Isn't that our true potential?"

From the look on Nathan's face, I figured he had anticipated my concern. "But you're not evil. Not really," he insisted. "You've got Hecate's blood in you, too. Right now, you're good. Your whole life, you've been good. In your heart, you're good. Both of you." He turned to glance at Alec before looking back to me. "The evil was planted, but it's not really what either of you are."

"How do you know? Heart isn't the same as soul," I pointed

out. What was in a person's soul ran much, much deeper.

A muscle in Nathan's jaw ticked. I knew he wanted to argue with me, but with a table full of curious eyes on us, he said nothing.

"I guess I'll go ahead and ask the question I think we all want to know the answer to," Alec said after a moment. "Did it work on Lillian?"

Since Nathan was locked in a staring contest with me, Jared volunteered an answer. "We don't know yet. Whoever drinks it is knocked unconscious for three days as it works its magic."

"We wanted to test it out on her first to see how it works before you and Alec take it," Nathan said to me, as if that should have made me feel better.

"*And . . .*" Jared jumped in. "We need Lillian's help in order for Callie to get better. She's the one who did this to Callie, and she's the only one who knows what we can do to fix her."

Now *that* I could get on board with. Yet the big difference between Lillian, and me and Alec, remained. Lillian had been born to be good, while Alec and I were born to be evil. What if Lillian woke up as her normal self, but Alec and I only sealed our fates with Hades—a little earlier than expected? What if we both woke up . . . the monsters we were trying to avoid becoming?

Lillian helping Callie would be huge, and I was happy about that possibility. Even if the same thing that saved her destroyed me. But I didn't want Alec affected.

"Okay." Alec propped his elbows on the table. "Assuming Lillian wakes up in—what, two days now?—and she's back to normal, then the theory is that it will work for Kris and me?"

"That's the theory," Jared said.

Alec looked at Nathan, his head bobbing in barely detectable nods. "Alright," he finally said. "If it works for Lillian, and we do this, then I go first."

I started to open my mouth, to inquire why, when Nathan cut me off.

"Agreed," he said.

I glared at Nathan for a brief moment, before shooting a curious look at Alec. "Why?"

He shrugged. "You're right. Lillian isn't exactly like us. It might work okay for her, but not for us." He glanced in Micah's direction. "Besides, we don't know for certain if Circe can be trusted. I want to go first to make sure nothing bad happens."

"No way," I argued. "I'm not going to—"

"That makes sense," Micah spoke up. "If it goes bad, only one of you will be affected. Not both of you."

Of course Micah would be in favor of this idea. But I wasn't a fan of letting Alec potentially sacrifice himself for me. What if something did go wrong?

"And if something does go wrong?" I asked him.

"Then you'll be spared."

His reasoning sucked. "Your reasoning sucks," I told him.

"But it's smart," Micah countered.

Everyone looked at me, waiting for my response, waiting for me to agree to go through with this. While I had my reservations, I didn't see where I had much of a choice. This was the most promising plan we'd had yet. Actually, it was the only plan we had. We had to give it a shot.

I nodded. "Yeah, okay. I'm in."

Chapter 17

{Nathan}

Today was day three. Today, Lillian would wake up, and we would see if Circe's potion worked. I was like a kid on Christmas morning, eagerly anticipating the moment we had all been waiting for.

And I couldn't find Kris anywhere.

After searching her dorm, the beach, the mess hall, my dorm, and her dorm again, it finally dawned on me where she was.

The rock cave.

I spotted Kim sitting in the dirt outside the cave, her back against the rock wall. She appeared to be asleep, but her eyes popped open as I approached—like a good Kala soldier. I smiled at her as I ducked through the opening.

Kris sat at the edge of the pool with her feet in the water. I knew the moment she realized I was there from the sudden straightening of her back. The fact that she pretended to not know I was there was my biggest clue that my intuition was right—something was wrong. Something more than uncertainty over a drink that may or may not work.

Aside from the anxiety she had regarding the potion, she had been fine the past two days. This sudden shift in her mood came out of nowhere. It didn't take me long to determine the reason behind it.

My steps faltered as I closed the distance between us. "What are you doing way out here?"

Though I knew the answer, I asked anyway. Sometimes I was wrong. It didn't occur often, and I doubted this was one of those times, but stranger things have happened.

"I like it here." Her feet splashed in the water, a weak attempt at feigning indifference.

I kicked off my shoes and sat beside her. The water felt nice, but not *that* nice. "Kris?" I waited until her eyes met mine, albeit briefly. "What's wrong?"

"Nothing's wrong," she murmured. "I'm just thinking."

Her talent for denial was almost as good as mine. I decided to confront the issue head on. Otherwise, this could go on for a long time.

"You know nothing is going to change, right?"

Her feet stopped moving as she registered the message behind my words, then began kicking again, slower, more calculating. "*Everything* might change today," she countered.

"Nothing about you and me is going to change." Her heavy sigh let me know that I was right. "You know that, right?"

"Nathan . . ."

"*Nothing.*" My hand shot out to cup her chin. I forced her to turn and face me. She needed to see it in my eyes. She needed to know how serious I was. "No matter what."

"Promise?"

"I promise you. It's you and me, okay?"

I got a weak nod, but a nod nonetheless. I would have pushed for more enthusiasm from her, if not for the sound of quickly approaching footsteps from outside the cave. We both turned to look over our shoulders as Micah appeared at the entrance, breathing heavily.

"I've been looking everywhere for you," Micah panted, looking at me.

"How did you know about this place?" I shot back.

Surely Kris hadn't brought him here while I was gone. I glanced at her and she shrugged. Turning back to Micah, I caught the look of uncertainty in his eyes as he surveyed Kris warily.

"I can always find her," he answered solemnly. "I assumed you were with her."

I hated that annoying connection they had. Everything about Micah annoyed me. I knew for a fact that he disliked me as much as I disliked him, so I was surprised that he had come here looking for me.

"What do you want, Micah?" I asked.

"Umm . . ." His eyes flicked nervously to Kris before he answered me. "They're looking for you. Lillian is awake."

I nodded, and maintained a calm demeanor despite the galloping in my chest. "Did it work?"

He nodded with a smile. "They think so." Again, Micah glanced at Kris and, just as quickly as it appeared, the smile faded.

"She's not making much sense though, and keeps repeating the same thing over and over."

I stared at Micah and waited for him to elaborate. Then it hit me. I knew what he was going to say a half second before he said it, and if I could have reacted faster, I would have stopped him.

With one last reluctant glance at Kris, Micah answered me. "She's asking for you."

*   *   *   *   *

Never in my life have so many people catered to me. Doors were opened ahead of my arrival as if I were a celebrity, and a high ranking Kala, whose name I couldn't remember, ushered me through the Infirmary toward Lillian's room. I let him show me the way, as if I didn't already know where it was.

I expected her to be awake, as Micah had said. I expected her to look like Lillian. I expected her to be . . . normal. Despite all my expectations, I wasn't prepared.

The Lillian I had come to know over the past few months was gone, replaced by the girl I had known, and loved, seven years ago. The transformation was incredible. Until then, I hadn't realized what being Skotadi had done to her—to her complexion, her eyes, her hair, and even her facial expressions. Whereas Skotadi-Lillian's eyes had been cold and her facial expressions hard, the Lillian I saw now appeared anything but cold and hard.

And she was crying.

Of course she was crying. She was surrounded by at least ten Kala, all of them spitting out stupid question after stupid question. None of them gave her time to answer before someone fired another one at her. Despite her visibly vulnerable emotional state, she was still strapped to the bed like a dangerous animal.

With one look at her, I knew she was no longer *that* Lillian. Couldn't they see that?

"Where are your superiors located?"

"What is the Skotadi's agenda?"

"Are you aware of the increase in . . ."

I shouldered my way through the mass of insensitive pricks. A few of the smart ones got the hint and backed away. Most of them stopped their incessant interrogation, but amongst an assembly of assholes, there was always that one who shined above the others. He stepped into my path, blocking me from closing the remaining few feet to Lillian's bed.

Regardless, she had seen me, and I had seen the relief in her eyes before I squared up to the world's most stupid Kala. He was obviously more brain than brawn, and that was the only thing that kept my fist out of his face.

"Who do you think you are?" he asked me, and I had to admit the guy had balls.

No, no. He wasn't ballsy. He was stupid, and he was asking for it. My hand instinctively clenched into a fist at my side.

A hand came down on my shoulder, stilling the forward motion of my arm. "Someone more important than you right now, Stiles."

Jared. To the rescue . . . and just in time.

The weasel named Stiles grudgingly moved to the side and I stepped forward, toward Lillian. Her tears had slowed and her fear was gone, replaced by hope.

I was vaguely aware of Jared clearing out the room behind me, and when I glanced over my shoulder at him for guidance, he merely nodded his head at me in encouragement, as if I should know what to do.

Like any guy would know what to do when confronted with his ex-girlfriend who had just magically returned from the land of the evil-dead after seven years.

"Are . . . are you okay?" I asked pathetically, and rolled my eyes at my own lameness.

That was a stupid question. Of course she wasn't okay.

Dr. Ribbons was the only other person Jared had not kicked out of the room, and I turned to him now. "Can someone undo the restraints? Obviously she doesn't need them anymore."

The doctor looked to Jared, and I followed his gaze to my old friend. If he even considered saying no, we were about to have a problem. Fortunately, he didn't even hesitate.

"Of course." Jared opened the door and called in someone by the name of Willis.

I didn't recognize him, but Willis had a set of keys. He maintained a ridiculous distance between himself and Lillian, extending his arms as far as he could to insert the key into the lock. Once the cuffs were undone, he backed away cautiously and looked to Jared for permission to escape.

Like a coward. As if he actually thought Lillian could hurt him.

Jared let Willis out and, although Jared stayed in the room, he remained near the door. His distance made it feel like Lillian and I were alone in the room, the seven years we had spent apart the only thing separating us. Though she didn't know it yet, much had changed in those seven years—for me. She was the same Lillian I had once loved, but yet she wasn't. We had once easily bantered, but now I found my tongue tied, the words that should have come easily now impossible to find.

Jared must have recognized my struggle, because he walked up beside me to lay a comforting hand on top of one of Lillian's—something I probably should have thought to do.

"Hi, Lillian," he said easily. "I'm Jared. I don't know if you remember me . . ."

She nodded, and her eyes flicked to mine briefly before returning to him. "Of course I do, Jared. We went through development together."

"That's right," he said soothingly. Clearly he was much better at this than I was. "We were all devastated when you left us." He patted me gruffly on the back in an attempt to include me in the discussion.

I opened my mouth, but my tongue still wasn't ready to cooperate.

"How long?" Lillian asked, glancing between us. "How long ago was that?"

Jared and I shared a look. She didn't remember?

"Seven years," he answered.

Her face blanched as fresh tears welled up in her eyes. Her mouth opened and closed several times, but all she managed was a strangled cry.

Her severe reaction took me by surprise. It was genuine and

gut-wrenching, and it was obvious that she really had no idea that she had missed seven years of her life. Until now.

"You don't remember, do you?" I finally said.

"I remember bits and pieces of my time as a Skotadi," she stammered, "but not seven years. It's as if I've been asleep the whole time. I feel like it was just yesterday that we were here on the island, together."

Jared and I shared another glance. This wasn't good. Not for what we had hoped to accomplish by bringing Lillian back. If she didn't remember much about her time as a Skotadi, how could she help Callie? Or all the humans dragged into this mess? Despite the hollow feeling building up in my stomach, I managed to keep the devastation off my face for Lillian's sake.

She lifted her gaze to mine, and held it. I saw it clearly then, and I knew. Her time as Skotadi-Lillian was nothing but a long, bad dream to her, and she was living seven years in the past. A past in which I remained the one and only in her life, and we were madly in love.

No wonder she had asked for me upon waking up. Not only had she not known how much time had passed, but she had no idea how much I had changed over the past seven years. From the saddened look in her eyes as her gaze held mine, I figured that she had just realized my feelings for her were not what they had once been. How could they be? How could she expect them to be? It had been seven years.

I was in love with someone else. Though that was the painful truth, I didn't think now was the best time to tell Lillian that. Not when she was this emotionally unstable. First, she needed time to absorb the fact that she had lost the time she had.

A knock at the door saved me from saying something stupid. Jared left to answer it. A few hushed words were exchanged before Jared returned to my side, the warm smile on his face directed at Lillian.

"What do you say to having an actual room again?" he asked her. Gesturing to the drab exam room we stood in, he added, "It won't be much, but it'll be better than this."

Lillian nodded eagerly. "That would be great. Thank you."

Hovering in the doorway was a scowling female Kala. I suspected that she was there to serve as Lillian's bodyguard. Of course. Seeing Lillian's drastic transformation wasn't enough for them. Once guilty, always guilty. Once a Skotadi, always a Skotadi. Lillian would more than likely be subjected to the same restrictions Kris and Alec were subjected to. Perhaps more.

At least they planned to let her out of this room, though I bet her room would be treated as more of a prison cell than a sanctuary. Nonetheless, Lillian smiled gratefully. For now. Until she realized the nasty truth. Not only the truth about how the Kala would treat her now, but also the truth about us—that there wasn't an 'us' anymore.

Several more Kala filed into the room, and I moved off to the side, out of the way. I didn't recognize any of them, but they were all talking at once to each other, and above each other, as they discussed the move.

I doubted anyone noticed when I slipped out. As I walked away from the room, I told myself that I left to avoid hurting Lillian with the truth now, when she could least handle it.

Leaving was for the best. I really thought that. Yet, for some reason, each step I took made me feel more and more like I was running from something.

Chapter 18

{Kris}

"What if it doesn't work?"

"It will work." Nathan sounded like a broken record, but only because I kept asking the same question over and over again.

I didn't share his confidence that this concoction, or whatever it was, would work. I was surprised when he told me that it had worked on Lillian. Though her memory remained fuzzy, she was no longer a Skotadi.

But just because it worked for Lillian didn't mean it would work for Alec and me. The fact that our circumstances were very different kept me from getting too excited.

Even Alec was more optimistic than me. "Yeah, come on Kris," he said. "You're kind of taking the wind out of my sails right now."

I shot him a sheepish smile. "Sorry. I've just gotten so used to . . ." What? What prevented me from getting excited about this?

"No hope?" Alec ventured.

I nodded. That was exactly how I felt. Completely hopeless, and sure that *nothing* would work. Ever. I had gotten so used to knowing I was doomed that I had come to sort of accept it. I had a hard time thinking or feeling differently.

On some level, I knew it was the Skotadi in me that had those feelings. Not me. Not really. I hoped she was scared, and knew that she would be getting her eviction notice soon.

We slowed as we approached the entrance to the boys' dormitory, and Alec turned to put a hand on my shoulder, as if trying to instill some of his hope in me.

"It will work," he said. He waited for me to nod, before turning to face Nathan. "Three days, right?"

"Yeah," Nathan said to Alec, then turned to address Bruce. "You have any questions?"

Bruce threw his hands up. "I'm good."

Nathan had spoken to him earlier to make sure he had no problem with what we were attempting. As I suspected, Bruce was cool with it, and had promised to not report anything that he saw to upper level management—as long as Alec behaved. Considering he would be unconscious, I doubted Alec could cause too much trouble. Then again, he was notorious for surprising me, and especially good at being bad.

"Just don't let me die, alright?" Alec pleaded, looking back and forth between Nathan and Bruce. He didn't wait for an answer before he turned toward the entrance, with Bruce on his heels.

"I'll be by to check on you later!" Nathan called after him.

Alec's hand lifted over his head in a dismissive wave, the

only indication he gave that he heard Nathan. He didn't seem thrilled about his plans for the evening, and I wondered if Alec had the same doubts and concerns I had—that this potion might not cause the results Nathan and Jared expected it to.

My thoughts preoccupied me as Nathan and I continued to the girls' dormitory. Not until we were back in my room, and I looked up to find Nathan staring at me, did I realize I hadn't said a word in nearly ten minutes.

Nathan sighed. "Alright, what is it?"

I smiled as I kicked off my shoes. I thought about blowing my concerns off as nothing. Then I remembered who I would be attempting to fool, and knew that wouldn't work. With a shrug that I hoped downplayed my concern, I said, "It's Alec."

Nathan looked surprised as I glided up next to him, seeking his reassuring presence. His arms automatically encircled me, pulling me inside their protective barrier. "He'll be okay."

"It's just . . ." I mumbled into his shirt. "Was it just me, or did he seem a little reluctant?"

I felt Nathan shrug. "Who wants to go to sleep for three days? He doesn't know what to expect, but the end result will be worth it. He knows that."

I pulled back far enough to see his eyes. "How are you so sure?" It wasn't so much a question as a statement of awe.

Because he wasn't just optimistic. He was positive that we had found the answer. He had a confidence about the whole thing that I lacked.

His fingers brushed through the hair framing my face, pushing the strands behind my ears. "Because Circe gave me that hope."

I thought about that. Having a goddess behind the whole thing was reassuring . . . "But what if—"

"Stop." He softened the order with a chuckle. "You're too worried about this."

I took a deep breath, then expressed my fear in a rush. "I'm just afraid that my true potential is for evil, not good, and I'll wake up the monster I am trying to avoid becoming."

His eyes softened with understanding. "You know why I'm *not* worried about that?" He paused long enough for me to shake my head before he continued. "Because of how much you *are* worried about that."

My teeth caught my lip. I rolled his words around in my head a few times, and no matter how hard I tried, I couldn't make sense of them. "I don't get it."

"You're *good*, Kris," Nathan said. He gripped my shoulders and gave me a little shake for emphasis. "You're good to your core. If you weren't—if evil drove you—you wouldn't be this worried about becoming evil. You would welcome it. Instead, you fear it so much that I know you—the true you—is good."

I opened my mouth to protest, but he stopped me with a look. "You've got your mother's blood in you, giving you that goodness, and that is what this potion is going to find. It's going to strengthen that part of you so much that the evil hiding in there somewhere won't stand a chance."

Well, when he put it that way . . .

It sounded alright. And it came from the gods. It wasn't some cockamamie attempt at a spell that I had stumbled upon in a book. We knew it was legit because it had already worked—on Lillian.

She was back to her normal self. Other than getting rid of the occasional extra voice in my head telling me to think bad thoughts and do bad things, I wouldn't really change. Same with Alec. We would just . . . be prevented from changing for the worse later. I hoped that was all that would happen to us. But how could we know for sure?

"Do you think we'll be the same people we are now?" I pondered out loud. "Or do you think this will change us? Not just in the good and evil kind of way, but change who we are?"

Nathan considered my question, and the thought occurred to me that I had brought up something he hadn't thought of. But maybe Alec had? Maybe that was the cause of Alec's reluctance? Maybe it wasn't just a fear of unknowingly sealing his fate with evil? Maybe he didn't want to wake up a completely different person?

"I don't think the change will be that big." Nathan pushed me back, far enough to look down at me. "In your case, it's preventing you from completing a transition into something. I don't think it will actually change who you already are. Or Alec."

"I hope so."

I couldn't imagine Alec not being . . . Alec. Or waking up feeling differently about Nathan. Oh, hell no. That potion better not change anything like that.

I wondered how the change had been for Lillian. If anything else about her had changed, or if she was back to her old self. Nathan hadn't really said much about her condition since returning from the Infirmary. This was the first chance we really had to talk about Lillian's transformation.

I pulled out of Nathan's hold so that I could see him better. "How is Lillian adjusting?"

He looked a little taken aback by the change of subject, but shrugged with a carefree ease. "Time will tell. I think she's just glad to be back to herself."

"You said she didn't remember much when she woke up?" That he had told me right away, and that had been a big blow to our campaign to help Callie.

"I doubt that was the potion," he said quickly. "More likely a byproduct of whatever spell the Skotadi had her under."

Yeah . . . I wasn't worried so much about the potion anymore. That would change in three days, when it was my turn to drink it. For now, I was more curious about Lillian, and what exactly she remembered and didn't remember. If she didn't remember much from her time as a Skotadi, did she remember me? Did she remember anything she had done to me? To Nathan?

"So she doesn't remember the things she has done?" I attempted to choose my words carefully, but the question still came out sounding a little harsh.

After all she put us through, it was hard not to hold some resentment. I doubted I would ever be able to look at her without feeling the sting of her hand on my cheek, or shake off the terror I felt watching her hold a gun to Nathan's head.

"No. She's sort of stuck in the past," Nathan answered. "Like her time as a Skotadi was just a nightmare, and she doesn't remember much about it."

Stuck in the past? I pulled a little farther away from Nathan. "Did she wake up thinking that the last seven years didn't happen?"

Nathan started to nod, then he realized the direction my line of questions was leading, and stopped. His mouth started to open, but I cut him off.

"Does she think you two are still together?" I asked, and inwardly cringed at the shrill edge to my voice.

An emotion I didn't recognize flashed in his eyes. Again, he started to say something before I beat him to it.

"If she woke up thinking the last seven years were only a bad dream, then she woke up still in love with you. That's why she was asking for you," I continued, piecing it all together.

This time, I gave him a chance to respond, but he didn't. And that could only mean one thing . . .

"And you didn't tell her," I concluded.

"If you're asking me if I set her straight within moments of her waking up and being told that she lost seven years of her life, that she had been living those years as a Skotadi, doing horrible things that she will have to come to terms with in her own time, then the answer is no," Nathan said stiffly. "I didn't tell her anything. She was a mess when I got there. She wasn't ready to hear it."

The sharp edge to his voice that let me know I had struck a nerve. The fears I had woken up with that morning—the fears that Nathan had squashed with the promise he had made to me in the rock cave—rushed back in a wave of panic.

"It's not what you're thinking, Kris," Nathan said, his tone much softer now. "She just—she's gone through a lot today. I couldn't add to it."

I nodded like I understood—and a small, rational piece of me did. I bit my lip on the emotions bubbling beneath my mask of self-control. It had been hard enough knowing that she was back to normal, back to the girl Nathan had once been in love with. But to hear that she was stuck in the past, still in love with him, and that he hadn't told her the truth . . .

It was awkward for so many reasons, and it brought out an insane amount of jealousy that I didn't know I possessed. Though I knew jealousy should have been the last thing on my mind, it was there. Nathan's defensiveness when it came to Lillian certainly didn't help.

"Kris?" he probed. When I didn't respond, his hand cupped my chin and tipped my head back until I reluctantly met his eyes. "Don't make it more than it is. If you had seen her, you'd understand why I couldn't do it."

"But you will, right?" I asked softly. "You will tell her?"

"Of course I'm going to tell her." He paused long enough to make sure I registered the sincerity of his words.

Though my presumably irrational concerns about Lillian weren't completely alleviated, I felt a little better hearing that. I believed him, and I knew he would tell her when he felt that she was ready for the truth. Hopefully sooner rather than later. Because surely postponing it would not only make it more uncomfortable for me, but it would also make it more painful for Lillian when she finally learned the truth.

It would be even worse if it didn't come from Nathan. Only a few days had passed since Nathan and I shared that very public kiss on the beach, and while I hadn't heard much talk about it yet, that didn't mean people weren't gossiping out of earshot. Lillian would eventually hear about it.

For now, I was okay with a delay, as long as it was for the right reason. Nathan had a good reason. I was glad he had the heart that he did. He may have odd ways of showing it at times, but he was a caring guy. He wasn't the type to hurt someone without doing everything he could do to prevent it.

Whether I liked it or not, that included Lillian.

"You're a good guy," I told him as I wedged myself into his arms, back where I belonged.

He didn't hesitate to wrap me up in a Nathan-cocoon. Unfortunately, I didn't get to enjoy it long before there was a loud rap at the door. Nathan's arms dropped with a sigh as my back straightened.

Micah.

For the longest time, he had claimed he could sense my exact location when I was within a certain distance from him. I never had the same ability . . . until recently. As annoying as it had been before, knowing that he could always find me, it was twice as bad now that my Micah-radar had kicked in.

Nathan saw it on my face, and an unhappy growl-like noise sounded from the back of his throat as he moved to the door. He swung it open, revealing the person I expected. Micah looked equally unhappy to see Nathan, and regarded him with visible distaste before swinging his attention to me.

"I just checked on Callie," he told me.

Callie updates were the only things that I would allow him in my room for. His lips curled into a barely visible grin—the only indication I had that I hadn't yet put up the wall around my thoughts.

"How is she?" I asked. I had left the Infirmary a little over an hour ago, but in her condition, a lot could change in an hour.

Micah waved at the entrance to my room, which was still blocked by Nathan. "May I?"

Even with his back to me, I could practically see that muscle in Nathan's jaw ticking. Though stiff with reluctance, he stepped aside to let Micah in the room. Once past Nathan, Micah turned his back to him to focus solely on me.

I knew that look on his face, and what it meant. As always, he was curious about Nathan, and about the state of our relationship. I enjoyed watching his curiosity shift to frustration when I put the wall up, blocking him from picking my head for the truth. Not that there was that much to keep from him, but I enjoyed watching his discomfort at not knowing. If he really got on my nerves, I'd give him flashes of some of mine and Nathan's more graphic make out sessions just for fun.

Once Micah realized he couldn't pick anything out of my head, he moved on to the reason for his visit. "When I was leaving, she wanted me to ask you to stay with her for a little bit."

I could do better than that. I looked past Micah, to Nathan, who still stood by the door with his hand on the knob like he was waiting for the first opportunity to shove Micah out of the room.

"I'm going to spend the night there with her," I told him. "I had been doing that a lot while you were gone."

He had already planned to check on Alec later, so we weren't going to be together anyway. From his carefree shrug, I knew Nathan didn't mind.

From the barely audible grunt Micah emitted, I suspected he had read more into my statement than I had intended—like I had otherwise been planning to spend my night with Nathan. Which I did on occasion, but Micah's imagination likely made them far more risqué than they were in reality.

I chose not to correct him, and quietly started to gather what I would need for the night. During the few minutes it took me to toss a change of clothes and my hairbrush into a small bag, no one spoke. An uncomfortable silence settled around us—so uncomfortable I spoke to Micah just to break it.

"So how did she look?" I asked him.

"The same." He shrugged. "It's weird though. The doctor seems to think that there is something unnatural keeping her alive at this point."

I froze with my toothbrush in my hand. "What?"

Micah glanced back and forth between Nathan and me, before settling on me. He sounded unsure, like he didn't know the right words to use. "He said that as sick as she is, he hadn't expected her to live this long, and that *something* he can't explain seems to be keeping her alive."

"Same curse that's making her sick in the first place?" Nathan suggested thoughtfully. "Maybe it's not ready to be fulfilled yet?"

"Or one of the spells actually did something?" I ventured,

though I was doubtful. Nathan's suggestion sounded more plausible. I remembered what Lillian had said about the events being put into motion . . .

The ball wasn't ready to be dropped yet. Hopefully, we found a solution before the time came.

I tossed my toothbrush into the bag and zipped it shut. Looking to both guys and gesturing toward the door, I said, "I'm going, so . . ."

Get the hell out of my room now, while direct and to the point, probably wouldn't go over well with either of them. Luckily, they both got the hint.

We walked in uncomfortable silence from my room on the top floor to the main doors on the ground floor. It worsened once we were outside, and Micah hinted at returning to the Infirmary with me.

I glanced at Nathan just in time to catch him roll his head from side to side. I have seen him do that dozens of times—always before squaring up to a fight, both in real situations and in training.

When his eyes shifted to mine, I saw the spark of his temper ignite. I shook my head before it erupted into a full-blown frenzy. "It's okay," I whispered to him.

He didn't look pleased, but didn't argue. I gave him a reassuring smile and turned in the direction of the Infirmary. I didn't get far before Nathan's hand snagged mine. In one swift motion, he spun me around and pulled me flush against him.

"I'll see you tomorrow," he murmured before pressing his lips to mine.

It wasn't unusual for him to kiss me goodbye when we parted ways, but usually those were chaste goodbye kisses. This kiss was anything but chaste. Oh, no. This kiss sent a message.

His mouth moved possessively against mine, and lasted a few seconds longer than what I considered publicly acceptable. Even after he softened and eased his lips from mine, he lingered agonizingly close, grazing my cheek with the back of his hand. Though I knew the ulterior motive behind his actions, I enjoyed every second of his touch.

I let the show go on only because I agreed that Micah needed a reminder every now and again. And only because I actually enjoyed his caveman-like declaration of 'mine', I gave Nathan a smile instead of the thump to the back of his head that he deserved when he finally let me go.

"Think he got the message?" I whispered conspiratorially.

Nathan grinned. "That should do it."

Nathan finally let me turn to leave, and then I had to hold back a laugh at the look on Micah's face. The daggers shooting from his eyes gave new meaning to the phrase, *if looks could kill.*

As I walked away with him, I shot a quick glance over my shoulder at Nathan. From the smug smile on his face, he knew it as well as I did—Micah got the message loud and clear.

Chapter 19

{Nathan}

Alec had a room on the top floor. I guessed the Kala thought they were safer keeping their *threats* up high. But then, I doubted the upper-level Kala knew that half the island had mastered the skill of scaling the buildings using the balconies, and just about everyone snuck out on a regular basis.

As fun as it was to scale the side of the building, I had no reason to sneak into Alec's room, so I used the stairs like a normal person. Bruce stood outside Alec's door, and nodded as I approached.

"Is he out?" I asked.

"Nope."

"No? How long could it take?" I shot Bruce a puzzled look as I knocked on the door. It swung open before I finished the third knock.

"Nathan!" Alec gushed. Or rather, slurred. "'Sup, man!"

I took a step back, putting distance between myself and the overwhelming aroma wafting from Alec's pores. "Did you confuse the potion with a bottle of vodka?"

"Try Tequila," Alec snorted. "Come in! Come in! I almost got that pesky little worm. He's hiding at the bottom of the bottle. If you want, you can have him."

Against my better judgment, I walked into his room and—Sweet Jesus, it smelled like an old bar that had a long night's worth of stale beer spilled all over the floor by sloppy drunks. I shot a wide-eyed look at Bruce as I closed the door behind me. His lazy shrug hinted that this wasn't the first time Alec was drunk off his ass, nor did he expect it to be the last.

The potion sat on his desk, untouched.

"I thought you'd be eager to get this over with," I said to Alec.

He stumbled to the bed, where he sat heavily. "Just having a little fun first. Before I either turn into the spawn of Satan or a goody-two-shoes who doesn't know how to have fun." He paused long enough to take a drink, then pointed a finger at me. "Kinda like you."

I let the insult slide, considering how wasted he was. "Having fun by yourself?"

"Hey!" He pointed at me again, this time with one eye closed—probably to merge the two blurry images of me he had to have been seeing. "I happen to be the funnest person I know. Besides, you're here now. You might not be as fun as me, but you'll have to do."

"I'm not staying," I returned. "I only came to check on you. It's a good thing I did."

Alec grunted.

It seemed Kris had been right about Alec earlier. He had the same concerns she had—except he also feared becoming 'too good.' I considered the possibility that Alec was beyond help, but shook that thought out of my head as soon as it started. If Lillian had come back from the land of the evil, surely Alec could avoid falling headfirst into it.

But it looked like he would need some help. At least help taking the first step.

I opened the door a crack and motioned to Bruce. "Do me a favor and go get a few cups of coffee from the mess hall. I'll stay here with him."

Bruce hooked a skeptical eyebrow.

"I'm good," I reassured him. "I can handle Alec."

God knew I had experience with it.

Shutting the door, I turned to find Alec with the bottle tipped back in his mouth as he drained every lost drop of tequila, including that damn worm, and I knew I was in for a long night.

One coffee later . . .

"You know . . . you're not as bad as I thought you were."

I glanced up from the music magazine I had been flipping through in an attempt to pass time. Alec was still looking at me with one eye, but the slurring had improved. I gave him a dismissive nod before returning my attention to the magazine.

"A-hem." Alec's grunt forced my eyes up again. He stared at me, apparently waiting for something.

"You're not all that bad either, Alec," I said. "At least, when you're sober."

He didn't say anything, and I returned to the magazine. I felt his eyes on me for several moments before he finally said, "I'm not sure I believe you." I stifled a smile at the wounded-pride sound of his voice. "You know, I'm usually a fun drunk. You're taking all the fun out of it."

I pointed at the Styrofoam cup, reminding him that it was in his hands before he spilled it all over himself. Again. "Drink up."

He lifted it to his lips shakily. "You suck," he muttered before taking a sip.

And another coffee . . .

"I let you have her, you know."

I groaned inwardly. The coffee was not working fast enough—or he had just been *that* drunk.

"If I had tried harder," Alec continued, "eventually she would have been mine."

"Maybe." I shrugged and returned Alec's hard gaze with an indifferent one of my own.

He had entered the mean phase of drunkenness about ten minutes ago. So far, everything from my personality to my haircut had taken a hit. And now, apparently we were back to fighting over Kris.

Well, he was. My goal was to get through the rest of the night with both of us in one piece. I needed him to sober up enough to drink the potion before I could leave. I didn't know what would happen if he mixed it with alcohol. It might not work right, or for all I knew, it might kill him. As tempted as I may have been to chance it, especially when he was being a jerk, deep down I knew I couldn't let that happen.

So I got cozy on the floor with my head propped against the wall, settled in as babysitter, and vowed to stay there for as long as it took.

Third, and final, coffee . . .

The mean phase had long passed. Compared to the overly emotional, sentimental phase Alec was in now, the mean phase had been a piece of cake. We were one man-bear-hug away from the worlds' most awkward bromance, and that was far worse than any of the verbal insults he had hurled at me earlier.

"She always loved you, of course. But just so you know," he said, pointing at me for what might have been the hundredth time. Drunk-Alec pointed, *a lot.* "There's a part of her that loves me, too. Maybe not the same as she loves you, but she does, even if she doesn't know it."

"I know," I returned quickly, and smirked at the look of surprise on Alec's face. I've known it all along. It no longer bothered me like he expected it to bother me.

He thought about my response a moment. A long silence stretched between us before he finally broke it. "Too bad that little piece of her that loves me will be gone in a few days."

I stared at the top of his head as it hung, bobbing side to side. I had never seen Alec like this before, and I didn't like it. I didn't know what to do with it, and I didn't have any clue what to say to him.

After all, I was partially responsible. I was the reason he didn't get the girl that he claimed, when sober, to be over—the girl that I now knew he wasn't over. Even if he might not act on his feelings, and she may never know about them, they were obviously still there.

Not knowing what else to do, I let the silence stretch. And stretch. Just before it got really uncomfortable, I jumped to my feet. "I think you're sober enough."

"Yeah," Alec agreed quickly. He stood and swiped the vial from the nightstand.

I glanced at my watch. 3:32. With some luck, I could be back in my room in five minutes. I looked up in time to catch Alec downing the fluid in one gulp.

"Uh, you need to lay down. *Now*," I said, moving quickly to his side.

"Why? Oh . . ." I watched as the drowsiness hit him.

I followed as Alec stumbled the few steps to his bed. Fortunately, he made it before his body gave out, and he sprawled out sideways across the mattress, his feet planted on the floor. Hooking my arms under his shoulders, I shifted him into a semi-reclined position, propped up against a few pillows stacked against the headboard. I took his shoes off, but didn't touch his clothes. It was his own damn fault for not doing this on his own like he was supposed to.

I backed away, leaving Alec to the potion, and his fate.

A lot would change in a few days. While severing Alec from the forces of evil residing in him was necessary, I wondered how

Alec might change as a result. Would he become a different person, as he and Kris feared?

Would Kris be the same?

Suddenly, I realized what I should have said to him before he slipped into unconsciousness. I knew that no matter how this potion changed either of them, some things would never change.

"That part of her that loves you will never go away," I said softly to an unhearing Alec.

Perhaps that was for the best. I didn't think I could handle him knowing the truth, and reminding me of it on a daily basis.

*   *   *   *   *

Alec was still breathing when I checked on him the next morning. I learned that the potion didn't completely knock him out. According to Bruce, Alec had several moments of zombie-like wakeful episodes throughout the night—enough to get himself to the bathroom and back—though Bruce didn't think Alec had been aware of his actions.

I checked on him a few times that first day, and got the same report from Bruce each time. Restless sleep. No awareness. Breathing. Alive.

I attempted to check on Lillian after breakfast, but got stopped at the door. Kala management had her under quarantine, where she would remain until they were confident she no longer posed a threat.

When I voiced my strongly worded opinion to Jared, he assured me that he would use his supervisor privileges to keep tabs on her, and to question her about Callie the first chance he got. When I saw him again at the end of the day, he told me that Lillian still hadn't remembered much about her life as a Skotadi, and remembered nothing about Callie.

The next day, I made it to lunchtime before I barged into Jared's office. It was one thing that Lillian didn't remember anything about Callie. I couldn't force her to remember, but I could express my disapproval of her being boarded up in her room like a convict.

"They're trying to get everything out of her that they can," he explained to me.

"You mean they're interrogating her?"

He shrugged. "I'm not involved, so I really don't know, but probably. They're getting concerned about the number of Skotadi that have been spotted on the mainland. They want to know what she knows about it."

"She doesn't know anything!" *What part of life changing, post-traumatic amnesia did they not understand?*

Jared held his hands up defensively. "Hey, buddy, I'm with you. Trust me. I don't like it either, but we have to let them do what they have to do so she can get past this."

Defeated, I sat heavily in the chair across from him. My hands were tied. Lillian was in the supervisors' hands, and whether I thought what they were doing was fair or not didn't matter.

"So what about these Skotadi? Any ideas what they're doing?"

Jared leveled his gaze on me. "They think it might have

something to do with Kris."

I pressed my palms to my eyes and rubbed until I saw spots. "Of course they do," I grumbled. As if I didn't have enough shit to worry about.

"Supervisor Jeffries asked me to assemble a team to investigate," Jared continued.

I lifted my hands to look at my friend. "You want me in on it, don't you?"

"Actually, I want you to lead it. Pick the team you want, come up with a plan, and execute. I'll help with the details, but I need you to lead."

"Jared, I told you I don't want to be involved with management—"

"I'm swamped right now," he interrupted. "I've got this second trip to Greece to organize, and just this morning, Jeffries gave me two more missions to plan. He wants all three teams to head out within the week. I need someone I can trust with this one. I could have anybody do it, but I want you because I know you can be counted on to do it right."

"I've got too much going on right now, Jared. There has to be someone else you can trust."

There were only hundreds of us on the island. Surely *one* of them was capable enough to lead a team in investigating the flood of Skotadi on the mainland.

Jared leaned forward in his chair, pinning me with his eyes. "I thought you would want this job, considering it could very well end up being centered on your girlfriend."

With those words, it clicked, and I understood Jared's

intentions. He wanted me to control the mission for one simple reason: to protect Kris. If Kala management discovered that the Skotadi were amassing because of her, they wouldn't hesitate to toss her over to the Skotadi to spare themselves. Giving me direct access to any intelligence gathered could give us the heads up Kris would need to escape the betrayal she would inevitably be subjected to if it were discovered that the Skotadi were here because of her.

Or. . . if I could find a way to take care of the matter without them knowing of Kris's involvement, I could keep them from turning their backs on her. Especially now, when she was so close to severing her tie to the Skotadi.

"When do you want this done?" I asked Jared.

"Think about who you want on your team, and let me know by the end of the day tomorrow. Then we'll work on strategy and objectives."

Coming up with names wouldn't be easy considering we had lost several good soldiers in Greece, and the ones that had survived wouldn't be happy about being chosen for another mission so soon. Not to mention, with the other two missions Jared had going on, there wouldn't be many soldiers left to pick from.

As I stood to leave, Jared stopped me.

"How's the, uh, magic drink working out?" he asked.

"Alec's on day two. He'll be waking up tomorrow."

"What about Kris?"

"She hasn't drank it yet." I thought Jared knew she was waiting to take it until after Alec.

"She shouldn't wait anymore," he said. "Especially if they're right about the Skotadi being here for her. If she drinks it, and it works . . ."

They would have no reason to want her to join them.

I nodded my understanding, and left to find Kris. She needed to know we didn't have the time to wait for Alec. Not now. Not with the Skotadi breathing down our necks. I wasn't thrilled about the idea, but she needed to take the potion now. She needed to get rid of that evil parasite hiding in her before the Skotadi came for her.

Chapter 20

{Kris}

Instructor Kand apparently woke up this morning with one goal in mind: today was the day he would orchestrate my fall. Again, he paired me with Tyson, but unlike the other times, he didn't stop us after I had taken a few solid, painful hits. This time, he let us go. Well, he let Tyson go.

I did more ducking and dodging than hitting. I lost track of how much time had already passed, and how much longer I had to endure before class ended. Glancing at the clock had already earned me a fat lip, so I didn't dare do that again. The rest of the class had stopped their own one-on-one training a long time ago, and were now gathered around us to watch.

I had landed a few solid hits, but had taken many more, including one really good one to the back of the head. The vision in my left eye blurred a little—maybe from brain damage, but I hoped it was only sweat. I would have even been happy with blood. Yes, blood was as likely a guess as sweat, but I didn't have two seconds to wipe at whatever it was to find out.

For as big as he was, Tyson could move.

His fist shot out, and I dodged it. I tried to land a kidney strike, but only hit air. He shoved me from behind, knocking me off balance. I spun around in time to see the blood on his knuckles before they made contact. While my head snapped back from the impact, his legs swept my feet out from under me and I went down on my back. The air rushed out of my lungs, and before I could catch my breath, he jumped on me—a blur of swinging appendages intent on inflicting as much damage as possible.

Instinct curled me into a ball on the floor with my arms over my head. First, to protect myself because the kid was fueled by unadulterated rage, and I knew internal bleeding wasn't a good thing. Secondly, the demon inside of me was straining against the barrier the charm around my neck had placed around it. I knew my eyes were close to, if not already, surging. I couldn't let anyone see them, or else I would certainly be on the next boat off the island.

But then. . . something snapped, and my demon broke free. It was she who propelled the side of my hand into his windpipe. And it was she who followed with a nose-breaking upward thrust of my palm. And she who rose to a stand over the now bleeding and moaning lump on the floor. She forced my foot up with the intention of breaking a few of the pathetic Kala's ribs, but the annoying sound of a whistle distracted her long enough for me to gain control over her, and my own body, again.

I crumbled to the floor beside Tyson as several students rushed at us. All of them focused on him, of course. While they helped him to his feet, I struggled to my knees. I kept my head down. I felt their critical eyes on me, and I didn't know if my own were still surging or not.

Then the mass of bodies surrounding me parted. Strong arms lifted me to my feet—arms that I recognized and knew, and welcomed more than anything at that moment.

"You okay?" Nathan asked me. He waited long enough for me to nod before he spun on Instructor Kand. "Is this what you've been doing since you took over my class?"

I didn't hear a response, and didn't look up to see if Instructor Kand offered one—a shrug, a nod, or *anything*—but whatever he did only infuriated Nathan more. Nathan rolled his head and took a step forward. I put a hand to his chest to stop him from going any farther. The last thing he needed was to get into trouble for standing up for me. Even if the jerk instructor deserved it.

"Nathan?" I pressed when he didn't back down. His eyes were fixated on Instructor Kand in outright angry, vengeful protector mode. I tried again. "*Nathan.*"

"What?"

"I think I'm surging," I whispered loud enough only for him to hear. "You need to get me out of here."

Finally, his eyes lowered to take his first good look at me since he showed up. His jaw clenched at what he saw. "You're not surging, but I am going to get you out of here."

Empowered by the security I felt with my hand in his and the knowledge that I wasn't surging, I lifted my head as he led me out of the classroom. Loud whispers and a few snickers followed us, but I couldn't have cared less.

Nathan had been the one concerned about everyone finding out about us, but right now, he didn't seem too worried about it. Once we were clear of the classroom, he stopped to check on me.

"Has it been like that since I left?" he asked.

I nibbled my lip. At the risk of putting him into a rage, I nodded.

His nostrils flared, but that was all. No rage, thank goodness. "Why didn't you tell me?"

I shrugged. He had only been back for a few days. "A lot has been going on," I offered. "Besides, today was definitely the worst."

This time, Instructor Kand waited until I fought back to blow the whistle. Good thing too, otherwise I didn't know how far my alter ego would have gone. As it was now, Tyson looked almost as bad as I did.

Nathan's jaw clenched tight, and his eyes fixed on the doorway to the classroom. I suspected that he was debating whether to walk away, or go back and maim Kand.

I made the decision for him, and grabbed his hand. "Let's go for a walk," I said. "I want to get away from here."

That worked to get him moving. Once outside, the sun eased the lingering tension and the light breeze blew it away. Not like I had never been beaten up before. I had gotten over it then, and I was nearly over it now. Nathan would take a little longer, but I thought I could speed the process up by distracting him.

"What were you doing there anyway?" I asked him.

He looked at me, and blinked as if trying to remember. "Uh . . . I was going to wait for your class to be over."

"Why?"

"We need to talk," he said, then proceeded to fill me in on the conversation he had with Jared about Skotadi on the mainland.

Once he finished, I turned to pace in front of him. "They're here to get me, and drag me back to be their . . ." Whatever they wanted me to be. Alec had once referred to us as weapons of war, but I didn't like that terminology.

"We don't know that for sure," Nathan said.

I stopped pacing long enough to look at him. "They are."

If the last few months had taught me anything, it was that Skotadi actions were usually related to me in one way or another. The Kala might not know exactly why the Skotadi were there, or exactly what they wanted, but I knew . . . I just knew . . . they had come for me.

What would they do if I were no longer the great evil wrecking ball they were counting on me becoming? I doubted they would just leave me alone. They would likely kill me, but I would honestly rather be dead than forced into the life they had planned for me.

"Nathan, I think I should drink that potion now," I concluded.

Nathan nodded. "That was actually the reason I came to find you," he admitted. "Jared thinks it would make you safer, if they are here for you."

I nibbled my lip. That was all assuming the potion did what

259

we all hoped it would do . . . and not speed the process along. Oh, God . . . what if we were wrong?

"Are you ready?" he asked me slowly, carefully.

Though I wasn't sure, I nodded. Because I *had* to be ready. I had to have faith that it would work.

Back in my room, I stared at the fluid in the vial and wondered if this was really it. If chugging some clear, enchanted liquid was all that separated me from a normal life with an evil-free soul.

Or if just the opposite would happen?

"You know you actually have to drink it for it to work," Nathan said.

I shot him a bland look. "I know that. I'm just thinking."

"It's going to be okay, Kris."

I wasn't in the mood to hear his reassurances. Nothing he said could lessen the deeply rooted fears I had. "How long will it take to knock me out?"

He shrugged. "Real quick. Alec went down hard and fast. But then again, he had just gone through a bottle of tequila."

"That doesn't sound like a bad idea," I muttered. I stared at the vial in my hand, wishing I had a nice shot of something else to calm my nerves first.

No one, other than Circe, knew for sure what would happen to me when I took this. We were trusting someone we didn't know. What if it was a trap—a way to lock me in as a Skotadi for good?

But she was a goddess. She was with us, on the good side. Maybe it was as simple as it sounded, and she had provided us with the solution. Maybe this fluid was all that stood between me and the life I wanted.

"Kris?" Nathan's gentle voice broke through the bipolar swing of thoughts bouncing around in my head, and tore down the wall I had built up around me.

"I'm scared," I whispered. "What if I wake up . . . different?"

He opened his mouth, but I moved to silence him before he could say anything. I kissed him—like a wrap my arms around his neck, tangle my hands in the wavy tufts of hair I found there, and hold onto him with a ferocity that surprised even me kind of kiss. I threw everything—every fear, every concern, every hope—into the kiss. For a brief moment, Nathan froze in surprise, but then he responded exactly how I expected him to.

He deepened the kiss with a noise that sounded like a growl, and slipped his hands under my shirt just enough to graze the sensitive skin at the small of my back. So, really . . . he only had himself to blame when my hands moved to lift his shirt over his head. Our mouths parted only long enough for the fabric to pass between us before crashing together again, and even that had been too long.

The bare skin of his chest and stomach were at my fingertips, and I took advantage of the opportunity to explore. Suddenly, his mouth wasn't on mine anymore, but on my neck— and oh, God did that feel incredible.

"Nathan?" I breathed.

He froze with his lips pressed to the side of my neck just below my ear. He said nothing, but he didn't need to. He knew what I planned to say next. From the look of sheer panic on his face when his head lifted and his eyes shifted to mine, you would think *he* was the one contemplating losing his virginity.

"You hear it in my voice this time?" I asked him.

He squeezed his eyes shut, and I knew he had. "Oh, Kris, not now."

"Why not now? We might not—" I bit my tongue on the rest of my argument, but it was too late. He knew what I had been about to say.

"You want to do this now, because you're *scared?*"

I wasn't sure if he meant it as a statement or a question, so I didn't respond. But I did grimace, and that was enough of an answer for Nathan.

He shifted to sit on the edge of the desk behind him, pulling me with him so that I stood wedged between his knees. "Look, Kris . . ."

"What if this is it? What if I wake up three days from now different? What if this is our last chance to be together . . . as us?"

His eyes softened. "While I don't believe that's what is going to happen," he started slowly, like he chose his words with great care, "I do think that you having that concern isn't the right reason for us to—"

I opened my mouth to argue—I knew he would say that—but he shushed me before I could start, his eyes piercing mine with a silent plea for me to listen to him, and understand. Reluctantly, I clamped my mouth shut.

"When this happens," he said, "it's not going to be for the wrong reasons, and it's certainly not going to be like this." My brow wrinkled at *'like this'*, wondering what was so wrong about this moment, so Nathan explained further. "Kim standing guard right outside your door?"

I made a face. Yeah, okay. He had a point there.

"Rushed," he continued with his list. "Moments before you take a drink that will knock you unconscious for three days . . ."

"Okay, okay . . ."

"Unprepared," he added quietly.

"What?" I leaned back to get a better look at him.

His face carried a sheepish expression I had never seen him make before. "I don't have any . . . protection," he clarified.

Oh. "You've got nothing?" I thought guys carried protection with them everywhere they went because, well, they were guys and if an opportunity presented itself . . .

Nathan shook his head. "Nothing."

I leaned farther back, forcing his hands to drop from my waist. "Why not?"

His eyebrows shot up. "It's not like they sell condoms out of vending machines on the island."

"So what does everyone do?"

He shrugged. "Stock up on the rare trips to the mainland, and hope the supervisors don't find out."

"You were just on the mainland," I pointed out.

He threw his hands up. "I wasn't expecting—"

"Well, from now on expect it." I had entered full-blown scolding mode, complete with hands on the hips. "You better be prepared next time."

His lips turned in to hide a smile. "Do you have any idea how sexy you are when you make that face?"

He tugged me closer, and I saw a fire in his eyes, a hint that he really regretted not being more prepared—because if he were, and the situation was different, we wouldn't be standing there talking about not being prepared.

In compromise, we kissed. A lot, and for a long time. At some point, we made our way to my bed. Since we both knew it couldn't go any further, we had fun exploring. Honestly, we were getting pretty good at that stuff, and it only made me wonder how much better it could get. Based on the way he could curl my toes with a simple kiss, I would bet on it being pretty awesome.

Eventually, Nathan announced the need for a time-out. As much as I hated hearing that, I knew it had been coming, so I didn't protest too much when he launched himself off the bed and snatched his shirt up off the floor.

I made a face as I sat up. "You could leave it off."

He shot me a grin before slipping the shirt over his head. Completely clothed again, his eyes leveled on me.

"So I suppose it's time to get back to business?" I sighed as I reached for the vial where it sat on the bedside table.

Nathan sat on the edge of the bed, close but not too close to me. He always maintained a safe distance for a while after we kissed, like he didn't quite trust himself yet. This time was no different.

Except it was completely different. He seemed to understand that, and his hand squeezed mine in encouragement. It was what I needed to take the final step.

It worked for Lillian.

That was what I told myself as I gulped the liquid down. I

puckered up, expecting an unpleasant taste, but found it slightly sweet. Like sugar water.

Nathan took the empty vial from me with a satisfied smile and laid it on the table.

"Stay with me until I'm out?" I asked.

"How about I stay all night?" He propped a pillow against the backboard and reclined back with his legs stretched out. He looked up at me and opened his arms in invitation.

I snuggled into his chest as the first yawn hit me.

"Told you it wouldn't take long." Nathan's chuckle vibrated me—serving as a lulling motion that nearly pushed me over the edge into sleep. I fought to hold on, just a bit longer.

"You'll check . . ." *On me*, I wanted to say, but it took too much effort.

"Every day," he promised. I felt his fingers slip through my hair as his lips grazed my forehead.

And that was it.

I slept.

Chapter 21

{Nathan}

Kim poked her head in the room about an hour later, and gave me *that look*. The same look she had given me from day one, like she had known about Kris and me all along, and though she didn't really care, she insisted on enforcing some ground rules. That included not allowing me to spend the night in Kris's room. When she knew I was there anyway . . .

"I'm not leaving," I told her with the perfect balance of respect and authority.

Neither of us moved as she stared at me for several heavy seconds. "I could get into trouble for this," she finally said.

"You won't."

Her mouth curved into a skeptical frown, but she shut the door without another word.

A few hours later, I found out what Bruce had meant by restless, zombie-like activity. Sometime in the wee hours of the morning, Kris scared the hell out of me when she got up, I thought, to go to the bathroom. Half way across the room, she stumbled and fell on her face.

The door swung open. Kim took one look at Kris on the floor and me scrambling to free myself of the bed sheets wrapped around my legs, and shook her head in disapproval.

"Could you help me?" I shot at her.

Kim helped Kris to the bathroom while I busied myself with straightening the sheets I had made a mess of. Kris came out walking like a drunk zombie a few minutes later, and fell into bed with the grace of a two-ton elephant.

The transition she was going through reminded me of the five-day transformation all hybrids took when they started development. Only this one lasted three days, and the sedation was a lot heavier. On the bright side, this transition didn't include a raging fever and uncontrollable vomiting.

Kris made it through the rest of the night without another incident, and was sleeping soundly when I left in the morning. Kim promised to check on her periodically throughout the day. She wasn't thrilled when I told her that I would be back to spend the night again, but I didn't care what she thought. I planned to stay the next two nights with Kris whether Kim liked it or not.

My first stop was to Jared's office, where I demanded to resume control of my two combat classes. He was surprised by my request. Considering I hadn't wanted the classes in the first place, so was I, but after seeing Kand's teaching methods, I didn't really see that I had much of a choice. I certainly wouldn't let Kris go back to the class three days from now if he remained on as the instructor.

I promised to have a list of names for the mission to Jared

by the end of the day, then I went to relieve Kand of his duties. Fortunately, he didn't put up much of an argument. He left without a bloody nose, and I taught the morning combat class.

By now, most of the students had heard about yesterday's events, and had come to their own conclusions about the nature of my relationship with Kris. I didn't let some of the crude and wildly inaccurate comments I overheard bother me. Considering how often we were seen together, and our kiss on the beach, I knew it was only a matter of time before speculation started. At least this way, everyone understood one thing: Kris was with me, and unless some idiot wanted to go through me first, she was not to be messed with.

I had intended to swing by Kris's room over lunch, but got stopped by Jared outside the mess hall. Supervisor Jeffries was breathing down his neck about the mission, and he couldn't wait until the end of the day for names.

We both grabbed a sandwich to go, and spent the next hour brainstorming in his office until we had assembled a team we were both satisfied with. The list of names was sent to Jeffries for approval. By the end of the day, the individuals selected would be notified, and the mission details would be worked out.

Jeffries' urgency to push this mission along so quickly worried me, but I didn't have the authority to question his intentions. Or the power to change anything.

I left Jared's office, and glanced at my watch as I stepped outside. I had half an hour before my afternoon combat class started. I could swing by Alec's room to see if he was awake yet. Or I could swing by Kris's . . .

I hurried through the lobby of the girls' dormitory, and took the stairs two at a time the whole way to the top floor. Thanks to all the work I put in to staying in shape, I wasn't even winded by the time I got to Kris's door.

"Nothing to report," Kim announced.

I didn't bother to tell her I wasn't there for a report, and let myself in the room. Kris lay curled on her side, exactly where I had left her that morning. Her hair was strewn over the pillow in a beautifully haphazard way, her face relaxed, her lips a kissable soft pink.

I hovered over her, looking for any signs that she knew I was there, but saw none. That didn't stop me from doing what I came here for.

I leaned down to rest my forehead against hers. "I don't know if you can hear me or not, Kris," I whispered, "but I want you to know I love you. More than you will ever know."

I heard the door open behind me, and sensed Kim's eyes on me as I pressed my lips to Kris's. Just for a second, just enough to let her know I was there, if she were aware at all. Actually, the kiss was probably more for me—just enough to get me through the next few hours until I could be back here with her again.

I turned to find Micah shooting daggers at me. Kim stood behind him in the hallway with an irritated scowl on her face. Richie hovered just beyond her.

"Kim, he's not to be let in here until she's awake again," I ordered. "No. You know what? Not even then."

"I'm not here for her, asshole," Micah jeered. "I'm looking for you."

I smirked. "What could you possibly want me for?"

"Alec's awake. Thought you would want to know."

Okay, that changed things, but I didn't let him know that. I kept my cool.

"And?"

Micah shrugged. "Nothing."

I moved to the door, forcing Micah and Kim out ahead of me. With one last look at Kris, I shut the door. Without waiting, I moved down the hall at a fast pace, forcing Micah and Richie to hurry to keep up.

"What do you mean by nothing?" I questioned Micah over my shoulder.

"I mean there's been no change. He claims he doesn't feel any different."

At least he didn't wake up worse . . .

But no, that wasn't the way it was supposed to work. He should have woken up freed of the evil lurking within him, freed of a future as a Skotadi. Like Lillian. He wasn't supposed to wake up . . . the same. Because that meant Kris would wake up the same too, and that couldn't happen.

The door to Alec's room was open when I got there. Bruce stood in the doorway, his big frame blocking the entrance. He moved aside when he saw me approach, and I caught the grim look on his face.

Alec stopped mid-pace in the middle of his room when he saw me. "Someone has got some explaining to do."

"No change, huh?" I asked as I entered his room.

"Oh, no," he said. "There's been a change alright."

I glanced at Micah, whose brow creased in confusion. "What?" I asked Alec.

"This." He pointed to his face, more specifically his eyes.

Instinct and training forced me to take a step back at the same time Micah muttered a string of curses behind me. I never took my eyes off of Alec's, and I didn't know how I hadn't noticed them sooner.

Alec's eyes were ringed in gold.

Skotadi gold.

*   *   *   *   *

Despite the change in his eyes, Alec claimed he felt no different. Most importantly, he didn't have an overwhelming desire to maim every Kala on the island—well, no more than he had before drinking the potion. Looking at him as he sat on the edge of his bed, I felt no more threatened by him than before. He still looked like the same Alec to me.

Regardless, I had no idea what to do about his eyes, so I sent Micah and Richie to get Jared.

"Well . . ." Jared crossed his arms as he looked down at Alec. "Let's keep this turn of events between the six of us for now, until we know more." He turned to Bruce, who stood in the doorway. "In the meantime, be extra vigilant, and let me know of any . . . concerns."

"Whatever," Alec grumbled. "I told you I feel fine."

"Yeah, well . . . until we know why your rings changed from black to gold, security is going to be a little tighter around you,"

Jared returned.

Alec shook his head, and looked at me. "Probably should have Kris hold off until we know more."

Jared and I shared a look, which both Alec and Micah caught.

"Tell me she didn't," Alec said.

At the same time, Micah lurched toward me, perhaps with the intention of hitting me, but Richie wisely intercepted him with a forearm to the chest.

Jared pinched the space between his eyes. His voice sounded as strained as he looked. "We couldn't let her wait any longer for her own safety."

"Bullshit," Micah spat. "What are we going to do when she wakes up looking like that?" He pointed a finger at Alec.

"Hey, Golden Boy," Alec returned, taking a few steps toward Micah. "Why don't you go f—"

Jared stepped between the two of them, placing a hand on Alec's shoulder. "Easy," he said, then turned to Micah. "Aren't you able to sense Skotadi?"

Micah nodded. "That's right."

Jared lifted a brow. "Well?"

Micah crossed his arms. "He doesn't feel any different."

I had almost forgotten about Micah's strange built-in Skotadi radar. Kris and Alec had never set it off before. That had to be a good thing that Alec still didn't set it off. While we could all agree that something had changed, it didn't seem to be anything really significant at this time. Alec was still Alec, only now with Skotadi gold eyes. It seemed he hadn't been freed of his Skotadi like we had hoped would happen, but at this point, I was glad it hadn't turned out worse.

Kris was going to be pissed if she also woke up with her eyes ringed in gold, but I would deal with her in a few days. Hopefully by then, we would have a better idea of what had happened to Alec.

*   *   *   *   *

It was a miracle that I walked into class only five minutes late. I wasn't in any mood for the whispers I heard as I walked in. I wasn't in the mood for anything. Period. I made the students work on group drills so I could hang back with minimal interaction. That left me to my thoughts and laundry list of problems to deal with, but after an hour and a half, I hadn't come up with a solution to any of them.

And I still had the mission to deal with yet. By now, most of the team Jared and I had chosen should have been notified. Next, we would work on a plan of execution, but with all the distractions around me, I had a hard time concentrating on what needed to be done.

For now, I wanted to get back to Kris and forget about everything else for the rest of the day.

As I packed my bag to leave, I spotted Lillian standing outside the door as the students filed out of the classroom. Her guard hovered nearby, prompting the students to stare as they passed.

I took a deep breath to prepare myself, and followed the last student out the door.

Lillian glanced up with a timid smile as I approached. "Do you have another class coming?"

I shook my head. "I'm done for the day."

She brightened, and I saw the start of a real smile. "Do you have a few minutes? Maybe we could go for a walk?"

My heart hammered in my chest, *hard*. I wasn't ready for this. Not yet. On some level, I had hoped they would keep her in quarantine longer, so that I could avoid seeing her again and avoid the conversation I knew we had to have. Because no matter how stable she appeared, I didn't think she would be ready for what I had to say to her.

Though after already telling her I was done for the day, I had no excuse not to talk to her. "Yeah, sure. We can go for a walk."

I let Lillian lead the way, and wasn't surprised when we ended up on the beach. She had always loved walking on the beach. We had done it often. Then, it had felt natural. Now, it felt awkward.

I glanced at her, and wondered if she felt it, too. Her face remained an empty canvas, but I knew from experience that didn't mean much. Lillian was good—almost as good as me—at masking her feelings. Right now, she was doing a good job of it. I, on the other hand, was not.

I clenched my hands to keep them from shaking.

"I keep waiting to wake up from this nightmare," she said. "I keep waiting for the moment that I realize I didn't actually lose seven years of my life."

She looked at me, and I nodded like I understood. But I

didn't. How could I? I might have been lost for a portion of those seven years without her, but eventually, I had moved on. I wasn't in that daze of mourning anymore. But she was. Only for an entirely different reason.

I watched as tears welled up in her eyes. My hand twitched with five years' experience at being the one to wipe her tears away. I kept my hands fisted at my sides, knowing that wasn't my place anymore.

I knew then . . . that she knew. Maybe not *everything*, but she knew.

"I know it's not the same for you anymore . . ." She paused, perhaps to give me a chance to correct her, to tell her that her gut instinct was wrong, that I *was* still in love with her.

Instead, I offered her a weak smile as a form of apology. "It was the same for me at first, Lil. For a long time, it was."

She nodded, understanding registering in her eyes before she looked away. "It's been seven years . . ."

"Yeah."

"Even if it feels like yesterday to me . . ."

"I'm sorry."

"I can't expect you to still be in the same place, waiting for me, after seven years," she concluded, though the heavy sigh that followed her words hinted that she had hoped for it.

"We thought you were dead," I offered as explanation. As if that made it better.

"I know." She turned to me with a forced smile. "I'm sorry you had to go through that."

Few knew what it had been like for me when I thought

Lillian had died. If anyone could imagine my devastation, it was her. At that time, she had known me better than anyone.

"And I'm sorry for all that I've done to you since," she continued. "I only remember bits and pieces, and what I do remember is horrible."

"It's okay, Lil."

"No. I tried to kill you, Nathan. Multiple times." She swatted at a tear as it slid down her cheek, and shook her head as if disgusted with herself for crying. Just like the Lillian I remembered. "And that girl? The first chance I get to apologize to—"

"She knows it wasn't really you," I cut in quickly.

"I still want to let her know how sorry I am. If she can ever bear to look at me." Lillian hung her head solemnly, and muttered, "I don't know how you can stand to look at me right now."

"It wasn't you." Placing a finger under her chin, I lifted her head. "I know that. We all know that."

"I'm going to make it up to you," she said fiercely. "To all of you. Everything that I did before . . ."

"None of that matters now."

She nodded slowly, as if reluctantly accepting that the things she had done as a Skotadi could be forgiven. No matter how long it took, she needed to forgive herself. She wasn't there yet, but she would be. Someday.

We retraced our steps back to the village center. Few words passed between us along the way, but after the heaviness of our discussion on the beach, I welcomed the silence. We naturally parted—Lillian turning for the girls' dorm and me for the boys'—like we had done hundreds of times before, and I couldn't help the sensation of déjà vu that slammed in to me.

I nearly faltered, but forced my feet to keep moving.

Her voice stopped me. "Oh, and Nathan!" I turned in time to catch her smile—the first real one I had seen since she had woken up. "Thanks for bringing me back."

I nodded, and watched as she turned away.

Lillian was back, but only partially. She needed more time to recover from the emotional wounds, but the healing had started. I would do what I could to help her. We were no longer what we had once been, but I still considered her a friend, and she seemed content to have that.

She knew things weren't as they had been between us. I had that off my chest at least.

It dawned on me as I watched her walk away, that though she knew I had moved on, I hadn't told her everything. She didn't know I was in love with someone else.

I never actually told her about Kris.

Chapter 22

{Nathan}

Lillian was waiting for me again the next day, after my morning class.

"Friends, right?" she greeted as I approached.

"Of course."

She flashed me a bright smile. "Are you going to lunch?" She sounded hesitant, but hopeful.

I had intended to get something quick at the mess hall and then swing by Kris's room. She had been fine when I'd left this morning, and Kim assured me she was in good hands, but I still wanted to be with her. It was mostly for my benefit, not hers, considering she probably wouldn't know if I was there or not. After failing to tell Lillian the complete truth yesterday, I felt like an asshole and wanted to redeem myself.

But then, I was the only friend Lillian had right now, and I felt bad about leaving her to fend for herself when everyone on the island looked at her like she was still the enemy. I felt the need to protect her. For now. Until she got back on her feet.

And right now, she was still pretty shaky.

"Yeah, I can go to lunch," I said.

"I don't want to keep you from something."

I shrugged like I didn't have anything important to do. "No. I'm good. Let's go."

Predictably, every Kala we passed along the way stared. Some even stopped in their tracks—literally—to stare. The bolder ones whispered as we passed. The boldest yet—and if I ever found out who it was, they would hear from my fist—had the nerve to shout, *"Demon!"* Of course, he had waited until we were past and I didn't see his face.

Everyone in the mess hall—and I mean everyone—looked up when we walked in. From the collective gasp of surprise that greeted us and the stretch of silence that followed us through the dining hall, I assumed that this was the first glimpse most of the Kala were getting of her.

Of course, I was with her for her grand entrance. It would appear to everyone that the fabled couple had reunited. I supposed it didn't look good. But then, aside from a few rumors, none of them really knew the truth about Kris and me.

Well, except for a few. And every one of *them* was sitting at a table together, staring at us along with the rest. One set of eyes in particular bugged me more than the others.

Micah sat at a table with Richie. Alec and Bruce were there too, and I assumed that Jared had decided it was okay for Alec to go about his normal daily activities.

I saw Micah's smug smile, and I wanted nothing more than to smack it off his face. I felt his gaze boring into my back as I collected a sandwich from the deli, and by the time I sat down at the table across from him, I was drilling him with a hard glare.

I barely noticed when Lillian sat down beside me a moment later. Until Micah's eyebrows rose in mock curiosity.

"What?" I spat, not bothering to reign back on the hostility.

He grinned, and if he weren't the Kala's golden boy, I'd call it a slightly evil looking grin. "Going to introduce us to your friend?" he asked, putting unnecessary emphasis on the last word.

"You already know who she is."

Micah looked pleased with himself. Belatedly, I realized that he enjoyed getting me worked up. I would have to remember to work on controlling my reactions around him, if only to rob him of the joy he got out of pissing me off.

Feeling Alec's eyes on me, I glanced in his direction. I shook my head at his bewildered expression. He knew I despised Micah, but even he was surprised by the level of disgust radiating off of me at the moment.

"Okay, anyway . . ." Micah drew slowly, forcing me to bite the inside of my cheek to maintain a neutral expression. He reached across the table, extending a hand to Lillian. "I'm Micah. I know we technically already met, but I haven't met *this* version of you. Much better than the former, I'm sure."

Lillian accepted his hand politely, but I recognized the wariness with which she regarded him. Either she had picked up on his smugness, or she was reacting to my obvious dislike of him.

I busied myself with my sandwich as the others at the table introduced themselves.

"Alec?" she asked thoughtfully, coming back to him after the others had finished their introductions. "I think I remember you."

He shot her a cocky grin. That certainly hadn't changed. "Most girls do."

She made a noise that sounded suspiciously close to a laugh, and I nearly choked on my sandwich. Figured. I should have introduced her to Alec sooner. Only he could succeed in healing seven years' worth of remorse, and resulting depression, in under two minutes.

"I don't doubt that," she returned.

And now they were flirting.

I shoved another bite into my mouth, suddenly eager to get out of there. The last thing I needed was to witness more of Alec's natural charm.

"So, Nathan?" Micah called.

I glanced up silently. With my mouth stuffed, I couldn't say what I really wanted to say to him.

"Have you seen Kris lately?"

I chewed quickly, suddenly eager to have full use of my mouth.

"Of course he has," Alec interrupted, dropping the flirtation with Lillian, which had to have been a first for him.

"It's day two," I answered stiffly—not that I thought he deserved any response from me, but Lillian was now watching us curiously and I figured I should play nice. "She'll be waking up tomorrow."

Micah opened his mouth to say something else, but Lillian

interrupted him.

"Waking up?" she questioned.

Alec volunteered an answer first. "She took the same potion they gave you. So did I, and I woke up yesterday with my eyes looking like this. I just might be a natural bad boy though, so we're all eager to see if it works better for her than it did for me."

"Works for her?" Lillian shook her head in genuine confusion, and I realized that she didn't remember who Kris was.

"Kris is the girl that the Skotadi created. You were apparently assigned with the task of tracking her down," I said to Lillian, hoping that was enough to jog her memory.

Lillian's face contorted. "Oh, God. That's her. That's the girl."

I nodded. "Yeah."

"And she's taken the same potion that changed me?"

"Yeah."

She turned to Alec. "And so did you, but it . . ."

"We don't know what it did," I finished. Looking at Alec now, he still looked the same. Even his eyes were easier to overlook than they had been yesterday. They flared more when he was angry now. Otherwise, the gold kind of blended in to the green.

"It sure as hell didn't do what you said it was supposed to do," Alec fired at me.

Lillian looked at me, a silent question visible in her eyes.

"I met Circe, and she gave me this potion," I explained. "She said that it would bring out someone's true potential, and protect their soul from evil." I saw a flicker of recognition pass over

Lillian's face. It passed so quickly that if I hadn't known her so well I might not have noticed it. "We gave it to you, Alec, and Kris."

"It worked on you," Alec concluded.

Lillian looked to Alec, then back to me. "You gave them both a potion enchanted with a *potential spell,* and it was created by Circe?"

I nodded uneasily. I had nearly forgotten that Lillian was an Incantator. She understood things that I couldn't begin to understand about spells and potions, and the wrinkle in her brow concerned me.

She turned away to study the table in silence. Finally, she murmured, "I've never heard of it being used in that way. But Circe knows a lot more than I do."

She almost spoke as if she *knew* Circe. Personally. "Did you ever meet her?"

Lillian shook her head absentmindedly. "I don't think so." She didn't sound so sure, but it wasn't because she was hiding something. No. She legitimately didn't remember.

"Do you remember much about Incantation?" I ventured, hoping for an opportunity to get some answers about the significance behind *potential spells,* and why the concept seemed to concern her.

Or Callie. As of yesterday, Lillian still hadn't remembered anything about Callie, but the doctor said her memory could come back at any time. We had to keep trying.

Lillian shrugged with little conviction. She was distracted by her own thoughts. "Some things have come back."

I was about to probe for details when her head snapped up, her eyes wide when they turned to me. "Is everyone still scared of Incantators like they used to be?" she whispered.

I understood her fear, and quickly tried to alleviate it. "We all know," I said, looking around the table at the others. "Kris is an Incantator, too, and we're all trying to help her. Your secret is safe with everybody here."

Lillian looked around the table, and must have seen what she needed to see for reassurance, but her expression still carried an edge of uneasiness. I decided to let the questions about the potion and Callie go for the time being, and let Lillian finish her lunch in peace. When she finished, she pushed back from her chair and excused herself, claiming a sudden bout of exhaustion.

What she didn't realize was that her time as a Skotadi hadn't changed her cues. I still recognized them, and I knew the exhaustion excuse was nothing more than that: an excuse. Something was bothering her. I just didn't know what.

Instead of digging for answers, I let her go with the intention of giving her some time to sort through the thoughts that were bothering her before I asked her about them. I would have let it go entirely, but I couldn't because a part of whatever was bothering Lillian was related to Kris.

I wouldn't—I *couldn't*—let something that might affect Kris go.

Alec slid into Lillian's now empty seat beside me. His eyes were on her as she walked away. "What do you suppose that was all about?"

"I don't know, but I'll find out."

Alec nodded thoughtfully. "So the two of you went out, huh?"

My hand faltered as I reached for my drink. "Yeah."

Alec let out a soft whistle. "I wouldn't want to be you right now."

I glanced at Alec and saw that his attention remained on Lillian's retreating backside. Though I knew I would regret it, I asked, "Why is that exactly?"

Alec looked at me like he thought I was joking. Or an idiot, because as far as he was concerned, the answer was obvious. He lifted a hand in gesture to Lillian, and made a noise that equated, '*duh.*'

I turned back to what was left of my sandwich with a groan.

"I just don't get it," Alec mused, speaking more to himself than to me. "I mean, you're not a bad looking guy, I guess, but still . . ."

I turned to glare at him. '*Not a bad looking guy*'? Really?

He finally looked away from Lillian, probably only because she had made it outside by now, and he could no longer stare at her ass. He looked at me as if I held the answers to all of life's mysteries.

"How do you get all the hot ones?" he asked. "I mean . . . there's *her*, and she is . . ." He blew out a puff of air, "and then you have the perfect girl, who for some reason wants you more than me, and she is . . . well, you know . . . but then there's . . ." He gestured to the door behind which Lillian had disappeared, "Well, you know . . . and then there was that hottie on the beach? I mean . . . I just don't . . . wow, that's all I can . . . just wow."

"Can you finish just *one* of your thoughts?" I snapped.

"Sorry. I get like this around the really hot ones," Alec muttered, and settled a look of disbelief on me. "Yeah, I really don't envy you at all right now."

I shook my head because . . . well, he should envy me. Only one part of his ridiculous ramblings rang true. I did have the perfect girl, and she was the only one who mattered.

As I turned away from Alec, my eyes swung up and caught Micah's gaze.

The smirk on his face combined with the slight shake of his head told me exactly what he thought. *Just a matter of time . . .*

*　　*　　*　　*　　*

After lunch, I met with Jared to go over some details for the upcoming mission. Supervisor Jeffries had given him a list of objectives. He wanted specifics on things like *how many, where, and why*, but he left it up to Jared and me to devise a plan to get the Intel. Then it was up to me to lead a team in obtaining it.

After an hour of planning, I left Jared's office with a throbbing headache. For the second day in a row, I ordered the students in my afternoon class to do group drills while I laid low with my aspirin and bottle of water. By the end of class, my problems hadn't gone away, and neither had my headache.

As I prepared to leave, I caught a glimpse of the one person who could make it worse.

I slung my bag over my shoulder and turned for the door with dread. Not only because it was Micah, and he was the last person I wanted to see, but that was especially true after the scene at lunch earlier.

Not to mention, since Kris had been in her semi-coma, there had been something *every single day* that had delayed me from getting to her when that was all I really wanted to do.

I cast a questioning glance at Richie as I approached. From his guarded expression and ready-for-anything posture, I gathered he knew just how little patience I had left for Micah. Considering Richie's sole purpose was to protect Micah, I wondered why he let Micah near me at all.

"What do you want, Micah?"

He shook his head with a smirk. "Just wanted to tell you thanks."

I knew better. I knew I shouldn't let myself get baited by him, but sometimes . . . oh, sometimes I let him get the best of me. "For what exactly?"

He smiled, and it was anything but friendly. "I told you."

I sighed, and shouldered past him, uninterested in playing his game—whatever it may be this time. I gave Richie a look that all but begged for him to keep Micah away from me.

"I told you that you would screw it up," Micah called after me.

Of course. I should have known what prompted this visit. I spun around, jabbing a finger at him. Out of the corner of my eye, I saw Richie flinch. "I haven't screwed anything up!"

"Maybe not yet." Micah shrugged. "But the events are set into motion."

I turned, determined to walk away this time. Determined, for once, to not let him get to me.

"I saw it, you know," he called after me. "It's just the start. You haven't told her about Kris!"

It took every ounce of self-control that I had not to turn around, to silence him with a strategically placed fist to the jaw. Somehow, I held myself back and kept it together. I wouldn't give him the satisfaction of a response. And no way in hell would I admit to him that he was right. I hadn't told Lillian about Kris yet. But it wasn't for the reasons Micah thought. He wouldn't understand.

As expected, Kim stood outside of Kris's room. She didn't question me when I wordlessly opened the door and let myself in.

Kris was curled up on her side, asleep and snoring softly. I watched her for a moment before I lifted my shirt over my head and tossed it to the floor. The numbers on the clock beside her bed read 3:42, but the time didn't matter to me.

Nothing would keep me from being where I wanted to be. Not today. As I pulled her limp body to me, and settled into a comfortable position, I concluded that tomorrow everything would be different.

Kris would be okay. And Lillian would know exactly who Kris was, and exactly what she meant to me.

Chapter 23

{Kris}

I tried waking you before I left, but you only rolled over and snored louder. I guess you weren't ready to get up yet. As fun as it has been listening to you talk in your sleep the last three nights, I can't wait to see you conscious again. I'll be back to check on you after class. If you're up, we'll grab lunch. I'm sure you'll be starving!

Love,

Nathan

I folded up the note with a smile and slid it behind the front cover of the leather journal Nathan had gotten me for my birthday.

I was only mildly mortified about the snoring. He had told me once before that I sounded like a purring kitten with a cold. No, the snoring comment didn't bother me. I was more disappointed that I had missed him.

Checking the time, I guessed that he had left recently. He'd had just enough time to make it back to his room, shower, dress, and should be strolling into class right about now. Which meant I would have to wait a whole hour and a half to see him.

At least the delay gave me plenty of time to shower and make myself presentable. Three days without a shower had left my hair a greasy mess, my face an oily pimple factory, and the rest of me smelling anything but fresh. Not nearly as bad as my transformation into a hybrid months ago, but enough to put taking a shower at the top of my to-do list.

Afterwards, I stood wrapped in a towel, staring at myself in the mirror for no less than five minutes. Even then, I had a hard time understanding what I saw in the reflection.

How could my eyes be *worse*?

I did a quick self-check. My inner Skotadi felt . . . calm. No, she definitely hadn't taken over control of my body as my appearance suggested. Oddly, I didn't feel anything. I felt no different than I had when I went to sleep three days ago. Maybe less scared . . .

But way more confused.

I checked the time again. The shower had only eaten up thirty minutes, but suddenly I had plans that would take up the rest of my morning. I threw on some clothes, pulled my still wet hair up into a hasty ponytail, and made a beeline for the door.

Kim quickly scampered to her feet at the sound of the door swinging open. I met her gaze briefly, but looked away before I could see her reaction to my eyes. She fell into step behind me without a word as I hurried outside and over to the boys' dormitory.

He had better be there, I thought as I climbed all the way to the top floor. Stepping into the hallway, I saw Bruce standing at his post and breathed a sigh of relief. I didn't bother to hide my eyes from Bruce. From the frown on his face as he studied me, I knew my suspicions were right.

I knocked, Alec's door swung open, and I stared into eyes that matched mine.

I pushed my way into the room without an invitation. "What's going on, Alec?"

I heard him mutter something to Bruce before he shut the door. When he turned to me, his expression remained neutral, calm. Much calmer than I felt. "We don't know yet."

"You woke up two days ago, like *that*," I pointed to his eyes, "and you still don't know what's going on?"

He shrugged, almost apologetically. "You weren't supposed to drink it yet."

"Yeah, well, things changed." A quick look at the crease in Alec's brow confirmed that he didn't know why I hadn't waited. "Apparently, there are a ton of Skotadi grouping on the mainland. I suspect they're here for me, for *us*. Who knows? We thought it would be best if I didn't wait, just in case the Skotadi decide to make a move."

Alec silently moved to sit on his bed. He stared at the floor for a few moments before he looked up. "One thing has changed," he admitted softly. "I haven't told anyone, but you know that pull we were feeling, to the ocean?"

I nodded, and waited.

"The past two mornings, I woke up on the beach. All day yesterday, the urge to go back there kept growing stronger and stronger."

I hadn't felt it yet. From the pained look on Alec's face, I knew I didn't want to.

"You think it might be the Skotadi?" Alec ventured. "Like they're calling to us, or something?"

That had been a theory of mine from the start. Learning that the Skotadi were grouping so close to the island strengthened that theory. And now? I didn't want to think about what waking up with Skotadi-gold eyes and a stronger pull toward something beyond the horizon could mean.

"I don't feel any different," I said as if that somehow made everything else okay. "I don't feel any more Skotadi than I did before."

"Me neither," Alec said. "Except . . . well, yesterday I was practicing my specialties. You know yielding fire has always been my weakest one, but yesterday, I did it . . . *well.*"

I plopped down on the bed beside Alec with a sigh. "Does Nathan know all of this?"

"He knows about the eyes, but that's it. I've kept the pull we've both felt and my strengthened specialties to myself. They've already got Bruce on *high alert* until we figure out what's going on."

Great. That was all I needed. Kim and Micah . . . extra vigilant. I knew Nathan wouldn't push for extra security on me, but I thought maybe it would be best to keep Alec's admissions between us for now. Until I found out if I would experience the same phenomenon as Alec. Definitely until we figured out a little more about what was happening.

Right now . . . I really just wanted to see Nathan again. If anything could make me feel better about the uncertainty of the recent events, it was seeing him.

I promised Alec that we would catch up later, and compare notes. Then I angled across the village center to the Education Building.

I waited in the hallway outside his classroom as the students filed out the door. Most ignored me; a few tossed curious glances in my direction. I wondered what gossip the rumor mill had been churning out the past three days, but then I saw him and none of that mattered anymore.

"I'll wait outside," Kim murmured.

I nodded without taking my eyes off Nathan, and Kim left.

The last student exited, and I hovered in the doorway as Nathan checked his watch and swung his duffel bag over his shoulder. My bright smile greeted him when he turned in my direction.

In an instant, he swept me into his arms. In the next instant, he pulled me into the room and backed me into the wall as he engaged the lock on the door behind me.

No words passed between us. Words would have gotten in the way of kissing.

We met like it hadn't been only three days since we had last seen each other, but *years*. Desperation and need fueled us both, and life's basic needs for things like air were no longer important. Re-familiarizing myself with the hardness of his chest, the curve of his shoulders, and lastly, the tuffs of soft hair at the back of his neck were all that mattered. Not until his lips slid from mine to leave a searing hot trail along my jawline did I finally allowed myself a breath.

Nathan's low chuckle in my ear was, at that moment, the sexiest sound I had ever heard. I attempted a head tilt that would put our mouths together again, but Nathan pressed his lips to my temple instead.

"You have to remember to breathe," he murmured before pulling back to look down at me. My hands were still clasped tightly behind his neck, preventing him from going too far.

"Didn't seem important at the time." I combed my fingers through the longer hairs within my reach.

If he went too long between haircuts, his hair started to curl slightly at the nape. I didn't dare say anything because once he noticed, a haircut was inevitable . . . and I preferred it like this.

Nathan leaned back to survey my face. His eyes were tinted with a trace of concern, and I knew we had moved on from greeting to getting down to business.

"Well?" he probed. "How do you feel?"

I reluctantly dropped my hands from their death grip on his neck with a sigh of defeat. "No different."

"You've seen your eyes?"

I nodded. "I already saw Alec, too," I added. "So nobody has any ideas?"

His head shook slowly, solemnly. "No. I'm sorry. I don't . . . I don't really know what to say."

"It's okay."

I saw that the outcome, and not knowing what it meant, tore him up. Trying so hard to find the solution, and finally thinking he had found it, only to be let down once again, had taken its toll on him. I wrapped my arms around his middle in an attempt to make him feel better.

"I'm no worse. Maybe it did work, and we just won't know right away?"

I wasn't hopeful, but I hated to see Nathan so defeated. It reinforced my decision not to tell him what Alec had told me about the pull and the increased strength of his specialties. Hearing that certainly wouldn't make Nathan feel any better, and he already worried too much. I would tell him once Alec and I figured out what it meant.

"I guess time will tell, right?" Nathan said.

"Why wait?" I pulled back with a grin. "Why don't you say something to make me mad, and we'll find out right now just how strong my inner Skotadi is?"

He barked out a laugh. "Oh, no. I'm not that stupid." He grabbed me by the hands and pulled me away from the door so that he could open it. He pulled me close, long enough to plant a hasty kiss to my forehead before ushering me into the hallway ahead of him.

"You hungry?" he asked.

"Starving."

"Lead the way . . ."

I knew the drill. The hallway was packed with Kala this time of day. Despite whatever speculation surrounded the status of our relationship, Nathan intended to maintain some level of distance between us in front of them.

Because I walked in front of Nathan, and rounded the

corner to the exit first, I was the first to see my biggest nightmare.

My steps faltered and I barely avoided crashing into Lillian as she hovered there in the middle of the hallway, almost as if she were waiting for us. That observation, combined with our history, immediately put me on the defensive.

At least she didn't seem all that interested in me. It took me a moment to register where her gaze was directed. Behind me. On Nathan.

I felt him behind me. My reassurance. My rock. His hand on my back, gently pushing me forward, kept me grounded even as I realized that he intended for us to greet Lillian.

Her gaze swept from him to me, and a timid smile graced her lips. "You're Kris?"

I gave a subtle nod. She sounded unsure, like she didn't know who I was, and she glanced at Nathan as if for reassurance. I desperately wanted to look over my shoulder to see his reaction to seeing her, but I didn't dare turn my back on Lillian. Sure she was cured, or whatever, but after all she had done to me, to Nathan—to everyone I cared about—I was a bit gun-shy.

Her hesitant smile widened and she took a cautious step forward, extending a hand. "I'm Lillian. I know you already know that, but I wanted to officially meet you, as the new me."

I accepted her hand, but dropped it as quickly as politely possible. It was just too weird . . . in so many ways.

"And I'm very, very sorry for everything I did to you while I was under Skotadi control," she continued sincerely. Her eyes darted over my shoulder, where I felt Nathan's firm presence. "I don't remember all of it, but I know I've caused you a considerable amount of suffering that I can never undo."

"It wasn't really you," I offered meekly.

She smiled again, and I hated that it accentuated her natural beauty. Even when she had been a Skotadi, and cold in every way, I suspected she had once been very pretty. I had, unfortunately, been right.

"Thank you for understanding." Again, she looked at Nathan. Her smile grew, and I saw the unmistakable twinkle in her eyes.

I recognized it because I had the same twinkle in my eyes when I looked at Nathan.

"You were right," she said to him.

Right about what exactly? I shot a look over my shoulder at Nathan. He glanced at me, and I recognized the worry that creased his brow.

Looking back at Lillian, and seeing the way she looked at him, it finally hit me. She sure didn't look like a jilted ex who had met the love of her life's new girlfriend for the first time. If I had woken after seven years still in love with a guy, and found out that he was in love with someone else, I knew I wouldn't be able to stand in front of her with a smile on my face. I definitely wouldn't be looking at my ex like Lillian looked at Nathan.

"Going to lunch?" Lillian asked, her eyes moving back and forth between Nathan and me.

"Yeah, in a minute," Nathan said. "I have to talk to Kris first."

"Okay. I'll see you there."

I stared after Lillian as she walked away, and a hatred-spurred heat spread from the roots of my hair to the tips of my toes. My body felt like it was on fire. Angry fire.

"Kris . . ."

I didn't turn. "You didn't tell her." His hand came down on my shoulder, and I shrugged it off. "It's been three days. I've been asleep for three days, and you still haven't told her."

In that instant, I knew that the potion had not worked. Not like it had for Lillian. I could feel my inner Skotadi straining to burst free. I held her in check—a feat only made possible by the charm I still wore around my neck. I had no doubt that I was still very much a Skotadi at my core.

Of all the people to make me realize that, and it had to be Nathan. The one who I had entrusted with my whole heart . . . and soul.

I slowly turned to face him, but kept my eyes down to conceal the devastation that I knew he would see in them.

"Kris, I'm sorry," he said. "I will tell her. I'm just not sure she's ready to hear it yet."

"It didn't work," I muttered.

His head shook once in confusion. "What? What didn't work?"

"The potion." Gritting my teeth, I took a step back, away from him.

When I finally met his gaze, his eyes widened at what he saw. My eyes had already been Skotadi gold, but now? Now I knew that they were surging. I spun away, intent on getting as far away from Nathan as I could. I didn't get far before he hooked my arm. As he twirled me toward him, his mouth opened, but I would never know what excuse he had to give.

"Let me go." I attempted to rip my arm out of his hold, but he was too strong. "Let go of my arm. *Now.*" I tried again, harder, and this time I pulled free.

"Kris . . ." He took a step forward, narrowing the space between us, and I held out a hand to stop him from coming any closer.

"I need some time alone," I said.

This time, he let me go. With each step, I expected him to stop me, but he didn't, and by the time I pushed through the doors of the Education Building, I was practically running.

I didn't know where I would go. All I knew was that I needed to put some distance between Nathan and me. For one, after the incident a few months ago when I had nearly killed him, I didn't want him around me ever again when my Skotadi pushed for control of my body . . . and right now, I shook with the struggle to keep her from taking over. Secondly, he had been the one to push me to this point, and because of that, I didn't want to look at him.

I marched through the village center in a blind rage. I didn't realize where I had ended up until I knocked on a door, and Alec's face appeared in front of me.

He took one look at me, and said, "Whoa. Get in here."

I crossed the room with long angry strides, but when I turned and saw the concern on Alec's face, I crumbled. In an instant, Alec wrapped an arm across my shoulders and sat me down on the edge of the bed.

Then I told him everything. From my initial concerns about Nathan's past with Lillian, to his promise that nothing would change between us, to the realization that, despite his promise, things were changing. I felt it, I saw it. I had feared it would happen, and it was happening.

My shoulders sagged in defeat once I finished my rant, and I realized that the anger, and my Skotadi's presence, had diminished in the process. Now, I felt nothing but sadness.

"Let's go for a walk," Alec suggested lightly.

I sniffed. "A walk?"

"Yeah." He pulled on my arm as he moved the door. "Come on."

As we walked through the village center, with Bruce and Kim trailing us, Alec gave me his blunt opinion.

"Nathan would be an idiot to screw things up with you," he said.

I laughed. "You're so good with words, Alec."

"I'm serious though. He knows how lucky he is." Alec's voice took on a distant, soft tone that made me turn to look at him. He quickly threw me off with an easy smile. "I think you should give him the benefit of the doubt."

"Coming from you, that's saying something."

Alec smirked. "Don't tell him I said that."

We continued in silence a few more minutes before I realized where we had ended up. I sucked in a sharp breath as a small wave of water lapped over my feet.

"Did you mean to come here?" I asked Alec as I stared out at the ocean.

"No." He glanced over his shoulder at Bruce and Kim, who stood several yards behind us. "But pretend we meant to do this."

I didn't feel the intense pull now, not like I had that first night, but I knew something had drawn us to the beach . . . again. Something—something just out of my sight—waited for us, and would come for us soon.

I bumped Alec's arm as I blindly reached for his hand. Without a word, he took it, and the warmth of his hand chased away the chills.

Though I feared the unknown that awaited us on the horizon, I felt empowered by the fact that I wasn't alone. I had Alec, and we would face it together.

Chapter 24

{Nathan}

My alarm sounded at its normal time, and I rolled over to smack the snooze button. I laid there in a state of semi-awareness for the entire ten minutes before the buzzer went off again. This time, I sat up, put my feet on the floor, and rubbed my head as if that could wake me up.

I needed a haircut.

I needed to fix everything with Kris.

Shit. I needed more sleep.

It wouldn't have been so bad if I hadn't been out until six in the morning with a small team, gathering Intel on the Skotadi on the mainland. It had been a bullshit assignment. In my opinion, a huge waste of time. But I had my orders and, according to Supervisor Jeffries, if I wanted to stay on the island, I needed to obey them.

It hadn't been completely bogus, I supposed. We now had an idea of how many Skotadi had assembled—at least five hundred from our observations—and the locations of three of their hideouts. But that was all we had learned. We still knew nothing about why they were there, or what their plans were.

Definitely not worth the exhaustion I was left with this morning.

And . . . it had prevented me from mending things with Kris last night.

Granted, she hadn't been in her room when I stopped by. I tried not to obsess over where she could have been. When I had finally crawled into bed this morning, I decided that it might have been a good thing, not seeing her yet. It would be better if I had resolved the issue with Lillian before I saw Kris again.

So that was my goal today. To make sure Lillian knew *everything*. And *then* mend things with Kris.

Because I had slept in as late as possible, I missed the usual breakfast hour, and grabbed an old pastry on my way to class. Afterwards, I didn't need to worry about finding Lillian.

She had made a habit of stopping by after class, and this morning was no different. But instead of going straight to lunch, I suggested we take a walk. We ended up on the pier—a short one unlike those found on most tourist beaches, but it provided us with enough privacy for the conversation I intended to have.

But before we got to that, I wanted to talk to her about something else that had been on my mind.

"Have you remembered anything else about your Incantation abilities?"

"You mean as far as what I did to your friend?" Lillian eyed the horizon as she tucked a chunk of hair, blown free by the breeze, behind her ear. "No, I don't remember anything about that yet."

I looked down to hide my disappointment. It wasn't Lillian's fault, but I was growing more impatient with each passing day—only out of concern for Callie. Though the doctor insisted she was being kept alive by something unnatural, none of us knew how much time she actually had left.

"I've tried doing a few basic spells," Lillian continued. "Can't do much of anything, it seems. It's like I could only do it as a Skotadi."

I had wondered about that myself—how Lillian had become an Incantator in the first place. It wasn't a skill she'd had as a Kala. But I hoped it was something she would continue to have the ability to do, for Callie's sake.

And that was assuming Lillian's memory returned, and she knew how to help Callie.

"How's the rest of your memory coming along?"

We had reached the end of the pier and I leaned against the railing on my forearms to look down at the water below. Beside me, Lillian rested her elbows on the railing, facing the other direction.

"It's coming in flashes. A little bit at a time, but nothing I can connect together yet."

I hesitated to consider my next words. I didn't want to scare her away, but I needed to know. "But you pieced something together the other day. In the mess hall."

She diverted her eyes, and I knew my intuition had been right.

"What is it, Lil?" I pressed softly. "You know you can trust me."

Her head bobbed slowly before her gaze lifted to meet mine. "I'm not really sure, to be honest with you. I don't completely remember, but when you mentioned Circe and the potential spell, something registered."

"A memory?"

"Yes . . . and no. More like a feeling of déjà vu," she murmured. "Like I was familiar with the spell, and with Circe, but I have no real memory of either. Do you think . . ." Lillian trailed off with a shake of her head. "No, forget it."

"What?" I grabbed her shoulder, forcing her to look at me. "Tell me."

"It was a *bad* feeling, Nathan," she eventually said. "I'm not so sure that this potential spell is going to produce the result you're hoping for. I'm not sure Circe had the best intentions when she gave it to you."

"She's a goddess," I returned with a little more vehemence than I had intended. "They need Kris . . ." I trailed off, and decided to drop it. I didn't want to get into it what all I had learned about Kris from the gods. Not now. Not with Lillian. I hadn't even talked to Kris about everything yet.

Besides, as far as Kris went, there was only one thing Lillian needed to know.

I shot Lillian a smile in the hopes that it would offset my near-asshole moment. "Let's not talk about that stuff right now, okay?"

Lillian sagged in relief, and her eyes held mine for a second too long, forcing me to look away first. Shit. This was going to be hard.

I actually felt my heart pounding in my chest, and heard the blood rushing to my head. My hands were damp when I rubbed them together, and I had to swallow a few times to dislodge the lump that had formed in my throat.

"Hey, Lil, I need to . . ." I started at the same time Lillian said, "Do you think it's possible . . ."

We both stopped and looked at each other. "Go ahead," I said.

Lillian hesitated, then looked down at the water lapping against the pier beneath us. "I know you're not in the same place we were seven years ago, but . . . do you think it would be possible for us to get there again, maybe start over?"

I grimaced. *Damn, I should have gone first.* My mouth opened to answer her, to say the words quickly—like ripping off a band aid—but they hung up in my throat.

Lillian misunderstood my hesitation, and turned to mirror me, excitement lighting up her eyes. "I know we could get back there again . . ." And then she did the last thing I expected her to do.

She stepped into me . . . and kissed me.

Her lips were on mine for only a second before my brain caught up to what was happening. Though something familiar that had been dormant for a long time stirred at the contact, something much stronger stomped it out.

My feelings for Kris were too strong. What I had with her was too real.

I pulled away from Lillian immediately, the words finally

ready. But as my mouth opened to say them, a streak of color out of the corner of my eye caught my attention. I turned my head toward the other end of the pier in time to see a blur of strawberry blonde darting off the beach.

I left Lillian standing there as I took off in a run.

*   *   *   *   *

{Kris}

I fought back the tears as I ran through the village center, with Kim hurrying to keep up with me. She had seen them kissing too, and when I had turned to leave, the pitied look on her face said it all.

Stupid me . . . I had been sitting at lunch, wondering where Nathan was, and wanting to see him after our argument yesterday. I had wanted to apologize for running off yesterday, to tell him I forgave him for not telling Lillian everything, and to let him know that I would let him take as much time as he needed to tell her. Micah had said he saw Nathan walking towards the beach, so I stupidly went there looking for him.

Stupid. Stupid. Stupid. I should have known.

I finally reached my room, and slammed the door shut behind me, leaving Kim in the hallway. Only then did I crumble to my bed and let the tears fall.

A moment later, a soft knock pulled my face out of the pillow. Suspecting Kim, I opened the door.

It was Nathan. "Kris—"

I slammed the door in his face, and locked it. I had seen him break a door down once before, so I stayed there, both hands splayed against the door as if I could will it to stay shut.

Instead of ramming the door, he knocked again. "Kris, let me in."

I stared at the tiny swirls in the grain of the wooden door, and listened. I almost willed Kim to say something, to stand up for me, to be the girl in another girl's corner.

I heard no voices, but another knock vibrated the wood under my hands. "Come on, Kris. Please?"

Nothing. I said nothing. I had nothing to say. I was in too much shock. I had heard the expression before, but never understood until this moment. I was actually shocked speechless.

I heard muffled voices on the other side of the door, but couldn't make out what was said. I pressed my ear to the door, but only heard silence. The hallway was silent. After a moment, I backed away from the door.

That was it? He left?

Granted, I didn't want to see him, but the fact that he wasn't fighting harder—fighting for me—stung a little. Almost as much as the reason I was upset with him in the first place.

Images of what I had witnessed on the pier played through my head like a movie, just as painful now as it had been then. The tears that stung my eyes now were fresh.

I went to the bathroom for a tissue, and grimaced at my reflection in the mirror.

This is what I have been reduced to? A tear-stricken weakling? Over a boy?

Granted, Nathan wasn't just any . . . boy. No. I was in love with him in the way I had always imagined love was supposed to be like—like I saw in the cheesy romantic comedies Callie used to make me watch. I had thought he was the real deal. I had thought that he would never, ever, hurt me. He had promised me . . .

Belatedly, I realized that my Skotadi wasn't even straining to make her opinion known. No. She was quiet because I wasn't really mad right now. I was upset. I was sad. My heart was *crushed*.

By the one person I thought I could trust.

Once the rolling, uncontrollable sobs had quieted to an occasional sniffle, I splashed cold water on my face to wash away the redness and cool my puffy eyes. As I patted my face dry with a towel, I heard the balcony door sliding shut.

My stomach dropped. *He wouldn't* . . .

Then he was there, standing in the open bathroom door like he had every right to be there.

"Get out," I demanded.

He shook his head. "Not until you talk to me."

I didn't want to talk to him. Not now. Not after what I saw. I didn't even want to look at him right now, but his wide stance made it clear that he wasn't about to go anywhere.

"Fine. I'll leave." I marched the short distance to the doorway, and wiggled through the narrow space between him and the doorjamb. He let me get as far as the bed before he moved to stop me.

One of his arms encircled my waist, and his fingers dug into my hip with the strain of holding me back. "What are you doing? Where are you going to go?"

Despite my best attempts at resisting, he managed to spin me around to face him. Fine. He wanted me to look at him? I would do the next best thing.

I lifted up onto my tiptoes so that we were nearly eye to eye, and sneered, "Anywhere but here! I don't want to see you. I can't stand to look at you right now."

I shoved against his chest in another attempt to dislodge myself from his hold. Of course, he was built like a tree, and didn't budge an inch.

"I don't care."

I scoffed. "That's obvious."

His eyes squeezed shut with a sigh and he shook his head. "Kris, you don't know—"

"I'd rather be spared the details. Thank you."

Again, I pressed my palms against his chest. This time, a little bit of angry-Skotadi strength seeped through, and I managed to push him back a step. Enough to rip myself out of his grasp.

I made it three steps before two hands came down on my waist. Before I could wiggle free, my feet were lifted off the floor and my back was pulled against an unyielding chest. The room spun as he hurled me back into the room. I didn't let it happen without a fight—complete with kicking the air and clawing at the arms around my middle.

Nathan's response was to toss me on the bed like a rag doll. Before I could scramble to my feet, he was on me, straddling my legs with his weight. He seemed intent on not letting me up, but that didn't stop me from trying. As his hold on me tightened, my anger intensified and my strength increased. Soon . . . soon I would be able to put up a decent fight. He couldn't hold me down forever.

He seemed to realize that too, and there was desperation in his eyes as he pleaded, "Listen to me, Kris! Nothing happened!"

I lifted onto my elbows, nearly touching my nose to his. "I saw you!"

"It wasn't what you think. It—"

I shoved his shoulders, nearly catching him off guard. He recovered quickly, grabbed ahold of my wrists and pinned them above my head.

He was still too strong for me. My arms rendered useless, I resorted to trying to kick him off of me. He thwarted that attempt by shifting his weight and wrapping his legs around mine until I couldn't move them. I couldn't move anything. He was just so much bigger and stronger . . . and heavier . . . than me. By the time exhaustion forced me to give up trying to escape, our limbs were entwined and twisted together like a deformed jumbo pretzel.

"You'd really be in trouble if Lillian walked in right about now," I smirked.

Nathan leaned down until his nose touched mine. "I. Do. Not. Care." He emphasized each word with a bite that made me cringe inwardly.

But his words made me do what I shouldn't have done. I met his eyes, and something deep down inside of me churned. I may have been furious with him, but I loved him. I always had. And, damn him, those eyes weakened me.

Nathan sagged a little in relief, but didn't loosen his hold on me. The only thing that softened was his voice. "Can you let me explain?"

I blinked back the surge of fresh tears. "There's nothing to explain. You kissed your ex-girlfriend."

"She kissed me," he corrected.

"It takes two people to kiss, Nathan," I returned quickly. "You didn't stop it."

"Yes, I did."

"I didn't see you."

"Because you left before—"

"It doesn't matter if it only lasted for a second. She should have never gotten close enough to kiss you in the first place!"

His mouth was open, ready to plead his case, but he shut it without a word.

I had a point and he knew it. I looked up at him triumphantly, except I sure didn't feel like I had won anything. He could have stopped it before it happened. He didn't. What did that mean?

Suddenly, I was too sad to fight anymore.

Nathan noted the shift in my mood. He let go of my wrists and sat up, lifting some of his weight off of me. "You're right," he murmured. "I shouldn't have let her get that close. I don't know . . ." He trailed off with a shrug.

"You still care about her."

"But not like that. Not like you think. Not anymore."

"How can you be so sure?" I didn't give him time to respond before I added, "Maybe you should spend some time with her to find out if there's still anything there."

His eyes widened at my suggestion.

Honestly, I couldn't believe I had said it either. I regretted it for a second, but ultimately decided to stand my ground. "I think you need to figure out if you still have feelings for her."

"Kris . . ."

"It's the only way to know."

Nathan cupped my face between his hands. "I don't have to *test* anything." He lowered his head, and I dodged a kiss—proving that it was possible to do so.

"Don't," I pleaded, shaking my head out of his grasp.

"I already know what I want." He tilted my head to his and brushed his lips against mine.

I didn't dodge him this time. I allowed myself a second of vulnerability, and opened myself to him as he slowly, cautiously penetrated my defenses.

My head spun from the minty taste of his kiss and I soared from the feel of his tongue tracing the curve of my bottom lip . . . and I came crashing down as I wondered if Lillian had felt the same way. With a strength I didn't know I possessed, I pushed him away.

"No," I grunted. "You can't just kiss me, and think that makes everything okay. It doesn't."

Nathan sat up straight and threw his hands up in surrender. "Okay . . . fine."

I stared into the space between us, unable to look directly at him, but unable to look away. I loved him so much . . . so much that the next words I had to say hurt too much to say. I swallowed, not sure I had the strength to mutter them.

"What do you want me to do, Kris?" Nathan's voice nearly cracked, and I had to close my eyes from looking to see if he was hurting as much as me. He couldn't, because no one could ever hurt as much as I hurt right now. "Huh? What do you want? I'll do whatever you want me to do. I'll go tell Lillian right now about us, if that's what you want."

It wouldn't be enough. My throat constricted in preparation of my next words, almost as if my body protested my need to say them.

"Remember when you insisted I figure out my feelings for Alec?"

He swallowed, and I knew he had an idea of where I was going with this conversation. And he didn't like it.

"I think you need to figure out how you feel about Lillian," I finally said. "I need you to figure out if you still love her."

"Kris, I love *you*."

I shook my head. "Then you need to do this, before the not knowing ruins us."

"Kris, I already know."

I repeated the same words he told me months ago, in reference to my relationship with Alec. "You need to make sure. *I* need for you to make sure."

His eyes narrowed fractionally. "What are you saying, Kris?"

I couldn't say it. My mouth worked, but nothing came out. Only more tears. They slid down my face and disappeared under my chin.

Nathan was silent as he watched me, but the clenching of his jaw and flaring of his nostrils hinted at his growing anger. "That's really what you want?" he asked. "The fact that I'm right here, telling *you* that *you're* the one that I love isn't enough?"

I took a deep breath to steady myself, but my voice still shook with the single word. "No."

Nathan launched himself off of me, off the bed. I sat up, already regretting that word. I was torn. I didn't want to lose Nathan, but I had to know if he had any lingering feelings for Lillian. I couldn't—he shouldn't expect me to— move on without both of us confident in our future together.

He was halfway to the door, when he stopped and turned. "We're done? That's what you want?"

No, not *done*. That wasn't what I wanted, at all. Unless he was still in love with Lillian . . . "Just a break. That's—"

"A break?"

I risked a peek at him, and immediately wished I hadn't. He was mad. Furious. I had never seen him that mad . . . at me, and I hated that it had come to that. Why didn't he understand? I didn't want a break. I didn't want any of this to happen, but it had, and now I needed to know with absolute certainty that he wanted to be with me.

"I need to know that you don't have deeper feelings for Lillian before we can move past this," I said softly.

He tilted his head to the ceiling with a shake. "Nothing even happened," he groaned. "There's nothing to move past."

"I think there is."

His eyes lowered to mine, and hardened. "Right. Because my words mean nothing to you."

He moved to the door, and this time he didn't stop. The

sound of the door slamming shut behind him made me jump, and tore down the damn that was holding back a new wave of tears. I feared, as I crumbled to my bed, that they would never stop.

Chapter 25

{Nathan}

Two days crawled by, and I didn't see Kris once.

She skipped combat class the first day, then as mission preparations heated up, Jared found me another replacement for the class. Whether or not she showed up the second day, I didn't know. She wasn't on the beach at her normal times. She dodged me at breakfast, lunch, and dinner. I honestly didn't know if she ever came out of her room. I never saw her. Never heard from her.

And it was killing me. Her absence was slowly. . . agonizingly. . . ripping my heart to shreds.

I didn't want this break—or break up?—or whatever it was. I knew, deep down, she didn't either. But she needed reassurance. I understood that. *Now*.

At the time, I had been caught off guard, and reacted out of anger. Now I knew what I needed to do. If spending some time with Lillian was what Kris needed me to do, I would do it. If evaluating my feelings for Lillian was what she needed me to do,

I would do it.

I already knew what the outcome would be, of course, but I would do it. I would do anything to put this break nonsense behind us.

Problem was, I hadn't seen Lillian since the incident on the pier, and I suspected that she was avoiding me, too. Not that I blamed her after the way I had taken off like a madman. I doubted she had seen Kris, or knew the reason why I had run off. I had some explaining to do when I finally managed to corner her.

But finding Lillian came a distant second to the agony I had suffered the past two days. I still couldn't believe how I had managed to muck everything up. I had done exactly what Micah said I would do.

"Little shit."

I stared into my cup of orange juice as if I expected a resolution to materialize out of the pulp—like an easy-to-follow checklist to guide me in fixing everything. Once I realized how stupid I probably looked staring into a cup of orange juice, I chugged it down with one gulp.

"Need a little vodka to go with that shot of OJ?" Alec pulled out a chair and took a seat across from me at the otherwise empty table. When I looked up at him, he grimaced. "Man, you look like hell."

I shrugged my shoulders. Who cared? Besides, I doubted I looked as bad as I felt.

Alec put both elbows on the table, cupped his chin in his hands, and looked at me. He didn't say anything, just looked.

"What?" I asked.

He shook his head once. "Boy, are you an idiot."

Apparently, Kris had come out of her room at some point. I shouldn't have been surprised that she had gone to Alec, and I shouldn't have had the urge to punch the wall because of it. They were friends. Sure, he was still in love with her, and she was probably still a little in love with him—even if she might never admit it—but I had made my peace with that.

Nevertheless, knowing that she had gone to him after I had screwed everything up kind of pissed me off.

I pushed away from the table. "I really don't want to hear this from you right now."

Alec jumped up and kept in pace with me to the door. "Well, you're going to hear it anyway."

My hands shot out to push the double doors open with a bang, drawing the attention of a few developing hybrids that were passing by. I ignored them, and Alec, and kept walking.

He didn't take the hint, and unwisely grabbed me by the shoulder. I stopped and made a fist as I contemplated whether or not I wanted to hit him. He took advantage of my hesitation, and backed me up against the side of the building, out of view of curious eyes.

"I was partially joking the other day," he jeered, "about how I didn't envy you because you were surrounded by all these tempting women. Truth is: I did envy you, because there was one thing that I said that day that was true. You had the perfect girl. Key word: *had*."

My fist unfurled and dropped to my side in defeat. Wow.

That hurt. Honestly, I would have preferred for Alec to pop me in the jaw than to hear him say what he had said.

And he wasn't done, either.

"You had the girl I loved so much, I let her go because she loved *you*. And what did you do with that?" Alec shook his head because, obviously, there just weren't enough words to describe the amount of stupid he thought I was. He jabbed a finger it into my chest, hard. "You better fix it, and you better fix it soon because if I have to see her cry one more time, I'm going to come looking for you, and it won't be pretty."

He turned to leave, and I thought, *what the hell?* "What should I do?"

He slowly turned. His eyes were hard when they met mine. "Are you seriously asking?"

I nodded. "I'm seriously asking."

Alec looked at the ground and inhaled deeply. When he looked up again, his eyes had thawed . . . some. "What happened?"

"She didn't tell you?"

"Oh, she told me. I want to hear your version of the events."

"Lillian kissed me," I said simply. "I didn't want it to happen, I didn't mean for it to happen. Kris saw it, and now she thinks I might still have feelings for Lillian, and she wants me to . . . explore them, I guess."

"You really didn't want it to happen?" His tone caused me to meet and hold his gaze. He lifted his eyebrows as if to say, *bullshit*.

"I didn't."

He held my gaze as if studying me for signs of deceit. I knew he wouldn't find any, and when he didn't, he sighed and came to stand beside me. He propped one foot against the wall behind him, put his hands in his pockets, and sighed. "She's pretty upset. I don't know what to tell you."

"You know what the funny part is?" Except it wasn't funny at all. "She's asking me to do the exact same thing I asked her to do . . . with you. It seems karma is coming back to bite me in the ass."

"You asked her to do that? To explore her feelings for me?" I heard the grin in his voice.

"Yeah."

"And you want to know what to do now to fix everything with her?"

"Yeah."

"I say . . . do it. Explore the feelings that may, or may not, be there for Lillian."

I tapped the back of my head against the wall with a sigh because, dammit, I knew he would say that.

"You probably don't want to hear this," Alec continued, "but she did it. Kris did what you asked her to do. We had some moments, some things for me to file away in my bank of memories. In the end, she determined she wanted you, but she did what you asked her to do. Maybe you need to do the same."

I hated it when Alec was right. His words really sunk in, really hit home. All of them . . .

I rotated my head to look at him. "Exactly what kind of *moments* do you have filed away?"

Alec's gaze slid to mine, and he grinned. "Wouldn't you like to know?"

"That was kind of the point of me asking."

Alec shoved away from the wall, and turned to me as he backed up. "I didn't give her up so that you could screw it up. So fix it."

He left without waiting for a response . . . or answering me.

*   *   *   *   *

I decided that my first stop should be to see Lillian, to put into motion the events that needed to happen for me to do the soul searching Kris had requested. But Lillian wasn't in her room.

Tracking her down was put on hold when an errand boy cornered me as I left the girls' dormitory, and handed me a note from Jared.

Jeffries is growing impatient. Wants us to attack. Team is meeting at the docks at dusk tonight.

After I read the three lines, I crumbled the paper in my hand and tossed it into the nearest trashcan. "God dammit."

Jeffries was an incompetent asshole. If I didn't know any better, I would have sworn he was trying to get us killed. We didn't know enough yet. The recon mission had barely scratched the surface of the Skotadi's agenda. For all I knew, we were about to walk into a huge trap, handed over to the enemy on a platter, wrapped up in a pretty bow prepared by one of our own damn leaders.

Moron.

I turned back toward the girls' dormitory. I had told myself that I wouldn't approach Kris again until I had fixed the Lillian issue, but . . .

This mission pressed the issue a little bit. There were a few things she needed to understand if I went and got myself killed tonight, like the supervisors seemed intent on.

They didn't seem to give a damn about the spies on the island . . . they had sent all of our best soldiers on numerous missions while the Skotadi strengthened their numbers in our back yard . . . they were forcing Jared's and my hands in this harebrained mission before we were ready, almost as if . . .

"Son of a bitch." I came to a sudden stop ten yards from the entrance to the girls' dormitory. "How did I not see it?"

I turned, and headed straight for Jared's office in the administrative building.

Rodney stood at his usual post, but I didn't pause to acknowledge him before I let myself into Jared's office.

He didn't look surprised to see me. "I assume you got my memo?"

"Yeah." I waved my hand as if batting that subject away, because that wasn't why I was there. "I have a question."

I took up position against the wall with my arms folded across my chest. I stared at my arms for a moment before I spoke, because the pieces were still aligning for me . . . and I had no idea where this conversation was going to go yet.

"Does Jeffries have any connection with Geography?"

"And by connection, you mean . . ."

"Does he have a hand in it?"

"All the head supervisors work together in organizing our

efforts. You know that." Jared leaned back in his chair with a sigh. "Nathan, I'm afraid to ask where you're going with this."

"This immortality conspiracy goes as high as the *demigods*," I said. "Who's to say some of our own supervisors aren't in on it? We know the Geography department has spies. What if there are others?"

Something flashed in Jared's eyes and he sat back in his chair. He studied me silently as he chewed over my words. "You think Jeffries is a spy," he concluded.

I nodded then added, "I think he's trying to distract us."

"From what?"

"Don't you find it odd that we have Skotadi sniffing around in our own back yard, and he has shipped all of our best soldier off the island during the same week?"

"The Skotadi are going to attack the island," he said, and I knew he believed it as much as I did. "But why?"

"For Kris. They're coming for her."

"So what do you want to do?" Jared asked.

I had no idea, but there was one thing I was absolutely sure of. "I'm not stepping one foot off this island tonight. Not without Kris."

*　　*　　*　　*　　*

Of all the times for me to not be able to find Kris, it had to be *now*. I knew something was about to go down . . . I just didn't know exactly what, or where, or when.

She wasn't in her room. I knew that for certain because I

climbed up the side of the building and snuck into her room to make sure she wasn't avoiding me. The sliding glass door was unlocked, but she wasn't there.

I went to her desk to grab a piece of paper to write her a note. I moved some junk out of the way to reveal an unopened envelope postmarked from Greece, addressed to her in my handwriting. I stared at it for a moment in confusion, then a goofy smile spread across my face when I realized what it was. The letter I had written her from the train before we raided the village.

It was unopened, which meant she hadn't read it yet, but I could use that to my advantage. This letter contained the words that, at that time, I thought might have been my last words to her. And now was when she needed to know exactly what she meant to me, more than ever.

If she didn't believe me when I told her, maybe she would believe me when she read my words.

I tore a piece of paper out of the journal, and wrote her a note, pleading with her to read the letter. I placed the note and the envelope in the middle of her bed, where I hoped she would see it.

Then I went back to my room to wait.

Chapter 26

{Kris}

I held Nathan's letter in one hand, and knocked on his door with the other. As I waited, I cast Kim a look that caused her eyebrows to shoot up.

"Do you want me to stay?" she asked quietly.

"No . . . yes . . ." I sighed heavily. I had no idea what I expected by coming here. All I knew was that, after reading his letter, I had to see Nathan. "No. You don't need to stay."

The words had barely passed my lips when the door swung open, and Nathan's imposing form stood before me. I almost told Kim I changed my mind, almost turned to her with a plea to stay, but she left while I was stuck staring at Nathan.

He ushered me inside, and it was just the two of us. Before the nerves got the best of me, I lifted the letter in my hand, and asked, "Is this true?"

He eyed the paper as he stuffed his hands in his pockets. "Every word."

I rocked on my heels as I fought the urge to run into his

326

arms. The letter, and the raw emotion in what he had thought were his last words to me, had floored me, but the way he looked at me now? That caused a painful, twisty sensation in my chest . . . that I knew could only be relieved by him.

He sighed heavily. "I miss you, Kris."

I pressed my lips together to stop myself from reciprocating. Because if I did, I would end up in his arms.

But wasn't that what I wanted?

I was so confused. He had hurt me, but I was hurting without him.

"And I meant everything I said in that letter. *Everything.*" He took a step closer. "When I said you mean the world to me, I meant it. When I said I never knew that love could be like this, I meant it. That you are the best thing to ever happen to me . . . I meant it all."

Another step brought him close enough to touch. All I had to do was lift my hands . . . place them on his shoulders . . .

"And when I said that no one compares to you," he continued, "I meant *no one*. Past, present, or future."

Another step narrowed the distance between us more, and I stepped back to maintain the space I needed to think straight. When the heel of my foot hit the wall behind me, I knew I was close to being trapped. I tried to skirt around Nathan, but he sidestepped to block me. My eyes lifted to his, and that was all it took. I was ready to surrender.

"You know how I feel, how I *really* feel. So my question is . . ." His hands pressed to the wall on either side of my head, and he leaned in to put his mouth next to my ear. "Do you still love me?"

My head involuntarily tilted toward his. Like a bee drawn to a flower, I was powerless to stop it. My breath escaped in a ragged burst, and my body trembled from being so close to him. Every part of me wanted to touch him, to kiss him.

The answer was surely written all over my face. Still, I whispered, "I've loved you my whole life. I could never just stop loving you."

Nathan hooked a hand behind my neck, and the inches between us melted away as his head lowered. He hovered over me, his breath warm against my skin, as his hand twisted into my hair.

"It's always been you, Kris. Only you," he murmured before he finally pressed his lips to mine.

With a sigh of submission, I leaned into him. My hands ran up his chest and across his shoulders as I reacquainted myself with every defined inch of his body. My fingers dug into his back when he took hold of my hips as he lifted me up and wrapped my legs around his waist in one smooth motion. He pinned me against the wall, my weight supported enough for him to use his hands freely.

And boy did he use them. His hands slipped under my shirt and slid up my sides, bringing on a whole body shudder when his hands grazed my bare skin. My response was to frantically pull at the hem of his shirt in a desperate attempt to remove it. His lips left mine as he helped me to pull it over his head, and I saw the desire in his eyes.

Who initiated it was lost amongst a blur of moving hands

and fiery kisses, but my shirt quickly joined his on the floor. He pulled me tight against him, his naked torso smooth and searing at every point it contacted my bare skin. He back stepped to the bed and slowly reclined, while pulling me down with him so that our lips never parted.

This is it, I thought, and my breath hitched.

His hand cupped my face. "You okay?" he murmured against my lips.

"Perfect," I said, trying to make it believable.

His eyes swept over me, taking in the sexy lace bra I happened to have put on that morning. Lust hooded his eyes when they lifted to mine, and I knew what he wanted. Because I wanted it too. His hesitation was only for me, and it made me want him even more.

"You don't happen to be prepared this time, do you?" I asked in a hushed voice.

He smiled sheepishly. "I actually had to make a trip to the mainland for something, and I didn't want you to yell at me again. . ."

I had expected him to say no, so my shock was genuine when I squeaked, "What? You got protection?" I leaned back and looked down at him with my hands on my hips.

His head tilted to the side as a slow grin formed on his lips. I realized too late the view I was giving him. My skin flushed under his observant gaze, but I made no attempt to cover myself.

Nathan's eyes lifted slowly and finally settled on mine with an appreciative twinkle. My eyebrows shot up when he didn't say anything.

"I'm sorry," he said. "What did you say? I'm a guy and. . . and, well, you don't have a shirt on."

"Nothing." I smiled nervously. "I'm just surprised."

My eyes dropped to take in the taut abs my hands were splayed on. There was nothing to stop us now. Except ourselves.

"But that doesn't mean . . ." Nathan started. "I don't expect—"

I stopped him with a look. "I know."

His eyes locked on mine, and his head nodded fractionally. I held his gaze for a beat before I lowered my eyes to my hands as I moved them up, over his ribcage and across his chest. I moved slowly as I memorized not only the sight, but the feel, of him at my fingertips. My hands slid over his shoulders, and then down his arms, thick and hard under smooth skin. He shuddered slightly from my touch, and when my eyes lifted to his, he let out a ragged breath.

"Come here," he ordered gruffly. His hands entangled in my hair as he pulled me toward him.

A knock at the door stopped my descent an inch from his lips. I looked at Nathan, and he shrugged.

There was a moment of silence, then Lillian's voice carried through the door. "Nathan?"

My eyes narrowed. I started to slide off of his lap, but his hands gripped my waist to stop me.

"I had no idea she was coming by," he whispered quickly.

"Nathan," she called again. "I got your note . . ."

Nathan tossed his head back with a curse, and I wrenched myself free. I shot daggers at him as I collected our shirts off the floor. I threw his to him a little harder than necessary, and slipped mine over my head.

"I know you're in there, Nathan. Please. You're right. We need to talk," Lillian pressed.

Nathan stood and grabbed my shoulders before I had a chance to turn away from him. "I was going to do what you wanted me to do, and spend time with her, and then tell her about you."

"Uh-huh."

"Nathan?" Lillian's voice lifted in concern.

"Just a minute, Lil!" Nathan called to her through the door.

I threw my hands up in the air. "What am I supposed to do?" I whispered harshly. "You want me to just open the door and walk right by her?" I gestured wildly with my hands. "Say *Hey, Lil, sorry, you caught us at a bad time. I guess it's your turn. See ya later!*"

Nathan looked down his nose at me. "You're way off base."

"Oh, am I?" I pushed against him, but froze when my hands met skin. "Put your shirt back on. I can't think with you walking around like that."

He slid his shirt over his head, rolling it down over his hard abs, and my brain cleared some of the fog, but I still wasn't any closer to a solution.

"You stay here," Nathan suggested in a low voice. "Lillian and I will go for a walk. I'll come back after we're done talking."

"What makes you think she doesn't have every intention of coming in here?"

He stared at me, and it was clear from his hesitation that he couldn't rule that out as a possibility. I wanted to throw something at him, but the only thing within reach was a pillow.

"I won't give her a chance," he said as he maneuvered me into the bathroom.

He glanced at me over his shoulder as he moved to the door. I wasn't sure what his expression was trying to portray. He might have been reminding me to be quiet, or he was trying to tell me he was sorry. Only he knew.

A second later, he opened the door and stepped outside.

Then it was just me, alone in his room, while he was out on a walk with the only other woman on the planet who came close to loving him as much as I did.

Chapter 27

{Nathan}

The sun set over the horizon as Lillian and I moved through the village center, and my thoughts temporarily drifted to the mission that was supposed to be kicking off, well . . . now. In the midst of making up with Kris, I had nearly forgotten, but now I wondered if my intuition was right about something happening soon. If so . . .

I needed to get through this talk with Lillian fast so I could get back to Kris. And then we would have to start making arrangements to get off the island.

Lillian remained silent beside me as we wandered closer to the beach. Finally, she cleared her throat, and said, "I know you probably want to talk about what happened on the pier the other day, but there's something else I need to talk to you about first. Yesterday, I remembered something about your friend, Callie."

"Okay . . ." She had my attention.

"I remember now. I remember doing that spell on her. There were others. Lots of others. I cursed entire towns, all over the world."

"I know," I said. "I mean, I kind of suspected you were behind it."

Her mouth dropped open. "Oh."

"Do you know why you cursed them?" I wondered if she had any knowledge of the demigods' ultimate plans.

"It's all a part of an immortality spell," she gushed. "I can't reverse it. I don't have that power."

I hung my head. "That's a blow."

"I'm sorry about your friend." Lillian's voice cracked as she held back her emotions. "But there is so much more to this than anyone realizes . . ."

"I learned about it in Greece. The demigods are after immortality. The gods asked us—"

"No." She grabbed my arm to interrupt me. "It's not the demigods, Nathan. It's Circe. She's behind the whole thing."

*　*　*　*　*

{Kris}

I paced Nathan's room until the walls started to close in on me, and I stepped out onto the balcony for a much needed breath of fresh air. I propped my elbows on the railing as the evening's events replayed in my head.

Had we really almost had sex? Would we have gone through with it?

Yes, I believed we would have. I smiled as I thought about

what had almost happened, what could have happened, and what might still happen when he got back.

My smile faded when the familiar throbbing started in the calves of my legs. An unseen force pulled me flush against the railing until I could go no farther, and I pressed my palms into the wood beam in an attempt to resist crawling over the side to seek the source.

"Not again," I muttered.

A scream arose somewhere in the distance, and my head snapped up to scan the horizon. From three stories up, I had a decent view of the island, but parts remained hidden. The advancing night, and deepening shadows didn't help, but nothing appeared out of place. A few Kala moved through the village center, coming or going from the dorms. Some sat on benches, talking. None of them looked alarmed.

Then another scream shattered the peace, and all heads turned in the same direction. Toward the beach.

In a move that caused me to cry out from the pain it caused in my legs, I turned and ran into the room. But I didn't stop there. I dashed down the hallway, then bounded two steps at a time up the two flights of stairs to Alec's room.

Bruce stiffened when he saw me coming. "What's wrong?"

"I don't know . . ." I slowed when I reached the door, and gripped my side as I fought to catch my breath. Before I could tell Bruce what I heard, the door swung open, and Alec stepped into the hallway.

"What's wrong?" he asked, looking between Bruce and me.

I grabbed Alec's hand, and pulled him into the room. Bruce

trailed behind us, but stopped when I slid the balcony door open and stepped outside with Alec.

"Do you feel it?" I whispered.

Alec glanced at Bruce before nodding. He dropped his voice for my ears only. "It started a few minutes ago, but . . . I mean it's happened before."

"Did you hear the screaming?"

Alec's eyebrows shot up. "Uh . . . no."

"*Listen.*"

A few seconds of silence followed before another scream came, closer and louder than the last one. The shrill cry abruptly ended, and my stomach soured at the realization of what that meant.

Bruce stepped out onto the balcony. "What was that?"

Before I could say anything, the pulling sensation intensified. Alec and I took collective steps forward until we were both pressed against the railing.

"What is happening?" Alec groaned against the strain.

"I'm going to go find out what's going on," Bruce volunteered. "You two stay here."

I gritted my teeth against the pull, pushing against the rail with my hands as I fought it. I wanted to tell Bruce not to leave, to tell him I didn't think it was safe, but I couldn't.

"Kris . . ." Alec ground out. "Look."

I lifted my head to look at Alec. His eyes were on me. On my hands. I followed his gaze . . .

And saw the wooden railing through my hands. They faded in and out, as if they were hovering on the threshold of invisibility. I lifted them to examine them closer, and saw that my arms were flickering in the same manner.

Suddenly, the force pulling Alec and I pulsed. When it subsided we simultaneously sagged in relief.

Alec turned and grabbed my shoulders. "What's happening? You're flickering."

"I don't know," I admitted. But I was scared to death of whatever it was.

"Pull yourself together," he ordered me. "No unauthorized Incantation shit right now, okay?"

"I'm not . . ."

"I know. That's what worries me." Alec pulled me into the room. "We need to find Bruce, and find out what's happening."

"Nathan's out there," I said. "I have to find him."

Before I made it to the door, it swung open and Micah burst into the room with Richie and Bruce behind him.

"It's the Skotadi," he panted. "I can sense them. They're on the island. A whole bunch of them."

I turned to Alec. "They're here for us."

"We need to get you somewhere safe," Micah said to me.

"No, I have to find Nathan."

I started to push past them, when a chorus of shouts and gunfire erupted outside.

*　　*　　*　　*　　*

{Nathan}

They advanced from the beach like a wave of death, overtaking everyone they encountered as they barreled toward the village center—hundreds of Skotadi, wielding guns and knives, and sparing no one.

I grabbed Lillian's arm. "Command Center, now!"

As screams and shouts of warning sounded behind us, the Kala in the village center shot to attention. Twenty of us raced to the entrance of the Command Center, and the closest weapons cache. I reached the door first, and stopped to pull the alarm to warn the entire island, but came up short when I saw that it had been smashed.

Lillian gasped. "Who would do that?"

"Spies," I muttered, but didn't stick around long enough to explain. I needed a weapon.

I met Jared as he walked out of the weapon's hold. He handed me a gun, and asked, "What about the fire alarms in the dorms?"

"It's worth a shot."

"Go. I'll buy you some time," he said, and then he disappeared out the door and into the advancing night.

"Stick with me," I ordered Lillian.

As I raced across the village center to the girls' dormitory, I heard Jared ordering the small group of Kala to form a line of defense directly in front of the building. A deafening eruption of gunfire opened up behind me as I reached the door.

Once inside, I pointed a finger at the guard on duty. "We've got Skotadi incoming. Pull the fire alarm. Unlock the weapons hold, make sure everyone arms up, and send them outside."

As the siren wailed throughout the building, I sprinted next door to the boys' dormitory. Behind me, the Kala struck down the Skotadi as they swarmed the village center. But there were so many of them . . .

Even with the female Kala joining in the fight, eventually the Skotadi would overrun us.

I yelled out orders as I swung open the door to the boys' dorm. Once the siren sounded, I turned to Lillian.

"What are they here for?" I demanded. "Do you know?"

She nodded hesitantly.

"They're here for Kris, aren't they?"

"I think so."

As confused Kala filled the lobby, I grabbed Lillian's arm to keep us from getting separated. "Go to my room. Tell Kris to stay there. Do not let her come down here."

Lillian blinked in surprise, and I realized what I had just admitted. But I didn't have the time to explain. Not now.

"Go! We can't let them find her!" As Lillian pushed against the horde of Kala pouring into the lobby, I called after her. "If she's not there, try room five-oh-seven!"

Surely Kris had heard the commotion by now. It wouldn't have surprised me if she had gone to Alec's room. It didn't matter where she was, as long as she stayed there, and we kept the Skotadi away from her.

As Lillian disappeared into the crowd, I turned to follow the others into the village center. We filed out the door shoulder to shoulder, and straight into hell.

Jared's line had been overrun, and the girls' dormitory had

been set on fire. Skotadi flooded the village center while Kala withdrew. The few experienced soldiers we had mixed with the inexperienced and the young hybrids, and struggled to maintain some order among the chaos. Lines retreated and regrouped closer to the boys' dorm before resuming firing positions against the Skotadi.

I spotted Jared among them as he barked out orders. I ducked low to avoid the bullets whizzing by my head as I scrambled across the open, and hunkered down behind the cover of a bench alongside him.

"Pretty shitty cover!" I told him as I rested my gun on the bench and opened fire. No point taking aim. There were so many, missing one meant hitting another.

Jared grunted. "We got overrun. Had to abandon the girls' dorm. Got about twenty girls trapped inside by Skotadi. Can't get enough organization together to go get them."

I took my eyes off the advancing Skotadi long enough to survey the situation. A line of a dozen Skotadi had grouped in front of the entrance to the girls' dorm. I couldn't see the Kala trapped inside through the thick black smoke that poured out of the door. If any of them were still alive in there, they wouldn't be for much longer.

"I'll take it." I turned to the two Kala on the other side of me, and yelled, "You two, with me."

They followed as I maneuvered through the sea of Kala toward the dormitory. Along the way, I spotted a face I recognized.

"My sister is still in there," Kira yelled.

I motioned for her to follow, and she and two of her friends joined us. As we approached the line of Skotadi, I motioned for the girls to veer to the right in a flanking position. We opened fire on the Skotadi from both sides before they saw us coming. A grenade from one of the men with me finished them off.

While the rest of us held the position, Kira ran inside the building. She came out a minute later with at least twenty soot-covered and coughing Kala. The fire would take the building, but it appeared that everyone was out.

I heard a blast come from somewhere behind me a second before the force of it knocked us to the ground. My ears rang as I scrambled to my feet . . . just in time to see a second explosion demolish the entrance of the boys' dorm. My feet were moving before I had fully regained my balance, and I stumbled toward the front of the building as a fire erupted in the lobby.

But how? No Skotadi had gotten past the second line. Not yet.

As I neared, I saw the entrance blocked off by a mountain of wood and stone. The fire created an orange glow that seeped through gaps in the debris, and illuminated the man-shaped shadow that stepped in front of me.

Supervisor Jeffries. My gaze dropped to the explosives he held in his hands, and my finger instinctively flexed on the trigger of my gun.

"The war has changed," he said to me. "We all had to make choices."

"And you chose to turn your back on your own?"

He scoffed. "It's not that simple anymore."

As he spoke, his hand moved slowly to his side, to the pistol I saw partially hidden under the waistband of his pants. My eyes remained fixed on his, and he would never know that I noticed.

"This is the only way to survive the war. You will see. You all will see," he continued as his fingers encircled the butt of the pistol.

His hand rose quickly, and I fired. One shot to the center of his chest dropped him to my feet.

"I'm not a traitor," I said to the wisps of his soul as it dissipated into the night.

Too late. The damage he had orchestrated had already been done. In front of me, flames engulfed the boys' dorm.

*   *   *   *   *

{Kris}

The building's fire alarm wailed as we stepped into the hallway. Kala raced past us, toward the stairwell. I started to follow when Micah grabbed my arm.

"Kris . . ." His eyes were pleading when I met them. "You need to stay here."

I jabbed a finger at Alec's open door. "Do you hear that out there?"

"All the more reason to stay here," he replied.

I stepped around him with a shake of my head. Alec and Bruce were behind me as I pushed through the doors to the stairwell, and Micah and Richie eventually followed like I knew they would. We didn't get far before we hit the line of Kala. Of course, we were the last ones.

As we approached the third floor landing, the building shook from an explosion beneath us, forcing me to grab the railing for support.

"That can't be good," Alec muttered from behind me.

I glanced at him, and noticed his hands fisted at his sides. His eyes were strained when they met mine. "You okay?" I asked him.

He nodded his head, but it didn't look convincing. I was about to press him when the third floor door swung open, nearly hitting Bruce. As he jumped out of the way, my eyes landed on Lillian. And she was alone.

"Where's Nathan?" I shouted at her.

An unreadable expression crossed her face as she climbed the steps toward me.

"Where is he?" I repeated when she didn't answer. *God, why wasn't she answering me?*

"Downstairs," she said. "He wanted me to—"

I pushed past Micah as I forced my way down the steps. The damn line wasn't moving fast enough, and I had to get down there. I had to find him.

Lillian grabbed my arm as I tried to slip by her. "He wants you to stay here."

"The hell I am!" I ripped my arm out of her grasp. I glared at Bruce until he stepped to the side, but then there were a hundred Kala beyond him, standing in my way.

"Kris, you don't understand," Lillian pleaded. "If the Skotadi find you . . ."

"What?" I spun on her. "So now your memory has returned? How convenient."

Micah stepped forward to address Lillian. "What if the Skotadi find her?"

Lillian glanced at Micah quickly before settling a troubled expression on me. "It's all part of Circe's plan."

"Circe?" Micah spat. "I knew it."

"She wanted you to take the potential spell," Lillian continued. "She needs you to reach your potential, because she needs *you* to finish the curse."

I glanced down at my hands. They were solid again. For now. When I looked at Alec, I knew our thoughts were the same. We had nearly reached our potential. Both of us.

Because of Circe's potion.

"What's going to happen?" I asked quietly.

Lillian stepped close to rest a hand on my shoulder. "Have you been practicing spells?"

"Yeah . . ." I nodded. "I'm not good. I haven't been able to—"

"It doesn't matter," she interrupted. "It doesn't work like that. Everything you've been practicing, once you reach full strength, you will be able to do . . . effortlessly. By practicing the spells, you've basically been filing them away for use later. For now."

"She was flickering earlier," Alec commented. "Almost like she was half invisible, only not."

I narrowed my eyes at Alec, and he shrugged

unapologetically.

"You have to hold your powers back until you learn to control them," Lillian said urgently.

I scoffed. "Yeah, because I'm so good at self-control."

Lillian turned to Alec. "How about you? How are you doing?"

Alec's eyes widened at her question. "Umm . . ."

"You're fighting it," I said to Alec, and his gaze slid to mine. "I can tell you are."

His jaw clenched. "I feel like I've been electrocuted," he said defensively. "Like all this power is running through me like an electrical current, and just waiting for its chance to get out."

"When this happens," Micah said slowly, looking at Lillian. "Will they be evil?"

"Ah, hell no," Alec sneered as he took a menacing step toward Micah.

"I don't know," Lillian admitted solemnly. "Really, with them being this close, they should have succumbed to the evil by now. Something else is preventing it."

Her brow furrowed as her eyes swept over Alec and me, and I knew she didn't understand how we were still us. Was it the charms Gran had given us? Free will, as my dead friends had once suggested? Or something else entirely?

"I'm not letting that shit take me over," Alec declared, and turned to me. "And I'm not letting it take you. And neither are the Skotadi."

He grabbed my hand as he started up the steps. He pulled me a few steps before I ripped my hand out of grasp. "No! I've got to find Nathan!"

I ran down the stairs until I hit the line of Kala again, now stopped halfway between the second and third floor landings. And they were running up, forcing me back as a cloud of smoke filled the stairwell from below.

Someone grabbed my hand and pulled me through the open door, into the third floor hallway. Smoke and Kala followed, and I heard someone say the lobby was on fire.

"We're trapped," Bruce muttered.

"No, weren't not. We can use the balconies to climb down." I moved down the hall, trying several doors until I found one that was unlocked.

I ran through the room, and stepped outside onto the balcony. Looking back and forth, I saw at least thirty other Kala on neighboring balconies, all with the same idea.

We were lucky enough to have found an unlocked room on the back side of the building, away from the village center and whatever was happening there. Though we could hear the sounds of fighting, we were spared from climbing down into the middle of it.

Richie climbed down first, followed by Bruce and Lillian. I started down once they landed on the balcony beneath me. I shimmied down the wooden post until I could go no farther, and then I let go. The drop was only a few feet, and I landed easily next to Bruce. Richie and Lillian were already on the ground below us.

"We need to find weapons," Bruce said to me.

I glanced up as Micah made his way down next. "Command

Center?"

"If we can get to it." Bruce swung a leg over the railing as Micah dropped beside me.

Alec and Bruce were both in mid-dangle when the sound of gunshots and shouting moved around the side of the building, along with a swarm of Skotadi. My head swiveled as I took in the defenseless Kala hanging from the balconies around me.

No. They weren't defenseless. They had me.

I felt the familiar tingle in my hand as I produced a fireball to whip at the Skotadi. Like a flaming bowling ball, it took down the first wave like they were nothing but plastic pins. Their shrieks of surprise and rage reached my ears as they dropped to the ground in an attempt to extinguish the flames that overcame them.

"Go!" I shouted to Micah. "I can hold them off!"

Alec dropped beside me with a fireball of his own ready. As Micah jumped to the ground, Alec helped me to repel a second wave of Skotadi. I kept an eye on the other Kala as they climbed down. They weren't safe on the ground either, but at least they weren't as easy to target as they had been suspended in the air.

Once the last one was on solid ground, I turned to Alec. "Go! I got this!"

Using both hands, I produced my largest ball of fire yet—something that resembled a flaming exercise ball—and shot it into another group of Skotadi as they rounded the corner of the building. The ball clipped the wall, and rained a mixture of stone and fire down on them. As they dodged debris, I jumped to the ground.

Behind me, the windows on the first floor shattered from an

explosion that threw me forward, facedown onto the ground. Alec helped me to my feet as flames shot out the open windows and a wall of black smoke rolled toward us.

"The whole building is going up!" Micah shouted above the roar of the fire.

I hoped everyone had gotten out.

I hoped Nathan had gotten out. I had to find him.

"Come on!" I took off at a run, moving toward the side of the building, away from the Skotadi.

The smoke thickened as we approached and, as we rounded the corner, I saw why. The girls' dorm was completely engulfed in flames. Covering my mouth against the onslaught of smoke, I hurried along the trail between the two buildings that led toward the village center. Once it came into view, I froze at the horror of what I saw.

Alec came to a slow stop beside me. "Oh, my God."

An orange glow from the two burning buildings lit up the night, and illuminated a battle scene straight out of my nightmares.

To our left, groups of Skotadi were scattered across the village center, and had formed a u-shaped line around a small group of Kala pinned down outside the mess hall. Toward the far side of the boys' dorm another standoff between two large groups took place. Directly in front of us was an opening covered with bodies, and occupied by only a few small clusters of a dozen or so combatants battling to the death with knives and fists.

Finding Nathan in this mess would be impossible. Looking at all the death around me, I feared I wouldn't find him alive.

"We need weapons," Bruce said, interrupting my worried thoughts.

Bruce and Richie took the lead as we crossed the village center and wove around the scattered Kala and Skotadi who fought behind the main battle line. Regardless, we were forced to duck low to avoid the occasional stray bullet.

We made it to the Command Center easily. Once inside, Richie scooped up something that looked like a machine gun movie prop, and stood guard in the doorway as everyone else selected from what was left in the weapons cache.

I picked up a silver pistol, but put it back.

"Kris, you need something," Micah chided.

I lifted my hands. "These are my weapons." I was much better, and more confident, at conjuring fire than shooting a gun.

As Micah gathered spare ammo and stuffed it into his pockets, his eyes slid to something behind me and his gaze hardened.

I turned to find Alec hovered in the corner with his head down and hands fisted to his sides.

"Kris . . ." Micah drew cautiously as I stepped closer to Alec.

"He won't hurt me," I tossed over my shoulder. As I neared, I heard Alec's labored breaths. My hand touched his shoulder and he flinched. "Alec? What's wrong?"

"I'm not doing so well." I heard the pain in his voice, and it tugged at my heart.

"Alec . . ." I stepped closer, and his head lifted fractionally. His eyes met mine, and my heart shattered. "Don't do this. Please, don't give in to it. I can't lose you, Alec. I need you to fight it with everything that you have."

His eyes shut as if he were in pain, and I took his hands in mine, though with the way mine were flickering in and out, I didn't know if he could feel me holding them. Nor did I know how much longer I could hold out. I was asking him to do something I might not be able to do.

"Can you feel me?" I asked him. His head nodded slowly. "Good. Stay with me, Alec. Please. I need you. I can't do this without you."

His head rose, his eyes met mine, and I saw his struggle. I had seen Alec have episodes before, and he had seen mine, but this . . .

This was it. Alec had reached the moment where his soul would no longer teeter between good and evil. He was about to fall to one side, and I hoped more than anything that he didn't let the evil win.

Suddenly, his hands cupped my face to hold me still as his lips crashed into mine with an urgency that stole my breath. The force of him drove me back, into the wall behind me. And then his arms were around me, his fingers digging into my waist as he held me to him . . . so tight that I could barely move.

And something made me think that I shouldn't. His mouth moved brazenly over mine, and I let him part my lips and deepen the kiss in the way that he needed right now.

Because something told me he needed this.

I felt the shift, and knew the moment everything changed. Alec's grip around my waist lessened at the same time his lips softened. Though he didn't exactly stop kissing me, he stopped kissing me . . . *like that.* Now, he feathered my lips with the faintest kiss before he slowly pulled away.

His forehead bumped against mine and when I opened my eyes, I saw the curve of a grin on his lips. "I'm good now."

"Oh, really?"

Alec stepped back, freeing me from the wall, and I saw Micah's scowl over his shoulder, and Bruce's widened eyes.

"You okay?" Alec asked me.

"Umm . . ." I looked down at my hands. They were solid again, and though they were shaky, it wasn't a fight to control the growing powers that ran through my body that caused them to shake. Not now. "Yeah, I think I'm good."

Though I still felt the power rising in me, I felt grounded for the first time since the attack started. And the kiss had obviously helped Alec . . . somehow, in a way I couldn't have begun to understand.

He flashed me a smile as he scooped a gun off the floor, then he trotted to the doorway beside Richie and Bruce. I ignored Micah's glare and Lillian's curious eyes as I followed in a partial daze.

"This is going to be dicey," Bruce warned.

"We need to find a way through the Skotadi line," Richie added. "Join up with the rest of the Kala by the mess hall."

"We need to find Nathan," I said. "I need to know that he's okay."

"I'm sure he's fine," Lillian mumbled. When I glanced at her, I noticed that she was already looking at me.

Micah pushed between the two of us, breaking up our short

staring contest, as he muttered, "Let's go."

Micah led the way outside, with Richie right behind him.

"Stay close to me," Alec said.

I wasn't sure if he wanted me near for my own protection, or if he felt that he needed to be close to me. Whatever it was, I nodded in agreement as we stepped outside together.

The situation in the village center hadn't improved in the few minutes we had been inside. If anything, it had worsened.

Both dorms were complete losses, and one whole side of the girls' dorm had collapsed into the village center, forcing the Skotadi to shift closer to the Command Center. Closer to us. Though the fires cast the fighting soldiers in an eerie orange glow, our little group remained in shadows. If we were careful, we could slip past the Skotadi line, and join the Kala on the other side. And I could find Nathan.

"Stay low," Bruce ordered as he started to the right, his back flush against the wall, as he took the lead.

"No, wait," Micah called, and he turned to me with wide eyes. "Kris, get inside *now*."

Before I could ask why, I saw what—or rather who—had alarmed him.

Moving through the crowd of Skotadi was a tall man, dressed in long black robes. But he wasn't just a man. I didn't recognize him and had no idea who he was, but I instinctively knew *what* he was.

A demigod. And it was too late. He had seen me. There was no running and hiding now.

"Temulus," Alec muttered. He spun to me, his eyes wide and

desperate. "I don't know if he can charm you or not, but don't make eye contact. Just in case."

Micah moved to stand in front of me, his arms spread out protectively. "He's not going to take you," he said over his shoulder. "I'm not going to let him."

The demigod stopped several yards away, in front of the large tree in the center of the village center, and faced us. With nothing more than a wave of his hand, he sent a wave of Skotadi at us. Richie jumped in front of Micah, and was the first to be hit. His body dissipated before it hit the ground. The scream that rose in my throat was carried away by a sudden gust of wind that swirled around us.

It left our group unaffected, but forced the Skotadi back. I heard a sharp cracking noise above the howling of the wind, and looked up as a large branch of the tree behind Temulus split from the trunk. Another gust of wind tossed the branch on top of the Skotadi.

One look at Micah's rigid posture and focused gaze, and I knew it was all him, using his powers of wind manipulation.

Temulus turned his attention to Micah, and his eyes flashed with the golden spark I had come to recognize in the Skotadi. His hand barely moved, but that was all it took. The remaining Skotadi marched toward Micah as if they were string puppets controlled by Temulus's hand.

"Micah, no!" I tried to push past Alec. He grabbed my shoulders to stop me as the Skotadi launched a string of star-shaped pointy objects through the air. A dozen, or more, all shiny from the diamond that coated them, flew into Micah with a chorus of flesh-piercing thumps.

The wind abruptly stopped as Micah dropped to his knees, and fell forward face down on the ground. I wrenched free of Alec's hold, and sprang to Micah's side at the same time Bruce got there. As I reached for Micah, Bruce was flung back by an unseen force. He hit the side of the building, and slumped to the ground, unmoving.

I rolled Micah over, and my hands flew to my mouth to stifle my scream. Blood poured from his mouth as he opened it to speak.

"Shhh," I cooed. "Don't try to talk."

His hand moved to his neck, to the vial he carried with him. His fingers were covered in his own blood as he extended it to me. "It's yours," he whispered. And then he was gone.

I rocked back on my heels as his soul dissipated into the night.

"The time has come," a dark, deep voice announced, and I looked up at Temulus through my tears. "You will join us now."

"No, I won't," I answered.

His gaze on me hardened with determination. "You will join us now," he repeated, and I realized what he was doing. He was attempting to charm me.

And it wasn't working. Knowing that filled me with a strength I hadn't had a moment ago, and I stood to face him defiantly. My anger over Micah's death fueled the powers that buzzed through my body, and I fisted my hands at my sides as if that could help restrain me.

"That's never going to happen," I said, and smirked at the

flicker of surprise that crossed his face. "You're forgetting two things. I've got free will on my side, and I don't want to join you. And . . ." My smile grew. "I'm Hecate's daughter."

Temulus chortled. "There are other ways, child." His arms rose to his sides, and he swept them forward, toward me. At the same time, Skotadi on both sides of him marched forward as if pushed by him.

Lillian's words from earlier came to me. I closed my eyes to compose myself, and willed myself to be ready. Because I *had* to be ready.

"*Obiectum motum,*" I chanted under my breath. My eyes snapped open as I lifted my hands out in front of me forcefully.

Nothing had happened the last time I tried it, but now . . .

Temulus flew back as if he was a flea flicked by a giant. He crashed into what remained of the tree behind him. As he fell to the ground, I advanced on him. My arms shot out, tossing Skotadi to the side with nothing more than a thought along the way. I came to a stop a few yards from him as he rose to his feet. He looked up, and I shot a swirling ball of fire at him.

He taunted me with a laugh as the fire hit his chest and burst open. He stepped through it unscathed. "You have much to learn," he jeered. "I'm a demigod. You cannot hurt me anymore than I can charm you apparently."

"Oh, no?" I returned. "There's one way to kill a demigod that I know of."

He smirked. "Yes, but it appears you are unarmed."

I needed diamond. Little did he know that at my feet, partially covered by my shoe, lay a diamond coated knife that had been dropped. And I was prepared to use it.

Chapter 28

{Nathan}

I watched in awestruck horror as Kris advanced on the demigod. Skotadi were tossed to the side, and out of her way, as if they were nothing. But Temulus?

I didn't want her anywhere near him.

I yelled her name, but she didn't hear me. I was still too far away.

Since the moment I first saw her as she darted across the village center and disappeared inside the command center, I had been trying to get to her. Though I had left a trail of dead Skotadi in my wake, many more still remained between me and her.

As I dropped one with a well-placed bullet, another rushed me with a knife. I quickly, and easily, ended him. The majority of these Skotadi were inexperienced newbies. Even with their greater numbers, and the fact that they had achieved the element of surprise, they would not overcome the Kala.

I doubted it had been their goal to overtake the base. No. I figured the attack was nothing but a distraction. Temulus's arrival confirmed my suspicion, and I knew that he planned to take Kris. And probably Alec, too.

I cut down another Skotadi in my way, and shouted Kris's name again.

I saw her lips moving, and I suspected she was talking to Temulus. She, at least, didn't appear under his control despite having made eye contact with him, so that was good. But then she bent to pick something off the ground. The light from the fire reflected off of it, creating a familiar sparkle, and my heart nearly stopped beating.

"Kris! No!" I yelled.

She rose with a diamond coated knife in her hand, and glanced in my direction, though I didn't think she actually saw me.

Temulus waved his arms as he stepped toward her . . . she disappeared . . . and I had no idea what was happening.

Skotadi and Kala—hell, *anyone* who stood in my way—were pushed to the side as I tried to get to where I had last seen her. I hadn't seen it, I hadn't seen Temulus hit her with a weapon. But had he?

Oh, God, had Kris been dissipated right in front of me?

My voice cracked as I yelled her name, over and over again, until my throat was raw. My body was tired and sore from fighting, my legs felt like lead, but none of that compared to the emptiness in my chest at the thought that I had just lost her.

I stared at the spot where I had last seen her as if willing her to come back. I stared at that spot so hard, I didn't see the butt of the gun intended for my head until it made contact.

Stars filled my vision as I went down. The Skotadi must have been out of bullets, because he came at me with a knife. I flipped over, catching him in the stomach with my foot. As he fell, I rose to my knees and finished him with a stab to the heart.

As I pushed myself up onto wobbly legs, Kris reappeared—ten yards from where she had vanished, and now only inches from Temulus. His eyes widened in surprise, and his hands shot out in front of him, but not before Kris plunged the knife into his chest.

Temulus roared as his hands connected with her. He didn't just shove her away. She flew into the wall of the Command Center like she had been shot out of a cannon.

I barely registered the fallen Temulus dissipating behind me. My focus remained on Kris where she laid unmoving on the ground.

Blood from the gash on my head blurred my vision and limited my view of her. Then, as Alec and Lillian crowded around her, I couldn't see her at all. The instant I got there, I forced my way between the two of them, and dropped to my knees at Kris's side.

"Kris!" In my head, I shouted her name, but it came out sounding like a hoarse whisper. I slowly reached for her, fearing the worst—because she was so still, too still, and her head laid in a pool of blood.

The instant my hand grazed her cheek, she sucked in a big breath. Her eyes popped open, and landed on me. "Oh, thank God you're okay," she breathed.

Why she was worried about me, I had no idea. She was the

one who had just taken on a demigod. And took a rock wall to the back of the head.

Her hand lifted to my forehead. "You're hurt."

"I'll heal." I gingerly lifted her up into a sitting position to examine the injury to her head. Her hair was matted with blood, but the wound itself appeared to have healed . . . already. My hands and eyes roamed her body for other injuries, but there were none. Finally, I sagged in relief and did the only other thing I needed to do.

I didn't care that we weren't alone. I didn't care that the battle still raged on behind me. I blocked everyone and everything out, and I kissed her.

I kissed her like I thought I had lost her and I couldn't believe my luck that I hadn't . . . and like I would never risk losing her again. If it were possible to tell her that with a kiss, I did it.

I barely registered the crunching of shoes on the ground as our small audience left us, and I pulled her in closer, holding her tighter, to let her know what I would never have been able to put into words.

When I finally let her go, she smiled and whispered, "Love you, too."

Her eyes slid over my shoulder to settle on someone behind me, and her smile faltered. I didn't need two chances to guess who she saw. I followed her gaze to a motionless, and expressionless, Lillian.

I helped Kris to her feet as I stood, then turned to face Lillian. I opened my mouth to apologize—not for the kiss, not for falling in love with someone else—but for not telling her sooner, when a shout from behind me stopped the words on my tongue.

"I need some help over here!" Alec yelled.

I ran to where he was crouched, tossing debris to the side as he worked to uncover someone. As I neared, Bruce's eyes opened. He was hurt but alive, and pinned under a fallen tree branch. Together, Alec and I moved the branch off of him, and Kris helped him to his feet.

"I knew it would take more than a tree to keep you down," Alec teased as he patted Bruce on the back.

I eyed the way Bruce's arm hung limply at his side. "We need to get you some medical attention . . ." Once we reestablished some sort of order.

I turned to survey the situation in the village center, and saw that more Kala than Skotadi remained. Finally. The remaining Skotadi must have realized their odds weren't good without Temulus, and appeared to have surrendered. They were being corralled into the Command Center by a group of Kala . . . led by Jared. Of course.

As if feeling my gaze on him, Jared looked up and nodded once when he saw me. Then his eyes swung toward Kris, and his expression changed from a look of relief to one of awe. He wasn't the only one. Several Kala glanced at her as they passed. They no longer regarded her with caution and contempt, but with admiration and gratitude.

I watched her as she wandered away, and dropped to her knees a few yards away. She retrieved something off the ground as I walked up behind her.

"Kris, you okay?"

She stood and turned, with a pendant dangling from a thin gold chain in her hand. Unshed tears rimmed her eyes. "Micah…"

I took her in my arms. "I know. I saw."

"So many died because of me," she cried.

"That's not true. Kris, what you did . . ." I pushed her back far enough to force her to look me in the eyes. Waving a hand at the passing Kala, I added, "You saved so many more. Look at how they're looking at you now. They know what you did."

"But they don't know the Skotadi came here for me. It's my fault they attacked in the first place."

"No . . ." I took her face in my hands. "Attacking us is what the Skotadi does, Kris. There were spies that set us up, set all of this up. It wasn't your fault."

She drew a shaky breath, and pressed her face into my chest as if to hide from what she believed was the truth. I knew it would take some time for her to see past the devastation, but eventually she would realize all the good she had done here tonight.

I gave her a moment before I pushed her back again, this time to study her. There was only one explanation for how she had managed to destroy Temulus, and survived that hit to the back of her head.

"You've reached your potential, haven't you?" I asked.

Her head nodded slowly.

"So?" Though her eyes still carried a blend of gold, she

appeared . . . okay. And she had destroyed Temulus, a demigod she should have wanted to join if she had truly followed the path she had been created for.

"I don't know," she admitted. "Something . . . happened, and I fought it. I think. I still feel something inside of me, but it's not as powerful as it had been."

"I saw it."

I looked over my shoulder at the sound of Lillian's voice.

"I saw what happened," she added. "You and Alec both were spared because of your connection to each other. I saw it the moment he kissed you, and I see it now. You strengthen each other, and that enabled you both to fight it. The kiss pushed it away . . . for now."

I had no idea what she was talking about, and the way Kris stiffened in my arms at the mention of a kiss warned me not to press for more. Though I was definitely curious, whatever Lillian was talking about, and whatever had happened between Kris and Alec, wasn't important right now.

"You feel okay?" I asked Kris tenderly.

Her eyes shot daggers at Lillian before they lifted to me. She nodded. "Yeah. But Nathan . . ."

I stopped her with a quick shake of my head, and jutted my chin over her shoulder. "There's somebody who wants to see you."

Kris turned as my indestructible grandmother emerged through the haze of smoke that blanketed the village center. Gran shot me a weak smile as she pulled Kris into her waiting arms, and gave her the kind of hug that only a grandmother could give.

The kind that healed the worst kind of pain.

*   *   *   *   *

{Kris}

We spent most of the night assisting the wounded and trying to restore some semblance of order. Fortunately, the Infirmary had been untouched, and Dr. Ribbons had survived the attack, so the injured had somewhere to go for help.

As the night progressed, it became painfully obvious that many had not survived. I heard early casualty estimates were in the two hundreds. Sadly, Richie and Micah were among them. As well as Kim, I eventually learned.

I tried to overlook the devastation and see the positive, as Nathan insisted. That many more could have been killed if I hadn't stopped Temulus when I had. But in the immediate aftermath, it was hard to see the silver lining.

Callie had been unharmed, and for that, I was grateful.

After hours of tending to broken bones, burns, and superficial wounds, the adrenaline wore off and I started to feel the exhaustion that came from using my powers. I hadn't realized at the time just how much energy I had expended in fighting Temulus, but Nathan noticed. Sometime in the early morning hours, he insisted that I get some rest.

Instead of bedding down on the floor in the mess hall with everyone else who sought a few moments of rest, I crawled into bed with Callie. My eyes shut the moment my head hit the pillow.

Despite the events still fresh in my memory, I enjoyed a few hours of dream-free sleep.

Alec's grin greeted me when I woke.

"Thought I would find you here," he said softly, careful not to wake Callie.

I sat up gingerly, and cringed from the soreness that had settled in my muscles. My body protested as I climbed out of bed. As I stretched life back into my limbs, I looked over Alec's wrinkled and blood stained clothes.

"Did you get any rest?" I asked him.

He shook his head. "Too wired. Maybe later when the adrenaline wears off." He paused, and stared at me intently. I almost asked him what was up, when he extended a hand and said, "Walk with me."

His intensity alarmed me, but I took his hand and let him guide me out of the room. We were outside, and well on our way to the beach, before Alec spoke again.

"How do you feel this morning?" he asked.

Aside from feeling the effects of being thrown into a wall by a demigod the night before? "Umm . . . okay, I guess."

"Your powers, Kris," Alec clarified. "How are your powers? Your repressed Skotadi? How does that stuff feel?"

I looked down at my hands. I hadn't experienced the weird half-invisible phenomenon since last night. And despite feeling like I had been on the verge of a future as a Skotadi only a few hours ago, my inner Skotadi had been surprisingly quiet. Still there . . . but quiet.

"I thought I was about to lose it last night," Alec said quietly.

"I thought that was it."

"Me too."

Alec spun to me quickly. "So what happened? What stopped it?"

"Maybe it didn't stop, Alec. I still feel it . . . just more under the surface like it was before."

"So what restrained it again? Kris, we were *there*." He looked at me pleadingly, as if he hoped I had the answers that he so desperately sought.

But I didn't. Not unless I believed Lillian's claim, which I still hadn't made up my mind about . . . despite what I had felt.

"I don't know."

Alec took both of my hands in his. "You know when the turning point was. I know you do."

The sun reflected in his eyes, creating an illusion difficult to look away from. Though they were still ringed in gold, they didn't appear evil to me. If anything, the gold only made his eyes look more stunning—and magnified his persistence as he gazed at me. But I had no idea what he wanted me to say, so I shook my head.

"I heard what Lillian said last night," Alec said. "About us giving each other the strength to overcome it."

"Yeah, but . . ."

"I believe her," he added confidently. "I felt it, Kris. I was right there . . . and the moment I kissed you, I felt this strength, this ability to overcome it that I hadn't had before then."

I looked away, hesitant to admit that I had felt it, too. Because what could that mean? For Alec and me to have a connection like that? Did it mean anything?

Alec dropped my hands, and started walking again. "I don't know what to make of it, but I know that it did something . . . to both of us."

"Maybe it just distracted us enough to . . ." I trailed off, because I really didn't have an explanation.

Alec chuckled as he glanced at me. "It was definitely a distraction."

We walked in silence for a few moments, both lost in our own thoughts about what the kiss had done . . . if anything. Despite having been there and having experienced it, I was reluctant to accept Lillian's theory. Part of me suspected she had only said it in front of Nathan to cause problems.

Finally, Alec said, "So I guess the next time I get the evil vibes, I'll kiss you, and see what happens." One side of his mouth curved up.

"Alec . . ." I started.

His grin dropped as he turned to me. "Look, Kris, I know you're in love with someone else." He exhaled heavily as he looked down at his shoes. "But just because you love him doesn't mean I stopped loving you." My eyes widened, and he continued quickly, "Relax. I'm not going to act on it. Not until the next time I need to test this theory anyway."

"Alec . . ."

"Kris, that was a joke."

"Was it? Was it really just a joke? I thought it was possible for us to just be friends, but . . ." Now I wasn't so sure.

Alec gripped my shoulders. "Kris, I'm going to make it possible for us to be just friends, okay? How I feel about you doesn't matter."

"How can you say that? Of course it matters."

He shook his head adamantly. "Your friendship matters more. You're the best friend I have, and I can't jeopardize that. I *won't* jeopardize that." There was a long silence before he added, "Nathan knows, so don't worry about that."

"He knows what?"

"He knows how I feel about you," he amended. "Apparently, I get a little sappy when I'm drunk, and we had a moment that I'd rather not relive right now . . . or *ever*."

Alec shivered as if the memory caused him distress, and I laughed. That was when I knew that we would be okay.

We had to be okay. Because I felt the same about him. Callie might have been my oldest friend, Nathan may have had my heart, but Alec had claimed a big part of me that would always be his. Despite our past, and our history, he would remain one of the most important people in my life. Always.

We didn't talk about kisses and feelings, death and dying, or powers and evil impulses again as we strolled back to the village center. After the heaviness of our earlier discussion and the events of the night before, I welcomed the meaningless banter that Alec and I shared over the ugly sand creatures we scared along the way.

When the village center and the devastation caused by the attack came into view, my mood sobered. Though the wounded had been moved and all the scattered weapons had been gathered, blood still stained the ground and smoke still rose from the smoldering mounds that had once been the two dormitories.

Only a few Kala continued to work, and I wondered if everyone else had finally retreated to the mess hall for rest.

I wondered if I would find Nathan there, but as Alec and I neared the mess hall, I spotted him walking toward us. Though his droopy eyelids suggested that he desperately needed a break, he managed a small smile.

"I'm glad you're here," Alec said to him. "We need to talk."

I shot Alec a curious look, but his eyes remained fixed on Nathan as he covered a yawn with his hand.

"It can't wait?" Nathan asked.

Alec glanced at me before he answered. "I'd rather not."

Nathan yawned again, and pointed to a nearby bench. Though splintered from bullet holes, it was one of the few benches still upright. "At least let me sit down for this."

I took a seat next to Nathan, inviting myself into the conversation. Alec stood in front of us, and hooked an amused eyebrow at me before addressing Nathan.

"Last night, before all hell broke loose, I got that letter you sent me," he said.

Nathan lifted his head out of his hands. "Well, as you can see, I survived, so there's no need for you to honor my request."

My curiosity piqued at Nathan's hard tone, but Alec waved a hand in dismissal.

"I'm not talking about that," Alec said. "You said the gods were going to have the demigods who were going after immortality destroyed?"

"Yeah. Before we left, they asked Jared to put together another team to assist in tracking them down. What's your point?"

Alec glanced around, taking in the chaos surrounding us. "How is he going to do that now?"

"I don't know," Nathan groaned. "I heard that everyone is going to relocate to the Australian base while the dorms are rebuilt. A few will stay behind to get things running again. I guess he'll get the Australians to help."

"What if we do it?" Alec suggested eagerly.

Nathan stared at Alec for a few seconds, as if he didn't understand what Alec was suggesting—or didn't believe that Alec could be that crazy. My initial reaction mirrored his.

"*You* want to go after the demigods?" Nathan finally asked.

"This relief that Kris and I have now . . . it's not going to last," Alec responded. "I think Lillian might have been right about how we managed to overcome the evil in us this time, but it's still there. It's going to happen again unless we can sever our ties completely."

"Yeah . . ." Nathan cocked his head to the side as he studied Alec. "About that . . ."

"Yes, I kissed Kris," Alec blurted out. "But I'm not going to apologize for it, because . . ." Alec trailed off as his gaze shifted to me. "Well, I'd do it again if I had to, and it did help. We're here, not evil, because of some connection we have."

My eyes swung toward Nathan nervously. He had yet to say anything to me about the kiss, but from the chill in his eyes, I suspected he had a few words to say to Alec about it.

So much for them finally getting along.

"You're saying you would do it again?" Nathan asked Alec

with forced control. Only the tick in his cheek hinted at his anger.

Alec glanced at me. "I told her I wouldn't . . . unless I had to, assuming Lillian's theory is right." Before Nathan could respond, Alec continued, "And that's actually what I wanted to talk to you about."

"Lillian's theory?" Nathan questioned. "Or the fact that you think you can kiss Kris whenever you want?"

Oh God. I slumped down in an attempt to make myself smaller. Suddenly, I wished I hadn't invited myself into this conversation.

Alec, on the other hand, didn't seem bothered at all. "If Lillian's right, and if Circe needs Kris to finish this curse, then she's going to try to eliminate me," he explained. "And if I *am* helping Kris fight her evil, what's going to stop her from joining Circe when I'm gone?"

Nathan remained silent as he glared at Alec, and I wished now more than ever that I had prophetic abilities. Because I knew Nathan was screaming some silent thoughts.

Then again, it was probably best for me to not know what they were.

"That is assuming Lillian's theory is correct," Nathan finally said.

"Of course," Alec agreed. "But I think she *is* right. That means Kris and I need to sever our ties to evil before it's too late."

Nathan glanced at me before turning back to Alec. "We tried. I don't know what else—"

"I think I know how to do it," Alec interrupted.

At that, I perked up. "How?"

Alec turned to me. "I know your charming specialty wasn't your best, so you might not have noticed like I did last night. After you destroyed Temulus, I felt . . . lighter. More free than I had in a long time. Even more so than after I kissed you."

"What are you getting at, Alec?" Nathan asked.

"I tried to charm someone this morning, and I couldn't do it," he gushed excitedly. "It's like I lost a piece of my Skotadi that was connected to Temulus. I feel like a weight has been lifted off my shoulders. Not all of it, but enough. I think destroying Hades' other three demigods might set us free completely."

"You do know where Hades' demigods are hiding, right?" Nathan questioned.

"I do," Alec answered breezily. "The way I see it, I've been told to go to hell so many times, I figure it's about time for me to go see what all the fuss is about. I'm looking forward to it."

Nathan covered his face with his hands as he groaned. "You know Kris is going to have to be the one to destroy them?"

"I thought you said in your letter that there were others," Alec said.

"Two other demigods who aren't in on this immortality scheme," Nathan replied grimly. "But once the other nine know what we're doing, they're going to come at us with everything they've got."

"Perfect." Alec shrugged. "Let them come to us."

"I'm not going to risk her safety," Nathan returned heatedly. "Not for something you just . . . have a theory on."

"Wait a minute." I placed a hand on Nathan's shoulder.

"They're going to come after me anyway. Circe needs me. Temulus was just the first. The others will come soon."

Alec looked at Nathan with a satisfied nod. "Wouldn't you rather strike first?"

"Or at least be prepared," I added, forcing Nathan to look at me like I had grown a second head.

"You're serious? You want to go hunt down the demigods?" he asked me.

"I'd rather do that than wait for them to come for me again, and prevent more meaningless death and destruction." I waved a hand to indicate the damage done last night. "And besides . . . I think Alec might be right. Getting rid of them might be the only way to free us from them completely."

Nathan looked down at his feet for several seconds. Finally, his head nodded fractionally. "Okay. If that's really what you believe it's going to take." His eyes lifted to Alec. "But we do this the smart way. With careful planning."

"Of course," Alec replied.

"I'll talk to Jared," Nathan offered. "We're going to need . . . everything. Weapons, money, and manpower."

As Nathan and Alec discussed necessities, my mind wandered to what exactly I had gotten myself into, and I started to question my ability to pull this off. Just as quickly as the doubt crept in, I pushed it away in favor of determination. I could do this. I would do this.

Because I had to. My life and my future, along with everyone else's, depended on it.

"We'll start making arrangements now. Just let me talk to

Kris for a minute."

Nathan's last few words broke through my thoughts. As Alec left, I nibbled on my lip in anticipation of what he wanted to talk to me about. I suspected I knew—the only thing we hadn't talked about yet.

Before he could say anything, I spun to him. "It wasn't what you think," I gushed.

He smiled faintly. "What do I think? What was it?"

"Alec was *there*. He was about to go over the edge, and then he kissed me. I happened suddenly, and I didn't know what he was doing until it was too late. But then, I didn't actually stop him when I did realize because I knew he thought he *needed* to kiss me..." I stopped with a shrug when I realized I was rambling.

Nathan's lips quirked up. "You're saying he kissed you before you realized he was going to kiss you?"

"Yes. I didn't have time . . ." I stopped when I realized the point Nathan was making. "Okay, I get it. The same thing happened with you and Lillian."

"Only I stopped it right away," he muttered.

He wasn't even mad. But the uncertainty I heard in his voice caused me to lower my head in shame. "I'm sorry," I mumbled.

"Look, Kris, I know you and Alec have . . ." He looked away with a shrug. "Hell, I don't even know what it is, but I told you before, I'm done pushing you away from me because of it. I told you I would fight for you, and I meant it. And if you tell me it was nothing more than what you just said, then I believe you. I don't want to fight with you anymore."

"I don't want to fight either."

"Good." He planted a kiss to my forehead. "Besides . . . that wasn't really what I wanted to talk to you about."

"What then?"

"Well, I guess it's kind of related," he amended. "I just. . . is everything okay. . . with us? After everything that has happened?"

I took his hand in mine. "I'm okay with us. If you are."

"I'm more than okay," he replied with a smile. "What we're about to do . . . we're going to do it together, every step of the way. And when this all over . . ."

He trailed off without finishing his thought, but he didn't need to say the words. I knew what he was thinking.

"I can't wait," I said as I wrapped my arms around his neck.

I couldn't wait to do simple for the rest of my life. With Nathan.

Epilogue

Callie's eyes fluttered as I pressed my lips to her forehead, but they didn't open. I didn't know if she could hear me or not, but I spoke to her as if she could.

"I'm going to fix this," I promised her. "I'm going to get you out of this mess, and once I do, I'll come back for you. We'll take a nice long trip to the mall . . . get some highlights in that hair of yours."

I lifted my head to look pleadingly at Gran, who sat in the chair beside the bed. "Take good care of her. Please." My voice cracked, and I swallowed to contain the emotion that threatened to pour out of me.

I had expected it to be difficult to leave her, but damn. I had been trying for five minutes to leave, and hadn't made it any closer to the door. I kept thinking that this could be the last time I saw Callie alive, and the possible finality of this visit terrified me.

Gran's hand covered mine. "I'll take care of Callie. You just take care of each other." Her eyes shifted to the door, where Nathan and Alec waited, having already said their goodbyes.

I nodded decidedly, and rounded the bed to hug Gran one

last time. I swatted a tear from my eye as I turned away from her, and Nathan slipped a comforting arm around my shoulders as we left.

We had nothing but the clothes we were wearing, and a few weapons stuffed into the duffel bag slung over Nathan's shoulder. We would have to start over. Jared had already moved some money into an account in Nathan's name to help us. Our first stop when we got to the mainland would be to buy some clean clothes, and more weapons.

Most of the Kala had already left for the Australian base, and the few who remained were busy with the recovery efforts. Eerie silence greeted us in the village center, and followed us as we made our way to the beach, and the boat that waited for us.

Sitting on the bench before the trail was a familiar face. I hadn't seen Bruce since the night of the attack, and he looked much better than I remembered. The only reminder of the injuries he had suffered was the sling around his arm.

"I hope you weren't planning to leave without me," he said to Alec as he came to a stand.

I shot Nathan a puzzled look. Jared had assured us that we were free to go. After the discovery of several traitors in their midst, what was left of Kala leadership was in shambles. Surely they had bigger things to worry about than ensuring Alec had his guard follow him on our vigilante mission.

"You're going to need some muscle to wrangle up those demigods," Bruce added. "And I got that, once this sling is gone, of course."

I bit my lip to stifle the smile on my face as I looked between

Nathan and Alec. Nathan was the first to wipe the astonishment off his face.

"We sure could use the help," he said to Bruce.

Alec slapped Bruce on the back to welcome him into our group as we resumed our walk to the dock. As it, and our waiting boat, came into view, I spotted two more people who appeared to be waiting for us.

I recognized Jared first, and started to smile until I realized who the second person was.

Lillian.

Nathan greeted Jared with a back pat-hug combination. "I thought you already left for the Australian base."

Jared scratched his chin. "I was going to. Then I thought, what the hell? Dangerous missions are our thing, and I couldn't let you go on this one without me."

Nathan nodded decidedly, and I was relieved that our team was growing, and getting stronger. Then I caught a glimpse of Lillian over Jared's shoulder, and I fidgeted nervously as I wondered what purpose she had for being here.

I really hoped she didn't plan to cause a scene over Nathan. I bit my lip as she stepped forward . . . toward me.

"I want to help, too," she said to me.

I glanced at Nathan, waiting for him to tell her no. He met my eyes with a shrug that said, *it couldn't hurt*.

"My memory is starting to come back. *Slowly*," she emphasized, "but maybe I'll remember something valuable. And . . ."

She looked at Nathan this time, and I saw it. There was no

doubt that she loved him.

"Maybe I can help you with your spells, and teach you how to control things better," she added.

I folded my arms as I surveyed her cautiously. Though I suspected she may have other reasons for wanting to come along—specifically, the fact that she was still in love with Nathan—I was intrigued by her offer to help me with my control.

Since the night of the attack, I'd had a few . . . episodes. My body flirted with invisibility, objects moved, glass shattered, my hands tingled without conscious thought of producing fire. Without Micah's guidance, I found that I was struggling.

And Lillian had been an Incantator as a Skotadi. If her memory, and abilities, came back perhaps she could be of assistance. Not only to me, but to our cause.

"Yeah, okay," I muttered with a nod. I looked up and caught Alec's smirk. I narrowed my eyes and mouthed, *shut up*.

"Okay," Nathan declared. "It's the six of us then."

Within the span of five minutes, our team had doubled. Though my guard would be up with Lillian around, I was more optimistic. Six was much better than three.

"Next stop . . . a clothing store," Alec announced as we boarded the boat.

As Jared took a seat at the controls, I moved to the back of the boat, away from the others, to sit. If anything, to collect myself and my thoughts.

Though I was scared to find out what would happen next, I was eager to get my life back. I was done with being the victim, and letting things happen to me. Now, I was prepared to make things happen . . . *for me.*

Nathan took a seat beside me as Jared steered the boat away from the dock, and I offered him a smile to let him know I was okay. Because I knew he worried about me.

His arm wrapped around my shoulders, and I turned to face the horizon, not with trepidation this time, but with hope, because I knew that somewhere out there awaited the key to my freedom.

Made in the USA
Lexington, KY
10 November 2016